"I want to kiss you again, probably lots of times. And I have feelings that I must think about."

"What sort of feelings?" Dominic allowed himself to smile at her.

"I can't say without examining myself, my reactions. There may be a whole new side to me, one I could never have imagined. If so, I shall need your help dealing with it. If you could spare a little time, that is."

What had he created? "How would you expect me to deal with this…this whatever it is?"

Fleur smiled back at him and stepped away. "I've intended to share my requirements in a husband with you. To help you eliminate men who just wouldn't do. But with this new development, this obviously *passionate* side of my nature that has shown itself, I must have the help of an experienced person to teach me how to keep my impulses in check."

Stella Cameron was born in Weymouth, Dorset. She was editing medical text and working in London's Harley Street when she met her husband, an officer in the American Air Force, at a party. He asked her to dance, and they've been together ever since. They are now the proud parents of three grown children.

Stella Cameron writes both historical and contemporary women's fiction. She regularly hits the bestseller lists and has a strong international following.

You are invited to visit the author's website at www.stellacameron.com.

TESTING MISS TOOGOOD

Stella Cameron

*MILLS & BOON and MILLS & BOON with the Rose Device
are registered trademarks of the publisher.*

*First published in Great Britain 2006
by Harlequin Mills & Boon Limited,
Eton House, 18-24 Paradise Road, Richmond, Surrey TW9 1SR*

© Stella Cameron 2005

ISBN 0 263 84429 3

153-0106

*Printed and bound in Spain
by Litografia Rosés S.A., Barcelona*

For Jerry
Thank you for sharing my life

1

Covent Garden
London, 1815

Success…or failure…depended on this, on what happened now, here, in a shabby park in one of London's sleaziest districts.

He reached a hedge, pushed through an overgrown gap that passed as a gateway and hurried inside. He saw her. A girl huddled in the middle of a pathway where what moon there was played hide-and-seek and picked her out for any interested eye to see.

Running, he hissed, "It's all right. You have nothing to fear. Get off the path. Sit on the bench over there—by the bushes."

"I'd rather stand, sir…father."

"Keep your voice down, I beg of you. They call me Brother Juste and I insist we sit. We could be too easily spotted standing here." He caught her by the arm and rushed her along. She kept quiet and didn't shrink from him. His real name was Lord Dominic Elliot, but the disguise served him well.

The girl's courage impressed him. He hadn't been sure she'd come to meet a stranger in this deserted place after sunset. From what he could make out, she was young, wholesome and simply dressed.

Jane Weller, a desperate servant wrongly dismissed from her place, sped along at his side, her breath coming in frightened gasps, until she plopped down on the stone seat he'd indicated. Tucked in the deep shadows of tall laurel bushes, anyone there would be all but invisible. He followed, his habit flowing around his feet, the rough brown wool heavy with moisture from the fog.

"I'd best be quick," Jane said. "I want to get back." She sat down, crossed her booted feet, wrapped a prim dark coat tightly about her and held it together at the neck. She bowed her head and an unadorned bonnet hid her face completely, not that there was much to see in this light, even if he had become accustomed to getting around very well in darkness.

She touched her chin and drew in a sharp breath.

"Are you hurt?" he asked.

Miss Weller shook her head, no, and muttered something inaudible.

Laughter carried on the heavy air, drunken voices bellowed and Jane muffled a cry with her hands and looked up at him. He saw her face better then, her eyes glittering up at him.

"Hush," he said, sitting beside her but with an appropriate distance between them. "You are safe with me, I promise." Acrid smoke from too many chimneys to imagine stung the eyes.

A long walk from ancient St. Mary's Church in Pearl Lane had given him time to think about the most efficient way to deal with the best, possibly the only, chance he might get to solve a most disturbing mystery before it was too late.

"I shall accompany you home to your rooms," he told Jane. "No harm shall come to you. Now, tell me your story." He already knew most of it, as reported by the son of her former employers while that young man wallowed in his cups at a certain gentlemen's club.

"It's not true what my mistress said." The girl's voice wobbled but she didn't cry. A brave one, this. "I didn't stay out all night with my young man—last Thursday that would be— I didn't. I don't have a young man. I was taken, that's what I was, taken. Kidnapped. And I know why."

You do? "And why would that be?" He knew very well but couldn't imagine how Jane Weller would have any idea why she was abducted in Hyde Park—opposite her employers' mansion—and spirited away.

"The gentleman thought I was Miss Victoria. On account of I was wearing one of her cloaks. She gave it to me," she added hurriedly. "Miss Victoria gets tired of her things and likes to give them away. It was her he wanted—he said as much when he was so angry at seeing he'd got a nobody for all his trouble."

The Victoria she spoke of was Victoria Crewe-Burns whose wealthy family was famous for, among other products, Crewe-Burns Serviceable Stockings—a mainstay of the working classes. There had been a time when Vicky's name had been linked to that of Dominic's brother, Nathan.

"You're sure of this, Miss Weller?" He kept his voice low.

She whispered in return, "Oh, yes. The man who took me never said a word till I was in that house of his." He noted she spoke quite well and tucked the fact away in case it might be useful to remember. "Look," she continued, "I will help you try to find this man. I want to because I think he'll hurt someone one day if he isn't caught. But they watch you at that rooming house where I'm staying and if I'm too late back someone will say things about me and I'll be out on the street again. I don't know if I could find another place as cheap."

He needed so much more from her. "Did you actually see this man's face?" Surely a good description would be too much to hope for.

"Yes and no."

Waiting for her to go on took almost more patience than he had.

"A painted face, that's what he had. He frightened me so, his face white like some ladies used to have, all stiff and hard from the stuff he'd spread on. And a little red mouth painted on and eyebrows almost up to his wig. A white wig it was, and white powder on his eyelashes so his eyes looked pink and nasty."

The next answer was expected but he asked the question anyway. "Would you know him if you saw him again?"

She didn't laugh or say no immediately. "I don't know. There was something about him—a feeling he gave me. He pushed me down and kicked me. He said I was a waste of time."

"I'm sorry." And he was furious. "Did you feel as if you'd met him before?"

"Oh, no." She shook her head vehemently. "I couldn't have. No. But when I say he gave me a funny feeling, I don't just mean the scared feeling. I wouldn't know his face unless he was painted the same way, of course, but...I don't know, I probably couldn't recognize him. He said he's a master of disguises so I suppose that means he changes how he looks." She looked up at him. "I'm sorry I'm not more help."

"You are a great deal of help." He must make sure they would meet again and soon. The thought of not being able to find her after tonight sent panic into his heart. "You cannot have a great deal of money."

She tossed her head and averted her face from him. "I know how to look after myself. I'll do well enough."

"How long can you manage without a position?"

Miss Weller fiddled with the neck of her coat. "Long enough."

"Let me give you some money."

"No, thank you." She stood up and he heard her rapid breathing. "I shall find a place soon enough. I must."

"You sound desperate," he said gently. "If you have enough money to manage, why *must* you find a place soon?"

"Because—because I must, that's all. Please, I wish I could be more useful but I'm going to that house now."

"Fair enough." He rose and offered her his arm. Jane Weller got up and stood beside him, ignoring his arm. "Very well, let us get you home but there's something I want you to do tomorrow morning."

"I can't do anything extra in the morning." She hesitated, cleared her throat. "The landlady said I could help pay my way by doing some work for her. I start first thing."

"In the afternoon, then?"

They walked to the nearest exit from the little park. He had to peer ahead to see where they were going.

"All right," she said at last. "If I can, I will."

"Miss Weller, remember you are not without a friend. I shall make sure you are cared for."

"I don't need—"

"You don't need help? Of course you don't. But would you please go to Heatherly tomorrow afternoon? You will be expected. Ask for my friend the Dowager Marchioness of Granville. Tell the butler you've been sent about a job and you're expected. You will be."

"But—" She stopped walking. "When the Crewe-Burnses let me go they said they wouldn't speak for me. They said if they were asked, they'd say about me being off with a man—

like you were told. And they'd say how I was a liar you couldn't trust."

"None of that will matter. I will speak for you."

"I don't know any Heatherly."

"You'll find the estate. It's immediately northwest of Regent's Park. Anyone in the area will direct you. You will do it, won't you?"

"I'll think about it," she said.

The horses stood quietly enough. He was grateful for that. With his habit safely stowed in a tiny secret room above the porch of St. Mary's Church, Lord Dominic Elliot strode toward the animals. He doubted if it would be long before he needed to don one of his Brother Juste disguises again.

Dominic's shadowy friend, Brother Cadwin of the Brown Monastery, had arranged with a priest at St. Mary's for Dominic to use the church as a haven when he needed one.

"Hurry up then." Dominic's older brother Nathan waited on one of the pair of blacks. "You're late, dammit. We can't afford to be seen."

Dominic held his tongue. He swung into the saddle of his own horse and took the reins while the animal skittered sideways, blowing. He and Nathan rode away at once, switching back and forth through a maze of narrow streets in the Covent Garden area. Fog ebbed and flowed and with it, visibility. Sometimes a patch of sky—gray stained with purple—showed, only to be snuffed out by another curling swathe. At last they clattered into a small square and paused to listen. They heard no sounds of pursuit.

"What took you so long?" Nathan said.

"The girl is brave but nervous," Dominic told him. "She wasn't quick to tell me everything. I made sure she got back to her wretched boardinghouse safely. Just as well since she finally told me what that cur said to her. And did to her. He was painted, by the way. Disguised as some sort of dandy but with a white wig and maquillage. Gaudy silks and white satin, I gather. Florid embroidery, gold thread, that sort of thing."

"You think you should be the only man allowed to pretend he's someone he's not?" Nathan said with laughter in his voice.

Dominic wasn't amused. "What we surmised about Bertie Crewe-Burns was correct. He wasn't as foxed as he pretended to be when the two of you spoke. The story about the servant was fabricated. She doesn't even have a gentleman friend, she says, and I believe her. They turned her out because they're afraid and they don't want to draw any attention to the probable truth."

"Did the girl say something to make you certain it was Victoria that man was after?" Nathan asked.

Dominic told him about the cloak, then went on with what Jane had revealed as he took her home. "She said he taunted her, pushed her down. Apparently he's got a fantastic—and awful—little house where he locked himself inside with Jane. Music boxes everywhere on a gallery and he set them all playing, one after another, twirling around like a madman as he did so."

The horses danced on the cobbles, their hoofs ringing. When they settled down Nathan said, very softly, "Perhaps he is mad. Not a pretty thought."

"I think it's all an extravagant pretense," Dominic said flatly. "He stopped that piece of nonsense and actually looked at his captive. She said he became angry and completely changed from the capering fool. He threatened her, said she was useless to him so she might as well die. Then he said he couldn't be bothered to kill her because she was no threat to him anyway—because she was a nothing. Why should he get blood in his favorite room just to murder a servant."

"Bloody hound." Nathan snarled. "Did she give you any idea where this place he took her might be?"

"Nothing really helpful. The Crewe-Burns mansion is on Park Lane—as you know—and Jane thought they traveled for about half an hour. She isn't sure but she thinks they went south, possibly across the southeast corner of Hyde Park. Then she felt the direction change—east or so she thinks. She appears to have a strong sense of direction."

"Do you think there's more, something she didn't remember to say?"

"If there is, and if she does as she's promised, we'll have plenty of opportunity to find out. She is to go to Heatherly tomorrow afternoon. Mother will offer her a position. It's arranged. Jane doesn't know I am the Dowager Marchioness's son."

Nathan clicked his tongue. "How do you accomplish so much in so little time, then forget to tell the brother who backs you up in all things? I had no idea what all this was about until this evening. I'm the one who brought this case to your attention, remember?"

"I didn't ask you to join me in my investigations at all," Dominic said. "You said you wanted to do it and that Mother would think better of you if you appeared to be busy and sober."

"Am I complaining?"

Dominic thought, but only for a moment. "Yes. But then, you often do. We can be grateful one of the Crewe-Burnses' servants could be bribed to say where Jane Weller went after she left Hyde Park or I'd never have found her."

"Yes, yes." Nathan sighed. "I've been celibate too long, that's the problem. My mind is becoming fevered."

"Exactly how long *have* you been celibate?" Dominic asked.

"Er—" Nathan closed his eyes and appeared in deep thought. "At least two days."

Dominic shook his head. "That long. No wonder your mind is affected. Nathan, there is more. You say your discreet enquiries lead you to believe several eligible, well-born girls have been spirited away by our evil clown. Spirited away and released again, most probably after payment of some ransom."

"Yes, and I'm even more certain he threatens to ruin their reputations if the families make a fuss." Nathan scowled toward the sodden sky. "Bertie let Gussy Arbuthnot's name drop. That was an accident, I'm convinced. But he rambled about other girls going missing and said it before he remembered his story about Jane Weller."

"I think Bertie's scared for Victoria and looking for help even though he's afraid to come out and admit it," Dominic told his brother.

"So am I," Nathan said quietly.

Dominic looked at his brother. "There's something between the two of you, isn't there?"

"From time to time I've thought there could be. She's too immature."

Dominic decided to back off the subject. "What did Bertie say about Gussy?"

"That she'd been what he called 'off for a day or more,' and how her family had worried she'd be ruined. I pressed him and first he said she was back and safe—which she is—then he said he was too drunk to know what he was saying and she'd never been missing at all. Made no sense except I'm sure he was telling the truth at the outset."

So was Dominic.

"We may be making too much out of this," Nathan said. "The villain is likely a harmless prankster."

"I think not," Dominic told him. "I intend to find a way to discover what Gussy knows. And Victoria's a forthright girl with strong opinions, even if she did bow to pressure and allow her maid to be sacrificed. If it becomes necessary I could ask Mother to invite Victoria to visit, then allow her to see we've employed Jane Weller. I hope we don't have to do it because it would be hard to explain without revealing Brother Juste, but it might lead to some potentially interesting comments."

"Gawd," Nathan said. "Mother hates visitors. A little of this intrigue will go a long way. She's likely to drive her heels in and tell you not to bother her. You know she only likes to be left alone to paint bunches of grapes, or whatever it is she paints."

Dominic was all too aware that his reclusive parent could decide not to help him, especially when he couldn't reveal Brother Juste or the work he did.

He urged his mount close to Nathan's and spoke softly. "As our clown grew more angry he started drinking. Three bottles of hock, one after the other, evidently. That was when he took out a roll of white satin and unwound it to reveal a number of wicked-looking knives. Jane Weller's description, not mine."

Nathan caught Dominic's upper arm. "Go on."

"He selected a knife and held it to the girl's throat. He could end her life so easily, he told her."

"But he didn't, so—"

"So we should call it a joke? I don't think so. Not yet. He said—and I repeat word for word what I was told—he said the time would come when someone would make the deadly decision to call his bluff, and when they did they would still get their daughter back—dead, her throat cut."

"What's his game?" Nathan said, clearly frustrated.

"Money," Dominic told him. "And lots of it. He could have been pulling in huge sums from any number of families who don't ever want to talk about it."

"We'd best be on our way," Nathan said. "We've loitered too long even if this is a deserted place. We'll talk in the morning. By then you'll have had a chance to become more objective."

Cold anger set Dominic's jaw. He pulled his arm away from Nathan. "We'll ride on. But not before I tell you that Jane Weller felt the point of Mr. White's knife. He made a small, quite precise cut beneath her jaw and said she was fortunate. The next girl to join him in his bizarre house and cross him would, he said, get similarly cut only some inches lower and much deeper so he could be sure she would bleed to death."

2

Heatherly House near Regent's Park, London

"Bloody hell, Dominic, what if one of the servants walks in here, one of the maids?"

"She'll be a very lucky girl."

Nathan strolled past his impressive, and naked, younger brother. "Best to err on the side of caution," Nathan said. "What the eye can't see is unlikely to be laughed at."

Dominic poured cold water into a bowl on his commode, dipped his fingers and aimed drops into Nathan's eyes. "That's deserved payment for your jealous cheek."

"You've got important things to do," Nathan said, smiling a little as he wiped his face. "Other than run Heatherly."

"Thank you for reminding me. I can hardly believe you're here at this hour when we were so late last night. I need to speak with Mother about the Weller girl but that means I must eat first."

"To gather your strength?" Nathan enjoyed this brother even if he was their mother's favorite son. "You'd best eat heartily."

Dominic stood still and regarded Nathan closely. There was something there in his manner, something more than he'd thought until this moment. "Let's have some honesty," he said slowly. "You caught me half-asleep but I'm fully awake now. There's another matter on your mind, isn't there? Not just the clown business?"

Nathan's inscrutable smile infuriated Dominic. "Very well," he continued. "Let's have it. No shilly-shallying—I don't have time."

"Get dressed," Nathan said, still smiling but with more glee. "Mother wants you at the Dower House."

"It's a cottage," Dominic said. "Are you telling me you've already seen Mother today?"

"I couldn't sleep," Nathan said airily. "She starts painting early so I wandered over."

Dominic narrowed his eyes. "Mother doesn't receive when she's painting. I've never even seen a single thing she's supposedly produced. Have you?"

Nathan shrugged and said, "Never. I know Mrs. Lymer buys fresh fruits daily—so perhaps that's what Mother paints. She's always been a shy woman. I don't imagine she'll be holding any showings after all these years. Regardless, she wants you there now because she's about to ask you to perform a service for her. Shouldn't take more than a couple of months at most."

Dominic's man, Merryfield, had already set clothes out on the bed. With one foot poised to shoot into his trousers, Dominic paused to give Nathan a bemused stare.

"You'll remember how Mother visited a girlhood friend several months ago," Nathan said. "A Mrs. Toogood. She's the wife of a pastor in some obscure parish in…a very obscure parish. In the Cotswolds if memory serves. Apparently Mother has decided to take the lady's daughter, one of five, I believe, under her wing."

"Good for Mother," Dominic said, putting on his trousers without taking his eyes off Nathan's face. "She needs more interests, and more female companionship. She and Hattie get along well—" Hattie was their brother John's wife "—but Hattie spends too much time in Bath and not enough here. It's a pity Mother didn't have a daughter of her own."

Nathan blinked and frowned. "That would have meant we had a sister."

"Many men do," Dominic said, amused. "You think you're going to give me a message I'll hate, don't you? Perhaps you have too much time on your hands and you're filling it by annoying me, but I think that's about to change."

"You are going to hate what I tell you, I assure you." Nathan chuckled. "And the man about to find himself with *no* time on his hands is you, not me."

Enough sparring, Dominic decided. Whatever Mother wanted of him was bound to be paltry. "Out with it. Now. I have that important business to do."

"Yes, with Mother. You can't begin to imagine how you'll hate this."

Dominic fastened his shirt, tucked it in and shrugged into a dark-green waistcoat. "Mother couldn't aggravate me if she tried. Not easily anyway."

"Miss Fleur Toogood has arrived from her father's obscure parish to stay here with us. Mother seems quite thrilled about it all and she's decided you will be the perfect one to squire the girl about—with a chaperon in attendance, of course—while she prepares for the Season. And during the Season—naturally—you'll make a fine, mature male protector with all the right connections."

"Don't be so blasted ridiculous. In the first place, Mother has no interest in such foolishness as the annual marriage mart. Secondly, she would never do anything that might require her to venture forth to some social events. You know how she hates those. Now concentrate. I wonder if I could trust you to sniff around the Arbuthnots and see if you get any hints about Gussy having had an ordeal."

"Bad idea. Gussy got too close for comfort once and I escaped, but she's still desperate for a husband. I can't risk having her think I'm interested in her. I meant what I said about Miss Toogood. And I could have let you go to Mother without giving you the nod about her plans. She didn't ask me to tell you. The least you could do is thank me."

Dominic, his shoulders slumped, walked slowly to the window and looked over the awesome grounds surrounding Heatherly. A soft rain fell, washing the lawns to fuzzy emerald. Great groves of trees in the distance marked the edge of the property on the side closest to Regent's Park. "I can't believe Mother would do something like this," he said.

"You'll be the darling of all, especially the mothers with offspring to unload. They'll have lots of time to share beauty secrets with you while you watch Miss Toogood dance at balls, or when you circulate at all those exquisite routs where you'll introduce her to the appropriate men."

"God help me."

Nathan snorted. "He won't if you don't completely dedicate yourself to Miss Toogood."

"It's not going to happen—although you're probably making the whole thing up—so I shall have no need to concern myself with such trifles."

"Miss Toogood is a reality."

"Really? Have you seen her?"

"No," Nathan said, "but Mother says she's a sweet little dumpling of a thing. *Comfortable* was another word she used, and *wholesome*. Of course, she also said Miss Toogood was a little bland from having grown up with no stimulation and will have to be made over, whatever that means. Mother was vague. Manners, I should think. She'll need to bathe at least occasionally and I understand it would be better if she kept her mouth closed in public."

Dominic tried so hard not to show what he felt, but the devil take it, *he was only a man.* "Why would that be?" There, he sounded most reasonable.

"Nothing important really." Nathan made a ridiculous motion in the air. "Just better not to draw attention. She has no teeth."

"Look—"

"Relax," Nathan said and pounded him on the back. "I should leave all this discussion to Mother. What a soul of generosity and kindness she is."

Dominic knew when he was being ribbed mercilessly, but Nathan would not have pulled this idea from the air. There was undoubtedly some element of truth in all the hog swill.

Quickly, Dominic returned to the commode and immersed his face in cold water. He didn't come up until he thought it possible he might drown. *Now there was an idea.* "You were right," he said. "I hate this and if it is true, I damn well won't do it."

3

Fleur threw herself on top of the bed and practiced frowning. Whatever she did she must overcome her reputation as the most sunny and reasonable of females. Not that people here in London knew anything of her reputation, or anything of her at all. To them she was a nobody, a charity case.

Still, a serious female would be passed over by all but the most discerning males—if any of those were likely to be present at the silly events she'd been told she would attend.

She rolled onto her face and spread out her arms and legs in a completely unladylike manner. This was all for Mama and Papa and her four darling sisters—to attempt to change their fortunes. Really, it was quite amazing how quickly one forgot all the annoying little habits of one's siblings once they were far away. The dear village of Sodbury Martyr, and home, did seem *so* far away from this great estate they called Heatherly—and its confusing house where she had been deposited the night before. *House?* It was big enough to be a castle.

Letitia, Rosemary, Zinnia and Sophie—yes, for them she was here, to give them hopes of advantageous connections through her own marriage. Fleur closed her eyes and let out a huge sigh. Therein lay the challenge because she absolutely would not marry a man she didn't love, and she wouldn't marry a man she loved if he didn't meet her standards. Safely stowed beneath the mattress on this very bed was her precious secret book. Inside, written neatly, The List set out those qualities essential in a husband, a husband acceptable to Miss Fleur Toogood.

Her eyes stung the tiniest bit but she blinked the feeling away. Self-pity was something she could not abide. Growing up poor, scrimping, had taught her to be grateful for what she had and to be strong.

She looked at the rows of embroidered daisies, dark purple, running up the lilac-colored drapery folds to the center of the canopy over the bed. On the fireplace wall painted sprays of daisies decorated porcelain medallions set into squares of wood paneling. This beautiful room represented a great kindness by the Dowager Marchioness of Granville and Fleur would not forget it.

She had not been greeted by her hostess yet, but she remembered her well from the startling visit that lady had paid to Mama in Sodbury Martyr.

After a light tap on the door a maid entered, the same pinch-faced girl who had helped her when she arrived late the previous evening.

"You're to go straight to the Dower 'ouse," the girl, Blanche, said and opened the impressive wardrobe where Fleur's clothes had been hung. Blanche's hands fluttered, touched garments lightly while she sighed and muttered.

"Where is the Dower House?" Fleur asked. She dreaded another coach journey so soon.

Blanche's head was inside the wardrobe. "On the other side of the rose gardens," she said, her voice muffled.

"There's another house here at Heatherly?" Fleur said.

"Of course," Blanche said. "The Dower 'ouse. Don't you know *anything*? It's where old Lady Granville lives. It's not far."

Fleur swung her feet over the edge of the mattress and reached until her toes met the step stool. She hopped to the fine, softly hued carpet and hurried to stand behind Blanche. "What are you doing?"

The maid gave her a pitying look. "Finding you a wrap. This will 'ave to do." She took out a pelisse of light blue wool and held it for Fleur to put on. Since a satin ribbon of the same color had been added to the high waist of her white muslin dress, the outfit looked well enough, Fleur supposed. Really, the thought of being primped at all times—for weeks— daunted her.

Blanche stepped back to study Fleur critically. "Hmm," was her verdict.

"Such goings on today. I've never seen the like before. Old Lady Granville usually keeps to 'erself and we'd all as well she did. A lot of trouble, this is. Running back and forth on account of you and some bee her ladyship's got in 'er bonnet. We're all wondering why you're 'ere, I can tell you."

"Do you think you should call her old?" Fleur asked tentatively. She decided not to mention the reason for her presence—particularly since there could be no guarantee the whole thing wouldn't be called off once the pointlessness of the effort became obvious. "I mean, her ladyship might find out."

"There's a young one, too," Blanche said as if that made the irreverence understandable. "The Marquis's wife. They live in Bath usually but I 'eard a rumor the young Lady Granville's coming to 'elp with you."

Fleur swallowed and felt goosebumps on her arms. Was

she so much trouble, enough trouble to require another important person to come?

Once Fleur's blue satin bonnet rested firmly on her head, the strings flying loose since Blanche insisted that was the thing, they left the lofty room and followed a long corridor to a flight of stairs and down to the great hall. The building, a large oblong with domed orangeries at its heart, seemed impossibly huge to Fleur. On the ground floor, one magnificent space led to another. Blanche took Fleur through the orangeries where trees flourished beneath the dome. Fine rain had coated the outside of the glass and a misty film clung to the inside.

Outside, they sped along pathways flanked by smooth lawns and statuary until they reached rose gardens where the first buds would soon burst into blooms. An archway in a privet hedge several times Fleur's own height led them into a courtyard and she saw the Dowager Marchioness's house for the first time.

Footsteps, heavy and fierce-sounding approached from behind. Blanche looked back. Fleur knew better than to show interest but she did glance up at the man who strode past.

He muttered something that might have been, "Day," and carried on to the front door of a square, three-story gray stone house.

"That's Lord Dominic," Blanche whispered. "Ever so lovely, 'e is. All of us think so. In charge of the estate, too, with that 'andsome Mr. Lawrence. Mr. Lawrence is the manager."

Fleur hadn't seen the gentleman's face but his form appeared *ever so lovely*. He marched along with great purpose, his big shoulders swinging. The heels of his boots clattered on paving stones and a black coat flew out behind him.

Fleur gave a little shiver. Mama wouldn't approve of any shivering at all under the circumstances but Letitia and Rosemary would understand. They had spoken together of such things many times while huddled together beneath the covers of Letitia's bed. There were, they had decided, male specimens who—with various attributes—could make females feel quite weak. A fine, powerful form was one of those attributes.

Lord Dominic had overlong black hair—or some would consider it overlong—tied back with a ribbon. Fleur found this most intriguing.

He threw wide the shiny black front door and left it open once he had marched inside.

Blanche giggled. "'E's ever so forceful," she said. "Quiet but strong and you can feel how 'e's wild somewhere deep inside."

Fleur decided Blanche was taken with his lordship and didn't blame her. Although perhaps he had an ugly face and a mean look about him, but she doubted it.

Just as Fleur and Blanche arrived at the door, a comfortable-looking woman appeared. She wore a black dress, and pieces of gray hair curled free of her fat chignon to frame a round, pink face. "Are you Miss Fleur?" she asked.

Fleur dropped a hasty curtsey and said, "Yes."

"I'm Mrs. Lymer. I look after her ladyship. Come with me, please. Run along now, Blanche."

Shut inside a perfectly square vestibule where creamy marble veined with green covered the floor and early spring flowers filled vases on tables against the pale-green walls, the first sound Fleur heard was a man's deep voice. Not exactly raised in anger, nevertheless it was loud enough for her to hear every word:

."What the devil are you thinking of, Mama? I'm a busy man. In fact, I'm here to ask you to do me a great favor, one which will ease my present burden. And before you mention it, of course I can't—and won't—squire some country parson's mousey daughter around."

When his mother was uncertain, she chewed her bottom lip. She did so now and Dominic felt like a cad. "Hush," he said to his ethereal parent. "I was too harsh in what I just said. My professional life is particularly pressing at the moment and when Nathan came to me with your proposition, I over-reacted."

His mother, wearing a paint-smeared smock over a dress of orange Japanese gauze, managed to appear at once exotic and, as always, unconventional. She wore her gray specked dark hair very short, but curls made it look soft. She had dark eyes and clear, almost unwrinkled skin. When she stood, as she did now, her slenderness and straight back belied her age—not that Dominic was sure what that might be. The Dowager Marchioness of Granville stood almost six feet tall and could still make every head turn on the rare occasions when she appeared in public.

At the moment Dominic's parent watched him with disconcerting concentration.

"Am I forgiven, Mother?" he said.

"What am I to forgive you for? You haven't told me the nature of this pressing favor of yours, so I don't know if I will approve. And since I haven't personally explained the very small service I wish you to perform for me, you can't have refused to do it, so I have no reason to forgive or not to forgive you—yet."

Dominic bowed his head and looked at her in time to catch

the upward flicker of her mouth. "How you do love to play with me," he told her. "No wonder you're my favorite parent."

"I am your only parent."

"Quite so. This afternoon a young woman, a girl, will come to Heatherly looking for a place. Her name is Jane Weller and I told her to ask for you. Her former employers will not speak for her but I will."

Mother nodded slightly. "Another of your underdogs. Wrongly dismissed, you think?"

"I know. She was Miss Victoria Crewe-Burns's maid and it's my hope that the Crewe-Burnses need never know she's here." He spoke of the story the family had used about the girl. "She is reduced to living in a room not far from Covent Garden and cleaning for the harridan who runs the place in exchange for a lower rent."

"I won't ask how you know this girl and all the details," Mother said and paused.

Dominic smiled, knowing she wanted him to tell her those very details. "Thank you," he said. "I believe I will be able to explain one day. Meanwhile, my impression was that she is a superior young person. Perhaps her family came upon bad times, and reduced circumstances forced Jane into service."

"Very well. Make sure McGee knows to bring her directly to me." Visitors did not get past McGee, head butler at Heatherly. "We'll see what can be found for her."

"You won't like this, but Jane Weller doesn't know who I am, and—"

"You said you knew her."

"Yes, but…Mother, I must ask you not to tell the girl I recommended her. Please say a friend spoke for her."

His mother regarded him narrowly for long enough to make him sweat. "Very well," she said at last. "To my knowledge you are an honest man. I'll do it as long as I don't decide it's against Jane Weller's interests."

"Thank you, Mother." He kissed her hand. "Forgive me, but now I must rush."

"No such thing," she said calmly, indicating an ancient Chinese chair strewn with satin pillows. "Be comfortable. We have much more to discuss. Have you had breakfast?" When she moved, the soft fabric of her dress floated and caught the light.

"Yes," he told her shortly. "And the moment I arrived I told you I'll have nothing to do with some silly scheme to bring out a country parson's daughter."

"Sit down."

He opened his mouth to protest but set his teeth together instead. His mother sat on a divan heaped with more brilliant pillows. Reluctantly, Dominic also sat down.

"Did you hear Vivian Simpson is engaged?" Mother said, offhand.

Dominic envisioned Lady Vivian. "No. I wish her happiness. She deserves it."

"You don't wish, even a little, that the lucky man was you?"

"Sweet girl, Vivian. But whatever may have been between us was over years ago." So this was only a ploy to get him here for one of Mother's reminders that she wanted him to marry. He would not hurt her by telling her he would never marry, that his work didn't lend itself to marriage, to family life.

"I wish I could hear your thoughts," his mother said.

Dominic made to get up. "I really must get on."

"Sit," she said, and he did.

"Miss Fleur Toogood," Mother said, "is the daughter of a

dear friend of mine. We hadn't met in years but a month or so ago I had reason to visit her and I decided—"

"To adopt the daughter you never had and fuss with a Season for her. Commendable, but—"

"Kindly allow me to finish."

Dominic looked into his mother's eyes and closed his mouth.

"And I will thank you not to make rude and belittling comments, young man."

He supposed that if he were sixty and his mother still lived, she'd continue to call him "young man" when she wanted to put him in his place.

"Nathan went from here in high glee," she said. "He always had a wicked love of torturing you, but that's one of the trials of the younger brother. I assume he told you the accurate gist of what I want you to do."

Dominic braced his elbows on his knees and buried his face. "I hope he made most of it up."

"This will not be difficult for you, Dominic," Mother said. "I have noted that in your work—the work you will never discuss with me—you find it necessary to move about extensively in Society. Taking a charming young girl with you should pose no problem. You can do whatever it is you do at those gatherings and all you have to do is keep an eye on her to make sure she meets the right people—men, that is—and that she is not taken advantage of."

"Wonderful," Dominic muttered.

"John says Hattie may act as chaperon while he's in Vienna on business, as long as you accompany the two women on all occasions."

"Gad." He scooted his rear to the edge of the chair, stretched out his legs and flopped against the back of the

chair with his arms trailing. "In other words, I'm to watch over my brother's gorgeous wife while she supposedly watches over this girl. Let me remind you that the Marquis of Granville's lady turns every head and I will be too busy making sure no man offends her honor to be about my own business. Brother John would kill me—and I mean that—if some drunken lout was to offend Hattie."

"But we know you're up to the task," Mother said, studying a red lacquer screen as if she'd never seen it before. "Hattie is a sensible woman and quite capable of putting unwanted attention aside."

He grunted.

"Of far more concern is the nubile Miss Toogood," Mother said. "You haven't seen *her* yet."

Dominic tilted his head forward and narrowed his eyes. "What does that mean?"

"Beauty, brains, wit, piety—"

"You should have stopped with the wit," Dominic interrupted.

"Piety," Mother repeated. "Reverence, a serious outlook, quiet—not one to speak unless she's spoken to—Miss Toogood is the perfect catch for some lucky young buck."

"Buck?" Dominic muttered. "Saint, you mean. Why me? Why not Nathan?"

"You know why."

"Ahem, my lady." Lymer came into the room, her ample figure leaning forward as it invariably did. "Miss Fleur Toogood is here to see you. Since you were engaged with Lord Dominic, I put her in the morning room but you did say you wanted to see her as soon as she arrived."

"Bring her in," Mother said.

Lymer hurried away and Dominic leaped to his feet. He made for French doors which opened on a side terrace.

"Remain," Mother said shortly. "Do this for me, please, Dominic. I rarely ask anything of you."

He rolled his eyes, but turned back from the doors.

Lymer reappeared, stood aside and ushered in Mother's Miss Toogood. A glance at her blue pelisse and bonnet left him in no doubt that he'd passed her on his way here.

Shabby was the word that came to mind, but there the negatives ended. My word, this serious-faced miss was no mouse, even if she did come from the country.

"Fleur," Mother said, getting up with her customary fluid elegance. "Come here at once and let me see you. I do believe blue is your color. What a charming bonnet. Meet my son, Lord Dominic. Dominic, this is Miss Fleur Toogood, daughter of a dear old friend of mine."

Bloody hell. Why couldn't the creature be plain and all but invisible? "Pleased to meet you, Miss Toogood," he said, taking her hand and bowing over a finely darned glove. "Welcome to Heatherly." He straightened and released her hand at once.

She bobbed a curtsey. "Thank you, my lord. I'm pleased to see you again, my lady. My mother and father asked me to convey their good wishes and their thanks. Papa said to tell you he prays for you at services every day."

"How good of him," Mother said and her smile looked delighted to Dominic.

Fleur Toogood's rich, dark red hair waved beneath the brim of her bonnet. At last she raised her pointed chin and looked up at him from beneath thick, sun-tipped lashes—and he contemplated protecting not one, but two beautiful females. Large and tilted up slightly at the corners, Miss Toogood's eyes were the brightest of blues. She had the pale, clear skin of redheads, a generous mouth, fine but definite arched brows and a straight nose. *Toothless and smelly?* Damn Nathan's hide. She was gorgeous, dammit.

And what a melting smile she had. He smiled back— couldn't help himself—and she immediately turned the corners of her mouth down and frowned, dash the girl's temerity.

"Where are you staying?" He winced a little. Since he already knew the answer, the question was the kind one asked when the brain had ceased to function.

"Here with us," Mother said, frowning at him. "In the main house, of course. It's too quiet for a young thing here with me."

"I like being quiet," Miss Toogood said quickly, surprising Dominic. "The room I was given last night is far too grand. I should be happy if there was a smaller space for me here with you."

"Rubbish," Mother said, smiling again. "But you are a sweet, unassuming girl. I want you to have the best of everything while you're in London and I intend to see to it that you are well set up for life by the end of the Season. Lord Dominic shares my determination, don't you, Dominic?"

He remembered to close his mouth again. "I hope you will enjoy being in Town," he said carefully. She had lowered her lashes again and he glanced down her length.

Fate could be evil. A lush little body if ever he saw one. Her proportions would make a less controlled man salivate. Dominic swallowed—several times. Usually he preferred taller women. This one wasn't short but neither was she average. Ah, yes, but nothing else about her was average, either.

"Dominic," Mother said in a soft tone that spelled danger. "Would you show Miss Toogood the house? I know it's confusing there at first and you're so good at that sort of thing."

"I should love to, but—" he spread his hands and grimaced

"—duty calls and I really must get on." He really must not allow himself to respond to their visitor like a man returning from years alone on a desert island.

"Nathan mentioned you had a lot on," Mother said. "He told me he'd take care of things for you if you need a couple of hours."

"Nathan should mind his own—" Dominic remembered his manners just in time. He looked at Miss Toogood once more and saw how color stained her cheeks. He'd let her know he thought her a nuisance, damn his carelessness.

"When did you say I should be ready to receive this person you think I should employ?" Mother said.

Blackmailed by his own parent.

"This afternoon," he told her. "Come, Miss Toogood. I have a great deal to show you."

"Enjoy yourselves," Mother said. "Lunch will be served for the two of you in the garden room. My modiste, Mrs. Neville, arrives this afternoon to start on Fleur's wardrobe. Since I know little of modern styles, I know you will make sure only the most flattering are chosen."

"Mother." This time Dominic didn't attempt to disguise a warning in his voice.

"Oh, you'll do beautifully. Hattie will be here in a few days to deal with most of the clothing. But we must have a few items to get started with. The modiste will have a list. Pay particular attention to color and fit. There's no truer saying than that a young lady in the market for a husband must make the best of her best assets. I'm sure you'll decide what those are."

4

He had smiled at her in his mother's house, hadn't he? Or had he? On the third floor of Heatherly House Fleur stopped on the threshold of the long room and turned to see why she couldn't hear Lord Dominic's footsteps anymore. She had tentatively mentioned that she liked paintings, to which he had said, "Long room," and led her out of the most beautiful ballroom she'd ever seen. Well, it was the only ballroom she'd ever seen—the Sodbury Martyr village hall where dances were held didn't count.

Lord Dominic's footsteps had ceased because he seemed to have forgotten to keep on walking. He stood a few yards away, looking at the floor, his expression distant and closed. What a shame for such a handsome man to appear so unhappy—not that it made him less good-looking. In fact, that remoteness might even make him more attractive, if that was possible.

He ambled on, hands behind his back, studying his feet, and Fleur waited politely.

But she didn't feel polite. Wretched man! Did he think a title and too much money made him important?

Yes, of course he did.

"Ouch!" What a widgeon she was; she'd allowed him to bump into her. "I'm sorry, my lord." *And sorry you are rude.*

He gripped her elbows to steady her. "Why? Why are you sorry because I was careless enough to collide with you?"

Breathless, Fleur felt her tummy flip unpleasantly. "I should have moved on, not stood in the doorway."

Lord Dominic's chest expanded, then he let out a long sigh. "You do have a great deal to learn about dealing with men, Miss Toogood. Never, *never* apologize if you can help it and absolutely not if there is the slightest chance that you have suffered even the most minute inconvenience."

"In other words, my lord, I am to turn into the kind of person I cannot abide—just to get a husband. That will not be possible. I have been brought up much differently from that."

He continued to hold her arms and he seemed awfully close. Fleur had to raise her chin to see his face. She had always wished to be taller but some things could not be changed.

"Principles are admirable," he said. "However, I gather finding a wealthy husband and bettering yourself and your family is the reason you're in London for the Season."

Fleur watched shadows gather in his startlingly blue eyes. "That was not my idea," she couldn't help saying. She continued hastily, "But I am grateful to the Dowager Marchioness for her kindness and I intend to do what I can for my family."

The way he looked into her eyes while she spoke, then dropped his gaze to her mouth completely unnerved Fleur. When her tummy reacted this time, the sensation wasn't unpleasant.

"If you were my daughter, I wouldn't let you loose on your own."

"I'm not on my own," she protested. "You make… That was a horrid thing to say. What can you mean by it? And what would you know of having a daughter my age when I'm an adult just as you are?"

He smiled slightly and released her. "Forgive me if I offended you. I meant that if you were important to me I would be afraid to have such a beautiful woman exposed to the type of rogue you are likely to meet while you're here."

His lordship said she was beautiful but still she felt a little sting. *If you were important to me.* Of course she wasn't, but why would he be so cutting? "With your protection, my lord, surely I have nothing to fear from rogues." He would think her saucy but that was better than having him consider her a vapid nothing.

"How old did you say you were, Miss Toogood?"

"I didn't. I am twenty."

He breathed in through his nose and frowned. "Mmm, I vaguely remember being twenty."

She laughed, put a hand over her mouth and laughed even louder. Ladies, she'd been told, chose when to laugh and did so charmingly but she had no idea how to plan such things. When something was funny, it was funny.

"Good," he said, smiling at her and taking her arm. "I've made you relax with me. Not that I intended any such thing, miss."

With no choice but to walk where he propelled her, Fleur giggled even though she struggled to be serious. He did have a smile worth remembering after all.

"There is no reason for me to tell you, but it's been ten years since I was twenty."

"Thirty?" she said. "So old? Women mature more quickly than men. Are you aware of that?"

"I'm aware that you like to spar. Indeed, I think you revel in trying to annoy me. What do you think of our paintings?"

Fleur barely glanced at a picture of fruit spilling from a bowl and moved on to study the faces of two women, one tall, one much smaller, both dark-haired. They smiled at each other, their arms threaded together.

"The Worth aunts," Lord Dominic said. "A very long time ago. My mother's older sisters. They live in Bath, near my brother John and his wife. The ladies are ancient but they keep us all on our toes."

"I should like them, then," Fleur said. "Spirited people change those around them for the better."

"So you say." He didn't sound convinced.

They walked, side by side, on wooden floors that creaked with each step. The room stretched the width of the house with large windows at either end. Dominic waved her to sit on a window seat. "I mustn't forget your long journey. Have you traveled a good deal?"

"No." She had scarcely been out of the village.

He raised his brows. Light caught glints of red in his hair. He appeared to be a strong, a really strong and lithe man. A sensation that he could move very fast and at any moment disturbed her.

"Look—" he paced in front of Fleur "—I think you have been given a heavy burden. You are charged with *saving* your family and that is absolutely too much."

She pleated the skirt of her dress between her fingers. Of course he didn't know she had heard him refer to her as mousey, or declare that he had no time to spare for her. Well, she didn't like the unkind words, but neither did she blame him for objecting to his mother's plan.

"How did the Dowager Marchioness manage to change your mind about me—about taking me about?" she blurted out, and shut her eyes tightly. "I'm sorry. I shouldn't have said that."

"No, you shouldn't. Why did you? No, no, don't answer that."

She opened her eyes to find him shaking his head.

"You must have overheard something," he said.

Fleur nodded. "I only heard that you didn't have time for me. And you are perfectly right to be annoyed at the prospect of trailing me with you. I cannot let you do it."

He stopped a moment, and stared at her. "That's not your decision."

"I won't be a nuisance," Fleur insisted.

"I am *going* to do it."

"No, I absolutely won't allow it."

He sat down, suddenly and hard, beside her. "I'm going to explain something to you. Watch my mouth and listen carefully. Concentrate."

Crossing her arms, Fleur used one of her best frowns but said nothing.

"It isn't for you to allow or not allow anything around here. Mother is anxious to help your family. Mostly she wants to help her old friend, your mother. I know I said this is too great a burden for you—that is what *will* happen. And I'll do my part because my mother rarely asks me for a favor."

"This is a burden to you. I don't care to be any man's burden."

He actually smiled again. "Of course you do—that's why you're here. I have—"

"Some men may not find a wife a burden," she said and heard her own sharpness. "Some may find her a helper, a supporter, a partner in all things."

She got another long stare before he said, "As I had started to say before you interrupted me, I have an idea. Why not allow me to pick out a few likely fellows for you to meet? It would eliminate all the fussing around." He raised a long-fingered hand and actually appeared enthusiastic. "That's exactly the thing. Why on earth isn't this marriage business always dealt with sensibly, the way I propose?"

"How exactly would you pick out these gentlemen? Since you have no idea what kind of a person would suit."

"Suit you?" he said, as if the idea of her having an opinion on the matter amazed him. "Far better for you to allow my experience to be the judge of who might suit. I know the background details, m'dear, the depth of the pockets and the family history. And any reputation I may not know I will find out. Don't give it another thought—leave everything to me. You may be sure I'll do well by you because Mother wouldn't allow less."

He *really* wanted to avoid spending time with her. Fleur slipped off her bonnet and ran the brim through her hands. Since Lord Dominic obviously didn't find her appealing, why should he think any other man would? What a pickle.

Fleur, you are a silly. You aren't attracted to him, either...are you?

"I see you're considering my idea. Wise of you. I'll talk to my brother, Nathan—he's the middle brother of the three of us—and ask him to make some suggestions. And I have several good friends who could be useful, too. Between us we'll work something out and make sure we all have a wedding to attend as soon as possible. The sooner the better. Of course the trousseau won't be a problem. Between whatever the modiste starts on today and then with Hattie's help, you'll be well fitted out."

Fleur didn't trust herself to speak. He thought she would enjoy having a committee appointed to marry her off. *Why couldn't he see how mortifying that would be?*

"I see you are overwhelmed. Think nothing of it. In my business I spend many hours thinking my way through problems."

"What is your business?" So now she was a problem. Ugh, this was hateful.

"I run this estate on the Marquis's behalf but I have other work that isn't something I can discuss. Other than to say it leaves me little time for frivolous things."

Like me?

"My lord," she said and put another inch or two between them. Once again he was too close for comfort. "My lord, I am grateful for your kind consideration of what you see as my problems, but I cannot accept the type of assistance you offer. I don't think I should be at all comfortable to have a number of gentlemen harvesting unsuspecting males for my perusal. In fact, I should be deeply embarrassed."

He snorted. "Your inexperience shows. I assure you this will be done in a way that will not embarrass you. Each man we present to you will come because our descriptions of you make him want to."

"Unfortunately I will be the one to watch the contenders' disappointment when they find out they have been deceived. Unless, of course, you would explain that I am penniless? That there is absolutely no dowry?"

"That would come later," he said. "After the man is besotted with you."

Fleur looked away before he could see her bitter smile. "I doubt if the Dowager Marchioness would be amused to learn you decided on such an unconventional approach. I suppose you would have me receive these people and try to engage them in lively conversation while you look on."

"Only until Hattie gets here."

Fleur stared at him and he had the grace to blush.

"And when your mother discovers you have devised a plan different from her own?"

"Mother doesn't have to know all about it. She will think I'm going the extra mile to make sure you do some of your socializing in the safety of this house."

Best not point out that he was admitting an intention to hoodwink his parent. Fleur imagined the rectory, worn but with every piece of furniture polished to a high sheen. A fire in the parlor fireplace and her sisters sewing or playing a game, or perhaps even writing to her. How she missed them. If she could find a good man who was also well fixed she could have the other girls do better for themselves, and ease Mama and Papa's way. Letitia was in love with the local Squire's son but it remained to see if anything would come of that.

"Come." His Lordship got up and offered her his hand, which she held. "Up you come. It's just about time for lunch. Cook is a genius."

"I ate breakfast and I agree," Fleur said. And now, for her own sanity, there must be a change in plans.

"Lunch is to be served in the garden room," his lordship told her. "In fact the garden rooms run the entire width of the front of the house. They were built to bring in more light. My great-grandfather had a hand in designing the place and he was a man of vision."

She must speak now and speak firmly. "Lord Dominic," she said as they walked out onto a balcony which surrounded the third floor and opened onto a view of beautiful flights of stairs descending to the first floor. "Please don't make any moves on these plans of yours until I have time to consider them. Whatever happens, I know I must have some suitable gowns made so that I will not mortify your mother. Today I will concentrate on that since I'm not accustomed to so much attention."

"Indeed," he said. "Very important and I'll speak with my friends later."

"You aren't listening to me." Fleur took a breath and let it out slowly, allowing her annoyance to calm down. "I just want to make sure you understand what I said about preferring you to wait before doing anything about…men, for me."

He pushed out his very attractive mouth. "If you're sure," he said faintly. "But I should have thought the sooner the better."

"We are discussing a lifelong commitment and I don't want, nor can I afford, a mistake."

On the second floor, where the ballroom and many receiving rooms were located, Fleur took her hand from Lord Dominic's arm. "My room isn't far from here. It's at the end of that corridor and to the right. I'm going to return there now and rest awhile."

"But lunch—"

"You are a big, strong man who must eat well. I'm sure cook will not mind if you eat my lunch also. I couldn't possibly touch a bite of it. And please don't let me keep you from your own important affairs any longer. I could tell you were horrified at the thought of accompanying me to the modiste. Quite unnecessary, I assure you. The modiste knows all about these things, I'm sure. And your mother gave her a list so I will rely on her assistance."

She backed away. "Thank you so much for looking after me. I promise to be as little bother as I can. Goodbye."

"Fleur," he said, startling her by using her first name. "I'd really like to have lunch with you."

Oh fie, his eyes were sincere. A piece of his hair had come loose and fell forward to outline a lean cheek with a dimple beside the mouth. Why did he have to be such a heart-stealer? Not, of course, that he'd stolen her heart but she did feel herself softening toward him.

Which was exactly the trap he intended her to fall into, the wretch.

"Thank you," she said. "But I am awfully tired. Or perhaps I should say overwhelmed. I'll feel better if I rest."

"You disappoint me, but I understand. I do want you to meet my brother, Nathan, soon. He is a good man, a brilliant man but with a tendency to waste his talents. He is kind and generous and I think you may enjoy him."

"I'll look forward to meeting him," Fleur said.

"Yes, yes, and meanwhile I'll have a tray brought up to you. You can't get through a whole day on breakfast alone." He took her hand and held it. "You have courage. I like that. We still have a great deal to see at Heatherly. Promise you will allow me to complete our tour."

Fleur swallowed and wondered if he heard the faint sound from her throat. "That will be lovely," she said.

He lifted her fingers to his lips and rested them there. Looking directly at her, he parted his lips the tiniest bit and allowed warm breath to drift over her skin. Then he bent her fingers gently down and softly kissed each knuckle. She thought she felt his tongue on each dip between bones.

Lord Dominic was a practiced lover and she was too easily seduced by his fine wiles.

"I'll go now," she said. "Have a wonderful lunch." Without thinking, she brought his hand to her lips and lightly kissed its back.

Dominic murmured. "In any other woman I should con-

sider that practiced flirtation but you, my dear, are a natural—
if impetuous—charmer."

She was a woman adrift with nothing but a List, and she'd
best study it well and quickly, before she made more stupid
mistakes. "Goodbye," she said and sped away along the corridor. This was a dreadful pickle.

5

He had been anonymous long enough—not that his true identity would ever be revealed.

His name—the name he had taken—needed to spread throughout the world of his enemies. He would not rest until mention of him made them tremble.

"Are you awake, boy?" he said to the twelve-year-old who lay on a pallet behind a rich curtain. "Pay attention! You live at my pleasure. Never forget it."

"Yes, sir," the boy said.

"I want them all to whisper about me, to make believe that the danger I bring will always be for someone else, never for them. Even those who have already felt my sting and paid a ransom for their daughters will pretend otherwise."

"Yes, sir."

Yes, he wanted the unspeakable spoken of, and lied about.

Aha, he couldn't ask for things to go better than they were now. The plot was remarkably advanced—especially since his inventive informant had as large a thirst for revenge as his own. Almost as large. There would never be a more determined, more malevolent pair of ill-wishers visited upon the ranks of the haute ton.

Fiddlededee, fiddlededum, who would have thought the

ambition of a malcontent would bring him his most valuable ally?

Freedom. He was free, free, magnificently free and day by day his fortune grew. The fattest pigeon was in his sights and, when he got what the bird was worth, she would be his last adventure, his last victim—unless he decided to remind London of the horrors of '15 during future Seasons—just for fun.

But it wasn't quite time for his most spectacular, his most daring abduction. First he intended to snatch another valuable virgin or two—just until the ransom rolled in, of course. Their families would pay, just as the others had, for his promise that no one would know their darling daughters had been taken and held by a man—alone.

The parents feared for the loss of their girls' reputations, and any chance of a brilliant marriage. And he, Le Chat Soyeux, *was only too glad to put their minds at rest by accepting generous gifts for his silence. He clapped and spun on his toes. The Silken Cat. His name was perfect.*

But now it was time to start rumors of the abductions, to set Society atwitter while "his girls" and their families trembled and sweated for fear their names would be revealed.

His spirits knew no calming. A gilded circular staircase wound upward from the receiving room to the glorious music box salon. Who would ever guess that inside a large, run-down warehouse with soot-coated windowless windows, a jewel of a residence had been built? Small, it was true, but perfect. After all, the builders and craftspeople had been brought from the Continent and returned there once the job was complete. A brilliant deception.

"Don't follow me," he told the boy on his pallet, and went to give him a sharp kick through the curtain.

Harry-the-bastard all but swallowed his cry, but not quite. "No, sir," he said, very low.

The Cat would forget the boy until he needed him again.

Whirling, whirling, he circumnavigated the room, hesitating an instant before each shadowy mirror to admire this, his most flamboyant costume. The maquillage didn't entirely please him so he rushed to the pots of paint and put a brush into some white paste. Holding a hand mirror high, turning a little to capture more light from the only candle burning, he put another coat on his cheeks, forehead, nose and chin— whited out his mouth and sat, tapping the toes of his high-heeled red-and-gold shoes while he waited for his face to dry.

Next came the pot of dark red rouge and he applied this precisely in two slashes over his cheekbones. He painted on the dear little rosebud mouth. A large black beauty mark made a fabulous addition and he drew thin arches for his eyebrows. The last touch to his face was an application of white powder on his eyelashes. The Pink-Eyed One had emerged to ready himself for the evening's games. He had considered publicizing his pet name for himself, but since only his victims got close enough to shriek at the sight of his inhuman eyes he'd decided to discard the notion.

The Silken Cat lived and would soon be a name on every pair of lips.

The wig, row upon row of tight white curls that reached his shoulders, and a short, curving fall over his forehead, delighted him. White silk stockings showed the fine shape of his calves and his thighs bulged in white satin breeches. His red-and-gold waistcoat fitted his admirable torso like a glove. His jacket of embroidered red silk clung to his wide shoulders and accentuated his muscular chest. He was not the tallest of men but his height was commanding enough.

Taking the ringing metal stairs several at a time, he sprang to the top and flung a leg over the bannister. Away he went, shooting down, around and around, shrieking aloud, his legs spread wide.

His informant was late. The Silken Cat pouted. His expectations must not be thwarted and if this inconvenience happened again, he might have to show his darker side—again. Apparently twice had not been enough.

The details he expected tonight would be essential, but he filled the time while he waited by studying his next marriageable heiress, and setting a fat price for her "untarnished" return.

And this time the whispered gossip would begin. He laughed aloud at the thought of how her family would join in the gossip about The Silken Cat even while they knew he held their daughter. They must if they hoped to protect their darling. Wheee!

Oh, the fabulous fun of it all. Tonight, tomorrow at the latest, would bring the start of a new era. There might be as many as three more young women invited to his gilded cage— at different times, of course—if for no other reason than to make his technique even more flawless. Above all, his mission must be to spread fear for the safety of England's most precious daughters.

He craved the money.

He relished the power.

6

Standing in the middle of her bedchamber, Fleur studied a fashion plate the modiste, Mrs. Neville, had produced for consideration.

"Perfect for the evening," the woman said. "The gathers at the back are very popular. And the half sash."

"Mmm." Fleur felt another rising blush, one of several since she'd been so flustered as to kiss his lordship's hand. Just as he had shown her, he could be polite, too. She should have had lunch with him instead of behaving like a child and running away. What could have got into her?

Neville waited and Fleur managed to smile at her. "I'm sure I will be delighted to have a dress like this," she said, tapping the paper. "Is that all? May I go now?"

"Go? We've hardly begun, miss. We have several outfits to choose and we haven't even taken measurements yet."

"Of course we haven't. I wasn't thinking." She was, in fact, thinking a great deal too much.

"A bit overwhelming, is it?" the modiste asked, her kind face all sympathy.

Fleur nodded. Why shouldn't this woman know she was dealing with an inexperienced country girl—everyone else here did?

"Yes, well, I took the liberty of making up some things for you to try and if you like them, we'll make the necessary alternations. The Dowager Marchioness described you to me. A marvel, she is. Such an eye, but that would come from her painting."

"Have you seen any of her paintings?" Fleur asked eagerly. She hoped to be invited inside Lady Granville's studio one day.

"Oh, no. I've made her clothes for years and I've never been in that room she likes so much. Her ladyship's very private about all that. But I do believe she gave me a fair idea of your measurements. See what you think of this."

From an oversize cotton bag she produced a dress made of a shiny fabric in pale, multihued stripes.

"A new material. French washing silk, they call this. Pop it on."

With Neville's help Fleur shed her own simple frock and wriggled while she was tied and pinned into an evening dress. "It's the one in the picture," she said. "How clever you are. But don't you think the neckline is a little…" It was a lot…

"No," the modiste said shortly. "With a figure like yours, why not show it off? Now stand still while I make some adjustments." She placed Fleur before a long mirror.

The neckline of the gown sank to a deep V front and back and long sleeves ended in points at her hands. A gored skirt didn't reach her ankles, except where the gathered section swept much longer over the heels of her shoes.

After a light tap, Blanche bustled into the room and whispered in the modiste's ear. Whatever she said got a nod, yes, and Blanche—her face very pink—returned to the door. "You're to come in, my lord," she said, then rushed to position a chair where Lord Dominic could sit behind Fleur but see her in the mirror.

Her heart leaping, Fleur watched him in that mirror, watched him enter her bedchamber without looking at her and saunter to the chair Blanche held for him. She would, Fleur thought, have to practice a great deal more before she'd be able to come close to the ferociousness of the man's frown.

"Thank you," he said to Blanche who left with evident reluctance. Finally he looked directly at Fleur. He crossed his arms, stretched out his long, strongly muscled legs and crossed his booted feet. "Good afternoon, Miss Toogood." He settled with his head tilted to give him the best possible view of her—and he used that view to its best advantage. By the time he finished examining every inch of her—minutely— Fleur's skin tingled.

"Good of you to take such an interest, my lord," the modiste said and bobbed a curtsey. "The Dowager Marchioness told me you insisted on advising Miss Toogood on her wardrobe."

He grunted.

For two pins, Fleur thought, she would remind him that she'd told him not to come. She'd have to be blind not to see that he didn't want to be here at all. What confused her most was that from Neville's reaction to their visitor it must not be an unusual event for a gentleman to be present for such intimate sessions. Things were so different in London.

"It's too big," he said suddenly, and sniffed.

The modiste bobbed again and said, "You're right, of course. The dress isn't finished and will be made to fit Miss Toogood perfectly." She went to work, deftly adjusting the garment.

"What do you think of it?" Lord Dominic asked, catching Fleur's eyes in the mirror. "Like it, do you?"

"Yes, my lord. I think it's beautiful. It's the most beautiful dress I've ever worn."

"Any dress you wore would be beautiful," he said, frowning as deeply as ever. "You are beautiful. Remember that. When you go about, people will remark on you. You carry yourself well and your voice is pleasant. Hattie—my sister-in-law—she will give you invaluable advice. The idea is to turn heads and you will certainly do that."

Fleur's heart beat faster yet. "Thank you for your kind words."

"There'll be curiosity about who you are, who your people are. You'll be asked questions you may find rude."

"I will be proud to tell anyone who my people are."

At last he smiled slightly. "I should have known that's what you would say. I suggest you say you are the orphaned child of my mother's sister-in-law and in Mother's care now. Should someone say they were unaware of Mother's brother, explain that he died in India—shortly before you were born. Killed by a mercenary. Your mother passed on recently and you came to us. Tell them the Dowager wants you to be the daughter she never had."

"I'll do no such thing," Fleur said, outraged by his idea.

"I did expect you to say that," he said. "The story is true, all but for you playing any part in it, or there having been a child at all. Now I'll explain some of life's realities to you. The bodice could be tighter, Neville."

"Not if I want to breathe," Fleur told him and not gently. She didn't point out that the neckline already revealed too much of her and if the thing were made tighter, her flesh would have no place to go but out—out of the bodice, that was.

Did his lordship smirk? He did. At least he had the grace to lower his gaze but his amusement deepened the dimples near his mouth and he looked…self-satisfied. The handsome rattle!

Neville tightened the bodice and Fleur looked at the way she blossomed out of the neckline. "I don't think it should be like this," she said firmly, all too aware of his lordship's presence.

"It's perfect, Neville," Lord Dominic said, and to Fleur, "very nice indeed, Miss Toogood. A woman dresses for a man, not for herself, and as a man I can tell you—"

"Is it necessary for women to be uncomfortable in order for men to be happy?" Fleur said, not caring if she interrupted him.

"Are you uncomfortable?" he said. "Where do you hurt?"

"Ooh," Fleur said, too irritated to contain herself. "*Men.* Why must you answer questions with questions? There are more ways to be uncomfortable than because of physical pain."

"The gown hurts you elsewhere? Surely not in your mind?"

He would not find her a witless pudding brain. "Certainly in my mind," she said. "The idea of popping out of a dress in public places gives me a headache."

"Better than falling into it, I assure you," Lord Dominic said. His nostrils flared and his smirk became a wide, purely evil grin. This man enjoyed torturing people he considered helpless. Well, she would show him. She would show him that Fleur Toogood had a strong mind of her own. The only questions were how she would do it—and when.

"She is so tiny here, my lord," Neville said, running a finger just beneath the bodice. "The lines will be irresistible."

"I can see that."

He saw too much and took too long about it. Fleur had thought of something to add to The List. A man might be human and weak—in fact she had every reason to believe this was the case for most of their kind—but with some strengthening of the backbone and more time spent in prayer for a pure mind, even men could mend their lascivious ways.

"Small here," Neville said, placing a hand on Fleur's hip. "When I'm working with a lady like Miss Toogood, I'm grateful for the simple softness of styles at the moment. They draw attention to, er, difficult areas on some ladies but in this case they show things off lovely."

"I'm grateful for that, too," Lord Dominic said.

Fleur felt his eyes on her face and couldn't avoid looking back at him. His intense regard, the intensity in eyes that seemed—hot?—stole away anything she might have said. The very corners of his mouth tipped up and his eyes narrowed the smallest amount.

She returned his gaze, aware that goosebumps climbed her spine all the way to her neck and her scalp prickled. And…my goodness, she almost put her hands to her breasts. They ached and the tips hardened. And she had no doubt what caused such a strange and, well, marvelous feeling. *Him.* Lord Dominic had some sort of powers over her and she thought she liked the result a great deal, which was probably harmless and part of the process of maturing sexually. However, where he was concerned she should not take such reactions seriously.

"Do you have jewelry, Miss Toogood?"

To have romantical notions, or worse, what could only be *carnal* desires in response to this man would be futile.

"Miss Toogood," he said. "I asked if you have jewelry."

She stared at him hard and wondered if she ought to say she considered his presence at such a time, and his opinions, unsuitable. "What do you think of a velvet band around the neck, Neville?" she asked, deliberately ignoring Lord Dominic. You can put a flower or a satin rosette, or even a little pin at the front and it looks very pretty. Mama sent her gold pin with me. It has a pearl in it and I should enjoy using that. It belonged to my grandmother. I know lots of tricks to make things pretty and spend very little money doing so."

Neville didn't answer and her round face lost its expression, but her skin turned pink. Fleur was certain the lady held her breath.

Lord Dominic stirred and leaned to rest his elbows on his knees. "I appreciate imagination," he said and Fleur glowed.

"Last year we had a dance at the village hall—that's in Sodbury Martyr where we live—and I wore one of my sister Letitia's frocks. Quite a plain frock but good material. Pale green. I tucked the skirt like this." She bent over and caught up seams between two of the gores. "At each tuck I sewed a deep green bow and the dress looked completely different."

Still holding the hem, she glanced up at Neville, then at Lord Dominic.

His interest was held rather lower than her face.

Furious, mortified, Fleur straightened up at once and put a hand to the neckline of the dress. Animals, that's what some men could be. This man's only salvation would be through lots and lots of prayer. That and by marrying and having a family of his own. Family life taught men the true value of things. Fleur's papa had told her as much and he never lied.

"I wish I had seen the green dress," Lord Dominic said. "Neville must make you something in green." It was possible he felt chagrined. He looked at her with gentleness now.

"I brought the one I altered with me," she said, pleased she could show that she wasn't the type of person to take advantage.

"Did you?" he said. "I should like to see just how tall you are beside me."

She spread her arms and smiled wryly. "This is all of me. I have wished to be taller like my sister Letitia who is so graceful."

"So are you." He got up and beckoned to her. "Come. A man doesn't have to be a great deal taller than his wife, but I doubt you would be pleased if he was shorter—not when you are a small person yourself."

Fleur remembered to pull her eyebrows together and walked hesitantly to stand in front of him.

"Hmm," he murmured while she looked straight ahead at the V where the front of his waistcoat crossed over.

His lordship had a lovely chest, solid looking and built to fill out fine clothes to advantage.

"Look at me," he said.

Fleur raised her face in time for him to slide a hand around to the middle of her back. He offered her his other hand and she placed hers on top.

"A little bit of a thing," he said with a short laugh. "How do you feel about the size of a man?"

What she felt at the moment was overheated. "I like a man to be substantial," she said and trembled inside. This was such personal talk.

"Substantial, hmm? At least you don't simper and waffle about your opinions. A substantial man is your preference. I shall bear that in mind."

He made a turn with her, and then another. His hand at her back burned. Or perhaps she burned because of his hand. A little pressure and their toes almost touched. Other parts did touch and Fleur retrained her gaze on Lord Dominic's waistcoat. She couldn't do a thing about a tumble of sensations. Their dance without music continued. His lordship's very solid thighs pressed against her, and her breasts brushed his chest.

The most ridiculous, most inconvenient urges all but overwhelmed her. She wanted to soften against him, to relax, to wrap her arms around his waist, rest her face against chest and close her eyes.

She would do no such thing and this had gone on far too long. "So now you know how tall I am," she said, stepping back, or trying to. He took a moment to release her.

He stared down at her, his face rigid, fists on hips, and a deep breath raised his chest. "I think I know a great deal about you."

Fleur doubted that.

"One moment," he said. "Raise your chin." Fleur did as he asked and his next touch turned her legs, and the very depths of her womanly places, both weak and overheated. With the back of his first finger, he started at the very lowest part of her neckline where he came in skin to skin contact with her breasts, and brushed ever so slowly upward, pausing from time to time while he rubbed almost imperceptibly and watched what he did. At last his finger rested in the hollow at the base of her neck. "Irresistible," he said. "I shall regard it as my duty to see that you are found by a man worthy of you. Both of your mind…and your body. A man of highly developed taste."

"You make me sound like a suckling pig," Fleur said, her voice too high.

Lord Dominic threw back his head and laughed, displaying his very white, very strong teeth. His hand remained on her neck and as his laughter subsided, he all but enclosed that slender neck in one large hand. "You are a marvel. Little wonder Mother is so taken with you. Only trust me, Fleur, and I will be a completely reliable champion." As he spoke he caressed her neck and his eyes never moved from her throat.

Fleur thought him a potentially dangerous champion, but the… She clapped her hands to her cheeks. Any thought of being wildly excited by the flamboyant and reckless Lord Dominic was forbidden.

Would he, she wondered, be a thoughtful but melting, mad-making lover? Oh, she must, at the earliest opportunity, spend a long time examining her conscience. And perhaps she should consider devouring fewer romantical novels. *Fie,* anything but that!

Again he massaged her neck and showed signs of returning his path to her decolletage. He did spread his fingers wide on her vulnerable skin. "This neck, these ears, these delicate wrists and fine fingers were made for adornment." His touch lingered on each part he mentioned. "We must make sure your toilette is the envy of the *ton.* Neville, continue. Pay close attention to fit."

With complete nonchalance, he strolled to the bed and tossed lengths of fabric aside, handling a piece here, wrinkling his nose at another there. He pulled out a bolt of heavy silk in a rich shade of orange-gold. "Make her something in this. It will turn her hair to fire. And I should also like to see her in red."

"*Red,* my lord?"

"Red, Neville. And now I must go. I've spent far too long here as it is."

Nathan met Dominic halfway up the lower staircase. "By God, man, where have you been?"

"Assisting Miss Toogood with her wardrobe for the Season."

Nathan's eyebrows rose. "You poor devil. What's she like? An ugly duckling, I imagine."

The temptation to tell Nathan he was right left Dominic quickly. Even the briefest encounter with the lady would prove him a liar. "She's comely, very comely. A completely countrified miss, though. Not the slightest idea how to conduct herself in the type of surroundings she's about to enter. Praise be that Hattie's coming. She knows how hard these things can be for someone who wasn't born to them."

"Yes," Nathan said, "But Hattie's the most gorgeous creature I've ever seen.

Dominic couldn't hide a smile. "She is indeed and I mustn't forget how beauty can ease the way of a girl without connections or blunt. Except for her connections to us, of course."

"Of course," Nathan said slowly, casting a deeply suspicious eye upon Dominic. "Miss Toogood isn't just comely, is she?"

"No," Dominic said. "Of course I don't have time for all this escort nonsense but if I were you I might wish Mother had chosen me for the job rather than my brother."

Nathan looked speculative and said, "You don't say." Then he grabbed Dominic's arm. "You distracted me, damn it. You'll never guess who's waiting for you in the study."

Dominic didn't have a clue and shook his head.

"I'll give you a hint. *Stolen away by a cavorting dandy in pretty clothes and paint.*"

"I'll have McGee's head," Dominic said, striding down the stairs two at a time. "The instructions were absolutely clear. Jane Weller was to be taken directly to Mother. What if someone with less than kind motives sees her in this house?"

"Miss Weller hasn't arrived yet, although she very well may at any moment—and therein lies the rub, brother. We must have a plan because the woman in the study is Gussy Arbuthnot, Victoria Crewe-Burns's closest friend."

7

McGee stomped to his hideaway in an enclosed butler's chair and climbed inside. He pulled his head back into the shadows—to hide his aggravated expression, Dominic supposed.

"Now we'll suffer," Nathan said, his eyebrows raised in the middle. "You suggested he isn't following directions when he is and always does. He could hardly get Miss Weller to Mama if the girl hasn't shown up yet."

Dominic took his brother by the arm, pulled him to the back of the great hall and behind the staircase. "Stay there," he said. "If Jane Weller does come, let McGee answer the door but be ready to pounce on the girl before she can enter, then carry her off to the Dower House. It would be a disaster if Gussy saw her."

"She'll scream. Have you thought of that?"

"Put your hand over her mouth until you've reassured her. Say Brother Juste sent you and she's not to mention him, not to anyone. Then just tell her about Gussy being in the house and that will be enough. She'll be grateful to be swept off her feet then. Mama won't be so easily diverted. Take her aside and explain how we're helping a monk."

"Dominic! If Mama discovers you've turned into a liar, she'll be crushed." Nathan looked truly concerned.

"Please do it," Dominic said. "Trust me. She'll do what we ask and she would do something similar if we were in need of help. Now I have to make sure Gussy doesn't get wind of anything."

Nathan wrinkled his nose. "I must say I was a bit miffed when I learned Gussy was here to see you. Always thought she had a thing for me."

"She probably isn't here to further any romantic notions."

"Why is she, then?"

"I hope to find that out shortly, don't I?" Dominic said, not looking forward to the interview. "Before I go in there…any rumors floating around? Anything that might be useful dealing with this kidnapper?"

"Not a thing. No hint of an abduction last night. But then, we wouldn't expect an announcement, would we? We'll have to rely mostly on luck and we need to question the Weller girl at length."

"And we will," Dominic said. He glanced at Nathan. "If she shows up, as I rather think she will."

"She could have lost her nerve and made a run for it. Gone home perhaps." Nathan looked glum.

"Cheer up," Dominic said. "A man doesn't think straight when he's feeling sorry for himself." When his brother's green eyes took on the quality of a depressed cat, trouble was almost always on the horizon. They said Nathan's flamboyant good looks drove the women wild but Dominic couldn't see it himself.

Nathan's mouth had thinned and only a fool would fail to sense a gathering storm. "It may be easy for you to take a devil-may-care attitude toward the flowers of womanhood being borne off by a pervert. Not for me. How long can it be before this twisted criminal decides he may as well have his way with them? After all, he's worked out his little plan very well. If they won't mention being stolen away because they're afraid of innuendo, they're unlikely to announce that they've been ravished."

"Quite." Dominic lost sleep over the same fears, but he'd allow Nathan to think he'd invented these black thoughts. "Let's not worry until we have to."

"All very well for you to say," Nathan grumbled. "From the look of you when you left your cozy session with Miss Toogood, your necessities had been—if not satisfied—pleasurably excited. A very healthy thing, that. My own necessities show signs of withering away. I need some stimulation."

"Withering away?" Dominic said, glancing toward the corridor where the study awaited him. "Not sure I should like to witness that. Do something about it, old chap."

Nathan crossed his arms and said, "Have your fun. The last laugh will be mine. Did you get a message from brother John? About Noel DeBeaufort?"

"Yes." Dominic closed his eyes. "Does John think he's the only Elliot with a great deal on his mind? Having new grounds designed at this point is overwhelming."

"The trouble is," Nathan said, "I think John's trying to show his interest and do something nice for the property and the family. And everyone's doing it so we might as well be prepared for upheaval."

"Heatherly is beautiful as it is," Dominic said, with more than a little anger. "We'll have to keep an eye out for marauding villains in heavy boots. I must get on. I can't put Gussy off any longer."

"Agreed," Nathan said helpfully.

"McGee," Dominic said, crossing to the butler's wicker

chair and sticking his head inside. "No offense, man. Things are a bit tense. Sure you understand. If this Miss Weller comes, Lord Nathan will stop her from coming into the house and take her to Mama himself. Not a thing for you to worry about." He sighed. "And now I suppose I must join Miss Arbuthnot."

McGee nodded and rested his head in a corner again.

Bloody servants, Dominic thought. The more you were inclined to treat a man with respect, the more he made you suffer for living at all.

Now to Gussy. Dominic entered the corridor with reluctance and scuffed over a long, dark, Chinese runner until he reached his destination. He applied a knuckle to the door and walked in.

Gussy Arbuthnot, with surprising purple marks beneath her brown eyes, stood motionless, a few feet inside the door. When she saw Dominic, she smiled and some of her natural impishness returned.

"Good afternoon, Gussy," Dominic said, disconcerted by the subdued manner of this long-term acquaintance.

"Hello, Dominic. Forgive me for arriving unexpectedly but I had to see you."

A leap of hope quickly followed Dominic's idea that she might be about to confide in him about the kidnapper. Although that might mean there was some suspicion about his own activities in this and certain other matters. "You're always welcome," he told her. "You don't seem your usual cheerful self. Does that have something to do with your being here?"

Gussy, of average height but with a voluptuous body, walked slowly around the paneled study, the rich materials of her dress and pelisse rustling as she went. Nathan always suggested she was plain but in fact Gussy's golden hair and bright eyes, her dimpled cheeks, her softly curving mouth—and her softly curving body—made for a delightful package and the failure of some man to snap her up only underscored Dominic's opinion that a good many fellows were light-brains.

"Sit down," he said, more abruptly than he'd intended. "Here, take this chair. I'll call for refreshments. Hot chocolate, perhaps." She looked as if a restorative would be in order.

"No, thank you." She clutched her gloved hands together in her lap. "Nothing at all. I wish to talk to you about my reputation."

It was possible, thought Dominic while his spine prickled, that he had in his presence the answer to his prayers. She was going to spill the beans about her ordeal.

"Has something unfortunate happened to you, Gussy?" he asked, pulling up a straight-backed chair and sitting with their legs all but touching. "Has someone…done something to you? Say it isn't so."

"No." Color rose in her pale cheeks. "That's just it. Nothing has happened and I'm about to enter my third Season. *Third.* I'm on the shelf!" She burst into wracking sobs and covered her face.

She took advantage of Dominic's vulnerable position, his being so close, and rose from the chair to throw herself into his arms—and land on his lap.

Hellfire. "Hush, Gussy, hush. Collect yourself."

"I c-can't." She gripped him around the neck and pressed her face against his shoulder. "I need a f-friend. I have been turned aside by the man I loved. Turned aside repeatedly…ignored. No, not ignored. He doesn't know I'm alive."

Dominic longed to ask the fellow's name. "Everything will be all right," he said and patted her back awkwardly.

"Will you help me, Dominic?" She raised her head and the misery in her face touched him. "Everyone knows you are to be at *every* affair this year because of your poor little charge. One of your servants spoke to one of ours, you know. You've taken in an impoverished relative? Really, you are so generous. Look after me, too. I won't be any trouble. Only dance with me now and again and show some interest in me and I shall be sought after. You—could—change—" She sobbed so hard she had to pause. "You could change—my life, Dominic. My very life. You could *save* me."

For an instant he'd feared the story of Jane Weller was out. But bloody hell. What to say? "You know I will be a friend, Gussy. Not that I think you need one when you are as attractive a woman as you are."

She sniffed and blew her nose in a tiny, lace-edged handkerchief. "You think so?"

"Absolutely." He must be mad, but the poor thing's confidence had been badly shaken and a dance or two wouldn't cost him anything. Although...by Jove, he needed help himself. Not one or even two, but three women would expect his attention. Dominic smelled disaster. That brother of his must do his part.

"I have to go, Gussy," he said. "I'm sorry to desert you at such a time, but estate business calls."

"Of course, my angel." She smiled adoringly at him. "And you are my angel. I will be very kind to your little relation, you know, and I'll make sure all the ladies welcome her."

"Thank you, Gussy. That's kind." He meant it but rapidly helped Gussy to her feet and gave her a moment to shake out her skirts and poke at her hair before ushering her from the room.

He heard the great front door open an instant before Nathan rushed past the end of the corridor. "My pet!" he roared, arms outstretched. "You're here at last."

"That was Nathan," Gussy said and hastened her walk to the great hall. "I wasn't very polite to him when I arrived. Nathan!"

Other than leaping to restrain her, Dominic couldn't imagine a way to stop Gussy's headlong flight after his brother.

They skidded into the hall where McGee, his wig askew to reveal a shock of graying red hair, made flapping gestures as if urging Dominic and his guest to return to the study.

Muffled squeals seemed very loud.

"Nathan," Gussy cried.

Dominic was barely in time to see his tall brother retreating through the front door with a pair of slim female ankles and well-polished black boots kicking up white petticoats at the level of his broad shoulders.

8

Fleur heard the rumble of men's voices. She paused, holding her precious journal to her chest, and strained to hear where the sound came from. The ceilings were so high that all noises rose and seemed to echo from everywhere.

And she was lost! *Lost, lost, lost.*

Furious with herself, she spun right and left in the wide, circular corridor surrounding the dome of the orangeries. White marble columns and walls hung with lemon-yellow silk looked the same in each direction. Widely spaced closed doors to suites which must overlook the dome lined the inner wall. Windows on the outer side of the corridor gave lofty views of the estate.

The dome was very large, the corridor very long, and one of the identical doors led to the stairs she'd used to get up here.

And this had seemed such a wonderful idea, to come up to the third floor in the quiet center of the house and find a place to sit and work on The List—which had become very long.

On tiptoe, the pretty pink day dress Neville had made moving softly around her legs, Fleur walked on. A chest with two doors in the front and a marble-topped table made her sigh gratefully. She remembered the chest and the blue bowl on top. She had come this way before she'd chosen a lovely, deep window seat where she could be all but hidden behind looped draperies. Before too long she should be able to get down to her own floor and make her way back to the front of the house. Most of all she wanted to avoid running into someone and having to make conversation.

Another window seat beckoned to her and she hurried ahead to peer outside. What would her sisters think of all this?

She knelt on the seat and wedged herself into a corner. This place, such beauty, would be in her memory forever. But leaving the loneliness behind to go home again would be a good thing—she'd seen only Mrs. Neville and Blanche in the past few days. The Dowager had sent a kind note about upcoming festivities and the excitement Fleur should feel, but there had been nothing else, not even a letter from Sodbury Martyr yet. She pulled up her knees and smoothed the muslin around her legs. How the girls would love this dress.

"If that's the way you feel, we have nothing further to say."

Fleur held quite still, her journal in a vise. She didn't recognize the man's loud voice.

"We have a great deal to talk about." This was Lord Dominic.

A door to a room behind her opened. Fleur tucked her feet far back.

"I warned you there could be disaster this time. You shouldn't have brought your Jane Weller here. How long do you think she can be kept hidden at Mama's?"

"As long as is necessary," Lord Dominic said. "As long as those involved keep quiet. Including the staff at the Dower House and McGee here, there are only six who know. Mama's servants would die for her and she's told them to say nothing. McGee would cut out his tongue rather than go against family wishes. Which only leaves you, Nathan…"

"Why, damn your hide, little brother. Snot-nosed upstart. What are you suggesting?"

Fleur wanted to put her fingers in her ears but didn't dare move. The angry man was Lord Nathan Elliot, Lord Dominic's brother. She prayed he wouldn't come this way.

Lord Dominic sounded angry, but calm. How like him, she thought. "I'm not suggesting anything," he said. "Just reminding the two of us of the facts. Did you make sure Jane got Brother Juste's note?"

"Yet again, *yes,* and if she's stupid enough, she'll keep the appointment at midnight in the little chapel."

"Nothing stupid about that," Lord Dominic said.

"There will be if she breaks her neck getting there in the dark tonight. Or if her heart stops from dread."

"The chapel," Lord Dominic said, "isn't five minutes from the Dower House. Jane is a courageous girl and will do what's necessary."

"Hah. Don't think I've failed to note that another of your so-called plain girls is an appealing morsel."

Lord Dominic laughed. "You're fast with your judgements, I'll give you that, Nathan. Enjoyed your encounter with Jane, did you?"

"I won't answer that. How are things with your little charity case?"

"Miss Toogood isn't *my* anything," Lord Dominic said. "And in case you haven't noticed, I've been a busy man these past days so I haven't seen the girl."

Fleur closed her eyes and rested her brow on her knees. How would she get through this degrading time?

"I'm meeting Bertie Crewe-Burns at White's this evening,"

Lord Nathan said. "He's promised to take me to some fast hells where he assures me the stakes are high and we won't be recognized."

"Wonderful," Lord Dominic said, clearly angry now. "You know our agreement."

"I'm to avoid gambling? I'm not going to gamble, just watch Bertie get foxed and pump him for information. He approached me, y'know. Said he had some interesting tidbits to share. Could be something about another kidnap victim."

Fleur held her breath.

"In that case, make the best of your opportunities. But watch your back. These hells Bertie speaks of will be low and dangerous."

"Have you ever found me careless when it comes to my health?"

"Mmm," Lord Dominic said. "This evening Brother Juste meets with Jane and we'll see what comes of that."

"How long will Jane stay here? We both know the position was made for your convenience."

"We'll see," Lord Dominic said. "But don't say something like that to Mother."

Fleur's eyes filled with tears. Another poor soul's future depended upon the whims of these people. She straightened her back. Perhaps there would be a seventh person to know Jane Weller, whoever she was, someone who would befriend her. Lord Nathan had called her Lord Dominic's Jane Weller…and he'd said she was a convenience. Back home she'd heard it whispered that a certain wealthy landowner kept a woman as a convenience and, as a warning, Mama had explained what that meant to her daughters.

"I'd best be on my way," Lord Nathan said. There was a short silence. "Look, Dominic, have a care, will you?"

"It's Brother Juste who should be cautious."

"As you say. But Jane Weller came to Heatherly so readily. She could be a setup. What more perfect place to waylay and kill a man than in the trees around the chapel?"

"Indeed," Lord Dominic said. "But remember that the men in this family are all experienced in life-and-death situations and so are their closest friends."

Fleur heard Lord Nathan walk into the corridor and held every muscle rigid. Slowly, she let out a breath. He walked the other way and before long his footsteps receded.

"I've *got* you!"

With a cry, Fleur tumbled from her hiding place, or rather she was pulled from behind the drapery by Lord Dominic who held her wrist so tightly she dropped her journal.

"What are you doing here? Eavesdropping, yes?" He didn't shake her but he looked as if he wanted to. Instead he pulled her with him toward an open door. She barely managed to stoop and snatch up her book before he hurried her into a large, handsome room.

"I wasn't eavesdropping," she said, trying not to tremble but failing. "Not exactly." Papa said the truth was always the best thing.

"Not *exactly*. Do you take me for a fool? Fortunately for you, Lord Nathan had his back to that window or you would have felt his wrath and I, my dear girl, am a strawberry syllabub by comparison."

A strawberry syllabub? Anyone less like a soft, creamy confection than this glowering man couldn't exist, but she must not laugh—even if anxiety brought her close to hysteria.

"So," he said with icy menace, "what have you to say for yourself?"

"I'm lonely." She all but swooned with horror. Why would she say such a thing? "I mean, I was alone and decided to look for a comfortable place to write."

"Lonely," he said, thoughtful but still without a gentle feature in his face. "Hmm. And you just happened to choose the window seat outside my rooms as your comfortable place?"

"I didn't know you…these were your rooms. And I didn't sit where you found me, anyway."

He looked toward the heavily carved and painted ceiling. "Well, that explains everything. Especially how it was I found someone who wasn't sitting there sitting on that window seat."

"That's not what I meant," she told him, too shaken to be cross. "I went much farther along the corridor to find a place. Then when I was coming back I heard voices and hid out there so I wouldn't be seen."

"So that you could eavesdrop."

"No! And now I'm going back to my room."

He didn't touch her, but he stepped between her and the door and backed up until he stood against it. "You will go when I tell you to."

The door opened against his back and he stepped forward.

"I say, Dominic. Don't know what I was thinking of but I wanted to mention a boy to you."

Another tall, broad-shouldered man came into the room; this one's long hair even darker hair than Lord Dominic's, and worn loose over his collar. Fleur could feel the strength in him, that same overpowering maleness Lord Dominic had.

"Nathan," Lord Dominic said, "this is Miss Fleur Toogood, Mama's charge. Miss Toogood, my brother, Lord Nathan Elliot."

"Really?" Lord Nathan smiled at her, a wide, interested smile, and his eyes glittered. She couldn't tell what color

they were but they weren't the shocking blue of Lord Dominic's.

"Yes, really," Lord Dominic said in a tone that caught Fleur's entire attention. His face showed nothing at all but he didn't sound pleased.

"Finally I meet the lovely girl my mother has befriended," Lord Nathan said. "And a very wise woman Mother is, too—with impeccable taste. You will be a great success, my dear. But we will have many opportunities to talk when we attend the same events. It is rumored that this will be the most memorable Season in years."

Fleur bobbed a curtsey. "You are very kind."

"Think nothing of it. You'll dance like a fluttering rose petal, or I am not the judge of female grace I know I am."

Lord Dominic made a strange sound but his face hadn't moved.

"I have only danced at country affairs, my lord," she told Lord Nathan. "In Sodbury Martyr where my family lives. But I do love to dance."

"And dance, you will," Lord Nathan said, coming closer and bowing his head benevolently. "We shall make sure Miss Toogood is the talk of the *ton,* shan't we, Dominic? You will soon dance better than any other woman in Town. Did I hear that Neville is making your wardrobe?"

Fleur bobbed again. "Yes. Such a kind and clever lady."

"I should say so. Ye-es—" He considered her dress closely. "A perfect frock for a perfect girl. I do take issue with only one comment you make. Neville is kind, but with perfection like yours, she doesn't need to be clever."

The noise came from Lord Dominic again and when Fleur glanced at him she noticed, to her surprise, that his face had turned a dull shade of red. He looked back at her. "I am a fortunate man," he said, his smile tight. "I am to escort you, Miss Toogood, and my gorgeous sister-in-law, Lady Granville—*and*—my old friend Gussy Arbuthnot. With such a band of beauties all to myself, I shall be the envy of every man in London."

"Gussy?" Lord Nathan said, frowning, wrinkling his fine, straight nose. "When did that happen?"

"Did I forget to tell you?" Lord Dominic said. "Gussy does hate these things and when she came to visit me the other morning we agreed she would go about with Hattie, Miss Toogood and me. I know you have to leave, Nathan. We'll talk more about the other later on."

Lord Nathan blinked. "Yes. Very well, we'll do that. And if you get a chance, have a word with Noel DeBeaufort. He thought John was in residence and came to talk to him about the grounds."

"Dash it all," Lord Dominic said with feeling.

"Quite," Lord Nathan said. "He returns in the morning to walk parts of the estate and I've told him to talk with you. He's eager to get started on one or two of the projects. Look, we'll take up the other matter later—could be useful."

A chill touched Fleur's spine. Lord Nathan would have said more about the boy he'd come to talk about, whoever he was, if she hadn't been present.

"Thank you," was all Lord Dominic said but his chest expanded with a deep breath and he stared meaningfully at his brother. "Until later, then?"

"As you say." Lord Nathan left.

"Sit down," Lord Dominic ordered when he was alone with Fleur. "There. Close to the writing table. I must work, but I can decide what to do about you at the same time."

Miserable, Fleur followed his direction to a big, black-and-gold-striped chair. She sat on the edge of the seat and made sure her feet touched the floor firmly.

"As if I didn't have enough to worry about," Lord Dominic muttered. "A meddler. An eavesdropper."

"I didn't—"

"Silence."

"Yes," she said quietly.

He flipped the tails of his coat aside and sat behind his expansive writing table—and he raised his eyebrows at her.

For so long that Fleur's eyelids began to droop, his lordship worked quietly over papers spread on top of the table. From time to time he signed his name and rolled a blotter over the ink.

"They have contraptions that allow you to sign several pieces of paper at once," Fleur said, and immediately closed her mouth.

"They do indeed," he said, and picked up a newspaper which he shook and began to read.

She opened her book and took up a pencil. At the end of many pages of notes she wrote: "Most men do not understand women at all. Nasty habits like behaving as if he is alone, rather than in a lady's presence, such as by reading while she waits for him to speak, show a man's disrespect and arrogance." At the back of the book she searched and found "disrespect" noted as number seven, and wrote a small seven in parentheses beside that word in her latest entry.

Fleur glanced up in time to see Lord Dominic watching her, his head tilted sideways from behind his paper. "Writing down all the things you think about me, no doubt," he said. "I hope they're suitably complimentary."

The pigheadedness of men. She set the journal on her lap and rested her fingers on its open pages. "I have always kept a journal."

"Whatever you heard from your perch out there is strictly confidential," he said suddenly and harshly, setting the paper down.

"I am no gossip, my lord."

"Are you a woman?"

She straightened her back. "We both know the answer to that."

"Yes. So you are a gossip. The only question is the degree to which you repeat what you hear in order to gain the attention of your peers."

"I have no peers in London," she said and smiled. "You really are quite funny, my lord. You take yourself so seriously."

Lord Dominic pushed back in his leather chair and laced his long fingers together over a flat stomach. "You are impertinent—but charming in your own way. You are also out of your depth. However, you are intelligent and, I believe, capable of learning quickly. My sister-in-law is uniquely qualified to put you through your paces and get you ready. Until she has polished the edges, your best course will be to say and do nothing, except smile and look as delightful as you do."

Fleur blinked slowly. "I'm sure I misunderstand you, my lord. You couldn't possibly have just told me I am socially unacceptable—completely so—and that my *edges need polishing.*"

He lowered his eyelids a fraction. "Perhaps that was a little unkind, but Society in Sodbury Martyr is not London Society. You have a quick wit, it's true. But wait till you're confronted with young women who have been schooled in the art of brilliant repartee. Then you will understand how much you have to learn."

Fleur seethed. "My lord, people are born with some things and wit is among them. No matter how much a stupid person is schooled, they will not develop a keen sense of humor and enough knowledge to be interesting. I am not stupid and I am schooled. My father believes in educating women. He taught us himself and continues to teach my younger sisters."

"So you say. And very admirable, too." His brow puckered and he met her eyes, and smiled a little. "You are no shrinking violet, Miss Toogood. You have spirit and, above all, I consider spirit—and courage—invaluable."

"Thank you." He needn't think he could toss a bone in her direction and change her impression of him as a man with every negative male quality she had identified.

"Now. What did you overhear?"

Lies were forbidden, but the truth could be dangerous and her family would not benefit from her being returned home in shame. "Words," she said. "Nothing sensible. Or nothing that meant anything to me. A boy. Lord Nathan mentioned a boy but he didn't say anything about him."

"True," Lord Dominic said. "What else?"

"I think you were arguing." She bent over to hide her face. Let him think she was embarrassed. "But you shouldn't be uncomfortable about that. I would never mention it. My sisters and I get cross on occasion. We say cruel things but then we make up and forget all about it. If I may be so bold, why not forget the harsh words you and your brother spoke? He seems a high-spirited man who would be slow to carry a grudge."

"Does he now?" He had relaxed in his chair and Fleur dared to hope she'd satisfied him that she was no threat. He said, "I believe you're right and I shall take your advice."

An ormolu clock chimed out the hour. "Later than I thought," Lord Dominic said. "But I would rather be here with you than elsewhere. Hattie—Lady Granville—arrives late tomorrow. Her adopted daughter, Chloe, will be with her and one or two members of the Bath household."

Fleur could tell he looked forward to the arrival of his sister-in-law, most likely because he expected her to relieve him of the onerous duties his mother had given him.

"Just as well," he continued. "On the following evening—" he consulted a list that looked similar to the one the Dowager had sent to Fleur "—there is a musicale given by the Herberts. Lady Granville will make sure you're as ready as you can be. You will meet Gussy Arbuthnot who insists she would like to help ease your way."

"Yes, thank you. How kind." A panicky fluttering set up in Fleur's stomach and she popped up from her chair. "May I look at your ormolu clock? They are so pretty."

He picked up his pen and tapped the handle against his lips.

Fleur tried not to look at his mouth but couldn't help herself. Another note needed to go into her book. An irresistible mouth was essential in a man.

"Of course you can look at the clock. It is pretty, I suppose. It was my grandmother's, which is why I keep it."

The clock was displayed in a niche in the fireplace wall. Fleur walked close and took pleasure in its colors, or as much pleasure as was possible with the certainty that Lord Dominic observed her every move. He probably assessed the way she walked and found it lacking. There were things about her that he didn't know, including her mother's upbringing in a well-to-do family—even if they did disown her for marrying a poor if learned parson. Mama had taught her daughters well.

"How do you know about these?" Lord Dominic—who had left his writing table without making a sound—reached past her and rested the heel of his hand on the niche.

Fleur felt her eyes widen and her throat close.

"Bronze and porcelain," he said, standing close enough for her to feel his warmth and his much larger stature. "See how they fashioned the white vine roses."

"So pretty," she said. "The French have an eye for flamboyance, and a unique style."

He took his hand from the niche, but then settled it on her shoulder and turned her toward him. "Where did you read that?"

"It's an opinion, my lord. I've studied many pictures and read about French artisans and craftspeople." His hand folded over her shoulder and made it impossible for her to move away without making a scene.

He took a step closer.

Holding her journal to her breast Fleur moved backward and met the wall. Her heart beat too hard and fast.

"So, in your village parsonage you read books about—"

"I read books about many things," she said, tipping her chin up to look steadily back at him.

He put his free hand on the wall behind her.

This was a man who might keep a woman as a convenience. A dangerous fellow to inexperienced young women if it was true.

"You are so much more than pretty," he said. "The word doesn't do you justice. But your mind is quick, and you conduct yourself well. I do believe you will make a fine wife for a man of position. Yes, indeed. Have you ever been in love?"

Fleur couldn't make herself look away. "I have found a young man interesting," she said. "But I don't believe I have been in love. Perhaps I won't know until I really am."

His smile, a downward twitch at the corners of his mouth, gave him a wistful air which puzzled Fleur. But he made her warm all through—hot in places. Lord Dominic was a complex man, and he shouldn't be where he was, doing what he was doing, in his rooms, alone with her. And he was doing something unsuitable, even she knew that.

"Did this interesting young man kiss you?"

Her blush made her feel silly. She lowered her lashes. "Of course not."

"Of course not," he whispered and when she raised her eyes again, his face was so close to hers that she felt his breath on her cheek.

Slowly, looking only at her mouth, he lowered his lips toward hers. He took his hand from her shoulder and spread it over the side of her face, brushed his thumb back and forth along her jaw. Their bodies touched.

Fleur felt her lips part and she ached and tingled—and wanted to hold him tight and have him hold her. But… "No," she said, ducking under his arm. He didn't move but she moved away until she stood in the center of the room.

He laughed! Actually laughed and turned around with an expression of delight on his face. "Good," he said. "Very good. You will do so well because there will be men who make advances, most not as subtle as mine, and you must rebuff them. You must be pure, untouched, until you go to your marriage bed."

"My lord, please." She had never been more mortified. "I should leave now."

"Soon. My brother is charming, don't you think?"

The abrupt change of topic caught Fleur off guard. "Er, yes."

"I never met a woman who didn't find him charming," he said. "But perhaps I should have asked my question differently. Do you find him…attractive?"

Fleur swallowed several times. What was she supposed to say? "Lord Nathan is a handsome man, but then, so are you, my lord. And having met your sweet mother I'm sure the entire family is handsome."

"You have a clever tongue." He walked toward her. "You have nothing to fear. What just happened will not happen again. As you heard, Nathan intends to accompany us a good deal during the Season. So I'm glad you find him pleasing company. As you will see, he is a better dancer than I am, so I will give him the pleasure of partnering you when you haven't already been swept off by some young buck. Yes, yes, indeed. Nathan is also far more sociable than I am. I'm known as a dour fellow and not at all easy to get along with."

"I think you are perfectly easy to get along with," Fleur said, "if you want to be."

Lord Dominic's expression set once more. He started to say something but put a closed fist to his mouth and walked past her to open the door. "Can you find your way to your rooms on your own?"

"Yes, thank you." Silly, stupid tears prickled in her eyes and she rushed past him.

He didn't say anything else before closing his door behind her.

Fleur set off. She turned and walked backward, lifting the back of her skirts as she went. Just as his rooms were almost out of sight she stood still and scowled. "You would try to palm me off on your brother just to get rid of me. I'm a nuisance to you. Well, even if he was interested, Lord Nathan wouldn't do at all. And I believe you dance every bit as well as he does, probably better. And you are not dour—or not too often."

9

No more than fifty people could sit in the chapel, Fleur decided. And only then if they squeezed together. She walked softly, using shafts of pale moonlight through leaded panes to find her way along the center aisle. Since she had been a tiny girl in her father's arms, houses of God had brought her peace.

Using the same route as she'd taken several days earlier with Blanche, she had crept from Heatherly House at eleven-thirty. Even though she wore her own heavy, hooded cloak, the night air chilled her and she was grateful to have on the stout shoes she'd worn for her journey to London.

After stumbling through undergrowth beneath the trees Lord Nathan had spoken of, Fleur had arrived early so that she could hide herself. The plan had seemed dangerous, but exciting, too, and Jane Weller might need help.

Bosh. The excitement had been the thing. That and the boring sameness of her routine at Heatherly. And she had been wrong to put herself in danger—and to interfere in something that was none of her business. Lord Nathan had spoken of killers attempting to murder a monk outside this very chapel!

In truth she thought Lord Nathan the type of joker who relished ghost stories told in the dark, and probably boyish but nasty pranks on occasion, too.

But if she left now there was still time to get away before anyone came. Lord Dominic had not taken his brother seriously and seemed not at all concerned for their friend, the monk. Still, the better part would be to get back to her room and resolve not to interfere again. The chapel doors were all unlocked and she walked quickly toward a side exit.

A door handle grated. Someone was entering by the double front doors. Fleur hurried to get out—until she reached a carved wooden screen around the family pew.

There was no time for dithering. She left or she stayed—now.

Fleur stayed, popped up a single step to the raised pew and sank to huddle on the cold marble floor. And just in time to hear the heavy door swing inward and then a scuff-scuffing of shoes. She had made the best of moonlight through the windows, but the newcomer lit a candle and faint yellow light flickered.

She had done foolish things, but this must be the most foolish of all. And only moments before she had promised to reform. Now there was nothing for it but to wait and pray she would not be discovered.

Curiosity killed the cat. She put her hands over her ears. Zinnia's voice, taunting her for some childish prying into a box they weren't supposed to open, was an ill-timed memory.

This was what she would do: wait and watch until the meeting was over then go back and raise the alarm—if there was any reason for alarm. And if she saw no reason to worry about Jane Weller, well, Fleur would hurry to the house as quickly as she could, go to bed and never, ever, meddle again.

This time she meant it.

Whoever was out there didn't stand still. The scuffing sounds continued as the owner of the feet kept on moving.

If it was Jane… No, trying to talk to Jane now would be incredibly dangerous.

Slowly, carefully, Fleur climbed from the floor to the seat of the family's carved wooden bench. She scooted to the end and raised her head enough to see over the arm at the end of the pew. Over the arm and through the screen.

She saw the monk at once. He sat on a chair not thirty feet from her, with his head bowed and the hood of a dark habit obscuring his head and face. The candle flame bobbed in a holder he'd placed on a nearby collection box. His prayerful attitude squashed the butterflies in her stomach. Papa always said there was refuge in church, in the company of people of God.

The man whistled! Softly, it was true, but a whistle nevertheless.

Fleur frowned, concentrating on the tune, then almost laughed aloud. The monk whistled, "Lavender Blue," and she held her breath. How she and Letitia had been taken to task for singing such lines as, "You must love me, diddle diddle, 'Cause I love you," from that song. Mama said the words were risqué and Fleur thought the melody did sound strange coming from the man in a brown habit.

Light, rapid footsteps on marble wiped away her smile. A slight female in a dark coat and bonnet went to Brother Juste with no sign of fear. "Thank you," she whispered hurriedly, even before she stood beside him. "I've got ever such a nice place. Mrs. Lymer is teaching me things I never knew about being a lady's maid and I'm helping her with her duties. She's not so young as she used to be."

The monk chuckled and got up. He waved the girl into his chair and got another for himself. "A good woman," he said, his voice raspy and a little muffled. "We must not keep you here long. Were you frightened on the way?"

"No." She flapped a hand. "I'm used to looking after my-self."

"You weren't able to look after yourself when you were spirited away, were you?"

"No, no, I wasn't. But I don't think that one would touch me again because he'd know me the next time and I'm not worth anything to him."

Brother Juste searched the folds of his habit, then reached toward Jane. "Hold out your hand. These were a gift from a French visitor—chocolate drops rolled in honey and nuts—and there are far more than are good for one person."

Jane actually squealed. She coughed and said, "I'm sorry. I don't think I ever had anything like this before." And she reached beneath her coat to put her treasure in a pocket hung around her waist. "Why did you give them to me?"

"Because I like you," he said, leaning closer. "I want to help you find whatever it is that would make you happy in this world, but that may take time. For now I can give you a few sweets and take pleasure in your happiness."

Jane giggled.

"Have you thought of anything new, anything you didn't recall the other evening? Have one of these now." He dropped what Fleur assumed was one of the sweets into Jane's palm and unwrapped paper from another before fumbling beneath his hood and putting one in his own mouth. "One for you and one for me. To sharpen our wits."

Jane giggled again. "I don't know about that. You've got something over your face, haven't you? I don't mean the hood."

Brother Juste mumbled something, presumably to indicate that he couldn't talk with his mouth full. Then he said, "A pre-caution, Jane. It would be bad for others if I was identified by a rogue who might use the information against us. I don't mean you would use it, of course, but one never knows when a moment requiring caution will arise."

"I've been thinking about that night," Jane said. She had a way of sitting quite still. "He took me by carriage."

"But he didn't drive himself?"

"Oh, no. A lad did. And the man was inside with me. He held me down so I couldn't see out of the windows. But I heard a good deal and it was— The place we went was a noisy area. A lot of shouting, and carriages and horses passing. Forgive me for mentioning it, but I think there was intoxication—at least from the way a lot of gentlemen were speaking."

Jane unwrapped her sweet and popped it into her mouth. "Ooh, this is ever so good. Best I ever had." She hunched her shoulders. "Not that I've had much chocolate. When my dad could work he'd bring home some bits and pieces left over from big doings at the hall." Jane fell silent and Fleur liked the monk for allowing the girl time to reminisce without asking her any questions.

"So this thing happened late in the evening?" he said eventually.

"Very. Miss Victoria had me run an errand."

The monk crossed his arms. "Late at night and on your own?"

"All I had to do was take a message to someone who was waiting for her. She'd been going to meet him see, but she changed her mind. I only ran across to the edge of the Park."

"That would be Hyde Park. The Crewe-Burnses live on Park Lane."

Fleur could tell that Brother Juste didn't think much of a girl being sent out on such a mission.

"Who was Miss Crewe-Burns to meet?" the monk asked.

"I don't know, but I do know she wasn't keen to go. Well, at first she was but she changed her mind."

"Did you deliver your message?" he said.

"No. The young man wasn't there but that lad who drove the carriage was. He was a poor thing dressed in rags and I could tell he was afraid. But the other one was nearby. Hiding. Ready to grab me."

"And you don't think it was Victoria's young man who abducted you?" the monk asked.

"Oh, no. This one was older, I think. The painted face made it hard to be sure, but I think he could be as much as forty."

"That old?" Father Juste said and Fleur heard his amusement. "What happened next?"

"I know we went straight down Park Lane," Jane said. "At first I was thinking we went into the Park for a bit, but now I don't. We went left. I know because of the way I fell over his nasty legs in those white satin breeches."

So, Jane Weller, on an errand for her mistress, had been abducted. How horrible.

"I think it was at Piccadilly we might have turned left and then we went straight on for a bit. But after that it was all turns, this way and that," Jane said.

"You've done very well."

"Oh!" Jane lifted her hands and stared at them, she held them to her face. "Chocolate. I almost forgot because there was so much muddle. I smelled chocolate that night and it was strong."

"He took you into a shop that late?"

"Oh, no, I mean I smelled it when we were in the carriage—not too long before we got where we were going." She clasped her hands together. "He blindfolded me when we got there so I never saw the outside of the place. I don't think I want to think anymore tonight."

"You don't have to. You've thought and said a great deal and you have helped me. I'll see you to the Dower House. Do you send money home, Jane?" He asked the question so nonchalantly that Fleur almost missed it.

"What makes you suggest that?" Jane sounded sharp.

"When we first met you said you *must* find a place. Now you mention that your father used to work. If he's no longer employed, times may be hard at home. You have brothers and sisters?"

"Three brothers, all younger. My dad broke his back and now he can't stand. My mum does everything."

Brother Juste patted Jane's arm. "I'm glad you have a place and can help your family again. Now, we should go."

"I worry I'm a nuisance, having to be hidden and all," Jane said.

"You are not a nuisance. What happened to you was wrong and I intend to get to the bottom of it before more young women fall prey to this scoundrel's tricks. There have already been others, you know."

"No," Jane whispered. "Oh, those poor things. I was lucky to get let go the way I was. There wasn't anyone to pay money for me so he couldn't be bothered. But what if he takes a girl from a rich family and they still won't pay the ransom? He said he would kill someone like that."

Brother Juste said, "Don't fret. Make a note of anything else you think of, that's all. I'm going to study an area I think may be the one you describe, or close to it. I shall arrange to speak with you again quite soon. Meanwhile, don't worry."

"Thank you. I'll try not to."

They got up and Jane walked ahead. Brother Juste said,

"Jane," and she turned back. "I am concerned about one thing and I want you to bear it in mind. Keep your eyes open at all times. I believe our man in satin may be someone known in Polite Circles—possibly quite well."

10

He had to be wrong. He wanted to be wrong. He wanted to have wasted his time scrambling out of the habit to reveal the evening clothes he had worn underneath. And he hoped it had been a waste of time to reorder his hair, and dashed well put a cloak around his shoulders when he would rather be naked and cool off, dammit.

But he was blessed and cursed with an overdeveloped awareness of concealed presences. He'd felt it in the chapel, but with Jane there he couldn't go looking for an intruder.

Dominic grabbed hat and gloves and left his rooms at a rapid clip. Even though he'd seen Jane Weller home, anyone following and staying far enough back not to be seen would be some minutes behind him if they were heading for this house and didn't have the advantage of entering it the way he did.

He was doing exactly as he'd planned. If he did meet someone returning to the house, his evening clothes provided the perfect excuse for him to be heading toward the front door and apparently going out, not that it really mattered. He had made a leap in suspecting her, but if Fleur had heard more than she let on of the conversation he had with Nathan that afternoon, and had been foolish enough to hide in the chapel and listen to what was said this evening, then he had a right to confront her however he pleased.

If he was proven wrong, so much the better. But he'd felt her hiding behind the curtain outside his room and been right. The sensation in the chapel had been exactly the same.

A strong smell of chocolate. Jane's announcement had rung in his head since he'd left her. Getting on with removing this wretched kidnapper from Society was the important thing, not Fleur Toogood's search for a husband.

He ran downstairs to the second floor, dashed along corridors to the balcony above the great hall, and hovered there. Since he really had nowhere to go there was no reason to continue on—unless he heard someone coming his way. Anyway, this was all so much twaddle, this so-called instinct. Fleur wouldn't go out in the dark.

Someone was walking through the hall.

Dominic timed the interval before he started down. He descended two stairs as Fleur Toogood, in a voluminous hooded cape, took her first step up and grasped a bannister.

"My goodness, young lady," he said in his best shocked voice. "Where can you have been at such an hour?"

Her head jerked up with enough force to knock her hood off. Her deep-red hair hung in curls around her shoulders and she had dirt on her face.

He marveled at the speed with which defiance replaced shock. "I could ask you the same thing, my lord, but I'm too polite," she said.

"I'm going out, not coming in, and what I do is absolutely none of your affair. Your behavior bewilders me. Have you been outside?" He walked slowly downward, thrusting his head forward as if to examine her more closely. "You don't look yourself. What has happened?"

"I'm accustomed to a good deal of walking, my lord. Heatherly is a beautiful house but it also has beautiful grounds and I felt like—" She coughed and doubled over as if in some spasm. When she was more or less herself again she said, "I was probably unwise to walk outside when it's damp. If you'll excuse me, I'll go to my room and get warm."

Dominic reached her, took one of her hands and clamped it firmly under his elbow. He set off upward again, turned right instead of left on the second floor and started toward the center of the house and the way up to his suite.

"My room is behind us," Miss Toogood told him.

"And mine is on the third floor. But you know that. You will sit by my fire and have hot chocolate. I'm quite the expert with chocolate."

Her expression didn't become knowing at the mention of chocolate, but she did resist him. Her spirit was remarkable. "The last time I was in your rooms, my lord," she said, all but inaudibly, "there was an event. An insignificant event, it's true, but not to be repeated. I think we both agree on that."

He cocked his head to look down at her and walked faster. "*Insignificant?* What can you be referring to? Come. Allow me to look after you. Mother would never forgive me if I allowed you to become sick so close to your first big engagement. She's counting on you being a huge success and you will be."

She made an outrageously funny face and said, "You think so?"

Dominic laughed and set a foot determinedly on the third-floor staircase. He liked Fleur Toogood, dammit. She had courage and brains—an irresistible combination in a woman, particularly a beautiful woman who could laugh at herself. Unfortunately she also had a giant dose of curiosity and he now knew she'd heard a great deal more than she'd confessed to earlier in the day.

The charge he had reluctantly accepted had become a challenge and a liability. And how, he wondered, should he deal with that situation? He believed he could make sure there were no more escapades like this evening's, but a few words about what she already knew, spoken in the wrong place, might well spell disaster.

At least he could be sure she had no idea that he and Brother Juste were one and the same.

When she entered his rooms without a fuss he breathed more easily. "Come along," he said. "The green velvet chair by the fireplace is comfortable. I'll stir the fire and start the chocolate. First, let me take your cloak."

"No!" She held the cloak tightly about her. "No, thank you. I feel the cold badly and take so long to get warm. I'd prefer to keep it on."

You'd prefer to keep it on because you're hiding something underneath it. "Just settle in that chair." He rubbed his hands and blew on them. "I do believe I'll enjoy some of that hot chocolate myself." He removed his own cloak and set it across the arm of a couch with his hat and gloves on top.

Fleur took the chair he'd offered and what a picture she made with her curly hair brilliant in the firelight and her young, smooth face still glowing from the fresh air. Too bad the situation wasn't different.

He stirred the fire and added coals.

"You're a capable man," she said suddenly.

Dominic, on one knee before the fireplace, looked at her over his shoulder. "I can well imagine that you're just as capable." Her feet caught his attention but he was careful not to stare. She wore black leather boots that laced. They were solid with thick soles and not at all what he was accustomed to seeing on young women of his acquaintance.

He put the kettle on the hob. Merryfield knew his master's preferences and the tall chocolate pot waited, already half-filled with cold milk. "The water shouldn't take too long to boil," he said.

"And while we wait—" Fleur's mouth had a determined set "—you have a good deal to say to me about some wrongdoing of mine, correct? Or something you think I've done wrong."

"You are a great deal too blunt, too quick-witted and too surprising. I rather like the surprising part, and quick wits are a good thing. Even being blunt can be refreshing, but you might give a man a chance to speak before you tell him what he's going to say." Working so close to the fire overheated him and he took off his coat. If his shirtsleeves and neck-cloth had been excessively crumpled by the habit, there was nothing he could do about it. He rolled his sleeves up to his elbows.

"So, my lord?" she said.

Still kneeling, Dominic sat on his heels and spread his hands on his thighs. "Your face is growing red, Miss Toogood. You're hot. I know you have something under the cloak you'd rather I not see, but does it really matter now?"

"Yes, it does. I should be embarrassed."

"Let me guess, you're naked."

"My lord!"

"People do go without clothes, y'know. I've always been rather fond of the freedom myself." He looked her over slowly and deliberately, not that he could make out a thing while she remained bundled up. "There are times when the body—particularly if it's beautiful, sensual to look at, or, in the case of a man, strong and well made—well then, there are times when to cover the body is a tragedy. A tragedy and a waste."

She pushed her soft lips forward and he could almost hear her mulling over what must be a completely new type of approach to her, especially by a man. Her blue eyes turned luminous by firelight, but they showed more interest than dismay.

"Don't you have anything to say to that, Fleur? May I call you Fleur since we are to spend a goodly time together?"

"Please do call me Fleur. What could I have to say? Statements don't need answers, but I'm glad you take pleasure in the human body. I admit to a good deal of curiosity about it myself."

The kettle steamed on the hob and he thanked providence for the diversion. She admitted to curiosity, did she? After pouring in exactly the same amount of boiling water as there was milk, Dominic added the chocolate shavings. When the brew was frothy, he filled two cups and gave one to Fleur.

She set it down immediately.

Dominic sat in a chair facing hers and drank. "If I say so myself, I make the best chocolate in the land."

This time he thought he saw the faintest flicker in her eyes. She had heard every word in the chapel and he had yet to decide how to stop her from talking to others about it.

"I should go to my room now," she said abruptly, moving to the edge of the chair. "It's wrong for me to be here at all."

That was true enough but he couldn't let her go yet. "I believe you want to leave because you're being roasted alive, but you're too self-conscious to remove your outdoor clothes."

She hopped to her feet, glaring at him, and unhooked the neck of the heavy wool cloak. Then she shrugged out of it, saying at the same time, "I shall not appreciate any laughter from you, my lord. I believe in doing what's expedient." She resembled a person who was in the habit of wearing all the clothing she owned to safeguard it from thieves. A brown dress gaped apart between the bodice buttons and puffs of white lawn poked through. The skirt of the dress fell in lumpy folds and voluminous amounts of pastel lace bulged beneath the hem.

Fleur narrowed her eyes at him and sat down again. She drank from her cup and said, "You're right. You make the best chocolate in the land."

He burst out laughing. Even doing his best to restrain the guffaws he couldn't hold them in. Finally he sputtered to virtual control and said, "You've got your nightclothes on under that dress." Very much as he'd worn evening clothes beneath the habit, only the habit allowed plenty of room.

"Observant of you. I wanted to be able to change and get into bed as quickly as possible when I returned." Without warning, a button popped from her bodice and another followed when it couldn't take the force. "These are some of the new nightclothes the Dowager was sweet enough to give me but there is so much material. They are very pretty on their own, but the dress isn't… Fie, I'm prattling about the obvious."

"Many of us talk too much when we're flustered," Dominic told her. He could not allow himself to think about the outlandish combination of the sturdy black boots beneath yards of white lace.

"I am not flustered." Fleur got up and bent to collect her buttons, and popped another. "Oh, really, this is dreadful. Help me with the tapes, please."

She turned her back to him and he got up, feeling as if he

were in a trance and bound to wake up at any second. He undid the tapes, and a sash at the waist. "I should think loosening the thing would save the rest of the buttons," he said.

"No such thing." This miss had a temper. "The fates have conspired to make an idiot of me. The dress comes off. What I'm wearing underneath is unsuitable but covers every inch of me well. Please, please, try not to laugh again."

In seconds Fleur stood in a robe and nightrail which were, as she'd said, made of so much material. Tiny tucks decorated yards of virginal white lawn and satin roses dotted lace at the hem.

Dominic smiled, remembered himself and held up a hand. "I'm not laughing, absolutely not. I'm thinking how much Mother must be enjoying buying things for a girl about to make her Season. I believe she truly is doing what she might have done for a daughter. The gown and robe are very fetching."

Fleur frowned one of the amazingly hostile frowns she occasionally produced. "You brought me here because you want to chastise me for something. Chastise away and I'll be off."

He would far rather gather her in his arms and sit with her before the fire. *Your mind has softened, Elliott.* Since when did he think of such tame sport when he was in the company of a woman ripe for far more?

"Where did you go this evening?" he said, regarding her sternly. "And don't tell me you only went for a walk. I believe you went out to rendezvous with someone."

"You…you cad. Who would I go to meet in the middle of the night?"

"You tell me," Dominic said. He just wanted her to confess her destination and the reason she went there so he could warn her to hold her tongue. "Did it have anything to do with the things you said you didn't overhear this afternoon?"

Once more she turned pink, charmingly pink.

"Fleur?"

"Oh, very well. I did overhear you and Lord Nathan discuss a meeting in the chapel between a Brother Juste and Jane Weller who lives at the Dower House."

"And you felt it was your business to go and do some more eavesdropping?"

"You're mean." She got up and stood with her hands on her hips—looking down at him. "You manage to make things sound so—sordid. I heard Lord Nathan speak of Jane not really being needed here and I felt sorry for her. I know how it is to be tolerated when you are not valued. It was my hope that if I went to the chapel early I might be able to talk to Jane, and help her."

Firelight turned Fleur's body into a titillating shadow inside the filmy lawn night clothes. He looked away.

"I don't suppose you would understand my feelings," she said. "I'm only supposed to care about all these silly *events* and the pretty clothes and standing around like an ugly duckling waiting for someone to take pity and ask me to dance, or to get me some lemonade. Well, I have to tell you, it all sounds exceedingly boring to me."

"It is," he said, looking at her shadowy body again. "But it's tradition. It's the way things are done and you did agree to come."

"Not… Yes I did and I shall do my best to help my family. So far I'm not doing very well. All I do is get myself in trouble even though I've had no intention of being bad."

Telling her she was not bad but good would be too easy. "Don't say you're an ugly duckling again. It's silly. Now, Lord

Nathan will come to me in the morning to discuss what transpired between Brother Juste and Jane Weller. I'd prefer not to have to mention your escapades tonight."

She actually smiled and his heart turned. "Don't then," she said. "I have already promised myself that I'll avoid a single other effort to interfere where I don't belong. That's what I did and I realize I couldn't have helped Jane but I put myself at risk just going to the chapel."

"You meant well," he heard himself say. She had cast a spell on him. "But you're right to avoid such things in the future. Fleur, Nathan and I believe there are serious problems going on and we intend to do what we can to help Brother Juste stop them."

"You mean the kidnapping? Isn't that an evil thing?"

He took a deep breath. "Yes, it is. And my request of you is that you don't say a word about any of this, anything you heard, to a soul. You may be questioned. At the moment I don't know by whom but the situation is a confounding one. If you were to say something to the wrong person, another woman might suffer terribly." Or she herself might become a victim.

She fell silent and threaded her fingers together.

"I don't mean to frighten you," he said.

"I'm not frightened, I'm worried. I shall not say a word but I'm still concerned that this monster will do something terrible. A man who is without conscience, and who prays on helpless women, and forces a lad into a life of crime should not be left at large and in a position to terrify people."

"You're absolutely right."

"Fear nothing from me, and if I can help in some way you have only to ask."

"Thank you," he said, hoping he appeared sincere. "You

will help me most by allowing me to get on with my own business and by not causing me to worry that you may be getting into mischief."

He saw how she longed to tell him what she thought of his assessment of her character. She said, "Don't give it another thought," and bent over to gather her clothes.

Dominic got to his feet at once. "Don't go yet," he said.

"I've already kept you long enough from your engagement. You must be anxious to leave. I expect someone is waiting for you."

He searched her face. Fleur's eyelids were lowered and the corners of her mouth jerked down. What was all that about?

"I've decided not to go out now. It's too late and I'm comfortable here." He lied about his own comfort. He had responded to the girl and the evidence felt heavy and demanding.

"Sometimes it's the best thing to be at home," she said. "I am a homebody, or so my mother tells me."

Could it possibly be that she had a slight interest in him? Regardless, it would not do. He would always pursue danger and anyway, he wasn't ready to settle down. He probably never would be. On the other hand, Nathan needed a sober woman to clip his wings and this might just be the one to do it. Nathan had never shown any interest in marrying to ally the family with more power. Nathan had never shown any interest in marriage at all. But, dash it all, if Nathan could come to see Fleur's considerable charms as irresistible, the whole matter of finding the girl a husband would be solved with minimum effort.

Dominic took the cloak and swung it around her. "Carry the dress underneath, you'll be more comfortable."

"Thank you." Her eyes were serious and clouded with deep shadows.

In the act of fastening the neck of the cloak, Dominic stopped and watched her face. "You aren't happy here, are you?"

She tried to look away but he held her face in his hands and gave her no choice but to return his gaze. "Heatherly is a lovely place," she said.

"But?"

"But I'm nervous, I should think. I'm not used to great houses and wealth and routs and balls and musicales—and all the things I'm to do. Oh, and assemblies. I would like to know much more about this Almack's place, too. Mrs. Neville makes such a fuss about how important it is.

"I'm interested in everything. I must settle down and make the most of this wonderful opportunity. I owe it to the Dowager to show how grateful I am to her for all she's doing. And I want to do my best for my family because I may be able to improve their lives."

"If you marry well?"

"Yes! Only that won't happen so I'm wasting everyone's time."

Dominic liked the feel of her smooth hair and soft skin and continued to keep his hands on her face and the sides of her head. "Now why couldn't that happen? I think there is every chance you will be engaged by the end of the Season."

"I won't find the right man."

"How do you know?" Her conviction sounded sincere and he didn't like to hear it.

"Because I…because there are things about a man that are important to me and I shouldn't like to spend the rest of my life with someone who made me unhappy."

He had never, ever, had a conversation like this one. "Very wise of you, but are you so hard to please?"

"Yes." What looked suspiciously like tears gathered on her bottom lashes.

Very lightly, Dominic touched his lips to her brow. A reassuring thing to do, the kind of thing expected from a thoughtful friend. Certainly not inappropriate…or was it?

Rather than resist him or even, perish the thought, cry out, Fleur rested her forehead on his mouth and said, "You are a kind man. In fact I think you probably have many more fine qualities, most of which I shall never discover. Whatever happens here—while I'm here—I will remember you fondly, perhaps as a sort of kindly uncle."

Bloody hell. Kindly uncle? What sort of uncle would feel fire in his loins and a possessive, aroused urge that threatened to ruin any chance of his playing the benevolent escort to this lovely woman?

Dominic used his thumbs to raise her face and looked deep into her eyes. He knew she would see a hunger in him—even if she didn't recognize what his emotions meant. And he didn't care. However she thought of him, it ruddy well wouldn't be as a *kindly uncle!*

He bent his face to hers, pressed his lips to her temple, her cheek, and leaned away a little to look into her eyes again. Excitement—good. Confusion—good. Anticipation—perfect.

Firelight turned the tips of her lashes gold and cast the shadow of her jaw across her neck. The image of how she would look naked before the fire heated his mind. He kissed an ear and blew into it softly.

"Um, my lord—"

His mouth silenced Fleur. He kissed her carefully, firmly, but made sure he remained in control of himself. More or less. The one liberty he allowed himself—yes, yes, he was already taking others—his one extra liberty was to part his lips a little and press the tip of his tongue into one corner of her irresistible mouth, to follow the smooth place where bottom lip met upper lip, and finish at the other corner.

Fleur shuddered. She put one hand on his chest, slipped it just beneath his waistcoat and dug in her fingers. She didn't make a sound.

His blood raced. What he had just done was unforgivable—and unforgettable. This girl was meant only for marriage and if he coaxed her into lying with him, he was as low as the lowest of men. Still his mouth rested on her cheek and swept across the soft skin.

Dominic straightened and held her shoulders. He wasn't sure what to say or how to proceed but he'd better be sure very quickly.

"That felt wonderful," she said. "But I have to be honest."

He raised one brow and waited to be insulted.

"I want to kiss you again, probably lots of times. And I have feelings I must think about."

"What sort of feelings?" He allowed himself to smile at her.

"I can't say without examining myself, my reactions. There may be a whole new side to me, one I could never have imagined. If so, I shall need your help dealing with it. If you could spare a little time, that is."

What had he created? "How would you expect me to deal with this…this whatever it is?"

Fleur smiled back at him and stepped away. "I've intended to share my requirements in a husband with you. To help you eliminate men who just wouldn't do. But with this new development, this obviously *passionate* side of my nature that has shown itself, I must have the help of an experienced person to teach me how to keep my impulses in check. I know you can be my guide in these matters."

This was all his own fault but who could have expected such a reaction? "I'm sure your feelings are muddled because you are far from home and lonely. I have shown how willing I am to be a friend—" so willing "—and what you really feel is gratitude to me for that. There's no need, Fleur, because you are a dear girl and it gives me pleasure to make you feel welcome here."

"You don't understand at all," she told him. "In your generosity you reached out to me this evening, but I took advantage of you. I now know what carnal urges are and I apologize for using you to further my education."

11

The Marquis of Granville's dark green traveling coach rolled up the mile-long drive to Heatherly House at a smart clip. The sun grew lower and shadows of great oaks rippled across the handsome vehicle.

With a smile on her face and apprehension eating her stomach, Fleur waited with the Elliot family to greet the Marchioness of Granville and her daughter, Chloe. Two lines of servants flanked the steps leading to the front door.

Never, in her entire life, had Fleur felt more out of place. Earlier Lord Nathan had caught her with a grim expression on her face and he hadn't stopped prying until she explained her misgivings about being part of the family reunion. He had actually taken her in a bear hug that lifted her feet from the ground, set her down when she started to laugh, and said, "There, that's better. I knew I could shake you out of yourself. Just remember that the only reason Lady Granville is coming at this time, and bringing her little entourage, is to help you. And she's doing it because she wants to. Of course you're not out of place being included with the family."

She liked Lord Nathan. She had discovered his eyes were green and distracting, but not with the disturbing intensity of Lord Dominic's. Truthfully, Lord Nathan was a cheerful man, handsome, almost too handsome for the good of many a female eye, she suspected, and he made her feel at ease.

That very morning he had escorted her to the Dowager for breakfast and she had expected him to scold her for taking matters into her own hands the night before. He hadn't even hinted at the subject which meant Lord Dominic had kept his word, and his silence.

A tall, thin, bespectacled coachman put the perfectly matched black horses pulling the Granville coach through their paces. He looped them in an extravagant curve before coming to a halt with his elbows raised as if the only thing that stopped the horses from running was the brute strength in the coachman's arms. A titter went up among the servants.

"I see some things don't change," Lord Nathan muttered. "Albert Parker is still a showman."

"Better remember he's also John's man of letters and valet," Dominic said. "Strangest combination I ever saw in a servant. But I'm surprised he isn't in Vienna with John."

Nathan elbowed his brother. "No mystery there. John's most prized possessions are Hattie and young Chloe. Albert's here because he's the only one John trusts to keep them safe if he can't be with them himself."

Fleur listened to all this with fascination.

The coachman climbed down from his box and placed steps in front of the carriage door. He flung it open and peered inside. A little girl holding a black cat jumped into view. She wore a peach-colored outfit, and auburn ringlets burst in all directions from beneath her bonnet. Albert picked her up and set her on the gravel where she hopped up and down, waving at everyone on the steps.

"How well Chloe has done," Lord Dominic said. "Don't you think so, Mother?"

"We can thank John and Hattie for that," the Dowager said. "When a child loses both parents as Chloe did it wouldn't be surprising if she took years to recover. It was John stepping into his cousin's place so quickly afterward, and then Hattie accepting the child as her own that worked the miracle."

Fleur had assumed the Marquis and Marchioness were Chloe's parents. She wished she could ask the Dowager what terrible thing had happened in Chloe's life but didn't dare.

The coachman helped a lady to the ground. She called out, "Hello!" at once and caught up with Chloe. This must be the Marchioness of Granville, and Fleur doubted if the lady was much older than herself. Lady Granville glowed and when she came to be kissed by her mother-in-law and brothers-in-law Fleur could only stare.

Lady Granville turned to her and held out both hands. Fleur extended her own and they were seized in a firm grip. She curtseyed and said, "I hope you had a pleasant journey, my lady."

"I did. We all did. You are perfect, a fresh flower and you're going to become an *originale!*" She turned almond-shaped gray eyes on the Dowager. "She will, Mother. She just isn't ordinary. Look at that hair. Oh, you make me jealous."

"Fibs," Lord Dominic said. He held Chloe and her cat in his arms. "You're impressed with Fleur's hair. Who wouldn't be? But you know very well you're a beauty."

Lord Dominic's compliment warmed Fleur much more than it should but she also agreed with what he said about Lady Granville. She wore turquoise and it showed off her honey-colored hair.

Lady Granville took Fleur by the hand and she warmed to the other woman's impulsiveness. Up the steps they went, side by side with the servants performing a wave of curtseys and bows when their mistress passed. The estate manager, Mr. Lawrence, stood apart with the head gardener, Mrs. Chambers who was housekeeper, Mrs. Skinner, the cook, and McGee.

McGee and Mrs. Chambers hurried ahead to greet the party when they reached the doors. The family talked and laughed, their voices rising to speak over one another and echoing when they entered the hall.

"Lawrence?" Still holding Fleur's hand, Lady Granville turned back to talk to the estate manager. "My husband asked particularly that I inquire about the tenants."

"They're having a good spring, milady," Lawrence told her. He had gray hair but he was quite young and well favored, Fleur thought.

"We don't have any sickness?" Lady Granville continued.

Mr. Lawrence smiled and lines showed in tan skin at the corners of his eyes and mouth. "Nothing to speak of. May I tell them you asked?"

Lady Granville agreed and they followed the rest into the salon where everyone was seated. Chloe sat on Lord Dominic's lap and he stroked her cat while she whispered and used one small hand to keep his face turned toward hers.

"McGee," Lady Granville said. "It's so good to see you."

"Thank you, my lady," he said. He waited with an expectant expression on his face. "Your luggage is on its way to your suite. Is there something else I can do for you or would you like to rest now?"

"Tea," Lady Granville said. "Cakes, sandwiches, pies, lots of them. Their lordships will want something stronger but they'll help themselves, I'm sure." She took a seat beside the Dowager on a couch.

"It is blooming six o'clock," Lord Nathan said. "Bit late for tea."

"Language," Lord Dominic told him at once.

"Blooming six o'clock," Chloe said as if finding out how the word felt on her tongue.

Nathan grinned—until his mother shook her head at him.

"Will that be all, my lady?" McGee asked.

"Mmm." Lady Granville rubbed a finger between her brows. "Do you suppose Mrs. Skinner has a strawberry syllabub or two hiding in the kitchens?"

Fleur chuckled and caught Lord Dominic's eye at once. He winked at her and she was sure they were both remembering when he'd told her he was a strawberry syllabub in comparison with Lord Nathan—which was completely untrue.

Everyone had stopped talking at once. Fleur checked around and realized they were all watching Lord Dominic…and her. They must have noted the exchange between them.

"I'll see about the syllabub," McGee said and left, closing the door gently behind him.

Fleur felt uncomfortable. It wasn't suitable for others to think she shared some secret amusement with Lord Dominic.

Right away, as if he read her uneasiness, he told the rest about how he'd warned Fleur not to get on Lord Nathan's mean side. A chorus of boos and shouts of, "Nathan's a pussycat. You're the ogre," followed.

"Now, Fleur," Lady Granville said. "I'd like it if you'd stand where I can see all of you—if that wouldn't discomfort you."

It may make me faint! "Of course," Fleur said and made her legs move until she stood in front of Lady Granville.

"Hmm. Your carriage is excellent, Fleur. What a blessing. I remember how much I had to go through to correct mine."

Fleur couldn't imagine the other woman had ever been other than the perfect feminine creature she was now. "Thank you, my lady."

"And you obviously speak well quite naturally. I'm a cockney. I suffered through a great deal of elocution so that I wouldn't be an embarrassment." She beckoned Fleur closer and reached up to whisper in her ear, "Not too many people notice, but I still have a bit of the cockney."

She let Fleur go and smiled suddenly and brilliantly. "But I'm glad I'm a cockney. My father used to be a baker and my mother worked with him. Now, thanks to my darling John, they live quite near us in Bath and they both grow the most exotic roses."

"How lovely," Fleur said. Lady Granville was proud of her beginnings, and she'd managed to do what Fleur longed to do—help her family to have a better life.

The Dowager had been quiet, just smiling and watching the people she loved. "Fleur is the second daughter of an old friend of mine," she said now. "I went to visit them some weeks ago and asked if I might have Fleur come to me so that she could make a Season. I'm glad her parents agreed. There's a good deal she needs to learn but she will be easy to teach and as you say, Hattie, she has that certain something that could very well make her an *originale*."

Chloe climbed from Lord Dominic's knees and stretched out on her tummy on the soft carpet. Her cat nuzzled her neck until she cuddled her. "Let us take our nap, Raven," she said and Fleur realized the child spoke with a French accent.

Dominic sympathized with Fleur. She had suffered her examination and evaluation well, or so she made it seem, but these were difficult times for her. Still, if anyone could draw her out and help her enjoy the weeks to come it was Hattie.

"Tomorrow," Hattie was saying, "I shall take you to Bond Street, to a milliner there. Madame Sophie's hats are treasures. And we'll buy slippers. I'll speak to Neville about colors first. Floris! How could I have forgotten wonderful Floris? We'll go there to choose scents and soap and I want you to have a bone-handled brush for that hair."

"Hattie," Chloe said. "I'm not hungry. Please may I play outside."

Hattie smiled at her and said, "Leave Raven here and be sure to put your bonnet and gloves on again," before she allowed the child to leave.

Dominic caught Nathan's eye and gave a sign for him to come closer. He stood up before Nathan reached him. "How about a drink?" Dominic said. "I'll do the honors."

"Capital idea. Our Fleur's a beauty, don't you think?"

Dominic poured whiskey into two glasses. "*Our* Fleur?"

"Well, we have more or less adopted her for a bit. I'd say she was ours and I know you'll do a bang-up job of launching her."

He gritted his teeth. "If Hattie hadn't agreed to come and take charge, I should have washed my hands of the whole thing."

Nathan took a swallow of his whiskey. Dominic felt his brother's watchful eyes on him but pretended he didn't.

"You seem a bit strange, old man," Nathan said.

Dominic glanced at the ladies. The door opened and a succession of servants entered with tea and food enough for an army. The chatter grew louder again and he was amused to see how Hattie was the first to claim a syllabub.

He turned his back on the room. "You have no idea just how strange I am at the moment. And I've a right to be. Have you ever kissed a woman you had no right to kiss, only to have her apologize for liking it?"

"Come again?" Nathan said and his lips remained a little parted.

"I warn you," Dominic said, "don't aggravate me more than I already am. You heard what I said the first time, but forget my question. It's not important. It's time you were married."

Nathan choked on his drink and Dominic slapped his back.

"Nathan, Dominic, come and get something to eat," Mother called. "There's an egg pie so light it's going to float away at any moment."

"We'll let you choose what you want first," Nathan said. He hadn't taken his eyes from Dominic's. He lowered his voice. "What wrong with you? Why would you bring up my marriage—or lack of one? What the hell business is it of yours?"

"Just stating a fact. Mother and John think the same thing. It would do you good to get settled with a good woman who will help calm you down."

"Calm—me—down? Why you—"

"Snot-nose or something, isn't that what you feel like saying? Which helps make my point. It's time to put the things of childhood behind you and think of having children of your own. You'll make a sterling father and a fine, reliable husband. At least give it some thought."

Nathan tipped the rest of the whiskey straight down his throat and poured a hefty second serving.

"You'll get foxed," Dominic said. "Not a good idea in front of the ladies— especially at this time of day."

"Don't speak to me."

"What could be so bad about having a warm, willing, fetching woman in your bed every night? And taking care of you during the day—and bearing your heirs?"

Nathan dropped onto a deep blue couch and indicated for Dominic to join him. "Let's get back to kissing girls and apologies, shall we?" he said. "You're having a difficult time with some woman who interests you, so you're using me as a diversion. I don't hear you talking about your own marriage prospects."

"That's because I don't have any and probably never will," Dominic said. He felt a momentary quiet when he said, "I'm giving some thought to entering the monastery eventually."

"Bunk."

"I'd have expected that response from you." He shouldn't have mentioned what was still an almost unformed idea.

Nathan settled deeper into the couch. "You're changing the subject just as you always do."

"No such thing," Dominic said. "Oh, will you look at this? I didn't think Hattie had brought anyone but Chloe and the coachman from Bath. I suppose we should have expected Snowdrop to be with them, too. Hattie dotes on her and so does Chloe. Don't ask me why."

"Probably because she dotes on them and both Parkers dedicate their lives to the family."

"That woman is addlepated," Dominic said. "The development of her mind must be arrested, just as her growth is arrested."

Snowdrop Parker, Albert Parker's wife, had slipped into the room and hovered near the door waiting for Hattie to notice her. Snowdrop was what John kindly referred to as "a character," but Dominic considered the woman unpredictable, disconcerting and headstrong.

"Snowdrop," Hattie said. "Come and have some tea."

"Oh, I couldn't, my lady," Snowdrop said, her eyes demurely downcast. She had wound blue-black hair that reached her waist into a heavy chignon threaded with white flowers.

Dominic and Nathan exchanged a knowing glance. "Look at the dress. What nursemaid have you ever seen decked out like that?"

"Nursemaids often wear gray and white," Nathan pointed out.

"Gray velvet with white satin piping?" Dominic said. "And soft, gray leather slippers, and flowers in their hair?"

"Keep your voice down," Nathan warned.

"She couldn't be five foot, even on tiptoe. I'm wrong, she would be more than an inch under five foot even on tiptoe."

"Dominic." Nathan glowered at him. "All of this is because you have other problems. Share them. Let me help you."

"No."

"Well, Snowdrop Parker is her husband's pride and joy and I understand he won't hear of her not being dressed like a lady."

"Clothes don't make a lady," Dominic said.

"You, Dominic, are in a foul mood and I don't think I want to talk with you further."

Dominic ran his eyes over the blue-and-maroon salon. Ridges in white marble pillars on either side of the fireplace were edged with gold leaf, and dainty furnishings reflected their French origins. His attention returned to Fleur, who stood behind Hattie where Dominic could see her green dress and the way the pleated back of the skirt showed off her rounded hips. Each time she turned a little he got a view of her breasts spilling firm white flesh at the neckline of her bodice.

He groaned and leaned forward, rested his elbows on his knees and looked at his boots.

When Nathan didn't say a word—for far longer than was normal for the man—Dominic glanced sideways at him. Nathan watched him steadily, a speculative gleam in his eyes. "Are you sure there's nothing you'd like to share? Other than your religious leanings."

"Nothing," Dominic told him.

"I'd swear you have a woman on your mind and you're more interested than you've ever been before."

"That's piffle. Now watch your mouth because Fleur's coming this way."

Nathan turned on the couch to watch her approach and muttered, "She's marvelous. I'm still impressed by Mother's good eye for these things."

Fleur reached them before Dominic could respond. "Let me get you something to eat," she said. "Everything looks good. I could bring you a selection."

"No," Dominic said and just remembered to say, "thank you."

"Lord Nathan?" Fleur said.

"Move over a bit, Nathan," Dominic said. "Sit with us, Fleur. I for one am in a poor mood. Perhaps you can cheer me up."

She hesitated, then sat between them and Dominic could have kicked himself. Nathan must have the same gut-squeezing view of Fleur as he did, dammit. He caught his brother's eye over her head but Nathan gave no hint of being fascinated by Fleur's pale breasts, or the shadowy cleavage between them.

Dash it all, the rattle should show interest in Fleur. If Nathan thought he'd seen better than she he was wrong. The point was to make him fall for her quickly. Dominic shook his head. He was a confused man.

She may have thought he was doing her a service when he'd kissed her, but she could not possibly have benefitted as much as he had from the experience.

"I've been thinking," Fleur said to him in a rush. "Last night must have been very annoying for you yet you didn't speak to Lord Nathan about it."

He shook his head, no, but didn't answer her. He did pray she wasn't about to spill the details of their encounter.

"Oh, you're too much of a gentleman to complain," she said. "I owe it to you, and to Lord Nathan—" she glanced at him "—to make myself as little of a burden as possible. I heard a good deal of what you and Lord Dominic were speaking about yesterday afternoon." She went on to confess her presence in the chapel the night before and how she had hidden in the family pew to listen to what Brother Juste and Jane Weller said.

Fleur continued, giving every tiny detail of what the two had talked about and finishing up with an apology for her behavior.

Dominic leaned against the couch and spread his arms along the back. She showed no intention of broaching more personal matters. He sighed.

Nathan looked at him. "I do believe we've been entrusted with a rare gem. A scrupulously honest woman."

Dominic smiled.

Fleur said, "I know many honest women. In fact, I'm not sure I know a dishonest one."

"I was just having a little fun," Nathan said. "I should tell you a story or two about women I've known who tended to say whatever suited them regardless of truth."

"Please don't," Dominic said, but he grinned at the thought of seeing Fleur's face if Nathan did share some of his amorous relationships and the scrapes he'd been in.

"Just one," Nathan said. "Remember Isabella who needed to be kept in a safe place because some rogue was after her?

It was only the second day after I put her in that little St. John's Wood villa when she told me all her clothes had been stolen while I was out and she needed a completely new wardrobe. She met me at the front door in nothing but—"

"Just so," Dominic said, narrowing his eyes at Nathan. "Before long we'll have to get ready for dinner. I'd like to hear more about Fleur's family first. I'm very fond of the Cotswolds."

The Dowager Marchioness of Granville sipped tea and watched Dominic, Nathan and Fleur on the couch at the far side of the salon. She watched the way her middle and youngest son interacted with the girl, and the way she looked at each of them. Fleur couldn't be more comfortable with two men who were unrelated to her, nor could she be more animated, or more attentive to whatever they said.

The Dowager glanced away, afraid someone would notice her staring at the trio. When she looked again, Nathan was speaking to Fleur and her prodigal son bowed over the girl, giving her his full attention. While he talked, he looked into her eyes and, just once it was true, he touched the back of Fleur's neck lightly.

Dominic's dark expression made him more handsome than ever. She could see how his eyes deepened and his nostrils flared, and the way he set his mouth—and the sharp cut of his jaw. He studied Fleur with an intensity that might have pleased the Dowager had she not seen Nathan turning on his considerable charm for their young charge.

She had been too clever with her plan to involve Dominic with Fleur. He had seemed set on a path which would never include marriage, which had justified her actions. At least it made them understandable. How could she have guessed something might go dreadfully awry? What would she do if both of her sons fell in love with Fleur Toogood?

12

Augusta Arbuthnot could not have worse timing. Dominic wanted to be right where he had been, with Fleur and Nathan, but McGee had discreetly asked him to go to the study.

Dominic tapped on the door and walked in without waiting for an answer. He deliberately left the door ajar.

"Hello, Dominic," Gussy said, turning baleful brown eyes on him. "Forgive me for interrupting the family reunion—I didn't know Hattie was coming today."

Much as he would rather not receive Gussy, he reminded himself that she could always decide to reveal something useful. "Don't look so crestfallen," he said. "Out with it. Tell me what's on your mind and if I can help, I will." As if it wasn't already enough that he was to see a great deal of her in coming weeks.

"You have always been the most sensible man I know," Gussy said. "You deserve better from me than deceit. I wasn't completely truthful the last time I saw you. I've come to make amends. Oh, I should have told you everything before, but my family made me promise not to say a word to anyone."

"Perhaps you shouldn't go against your word."

She flopped into a chair and let her hands trail over the

arms. "I don't have a choice. This is no longer something that only involves me. I must try to warn others without anyone attaching my name to the matter. If everyone learns what happened to me, my reputation will be ruined and so shall I.

"Dominic, several weeks ago I was kidnapped and only released when my family paid a ransom for me. If the money wasn't paid, the kidnapper threatened to let it be known that I had spent a night in the company of a man. As if I didn't have enough ghastly problems already. It just isn't fair."

"It's an outrage," Dominic said, making a good job of appearing shocked, he thought. "But what makes you think this villain will do it again?"

"I knew he would before he set me free. He told me so and now I'm absolutely certain. He's becoming more crazed, you see."

"Crazed? Gussy, what do you mean?"

She gave exactly the same description of the man in maquillage as Jane Weller had. "And I've seen him again," she said, sniffing and blinking tears away. "He found me in the garden early this afternoon. *Pounced* on me when I was on my own. Just to show me how easily he could take me again, he told me. And he said he would take me again if I didn't spread a message for him. He is *Le Chat Soyeux,* he said, The Silken Cat, and every parent of a virgin should fear him because he slips through the night, gathering his prey in his claws and unless his demands are promptly met he will make sure the *ton* thinks of each victim as a jade."

"But why?" This development suggested the man was changing his pattern and that did not sit well with Dominic. "Gussy, he wanted to be anonymous but now he wants to create panic. Surely, once his warning is out his task will be more difficult and more dangerous—for him."

"I think he wants the thrill of causing panic," Gussy said quietly. "The thought of watching powerful people reduced to fear excites him, or that's how it seems."

"If it's thought that there hasn't been a crime, Society will convince itself that this is an empty threat and ignore it," Dominic said. "I can get the message out but I'll need to let it be known that the man has already struck."

"No!" Gussy sat forward in her chair. "There will be questions asked everywhere and eventually one of us will make a slip and we'll be spinsters forever."

"Us?"

"Oh!" Gussy jumped up and caught Dominic by the arm. She looked up into his face. "You see? Already I forget myself and say something I should never have said."

"There has been another victim?" He wanted her to think he knew only what she had told him. When he could, he'd attempt to speak to Victoria Crewe-Burns for whom he had little respect since she'd apparently made no effort to stand up for Jane and had allowed the maid to be so poorly treated.

Gussy shook her head slowly. A pretty thing, Dominic thought, but too obvious for his taste.

"Gussy?" he said gently.

"Yes," she said. "But don't ask me for her name. We promised we would guard each other's secret, although…well, I can tell you that her situation and mine are considerably different."

Yes, Vicky's maid had been the one to suffer rather than her mistress. "I've told you I'll help you with this," Dominic said. "Together we'll decide how you'll resist the temptation to say something damning. First, whenever the subject is raised, remember to shake your head. Concentrate on shaking your head and withdraw from the conversation as if you are frightened even to talk about—The Silken Cat. That will cover you for now."

"Yes, Dominic," she said, looking adoringly into his eyes.

"I'm going to ask Nathan to help me. I trust my brother completely."

"No!" She held both of his hands and shook them. "Please, I beg of you, not Nathan. Oh, I should not have come here at all but your reputation as a steadfast and loyal friend is unequaled."

"Nathan is also loyal."

"I don't want him to know." Tears brimmed in her eyes. Her distress struck at him. It also convinced him she still had a tendre for his brother.

He eased her back into the chair and bent over her. "Nathan would never hold this incident against you."

She frowned and he heard her swallow. "Why should I care about his opinion?"

"You do, or you wouldn't be so quick to refuse his help. You care for him. You also treat him badly. I'm sure he has no idea of your interest."

Gussy spread her fingers over her face. "It isn't up to a lady to pursue a man. And I absolutely don't treat him badly. He treats me badly. Whenever he might ask me to dance, I catch him smiling at me as if he's letting me know I'm insignificant. Of course, then he looks elsewhere and never, ever approaches me."

Confound it, Nathan had feelings for Gussy, too. It had to be. Silly pair.

"If that is so then he is a foolish man and he is also the loser. Don't give it another thought."

He decided not to continue the subject. If some mutual sign of attraction developed between Nathan and Gussy he'd just have to step back from his plan to involve his brother with Fleur.

But he hadn't imagined Nathan's response to Fleur. Nathan had hung on her every word and given her the kind of close attention Dominic didn't remember seeing his brother give to anyone else. At least, not for a long time. It could work well to "help" them realize their mutual attraction. Fleur didn't hide her pleasure in Nathan's company.

"Are you feeling well?" Gussy asked.

Dominic started. "Of course I'm well." He turned from her and went to the windows. No, drat it all, he didn't feel well. He felt muddled and angry and if he ever caught Nathan attempting a dalliance with Fleur he'd kill him, brother or no.

Perhaps he wouldn't go that far but he would surely remind his brother that it was Dominic who bore the responsibility—given him by their mother—to ensure Fleur's happiness and safety.

No, he'd just kill him after all. There would be no misunderstandings then.

The feel of her lips beneath his...her supple body... He was a bounder who had taken advantage of an inexperienced girl...and enjoyed every moment of it.

For once he wished brother John would get back from Vienna and show up at Heatherly. John would give him invaluable advice and without emotion interfering.

"Dominic?" Gussy said behind him, and sounding querulous. "I'll leave you now. I can tell you're giving this a great deal of thought and I bless you for it. What should I do next?"

Pull yourself together, he told himself. He faced her with a smile he hoped looked more genuine than it felt. "Dear Gussy. Thank you for your trust. You don't need to do anything. You may be a little taken aback the first time someone talks about our Silken Cat but all you have to do is remember to shake your head, and—"

"I understand," she said quickly. "Perhaps we'll speak some more tomorrow evening at the musicale."

"We definitely will. Let me see you out."

Her carriage stood waiting with the coachman standing beside the door. Dominic followed her down the steps and put her inside himself. Gussy was a good sort. There had to be any number of men who would bless their good fortune to have her as a wife. He would see what he could do to make some introductions.

Dominic looked toward the sky. When had fate decided his calling should be matchmaker to forlorn women? Not that Fleur was one jot forlorn—just in need of a wealthy husband.

Snowdrop Parker, her skirts lifted to allow her to run, met him as soon as he reentered the house. He looked from her to McGee who stared at him with something close to terror on his face.

"Snowdrop?" Dominic said.

"Help us, please. I don't want to say too much because it's not my place, but Lady Granville has been a little bit wobbly-like and I'd rather not frighten her if I don't have to."

"For goodness' sake, speak up, woman. What has happened?" He glanced at McGee. "You know, don't you?"

McGee nodded. "The staff has been mobilized."

"Mobilized," he all but shouted. "Mobilized, *why?*"

Snowdrop hopped from foot to foot. "It's Chloe. She went into the gardens to play. She was told to stay near the orangeries but she's not there. Lord Dominic, we've been searching but we can't find her."

13

McGee had come into the salon and spoken quietly to Lord Nathan. Fleur heard the butler say there was trouble and Lord Dominic needed his brother outside the orangeries—on the west terrace—at once.

Lord Nathan's face had paled and he waited only a few moments after McGee withdrew before leaving himself.

The Dowager and Lady Granville were deep in conversation, their heads close together, and Fleur slipped out, murmuring, "I'll return soon," when she passed them.

She had no idea what the trouble might be, but Lord Dominic had been the one to send the message, which meant he must be involved in whatever was wrong. Her pulse pounded as she sped toward the orangeries. The men might be angry but she didn't care. She was capable and could help in many situations where other females might be useless. Papa had taught his girls to be strong if they were ever in difficult situations.

There was barely a moment to take in the pungent scent of the orangeries. She saw Lord Nathan open a door to go out on the west terrace and her heart lifted. At least she wasn't too late getting there.

Snowdrop and Albert Parker, McGee and a large gathering of servants crowded around Lord Dominic who said something to McGee and looked at the house. The butler hurried toward the orangeries and Fleur slid behind the statue of a woefully underdressed nymph apparently crawling up the torso of a gentleman in a few floating pieces of cloth and with a laurel crown on his head.

The moment the coast was clear, Fleur walked quickly outside and tucked herself into the group of servants.

"Split up in pairs," Lord Dominic said. "Then fan out. About half of you go from this side and the rest from east terrace. Move rapidly but not so rapidly you miss little Chloe. Either she has become lost or she started out hiding—as a prank—and now she's afraid she's in trouble. It's getting darker. We must find her before the light fails completely."

Chloe was lost. Fleur felt sick and she broke out in a sweat. Her heart bumped hard. She started to move away with the group set to leave from the east terrace when a horrible thought stopped her. Brother Juste and Jane Weller had spoken about abductions. Oh, surely the fiend wouldn't take darling Chloe—not a little girl.

"Fleur! Stop right where you are!"

Lord Nathan, sounding quite unlike himself, roared her name and she turned around. The two brothers stared at her. *Idiots.* What made them think she couldn't be just as useful as the female servants they'd sent forth? Just as useful as the men, too?

"I'll go through and leave with the second group," she said. "We must hurry."

"Go inside and stay inside," Lord Dominic said. "Now."

"Don't waste another second of our time." Lord Nathan made a shooing motion with his hands. "And don't talk to the other ladies about this."

Fleur turned on her heel and went back into the house.

Through the orangeries and into a magnificent reception room she went. And from there she left the house again, checking in all directions to make sure she didn't run into her two overbearing masculine hosts.

Already the servants had set off and she picked out one pair heading for the rose gardens and the Dower House while another hurried off in the direction of the topiary gardens where three fountains surrounded by stone benches offered the calming sound of splashing water.

Fleur considered areas she had found in the grounds that she liked best. There were so many places. She would start with the narrow band of evergreen trees separating the ornamental gardens from pastures where sheep grazed and horses were frequently put out.

Mr. Lawrence cut around a corner of the house and across a flowerbed, heading straight for Fleur. "Oh, fie," she said under her breath. He stepped onto the path in front of her and she gave a little curtsey because she couldn't think of anything else to do.

That stopped him. She almost laughed when he skidded to a halt and bowed. "Good afternoon," he said, then looked at her with his piercing eyes.

"Good afternoon." She held her breath. He would tell her she shouldn't be out here—she just knew he would.

"I hope you're glad to be at Heatherly, Miss Toogood," he said.

So he knew who she was. "Very glad." And she wanted to go on and look for Chloe.

"It's getting dark, miss, so I wouldn't go too far if I was you."

Could she ask him not to tell Lord Dominic or Lord Nathan she was out here? "I'll be returning soon enough," she said. Of course she couldn't ask him to take her part.

She smiled and nodded and walked past him—and felt him watching her. Fleur didn't look back and puffed with relief when she heard him walking away.

The band of trees took a good number of minutes to reach. Fleur started at one end and ran back and forth through the straight trunks. They stretched a long way. Thank goodness she had grown up in the country and was accustomed to walking considerable distances.

Now and again she heard a voice call, "Chloe, where are you?" or, "It's all right, Chloe, you're not in trouble. Come along now."

"No dogs!" she heard Lord Nathan shout.

He sounded angry, and Fleur all but ran into a tree. She grabbed its trunk in both hands. *Dogs?* Heavens, no, not dogs. Chloe would be found without such extreme measures.

The sight of Lord Dominic stopped her again. She crouched and peeked out occasionally. Several workmen set down tools and left a large rock garden under construction to gather around him while he explained Chloe's disappearance.

"How long has she been gone then?" one man, a strongly built fellow with curly hair and his shirtsleeves rolled above deeply tanned forearms asked. He spoke with a surprisingly cultured accent. He had been taking notes and looking across the estate through a telescope.

"We're not sure, Noel," Lord Dominic told him. "Perhaps an hour. Maybe longer. She was told not to wander off."

The man wiped his hands on a handkerchief. "I just got here myself and I didn't see any sign of a child. My men and I can help. We'd like to."

"I'd appreciate it." Lord Dominic started to walk away but turned back and said, "My sister-in-law is pleased you'll be doing some redesign on the gardens. She particularly likes the idea of this big rockery your people are building."

"It will give some separation in this spot," the man said, using his hands to outline a pattern of how the project would look when it was complete. "The Marquis made a particular request that this be done now—for his wife."

He took off with his men behind him and Lord Dominic climbed to the top of a pile of rocks waiting to be used. He turned slowly, shaded his eyes and searched as far as he could see.

Fleur held still in the shadowy trees and watched him. She couldn't help herself. Her thoughts about him were unsuitable but how could she stop her thoughts and feelings?

Pieces of his hair, pulled loose from the tail at his nape, blew wildly and she realized she hadn't even noticed the wind until now. With his fists on his hips and his coat flapping, he resembled a pirate captain at the helm, keeping watch over the waters. She smiled and bent double to creep away.

Many minutes later, Fleur stopped again, winded, her throat dry. To go through the entire band of trees would take too long and she'd be in darkness before she finished.

She left the trees on the side of the formal gardens. Here and there she saw bobbing lanterns and wished she had one herself. Now she would return, searching a swathe to include little grottos tucked away here and there—obviously by a whimsical gardener, and the deserted gazebo too far from the houses to be useful…she would start with those.

One after another she eliminated likely spots and she turned her ankles too many times to count. The left foot felt as if it could be swelling. A frog pond surrounded by a grassy ledge and a wall lay tucked away near the gazebo and she approached carefully, afraid she might slip in if she were careless.

At least the moon had come out to spread eerie light over the ground. Wild animals scuffled in the brush and birds flapped in overhead branches. Fleur was glad of the lights at Heatherly, distant though they seemed.

Humming.

She bowed her head, closed her eyes and concentrated. Definitely some sort of high, out of tune, burbling hum, and coming from the area of the pond.

Fleur got down on her hands and knees and crawled through grass rapidly growing damp. Poor Mrs. Neville would be outraged at such treatment of one of her lovely dresses.

Her hand connected with the edge of a wall and she paused. This was the wall around the pond. On her stomach, she wriggled forward until she looked through a ring of tall grasses that surrounded the wall. She had to make herself stay calm, and stay put until she knew what she would say and do.

Curled on her side near the pond lay Chloe. She held her two hands together and whispered through her fingers into her palms. Fleur couldn't make out much but the occasional sentence. "P'raps I don't want you to be a prince. P'raps I can't kiss something so slimy and ugly as you."

Cautiously, Fleur crawled around until she was behind Chloe, then she climbed over the wall, landed on the grassy ledge and scurried around to sit between Chloe and the murky water. Who knew how deep it might be.

Chloe blinked at her, "'Lo, Fleur. I think you are most pretty."

"Thank you," Fleur said. "And so are you. It's cold and dark. Shouldn't you like to go home now?"

Chloe let out a loud puff and Fleur winced. Surely she was wrong. Where would the child get intoxicating liquor?

"You see," Chloe said, "I'm so tired and I think I shall sleep here tonight."

Fleur gathered the unresisting, bony little body into her arms, but Chloe gradually slid down until her head rested in Fleur's lap.

"I don't think I can carry you," Fleur told the child. "But we can lean on each other and find our way back."

"Too tired," Chloe said. "Lost my frog. He will never be a prince now."

The slightest sound caught Fleur's attention and she looked up. She couldn't see Lord Dominic's face but she'd know that tall, straight-backed form anywhere. The sliver of a moon shone directly on her and she shook her head, indicating that he shouldn't frighten Chloe.

"Did you drink something?" Fleur asked and sensed as much as saw Lord Dominic make an agitated shift of weight.

"No. Well, yes, I did. He said I shouldn't tell anyone and it was so nice. He only gave it to me in the little cup because the afternoon had grown hot. And I think he was sorry be-cause…because I got frightened when he insisted on show-ing me new things in the gardens and carried me off even when I said I mustn't go."

"And this is where he left you?"

"Only so that I could have a little rest. And he said it was quite all right for me—"

"Chloe?" Fleur leaned closer. "What's that on your face?"

The girl touched her cheek and giggled. "He painted it on from a little pot. It's a cat. Isn't that funny? He makes people laugh at the party gardens. A clown, that's what he said he is and he wears funny clothes."

Lord Dominic snapped his fingers to get her attention and indicated he would join them.

"Here comes Uncle Dominic," Fleur said. "Come to help me take you home."

Lord Dominic crouched beside them and gave Chloe a kiss on the cheek. He lingered long enough to look up at Fleur with fury in his eyes. "Are you sure the man didn't say, pleasure gardens, or Vauxhall Gardens."

"He might have."

"What else did he tell you?"

"Mmm. That he can play a trick on anyone he wants to. He can even make people disappear, but he didn't do that to me this time. P'raps next time, he said."

Lord Dominic took Chloe from Fleur's arms. He settled the child in the crook of his arm and offered Fleur a hand. When she took it he held her firmly and didn't let go while they climbed away from the pond and walked toward Heatherly House.

Chloe fell asleep and Lord Dominic said to Fleur, "You and I have a great deal to discuss. I'll have Snowdrop bring you to me later. It's time you showed me your silly list. The sooner we get that out of the way, the better."

"Yes, my lord," she said very formally.

"Now, my timing may be a mistake, but I have to find ways to make you trust me—and do as I tell you. I'm well aware of what is or is not the done thing but I hope you will call me Dominic."

She paused at once. "That would be disrespectful."

"Not if it's what I want."

Fleur felt strange, light-headed and oddly warmed. "You are so generous. Very well, I should very much like to call you by your given name when it's appropriate." He was generous—and confounding—and if she wasn't careful he would reduce her to a spineless creature who always did what he wanted. Pah! That would never happen.

"I have decided it will always be appropriate and the devil take anyone with another opinion. You are the most resourceful woman I've ever met, and the least concerned with her own safety. I think you may prove worthy of calling 'friend.'"

"Thank you." She was grateful the darkness hid her blushes. "Who do you think this clown person is? He could have done Chloe great harm. He did do her harm and think how easily she could have rolled into the pond and drowned."

"I know."

"I will not tell anyone you are such good friends," Chloe murmured and Fleur had to laugh—with Dominic's help. "The silk cat meant me no harm. That is his name, you know, *Le Chat Soyeux.* He said I could tell Hattie and Grandmama about him."

"Did he now?" Dominic said.

They reached the house and he held a door open for Fleur to enter. "I'll send for you later, remember. And I warn you, our interview is unlikely to be pleasant. You try me severely and that must stop. But I see your strength and I'm willing to see if you can be trained."

"How kind of you."

"Kindness has nothing to do with it. I have to try to maximize your worth on the marriage mart—it's important to my mother."

14

Snowdrop hurried Blanche from the room telling her, "The Marchioness knows what she wants and knows how to ask for it. I'm to take your place with Miss Fleur because she isn't quite so sure of herself."

"I know what needs to be done for 'er," said Blanche, puffing at stray wisps of hair and sounding flustered. "And you 'ave to look after that—Miss Chloe."

"Don't you worry about Chloe," Snowdrop said, sounding grim. "Lady Granville's expecting you now." She closed the door almost before Blanche was completely outside.

Snowdrop had arrived with a vase of spring flowers which she carried to a table between the two blue chairs. "Shall I put these here?" she said.

Bemused by all the coming and going, Fleur nodded.

With her hands on her hips, Snowdrop stepped back from the flowers and turned around. She smiled broadly and stood in front of Fleur. "I'm so pleased I'm to be your maid for the next few weeks and I'll do my best to 'elp make sure we 'ave fun."

Fleur said, "Thank you," but she was at a loss to understand what was happening, and why such a change was being made.

"It was Lady Granville's idea for me to cheer you up, and Lord Nathan agreed. Try not to think badly of Lord Dominic—he's just a deep one, and takes himself too seriously. He's a fine man and I've heard as he does a lot of good for people who need it."

"What sort of good?" Fleur asked and instantly wished she hadn't.

Snowdrop, whose skin was as pale as…snow, and very lovely, raised her pointed chin while she thought. She wore her black hair, of which there was a great deal, wound into a heavy chignon. "I can't exactly tell you details because I don't know 'em, but I know it's true and I also know his concern is for those less fortunate than 'imself—or it mostly is, I think."

Fleur recognized that Snowdrop had worked to pronounce her aitches but didn't always manage perfectly. Fleur found the result endearing, but she wasn't convinced by the young woman's explanations.

"I suppose you're here to take me to Dominic—Lord Dominic," she said.

"Not for a little while," Snowdrop said. She batted at her gray velvet skirts. "Isn't this a lovely dress? My Albert picked out the material—with her ladyship's help, of course. He will have me wear pretty things. Lady Granville's the best person I know—apart from Albert, of course. And her John, the Marquis, well, I hope you meet him because he's a prince among men."

"I should like to," Fleur said, waiting to find out the actual purpose for Snowdrops's invasion. "I expect you're helping make sure Blanche doesn't find out where I'm going tonight, just to keep down gossip among the servants, and she'll be back later, after all—"

"No, no, no." Snowdrop rushed to Fleur. "Oh, you poor thing, you've been through so much. Lord Nathan's angry with himself for shouting at you outside the orangeries, you know."

Fleur's head spun. She realized her mouth was open and snapped it shut.

"He said it was a good idea for me to look after you while you're here, with Lady Granville's help, of course. Blanche will do the necessary things for her."

"Chloe—"

"She's got to be guarded," Snowdrop said quickly. "Lady Granville had to rest after they told her what happened, but she's angry now and organizing things. It's been decided my Albert will guard Chloe by day, and Butters, one of the underbutlers, will sleep outside her room. You know what a strapping man he is."

"Yes." Fleur had been introduced to Butters. But she couldn't concentrate. All she could think about sensibly was the meeting Dominic had already told her would be unpleasant.

"I've got to put a smile on your face—and wipe the smile off Lord Dominic's. Not that he's likely to do much smiling in his present mood. He's ordering people around, accounting for every key. You should have heard him lecture Mrs. Chambers and McGee! There's to be a list kept all the time and everyone's to be accounted for. Who's in the house and who's not. And nobody's to be admitted without approval from himself, Lord Nathan, Lady Granville or the Dowager."

While she chattered, Snowdrop pulled clothing from Fleur's wardrobe and spread it on the bed.

"Surely I don't need to change," Fleur said. "As soon as Lord Dominic's finished with me, I'll be going to bed."

"*Finished* with you? There, it's just the way I thought. He's cowed you."

"No, he hasn't," Fleur said, indignant. "I wouldn't allow it."

Snowdrop smirked. "That's what you think. But you tell me this—is your tummy wobbly?"

Fleur breathed deeply. Her stomach flipped over as it had many times since she'd come upstairs. "Yes. But that's only because of all the upset this evening."

"What upset you most?"

"Discovering what had happened to Chloe," Fleur said. "It frightened me."

"She's safe now." Snowdrop raised one eyebrow and looked exceeding haughty. "What upset you most *after* Chloe's trouble?"

"I—" She felt alone here. "Very well, but I shall deny I said it if you tell anyone. Lord Dominic has been strange. He has told me he… He's been pleasant to me but he has also made me nervous. There, now I've told you."

"Oh, you poor thing. There, there, you don't 'ave to be nervous anymore because you've got good friends to help you." She took a break from going through clothes and patted Fleur's hand. "Good gracious me, I've crumbs in my brainbox. This is for you. It goes with the flowers." She took an envelope from her pocket, gave it to Fleur and returned to the wardrobe.

Her own name was written in large script on the front of the envelope. The initials *NE* on the back meant nothing to Fleur. She slipped out a card and read: *I was wrong to shout at you. Have courage, Fleur. You are special and will be cherished here. Remember that you can always come to me—Nathan Elliot.* The kindness of it brought tears to her eyes and she slipped the card between the flowers.

"Ooh, look at this." With one of the dresses Fleur had brought with her from the country held high, Snowdrop spun around on her toes. "Now this is a no-nonsense affair if ever

I saw one." She shook the white cambric dress out and turned it for Fleur to see. "Very high in the neck—I hope it doesn't choke you—and enough flounces on the bodice to hide any hint of a bosom."

Fleur laughed and it felt good. "I'll have you know that my mama made that dress for me with her own hands. It's her favorite."

Snowdrop minced across the carpet with the gown pressed against her. She twirled this way and that. "I should think it is. No man would have amorous thoughts with you wearing this. Not unless he already knew what was underneath. It's perfect. Let's get it on you."

Curious she might be, and caught up by Snowdrop's energy, but Fleur held her ground and made no attempt to change. "You'll have to tell me why I should do this first. I've been told not to wear any of my own clothes while I'm here."

"What you do in the privacy of your room is your own affair," Snowdrop said. "Here you can be the person you want to be. When you came back to your room this evening you changed into familiar clothes because they comforted you, and made you feel the person you really are. And if Lord Dominic behaves like an overbearing... If he's overbearing about your dress, 'e needs to find out he's no right to be. The Dowager wants you here and she wants you to be really happy. So does Lady Granville. And so does Lord Nathan. Now we have to teach the other one to stop thinking of you as a beautiful, empty-headed child."

He had already said he thought of her as resourceful and that he'd like them to be on friendly, first-name terms. "I don't think he considers me empty-headed." And he had kissed her as he would a woman.

"Let's make sure. Hattie—Lady Granville—says you are

to put him firmly in his place. Remind 'im why you're in London and tell 'im you don't want him as a bodyguard because you can look after yourself."

Fleur's mind turned blank.

"That'll be one of the things he says tonight," Fleur said. "He says he's going to know where you are every minute and if he thinks it's necessary, he'll guard you himself—whatever that means."

"He'll do no such thing," Fleur said, growing angry. "Why should he worry about my safety?"

"Because of the kidnappings, of course." Snowdrop clapped a hand over her mouth and her black eyes grew huge. "Oh, dear, what a paperskull I am. Her ladyship talks about everything with me but she'd be ever so angry if she knew I'd said something that could frighten you."

"You haven't. And you're not a paperskull because you told me the truth. Honesty is always to be admired. But there's no need to be concerned for my safety. That dreadful Silken Cat must have changed his mind about taking off with Chloe even though the family would have paid whatever he asked to get her back."

Snowdrop clutched Fleur's dress tightly. "He must 'ave done it to send a message. Why else wouldn't he take her?"

"Perhaps he has *some* scruples. But my family has very little money. They couldn't pay a ransom so Lord Dominic needn't worry about me being taken. The Cat's only interested in the wealthy…" Her voice trailed away. He had taken Jane Weller and now she was free again. Someone must have paid. It could have been Dominic doing one of his good-hearted deeds for a poor person. Since it was known that Dominic championed the needy, The Cat could well decide to strike at another person of lowly means again. Perhaps someone who was close to Dominic—in the same house.

The thought of Jane Weller made her tremble. Jane had seen the man. What if he decided to come for her once he found out where she was? He'd been here, at Heatherly, and for all anyone knew he'd come for Jane in the first place.

Snowdrop cleared her throat and Fleur jumped.

"Decided to put him in his place, have you?" Snowdrop asked.

"I most certainly have," Fleur told her. "But I won't need a different dress to make him believe I mean what I say. I want to go at once."

Snowdrop turned the corners of her mouth down and sighed. "Ah well, it would have been such fun. I wanted to see his face when you went in." She produced a beribboned, white satin cap. "This would have been the finishing touch."

Fleur giggled. "I think we'll have other opportunities for fun." She smoothed her hair in front of a mirror. The Dowager had given her a cream sarcenet stole—among many other things. Fleur found the stole and tied it around her neck and shoulders. She draped it with care to make sure no skin showed.

"He's met his match in you and that's what Lord Dominic needs, to learn that even if women can't be as strong as he is, they can be his equal in every other way. He's got an eye for a pretty body. That shawl's covering too much and it's going to make him cross." She gave Fleur a quick hug. "Come on then."

How unfortunate that men were so captivated by certain parts of a woman's body, but Fleur knew it was true. "Snowdrop, please do one little thing for me and turn around."

Instantly Snowdrop faced the wall and she covered her eyes for good measure. Fleur retrieved her journal from beneath the mattress and tucked it under her arm before joining Snowdrop for what felt like a very long walk to the third floor.

"Good evening, Fleur. I'm glad you finally decided to join me." Dominic did his best not to let his annoyance at being kept waiting show.

Fleur glanced at Snowdrop, who accompanied her, and the latter reached up to whisper in Fleur's ear.

With a sharp nod, Fleur said, "Snowdrop would like to see if Lady Granville needs her. Then she'd like to join her husband. But she'll send—"

"She'll send nothing and no one." A pox on the wretched, meddling woman. "Kindly inform Lady Granville we need to discuss arrangements for picking up Gussy Arbuthnot on the way to the musicale at the Herberts' in Berkley Square tomorrow evening. There is no need to worry about Fleur's well-being when she is with me. It's my job to make sure her time in London is successful."

"But—"

"It's all right," Fleur said. Dominic would have preferred to hear her reprimand the meddler.

"Very well," Snowdrop said. She dropped him a perfunctory curtsey and actually gave Fleur a light kiss on the cheek. *Upstart.* She went on her way but not before she had the audacity to say, "Don't hesitate to send for me if you need me. At any time. The pull is by the fireplace. Otherwise I'll see you in the morning."

"She's a menace," he said when she'd left. "Watch that woman carefully or she'll take advantage of you. She'll have you thinking she lives and breathes for the family."

"From what I've seen—and been told—she does."

Dominic seethed. No doubt his brother had found a way to

take Fleur aside and turn her mind. God knew how Nathan might have pressed his advantage by using the earlier debacle when he, Dominic, had been overheard speaking harshly to Fleur on their return to Heatherly with Chloe. Not that it mattered, really, since bringing Nathan and Fleur together would solve a great many of Dominic's problems. It would set him free.

He wanted to be set free.

There was no room in his life for a woman. Absolutely not a spare inch.

"My lord, you wanted to see me. You told me our meeting would be unpleasant. I'm here but I'm tired. May we please get through our interview quickly?"

He walked slowly closer to her, his hands clasped behind his back and his head thrust forward. "Please take a seat."

"I'd rather stand."

This would go even worse than he'd expected. "Stand, sit, do whatever you please. It's of no interest to me."

She flinched and he turned his back on her. "Why must you deliberately plague me with your contrary behavior? It's as if you deliberately set out to vex me."

"Because I don't want to sit down?"

Her voice wasn't quite so confident. Good. "Because you make yourself unattractive when you talk like an unmannered chit of low station."

"I am of low station. I am not unmannered, which is more than I can say for you, my lord. You are obviously making a special effort to insult me and make me feel unworthy of being here, and certainly unworthy of your attention."

He smoothed the scowl from his features before facing her again. "*Impudent.* You astound me."

Her pallor and the faint sheen of perspiration on her face

worried him. If she was ill, this interview could wait. "Do you feel unwell?"

"No, my lord."

"I told you to call me Dominic," he roared. He took a deep breath to calm himself. "Fleur, you are to call me Dominic. We agreed on that."

"We did but you've been shouting at me ever since. And I don't have any idea why you are so angry with me."

His eyes actually stung. Hell's teeth, what was wrong with him? Her blue eyes had widened and she stared. She constantly plucked at the fringe on a shawl he wished she hadn't worn. And she clamped the wretched journal beneath her arm.

"How have I made you so angry?" she asked quietly.

He covered the space between them in three strides and drew her roughly into an embrace. "Fleur, Fleur," he said and closed his eyes while he rested his cheek on top of her head. "I'm not angry at you, I'm angry at…at everything that confuses me at present. Please, if not for my sake, then for my mother's, don't take more risks. When I told you to return to the house, I thought you had. I had no idea you had defied me and wandered off in the dark."

"I didn't wander off. I decided how I would search for Chloe and set out. I had a plan. She's just a little girl and I was afraid for her. I found Chloe. I wouldn't have if I'd done as you and Lord Nathan told me."

"I would have found her. I was already close."

"Perhaps you would. But could it have been my voice speaking to Chloe that made you come in that direction?"

She had not attempted to leave his embrace. He thought about what she said. "I did hear your voice—and Chloe's—but I had already started that way."

Fleur made fists against his chest. "I was not wrong in what I did. Can't you just admit it?"

Dash it all but he hated to give in. "Very well, you did nothing wrong. But I have had time to think about the implications here and you can no longer wander in the grounds. You can't be unaccounted for at any time. Whenever you decide to go out, even if it's with Hattie, make sure I know about it. One of the men will go with you."

She took too long to say, "Very well."

"And when we are at some entertainment, you will not leave my sight. If a man asks you to go outside, refuse. You would refuse anyway, but it never hurts to be reminded. If he asks you to accompany him to the refreshments, feign tiredness and ask him to bring something for you. I'm not concerned for you when you dance because either Nathan or I will dance close to you."

Her body stiffened in his arms.

"What is it?" he asked her.

"You cannot stifle me...Dominic. I shall be very sensible, but if you make me a spectacle by hovering, I don't think I can bear it. And I do know you mean well, and that you are kind."

The olive branch was puny but he'd take it. And he'd better stop holding her before she realized how much he enjoyed doing so. He let her go. "I will make sure you are not embarrassed. I take it your list is in the journal?" He held out a hand.

She took the book and opened it to the pages she wanted him to see. Fleur sat down and he walked slowly back and forth in front of the fire, reading, a sense of disbelief growing with every second. When he reached the end of the list he closed the journal and stared at her.

Her expression showed no trepidation. She actually

thought there was a man on earth who could achieve the state of perfection she'd set out?

Dominic moved the second chair close to hers and sat down where he looked directly into her face. "Are you cold?" he asked. Best keep things civil.

"No."

"I thought you might be since you're wearing a heavy shawl."

"It isn't heavy, it's sarcenet and quite light. It's comforting."

Comforting. Why should she need to be comforted by some piece of clothing? "Very well." He put the open book on his knees. "I commend you on your detail."

"Thank you. I'm an organized person."

"You entitle this *The Man Who Wants to Marry Me*. Then you go on with your so-called questions."

"They *are* questions."

She would insist upon having the last word, a most annoying feminine trait.

"Now I'll read off the questions.

1. Does he accept and love my family?

2. Does his family respect my family and accept me?

3. Does he like cats?

4. Does he like dogs?

5. Is there the vaguest chance that he's a prig?

6. Does he think men are superior to women?

7. Does he love and like me more than anyone else?

8. Does he respect my opinions and give them equal weight with his own?

9. How will he react if I ask him to walk outside with me on a rainy night? (Note to myself—will he refuse when I ask him to lie on the grass so we may feel the rain on our faces?)

10. How does he behave with children? Will he make an affectionate, patient father?

11. Will he be gentle and teach me how to please him without turning into a cruel animal?"

Dominic paused for breath. He looked at Fleur with the intention of conveying the enormity of her expectations, but she stared into the distance with her arms crossed. "I'll go on," he said.

"12. What does he wear to bed? And will he share the same bed with me other than during his gratification? Mama said he would probably return to his own bed, this being common with men of a certain class. Used and abandoned—I'll have none of that."

"What do most men wear to bed?" Fleur asked suddenly. "What do you wear to bed?"

He barely stopped himself from laughing. Over and over again she amazed him. "Some men wear nightshirts. I don't wear anything to bed."

She tilted her head a bit and he'd never seen a more pensive expression on her face. Her regard slid down his length then returned to his face. "I see. Thank you for answering my question. I don't think I should like nightshirts."

Before long she would drive him wild.

"13. Will he include me in his business, talk to me about his problems and give consideration to my ideas?

14. Will he drink too much—even on occasion?

15. Will he find it necessary to spend raucous hours in the company of other men, gambling, drinking and encouraging loose women?"

Dominic ran a forefinger around the inside of his neckcloth.

"16. Will he manage to convince me that he doesn't have a woman of convenience?

17. Will he accept my need for love and close companionship? And will he enjoy my being a carnal person since I now believe I am?

18. Will he join me in learning exotic ways of lovemaking? I have heard such things mentioned and believe I should enjoy them. If he is the right man he will want to research these matters with me."

Closing the book quietly—just to be sure he didn't slam it shut and throw it—he placed it on her lap. "Do you have any idea how a man would react to your questions?"

"If he wanted anything to do with me, he would respond well," Fleur said. "Before a person gives their life to another they should be sure they won't regret doing so. You're a man. How did you react?"

Telling her he'd like to start showing her how well he could do with the exotic forms of lovemaking might not be a good idea. "I think you have a great many probing questions that suggest they are demands. No man in his right mind would respond without having a chance to give you a similar list."

"The more similar, the better, don't you think?" Her sweet smile touched him.

"Of course. But you want to find out a lot of intimate details I'm surprised you know how to put into words."

Fleur opened her journal to the back and took out a copy of her list of questions. "Here," she said. "I would appreciate any suggestion you might have for me. Places where you think I've been too outspoken. Questions I should add."

Dominic tossed the papers aside and stood up. Fury of a kind he'd never felt rose through him. This anger was out of control. He gritted his teeth and curled his hands into fists.

She had sensed his sudden flood of emotion and stood up

quickly, staring at him as if she expected him to change into a monster.

"You will go to your room now. I will walk with you until I see you enter and you tell me all is well."

He stayed behind her all the way to the second floor and to her room. She rushed inside and he heard her call out, "Good night," before she slammed the door and he heard the key turn in the lock.

But he had her to rights now. He knew exactly the nature of her devious plot and it wouldn't work. Her so-called list of questions to potential suitors was meant for his eyes only. Why else would she make a second copy for him. He hadn't been careful enough to hide his attraction to her. Hell, he hadn't hidden it at all. He'd embraced her, kissed her—and he'd enjoyed it. But he wasn't about to be tricked by a little fortune hunter capable of writing her "questions" in language provocative enough to arouse and, she hoped, ensnare him.

Very provocative language. He thought about that while he slowly made his way back upstairs. *Would he help her learn exotic ways of making love?* Were those the words of an innocent? He thought not. It was time for him to run a test or two on Miss Toogood.

15

"Everybody!" Their hosts stood in front of a dais where a string quartet waited to play. Sir Toby Herbert raised both hands, allowing cascades of lace to fall back from his wrists. "A debacle is about to happen."

Lady Herbert opened her eyes wide and clapped her hands in mock horror. "We shall be the failure of the Season."

Titters circulated in the small, elegant ballroom at Rose Place in Berkley Square.

Fleur, wearing the brilliant orange-gold evening dress Dominic had requested of Mrs. Neville, did her best to sink behind an exotic, broad-leafed plant in a Chinese pot. Dominic caught her eye and frowned. She nodded politely, even if the effort did cost her a good deal. This had been a day filled with his demands and his stalking about to check security at Heatherly. Fortunately they had not spoken alone since the previous night.

"You see," Sir Toby said. "It appears that our world-renowned baritone, Monsieur Vilepain, is dissatisfied with the accompanists we provided—even though they are the King's favorites—and he chooses to leave us."

A man who could only be the singer emerged from behind Chinese screens artfully used to create the back of the dais.

Swathed in a dark, floor-length greatcoat with a fur cape, he swept forward and from the dais, parting a path through the guests as he went. He flipped back an unruly bob of oily black hair and avoided settling his dark eyes on anyone in particular.

At the doors to the handsomely oversize music room, he paused and waved with the hand in which he held his hat. *"Au revoir,"* he said. "I shall shed tears to have missed my opportunity to thrill you, but the best can only perform with the best."

He glided from the room and Fleur said, "Poof," much louder than she had intended.

Lady Granville laughed and said, "Poof," just as loud and soon there were dozens of "poofs" circling the room.

"You were lucky that time," Dominic said from behind Fleur. She hadn't noticed when he moved. "Next time you may be left standing alone in a silent room with only your foolishness to keep you company. Why aren't you wearing the necklace my mother sent to you for this evening?"

Fleur touched her mother's pin on a band of black velvet. "For my first outing I wanted to wear this to remind me of Mama."

"This is a business venture, not an occasion for sentimentality. The diamonds and sapphires would have been so much better."

"And may all your hopes turn to worms," she said, stepping away.

"A terrifying curse," he murmured. His hand, firmly gripping her waist, brought her back. "Be quiet. Our hosts are dealing with a difficult situation."

"Quite. Try to reign in your nasty tongue."

"The chairs will be moved," Lady Herbert said. "And we shall pass the evening in dance and conversation."

Wonderful, Fleur thought. She faced the inevitable—that she would have to dance and make small talk with gentlemen approved by Dominic.

"And champagne and strawberries will be along," Sir Toby said, beaming at his guests. "Perhaps chocolate, too. I'm sure we all know how to get along without dance cards."

Another chuckle followed and a number of servants cleared rows of chairs to the sides of a dance floor.

The music struck up and couples took their places for a quadrille. Gussy Arbuthnot, fetching in mauve taffeta, craned her neck all about. Fleur felt awkward for her since she made it obvious that she searched for a partner.

Fleur looked sideways at Dominic. Then she checked to see how many female eyes were upon him. Just as she'd thought—almost all of them, and some of the younger misses huddled together to sigh over him and Lòrd Nathan. The girls watched for any promising moves they might make toward them. Dominic made no moves. He appeared as still as a statue and his autocratic features turned Fleur's heart. This man was deeply thoughtful and it showed.

A cheer went up and cries of, "Hurrah, hurrah." The host and hostess took to the floor, the myriad colors in Lady Herbert's gauze gown shimmering.

Fleur turned toward Dominic.

He had left. Just like that. She searched the room but didn't see him.

A tall, thin man with a rather supercilious air approached. He bowed to Fleur and said, "Fritz Mergatroyd, your ladyship," to Hattie. "We met at the Soamses' last year."

Hattie said, "I remember. Good evening," but didn't sound enthusiastic.

"May I have this dance with your charge?" Mr. Mergatroyd asked and Fleur turned cold with apprehension.

"Um…" Hattie turned about, looking for Dominic, Fleur assumed. When she didn't see him she inclined her head and said, "Take great care of her."

Fleur spent an unpleasant time with Mr. Mergatroyd, who leered down the front of her dress and repeatedly mopped his face with a large handkerchief.

"The Mergatroyds are an old family," he said, and gave a snort that turned into a braying laugh. "Very old. And much admired for our reputation as purveyors of fine merchandise for more than three generations."

He wrapped his fingers in hers, pulled her toward him, and trod on her toes. To which he said, "Ouch," quite loudly.

"How interesting," she said, trying not to wince. "What sort of merchandise?"

Mergatroyd made an airy gesture with the hand from which the damp handkerchief trailed. "All manner. Far too many to list. We are particularly well-known for our potted meats. Mergatroyd's Meat Pots are in every home."

Fleur had never heard of the stuff. When the music stopped she made a determined move to return to Hattie and Mr. Mergatroyd went willingly enough. "May I call on you at Heatherly House?" he asked.

"Well—"

"Oh, do say I may or I shall be destroyed."

She looked up into his moist face and said, "I can't have that. By all means, call." *Please don't, oh, please don't.*

The man gave another of his horsey laughs.

As soon as Fleur returned Lady Granville stood close to her and said, "You've earned your first medal. Now, shall we sit down with those ladies over there and I'll introduce you.

They don't approve of me, of course, but they're rather sweet."

"Why don't they approve of you?" Fleur asked, shocked.

"Because I don't have a pedigree." She dimpled at Fleur. "However, they are in awe of John so they hide their disdain well."

"We don't want to sit with *them*," Fleur said. "How dare they consider themselves better than you."

"They aren't better," Lady Granville said. "And I don't care what they think."

Fleur smiled and thought how right Snowdrop was in her opinion of her mistress.

They moved toward a gilt table where three ladies sat, their heads close together. When Lady Granville and Fleur approached the ladies stopped talking and their heads appeared to draw back into their necks but they gushed over Lady Granville and smiled suspiciously at Fleur.

"Hattie." Dominic arrived with another man in tow. "Do you recall Franklin Best? We were all at his parents' Surry home for a house party last autumn."

"I certainly do. How are you, Franklin?"

The pleasantries disposed of, Dominic made a formal introduction of Fleur to Franklin Best, a good-looking man in his late twenties or so with thick blond hair.

"Franklin's in his father's banking business," Dominic said and Lady Granville murmured, "I remember. Your father spoke highly of you."

"Fathers tend to see the best in their offspring," Franklin said, grinning. "To be honest, my hope is to become a barrister. Money is the most *boring* thing in the world."

Fleur laughed. "I suppose it might be if one had any," she said. Dominic's face lost all expression but Hattie put an arm around Fleur and squeezed her. "You, my dear one, have what money can't buy—a loyal heart."

"Excuse us," Gussy said, much louder than necessary. "Nathan and I are going to dance."

The two of them went onto the floor and Gussy looked so happy she trembled.

"With Lord Dominic's approval, Miss Toogood?" Franklin Best offered his hand and Fleur stared at it. Seconds passed and Franklin said, "Will you dance with me?"

Lady Granville gave Fleur a little push and she placed a hand on Franklin's wrist.

She liked him, Fleur decided. There was little doubt that the man had lots of money and, thanks to her careless mouth, knew she had none, but he made no secret of his pleasure in dancing with her.

They moved in and out of the intricate formations and bowed. Fleur blessed her mother for being the accomplished dancer she was and for teaching all of her girls to acquit themselves well. Fleur had always had the most flair but that was, she thought, because she enjoyed dancing so.

She caught the eye of a gentleman opposite and to the left. A big man, but solid, with no fat on him, and a tanned complexion that spoke to hours spent outside. He inclined his head at Fleur, bowed slightly, but kept his eyes on hers. She had to look away.

She and Franklin touched hands and reversed positions. The music could not have been more beautiful and she felt as if she moved in a dream, as if all this was a dream. They revolved again and as they passed, Franklin said quietly, "You are lovely, Miss Toogood."

Fleur glowed but she was sure the result must be a red face—and that he said the same thing to every female he danced with. Again she was opposite the man with a too familiar look in his dark brown eyes. He smiled at her and bowed again, keeping his face always turned so that he could see her. Thick fair hair curled over the top of his collar and when he smiled, deep dimples formed beside his mouth.

"You seem far away," Franklin said.

"This is my first outing in London," Fleur told him. "I'm a country parson's daughter and quite green, I suppose. Look at this room, at the colors and the grace. And the bloodlines. I'm overwhelmed."

He stared back at her and his smile fell away. "It all pales beside you." The moment before they swung around and moved on to another partner, he squeezed her hand tightly and stroked the backs of her fingers with his thumb.

Fleur's heart beat very fast. She knew nothing of all this. The village dances were gatherings of old friends and the young people had danced together since they were children. Very little art went into their exuberant exchanges.

A small pause to face a new partner and the patterns began again. The man with fair curly hair and brown eyes stood across from her and she had no doubt that he would recognize her if they met again. He studied her from head to foot and his broad chest expanded by the time he met her eyes again.

She had seen him somewhere before.

They inclined their heads and swept toward one another. "You must be Miss Fleur Toogood," he said, stepping away, turning, and stepping back. "The Dowager Marchioness of Granville's charge. You will set London on its ear, my dear."

She didn't know how to respond.

"I am Noel DeBeaufort. My parents' prodigal son. They

have never recovered from my decision to study the great landscape artists and try to follow in their footsteps."

The man she'd seen Dominic speak to in the grounds at Heatherly. "You are doing some designing for Lady Granville," she said. "I saw you there."

He bent his head then smiled at her. "This is true."

Noel held her hand and around they went. "Let's leave the dance," he said. "It's hellish hot. Have you tried champagne?"

Fleur shook her head. He seemed so worldly—and so sure of himself.

"Come then," he said, taking her hand.

As smoothly as if she'd only imagined it, Dominic stepped into the formation. He nodded at her partner, said something brief and took his place. She did blush then, and glance sideways to find curious faces watching her.

They came together and Dominic touched her hand. "Are you enjoying yourself?"

"Yes, thank you. I didn't think taking another dancer's place was—"

"It is now. That man is a good enough fellow but unconventional. And too worldly. He has a reputation with the women."

Fleur wished she could die on the spot. Dominic had spoken too loudly and everyone looked at her and whispered, and shook their heads. "He was just part of the dance," she told Dominic. "Why make such a fuss?"

"No fuss," he said. "Your imagination is too active. The gold is as perfect on you as I expected it to be. Perhaps cut too low, and a little tight in the bodice, though."

Fleur stood still and a lady bumped into her. Immediately, Dominic crossed smoothly to her side, apologized to the lady and walked Fleur from the floor.

"How dare you?" Fleur said almost under her breath. "You interfered with Neville when she was fitting the striped dress. She did as you told her with that one, then with this, and now you mortify me in public. I should like to go home."

"Grow up. Apparently my task will not be a task at all, apart from weeding out the wolves. In this room, there are too many interested and eligible men to count. They see the obvious. You are peerless. You and I shall have a long talk. There's no possibility that your experiences up until now can have readied you for this jaded world—or have they?"

She didn't know how to answer. Taking a deep, deep breath, Fleur let the air out slowly, working to calm herself. Finding Dominic looking directly down the front of her bodice ruined her efforts. "Lord Nathan is such a good-humored man," she said, determined to match the task she faced. "I think Gussy likes him. She smiles at him a great deal. I think they make a nice couple, don't you?"

"Mmm?"

"Lord Nathan and Gussy make—"

"I suppose they do. I saw you with Mergatroyd. The man's a boor."

"Perhaps."

He smiled at her. "What did you think of young Best?"

"He's charming and easy to be with. Not that I was with him long."

"Would you like to be?" He looked over the heads of those closest to him.

Fleur pressed a hand into her stomach. "I have no idea. How can I meet someone for a few minutes and know if I would enjoy them again?"

"Would you enjoy spending more time with the other man?"

"Other man?" She frowned up at him.

"DeBeaufort. The ladies find him irresistible. Must be all that outdoors ruggedness."

She knew who he meant but she said, "Which man is that?"

Dominic turned up one corner of his mouth. "*That* man. The one who made you fluttery. Noel, whom we already discussed in some detail as unsuitable. He isn't bashful in setting commissions for his work but he isn't retained often enough. There's talk that he lives mostly on an allowance from his father who intends to cut him off altogether if he doesn't join the family concerns. I shouldn't imagine he needs to research exotic lovemaking."

"That was despicable," she said.

He said, "Yes, it was. Forget I said it. Come, let's rejoin Hattie."

Grateful, Fleur placed a hand on the back of his forearm and hurried along to keep up with his strides. "Why doesn't she dance? Lady Granville, that is? You can see all the attention she gets."

Dominic looked sharply toward his sister-in-law who didn't seem happy in her conversation. "Hattie doesn't care to dance with anyone but John. Or Nathan and me in situations like this."

"You have a heavy burden," she said, hiding a smile. "So many females to protect."

"Hah," he said. And that was all he said.

"Do people have many of these things?" she asked. "When Lady Granville took me shopping for white slippers—did you know colored slippers are going out of fashion? No, no, perhaps you wouldn't. When we were in Bond Street there were so many ladies buying hats and ribbons and all manner of things. And they all talked about exciting events they were going to. Or they thought them exciting."

"You don't usually chatter so."

She didn't bother to hide her next smile. "Come now, Dominic. At least admit this is new and exciting to someone like me. Don't be a curmudgeon."

He rolled his eyes. "In answer to your first question, yes, they do have many of these *things*. There are *things* every day and every night and knowing Mama, you have invitations to all of them."

She couldn't help but say, "Then so do you. See, you have many wonderful things to look forward to and it's all because of me. Now I think of it, why waste time? We should be looking for a wife for you, too. What kind of wife should you like, do you think?"

Dominic bent over her and made a soft, growling noise close to her ear. Startled, Fleur could only stare at him—before she giggled and executed a little jig. "Oh, they're playing a waltz." Fascinated, she turned toward the floor as couples swung into the risque dance.

Dominic's hand stole farther around her waist and held on too tight. "Not a suitable thing for newly acquainted couples."

"Lord Dominic?" Franklin Best stood before them. "May I have this dance with Miss Toogood?"

Fleur gave Dominic a poke in the back and he actually grinned at her. "Yes," he said. "But I am entrusting her to your care."

Franklin swallowed and said, "I understand and you can trust me, my lord."

"Oh, phooey," Fleur said, as soon as they were on the floor. "He thinks he has to behave like my father."

"Most fathers are far more eager to have their daughters dance with eligible men. Lord Dominic stays so close to you that most men are afraid to approach. One might wonder—" Franklin stopped and turned bright red. "I'm sorry, Miss Toogood."

"Call me Fleur. And don't be sorry because I think it's funny."

He took her in his arms and she found her legs didn't want to move at all.

"Are you all right, Fleur?" he said.

"I've never danced a waltz," she told him. "Aren't I a silly?"

His smile showed his delight in her. "You are a wonderful dancer. Let me lead you and in no time you will feel as if you've been waltzing forever."

Around and around, they swung. Franklin's very straight back remained so and he held her carefully, maintaining a small distance between them.

Fleur raised her face and laughed. Whirling, whirling, they went and Franklin's laughter joined hers.

He stopped dancing abruptly and Fleur blinked at Dominic who stood at her partner's shoulder. Dominic gave an irresistible grin and said, "She can't be out all night, old chap. You'll have to share if you don't mind." Franklin muttered something and did his best to hide his disappointment as he walked away.

Dominic placed a large hand at her waist, took hold of her hand and away they went, swaying, revolving, as Fleur had with Franklin, but with a different kind of energy. Dominic's thighs met her body with each turn; they guided her. Her own legs shook, and so did her tummy.

"You've waltzed before," he said. "And you're very good."

"I've waltzed with Franklin Best. I was waltzing with Franklin Best when you took his place."

"Such proximity with a man shouldn't be for too long." He angled his head and studied her face. "Are you sorry I took Franklin's place? I can always get him back."

These were clever games she had never played but, as she'd often been told, she learned things quickly and she would learn the rules of this thinly veiled seductive charade.

Dominic's hand moved across the back of her waist and his arm held her close. She dared not look to right or left for fear of seeing disapproval on every side.

Her body pressed to his. Fleur looked down, and saw her breasts, all but naked in the tight bodice, crushed to Dominic's chest. Twisting, burning heat darted into her private places. Her breathing grew short. When she raised her chin again, Dominic looked at her eyes, her mouth, with his eyes narrowed and his firm lips curved in a possessive smile.

"Every male eye in the room is on you," he said. "There isn't a man present who doesn't want to be where I am. You are luminous."

"Excuse me." Nathan plucked Fleur's hand from Dominic's. "My turn, I believe, little brother."

Dominic released her at once and Nathan swept her away. He smiled, his teeth very white in a tanned face. Those green eyes glittered, but with fun Fleur, thought. How different the brothers were. She turned her head to look for Dominic but he'd disappeared. Noel DeBeaufort hadn't. The rigid lines of his face, the way he stared at her, turned her heart. But then Nathan swung her the opposite way and she caught the eyes of a heavy, richly dressed man whose small, moist mouth pushed out while he popped food in from a plate held by a flunky.

"Good…heavens," Nathan said, guiding Fleur rapidly out of sight of the older man. "The Prince Regent himself. Who would have expected him at the Herberts'?" He pulled her a little closer.

"Spare a few moments for a poor man," Noel DeBeaufort said, stepping beside Fleur and taking her from Nathan. As he eased her away he said, "You can't let a fellow die for want of a few minutes of bliss."

"Seconds will have to do." One revolution and they bumped into Dominic, who claimed her once more but gave Noel an affable grin. "You'll have other chances, old man."

They barely left Noel standing on the floor when the music stopped and Dominic guided Fleur back to where Hattie sat with the group of ladies which had grown since Fleur had left. Hattie, like a brilliant flame, had drawn all manner of chattering, gorgeously dressed females to her and each did her best to outdo the others in wit and by raising her voice ever higher. Several groups of men stood close, openly remarking on the women's charms.

Without warning, the women's voices dropped to whispers. Hands were cupped over mouth and ear to keep every word a secret. Fleur saw Hattie look at Dominic and frown. He nodded in response.

Gussy rushed up trailing an elegant blond girl by the hand. "Fleur, meet Victoria Crewe-Burns, one of my oldest friends. In fact she is my best friend. Vicky, this is Fleur Toogood who is staying with the Dowager Marchioness of Granville."

Vicky offered a gloved hand and seemed, Fleur thought, subdued. She was definitely watchful.

So this was the young woman who had sent Jane Weller on a mission, then done nothing to stop her from being falsely let go from her place?

But Fleur was too preoccupied to concentrate on the problem at the moment. She seethed. She might be a country bumpkin but she was not an uneducated fool with no knowledge of the polite world and how it worked. Dominic had just made a complete cake of her.

Also, something strange had happened among the group of women with Hattie, and Fleur was certain Dominic knew what that was.

The intrigue unsettled her and she wanted to leave.

One man after another found a reason to bow over her and introduce himself. Women raised eyebrows and tossed their heads if she met their eyes.

"Don't mind about them," Gussy whispered, pulling Fleur into a huddle with Vicky. "I see you feeling badly because of the way they look at you. All of them are so jealous they can't stand it. You are the success of the evening."

"Yes, you are," Vicky said, her voice soft. "I can hardly wait until you come to Grosvenor Square. The gathering will be much bigger than this one and by then I don't think anybody who is anybody will have failed to hear of you. The only question worth considering is what offers will come for your hand and who will be first."

"And richest," Gussy added.

"And the most handsome," Vicky said.

Gussy pouted. "This is my third Season, Fleur, and as yet not a single man has offered for me. I am going to be on the shelf."

"You're so pretty," Fleur said honestly. "And funny and full of life. Men can be dolts but you must be patient. When it's discovered I have no money I doubt I'll get a single offer and I'll be just as glad."

"What?" Gussy and Vicky asked in unison.

Vicky continued, "Of course you wouldn't be glad. Anyway, when a female looks the way you do, she doesn't need money. Did you see the Prince Regent? I almost fainted to be so near him."

Fleur didn't think she should remark on her thoughts about the royal gentleman.

"Where is Lord Nathan?" Vicky asked. "I thought he would be here."

Fleur said, "He is. Gussy already danced with him."

"Why didn't you say so?" Vicky asked her friend.

Gussy flipped her hand. "Because it wasn't important. I'm surprised Olivia isn't here." She stood on her toes to peer about. "I know she was invited and she told me she would come because there's a dashing military officer who has caught her fancy."

"You know she's secretly engaged to him." Vicky looked around the room. "With all the money her family has, she can do better than that."

"Don't talk about secrets." Gussy caught Vicky's arm and stared into her face. "You don't think Olivia's been…"

Vicky shook her head vehemently. "No, I don't. I'm sure Olivia is under the weather. I shall call on her in the morning. That is the officer in question, isn't it?"

"It certainly is." Gussy beckoned to a dark-haired man who looked splendid in his uniform. "Captain," she said. "What have you done with Olivia?"

He appeared uncertain about approaching them.

"Come now," Gussy said. "We are in a group and we are not at all fearsome. Join us."

"Olivia became ill at the last moment," he said and Fleur decided she understood why Olivia, whoever she might be, found him attractive. "I wouldn't have come myself but my aunt expected me."

Gussy slipped a hand around his forearm. "Well, I for one am glad you did come. In the morning I'll go and visit Olivia and take her some of our restorative. I'm sure she'll recover almost at once."

The music struck up again and Gussy raised her eyes to the soldier's. He cleared his throat and glanced around for her chaperon.

Gussy poked Dominic in the ribs and said, "This gentleman would like to speak with you."

The captain, his neck as crimson as his jacket, said, "May I dance with Miss Arbuthnot?"

Dominic said, "Look after her," and followed the couple's progress toward the dance floor.

"Excuse me," Vicky said at once and joined the ladies around Lady Granville.

"And that," Dominic said at Fleur's shoulder, "is why it's so damnably difficult to get Gussy married off. She's aggressive and a tease. She doesn't give a fellow a chance to act on his own instincts."

"You mean she emasculates him?" Fleur said.

Dominic pulled her to face him. "It's just possible that you are too daunting for most men, too."

"Good. I find I don't particularly like most men. In fact I find them foolish and obvious and altogether too overbearing."

"Really?"

"Yes, really. Please may I go home?"

Nathan arrived beside them in time to hear the end of the exchange. "This has been too much excitement for you, Fleur. You're a quiet girl and you need to be treated with care. I shall take her home, Dominic. You can handle Hattie and Gussy, can't you?"

Never had Fleur seen a more demonic expression on a

man's face. With his slitted blue eyes and the upward slash of his brows, Dominic conveyed his deep displeasure with Nathan. In fact he might as well have taken a blade and cut him. The only benefit of the former insult was that it didn't draw blood.

16

At least Hattie had been amused, delighted even, by Fleur's obvious popularity at the Herberts'. And she thought it funny rather than annoying, when Dominic suggested that he and Hattie and Gussy should leave not more than half an hour after Nathan and Fleur set off.

"You take your responsibilities seriously," she told him. "It must be a great trial to be saddled with finding a husband for a girl you couldn't care less about."

At first he feared she might be joking with him, but she appeared quite serious. Good job since the last thing Dominic wanted was for his sister-in-law to guess he split his time between being furious with Fleur Toogood, and so helplessly drawn to her he couldn't think.

He should be honest with himself. She was a tantalizing little piece and she attracted him. And last night she had made him furious with her not very subtle attempt to quiz him as if he were someone she might choose as a husband—if he came up to snuff!

All of that must be put behind him—although he still intended to ask her a few questions of his own.

Once they had delivered Gussy home and he had seen Hattie safely to her suite, Dominic waited in his rooms—and rewarded himself with a stiff brandy—while he gave the household time to settle down. Next on his agenda was a visit to Nathan to see if he was serious about Fleur. If so, they might as well get the thing over with, and no more for Fleur and Nathan's sake than for his own. More for his own, dammit.

I should never have waltzed with her.

That was it, the end. Any hope he'd had of getting through his encounter with Fleur and keeping himself from wanting her to distraction had gone. *Poof,* as she had said. He smiled a little. Natural, unaffected, funny and brave—and not afraid of him! The last item might have to change.

What was he thinking? *Get hold of yourself, man.* Her reaction to Nathan was the one that counted and she had enjoyed herself with him this evening. Dominic had seen that with his own eyes. Nathan would have to sit Fleur's test and pass it. Now that should be the most challenging event of the man's life.

Hattie had reported gossip and trepidation about rumors of abductions. She didn't know who had started the talk but at some point during her visit with the ladies, whispering had begun, and agitation. The ruination of young women by The Silken Cat was to become epidemic, they said.

At his desk, Dominic pushed papers around and thought about The Cat. Puffed-up idiot—giving himself a name supposed to invoke his ability to strike quickly and quietly, and to get away with it.

He could have stolen Chloe away. A film of sweat damped Dominic's skin. The man wasn't an amusement to be taken lightly. No, already he had changed his original pattern and he could change it again. The very dangerous incident with Chloe puzzled him. It seemed like a warning, an unspoken threat that The Cat could get at the women of Heatherly in particular. What other purpose could there have been for luring a small girl away and giving her liquor?

Dominic shoved his chair back from the desk and crossed his arms. This Cat was a menace, and who knew when he might turn from abduction to murder? Chloe might have been the first victim—if she'd drowned in the pond as she might well have.

An effort must also be made to find the boy who had been used to trick Jane Weller. Dominic had a bad, sickening feeling about that lad and his safety. When he got to Nathan, the two of them would decide how to go about searching the area Dominic believed this Silken Cat frequented.

In his shirt and breeches, with Fleur's list in his pocket in case he needed it, he got up and set off for Nathan's peculiar choice of a retreat. High at the very back of the house, where he had a view over the estate in every direction but Regent's Park, Nathan lived in two sparsely furnished rooms once the domain of an Elliot who fancied himself a painter. For most of the day the light in the rooms was unparalleled anywhere else at Heatherly—except for Mama's studio in the Dower House—or so Dominic had been told.

Nathan didn't paint.

Nathan did like privacy.

Moonlight squeezed beneath the door of the bedchamber. Dominic tapped lightly.

Nathan slept like a dead man.

"Wake up," Dominic said, walking in and approaching the bed. "We need to have a serious discussion. On two topics."

The moon silvered the bed—the smooth bed where no telltale bump gave away the whereabouts of Nathan Elliot.

Dominic frowned and strode to throw open the door to the adjoining sitting room. Darkness greeted him.

He went in slowly, casting about for where his brother might be...probably with Bertie Crewe-Burns in some hell-hole frequented by the lost.

Dominic lit a candle and looked around the room. Then he repeated the process in the bedroom. And he checked the dressing room. Nathan hadn't been in the suite recently. The fires were out—Nathan preferred to light his own. Surely he would have returned here after dropping Fleur off and before going out for the night.

"Confound it!" Why had he been so slow to consider the unthinkable—considering that very little was unthinkable with his brother? He slammed from Nathan's rooms and broke into a run. Soon enough he realized he'd wake servants if he wasn't careful so he moved as fast and quietly as he could all the way to the front of the house and down to the second floor.

"I'll kill you for this, Nathan," he muttered to himself. "No, not that, but you'll walk down that aisle so fast you'll rue the thrill of what you've done tonight."

Absolutely quietly he approached Fleur's room. He had disapproved of her being all but alone in this wing during the night but hadn't had the courage to raise the issue too many times for fear someone might question his motives. Damn it to hell, he should have insisted she be given a suite with maid's quarters attached—and a maid in them.

Beneath Fleur's door, not moonlight, but the wavering glow of candlelight shone.

Cozy, he thought. He detested what he must do but had no choice. Nathan and the girl must be caught in a compromising situation. And if Nathan had any idea of shirking his responsibilities, the threat of bringing their parent into the fray would put a stop to that. Dominic shook his fists in the air. At the very least he would beat his brother to a pulp.

He paused, struggling with his feelings. To embarrass Fleur, who was the wronged innocent in this, seemed too much to bear, but there was no choice if Nathan's hand was to be forced. The marriage must take place at once—just in case the scapegrace had managed to... Dominic closed his eyes. He hated this. And it didn't help that he was certain Fleur had judged him a potential candidate to spend the rest of her life with. By now she would have decided he'd seen through her trick and she might well think his intrusion was motivated by his desire to finish any designs she had on him.

Poor Fleur, it had been a very little deceit and without malice.

He turned the door handle, pushed, and said, "Nathan," just loud enough to be heard inside the room.

The door was locked. Of course it was. Dominic put his mouth to the narrow crack between the door and the jamb. "Open up at once or the whole house will start hearing this fuss and come running."

The key rattled and fell to the floor inside. Immediately he heard it picked up and after some fumbling it turned in the lock and the door opened. Before Dominic stood Fleur, still wearing her gold evening dress and with her red hair threaded through with pearls on black velvet ribbon, just as it had been at the Herberts'.

By all that was good, he might be in time to make sure she enjoyed every scrap of the respect and anticipation she deserved from her clodpole of a husband-to-be.

"Where is he?" he asked her, kindly enough. It wasn't her fault if she'd fallen prey to a born hunter.

Fleur backed away. "Who?" she asked in a small voice. "Is someone coming after me? He hasn't arrived, thank goodness."

Dominic hoped his brother would appreciate a faithful wife for the treasure she was. "Nathan—stop hiding behind this poor girl's skirts and show yourself." He closed the door quietly behind him. "Come on out."

"Dominic," Fleur said, "Lord Nathan isn't here. What could make you think he would be?"

"I know my brother, that's what, and—"

"He couldn't even stay at Heatherly because a man was waiting for him and as soon as I was inside, Lord Nathan left again."

Dominic let his head fall back. His ridiculous behavior all but overshadowed the relief he felt. "I have to be sure of these things," he told her in a voice he hoped would stop her from pursuing the topic. "You don't happen to know who this man was—the one waiting for him?"

"Not exactly. He wasn't at the Herberts', or I don't think so. Lord Nathan called him Bertie."

Dominic marched over and flopped into one of Fleur's blue chairs. "Do you mind?" he asked belatedly.

"No." But she didn't look pleased.

"I might have known there was some devious reason Nathan was in such a hurry to leave the Herberts'."

Fleur gave a wry smile. "You mean it wasn't because he knew I wished to come home and he wanted the opportunity to be with me? I'm wounded."

Dash it all, Dominic thought, watching her carefully. She had a sarcastic tongue and she truly didn't seem to give a damn about Nathan's motives where she was concerned.

A bowl of flowers—past their prime—stood on the table beside the chair. A card rested between the blooms and he read his brother's handwriting with ease. He couldn't tell when the token had been given, apart from the flowers being two or three days old, but he took some heart in knowing that Nathan had taken the trouble to send them. Surely that meant there was some interest there.

"Why would Nathan be here with me so long after he brought me home?" Fleur asked.

He deserved this, Dominic thought. If the truth be known, even though he wasn't willing to deal with the responsibility of a wife and family, if he were, Fleur might be a candidate. And that was why, although he'd decided Nathan's attachment to her would save a lot of time, the idea of Fleur with his brother drove Dominic wild. The idea of Fleur with any man destroyed his peace.

Fleur crossed the carpet and stood beside him, looking down into his face. She patted his shoulder awkwardly. "You never wanted any part of dealing with me, but because you are honorable, when you told your mother you would help, that meant you must do a good job. I regret that you felt I intruded on you by sharing my list with you."

She had left her hand on his shoulder and Dominic took her fingers in his.

"Don't worry about Nathan. I am not at all his type, although I do think he might enjoy a…a dalliance." Her lowered lashes cast shadows on her cheeks and Dominic could tell how difficult she found the conversation. "But he wouldn't pursue such a thing because the Dowager would be so angry with him."

Dominic's heart lightened and he wasn't sure why. "You amaze me," he told her. "I came here in a turmoil with a headache and fury pounding in my veins. But you are so reasonable—if you choose to be—that all that anger just goes—"

"Poof!" she said and smiled so charmingly he couldn't look away from her mouth.

"Come here and talk to me," he said and an artful tug landed her on his lap where he knew she shouldn't be and where he liked the feel of her far too much.

She put her hands down to push herself to her feet, made firm contact with a part of him that shocked her, and crossed her arms quickly. "It isn't seemly for me to sit here," she said.

"No, it isn't. But does it feel so unpleasant, Fleur?"

She wouldn't look at him but she said, "No."

"Then can it be bad for two people to find comfort in one another?"

"You know perfectly well I am not a child and that you are taking advantage of the situation." She poked his chest with a hard forefinger. "And you, you hypocrite, came roaring in here ready to accuse your brother of compromising me."

"Am I compromising you?"

She raised her eyes to his while she thought about the question. "Oh, I should definitely think so. And we know it isn't for the first time. If we were discovered, my reputation would be ruined—which would also be absolutely unfair since yours should also be ruined. The inequity of it all infuriates me."

"Ah, yes." He sighed. "Such inequity. Tell me, you and Nathan do get along well, don't you?"

"Oh, yes. He has been kind to me and made me see situations more sensibly on a number of occasions. And he's funny. I think it's past time for him to be married. He will be a good husband once he falls in love and I know his children will adore him."

Such an endorsement. Lucky Nathan. But hardly the words of a woman in love.

"I did wonder about Vicky Crewe-Burns," Fleur said. "She asked if he was at the Herberts' and looked all around for him. Perhaps there is an interest there."

As naturally as if he held her on his knees frequently, Dominic put an arm around her shoulders and eased her against him. Her body didn't relax. "You are in the mood to marry off the Elliot men tonight," he said.

She raised her shoulders and even with the highest of intentions, Dominic couldn't avoid a glance at her breasts. Somehow he must train himself to look no lower than her chin.

She had beautiful breasts, round, pressed together by the bodice, and with the slightest hint of pale-pink nipples visible. He considered her deep cleavage and decided a single large diamond there, teasing the eye, would be far more the thing than his mother's diamond-and-sapphire collar.

Yes, a single diamond so white it caught every light in a room to itself, and the red dress he believed Mrs. Neville had finally been persuaded by Hattie to make. Fleur would look even more perfect and he enjoyed anticipating the shaking heads of jealous, disapproving females at the sight of her. A redhead wearing red, and so young a redhead, and unmarried, and look at the size of that diamond, and, and, and… What a satisfying thought.

"Tomorrow evening there are three routs," he said. "Am I correct?"

"There are three things. Yes, routs. Snowdrop described them to me and they sound horrid."

"They are horrid, but we will make the best of them. The trick is to stick together——that's even more important at the moment."

She looked at his face directly and he realized how close it was, how easy it would be to kiss her. But he had already taken that liberty and now he must correct his evil ways. Hah, he sat with her in his lap, her bottom drawing his manhood to straining attention, and warned himself against evil ways. As she said, he was a hypocrite. But he wasn't about to release her until he had to.

"I've been concerned about the boy who waited at the edge of Hyde Park and guided Jane to that man," she said. "She told Brother Juste he seemed a poor thing. He could be in danger as we speak."

"Yes, he could. And I wish there was a way to pluck him out of the thousands of street children who make their way alone in London. That whole situation must change. I intend—" He stopped himself. There was nothing Fleur could do to help him with the campaign he intended to wage against the exploitation of children.

"You intend to help the children, don't you? I should like to be useful, too." She turned in his arm and leaned on his chest. Oh, cruel, oh, wonderful fate.

"Not yet," he said. "But I will let you know if you can do something to help." Would he? That would depend on how all this turned out.

"Do you know a young woman called Olivia?" she asked him.

He blinked at the sudden change of subject. "I know more than one."

"This one should have been at the Herberts' this evening— or last evening now—but she wasn't. Her beau came late, a military gentleman and very dashing."

Dominic said, "Ah. That would be the one Gussy thrust herself— Gussy danced with him. And you're talking about Olivia Prentergast. A nice young woman. What of her?"

"I was with two ladies who appeared surprised by her absence. They thought she might be ill and spoke of visiting her in the morning. But then they became quiet and looked at one another strangely. I thought they were about to say she wasn't sick at all and to suggest where she might actually be."

"Are we talking about Vicky Crewe-Burns and Gussy?"

"Yes. I'm sure it all meant nothing, but there was a look that passed between them and, thanks to my snooping, I know Miss Crewe-Burns has had an unpleasant experience."

Dominic flexed muscles in his jaw. He set Fleur on her feet and stood himself. Desire could so easily turn to lust, and it already had. Not a suitable situation. "First thing in the morning I will find an excuse to go to the Prentergasts. I won't have to see Olivia to know if something is awry. I should leave you now." He didn't want to, but he had a reason to go to a certain part of London at this time of night.

"Do you think Gussy likes Lord Nathan a lot?" Fleur asked. "I think she does."

Enough. How surprised Fleur would be if he told her she was the only woman who interested him, in any manner at the moment, and he didn't care about any other woman's matters of the heart.

"She pretends she doesn't really give a fig about him but that is an obvious fib, don't you think? She's only saying it because she thinks it throws people of the track."

"It could be," he agreed. Mother had always spoken of having certain hopes for Dominic's future and his marriage, but she had never elaborated. She liked Fleur… But her plans for him would not include marriage to a parson's daughter and neither should his—if he ever had any. However, his dear conventional mother—conventional when it came to her sons—considered Nathan in need of a steadying influence when he married and Fleur could be perfect for him. These were early days. There was time for Nathan and Fleur to fall in love.

Dominic's gut clenched. He didn't judge people on their station—never had.

"Dominic," Fleur said quietly. "It would be easy to avoid this topic when you already appear to have forgotten it, but I would be a coward if I didn't ask—"

"If I've given more thought to the list you gave me last night? Yes, I have." It would be best to give her a blunt response. Then she would understand where she stood with him. "I believe you made an extra copy of your list and left it with me because you are considering whether or not I would make the kind of husband you demand."

Fleur stepped backward and her hand went to her throat.

"Your idea of letting a man know what you want of him might be a good idea. Who am I to judge? But I cannot become your husband."

"I didn't suggest I wanted you to think about marrying me," she told him in a tiny voice. "How could you embarrass me so?"

"You didn't mind embarrassing me by handing me your demands. Many of them completely unreasonable, by the way. Can you honestly say you didn't do that because you had decided to set your cap for me?"

She exclaimed and turned from him. "Yes, I can honestly say that. Of all the arrogant, inconsiderate men on earth, none can be more so than you. Oh, I am destroyed. Please go. Now. I will pack up and go home tomorrow."

"No, you won't," he said, well aware of how harsh he sounded, and how confused he felt. "You have made a promise to your family and to mine. Hattie traveled all the way from Bath to help you. I have agreed to squire you around and make sure you find a suitable partner in life, and *you* will stop interfering and do as you're told."

"My only mistake was to start considering you as a man of experience who could be of some help to me in a situation which is new to me," she said. "But I understand my position. Very well, I'll stick it out and if something wonderful happens, I will be grateful. If I go home as unattached as I arrived, I will also be grateful and then I will be as much help to my family as a spinster can be."

"You will not go home unattached. That I promise you."

"Don't concern yourself with me, please. Now I need time alone to compose myself. I must show nothing but gratitude to those who have been so kind to me."

"You haven't entertained any thoughts of becoming my wife?"

"No-o." Her shoulders shook. "I know my place."

Drat, but he believed her—and felt like a worm. "Then I apologize. I only thought... I made an assumption. I'll continue to do my best for you."

She remained with her back to him.

"I know you haven't had much chance, but has anyone at all taken your fancy while you've been with me—us?" He managed to make it sound as if she might be looking for a pet dog. "At the Herberts', perhaps. Young Franklin is a good fellow. And I dare say Noel DeBeaufort has his good points but I do think he's seen too much of the world."

"Franklin Best is a good man. I felt that. But don't concern yourself further." Her voice shook. "If I am meant to meet someone appropriate, then I shall."

"You mean someone who fits all the items on the list."

Fleur swung to face him. "Showing you the list was a mistake. I only thought you might be able to give me some advice. I was wrong."

Dominic pulled her damnable list from a trouser pocket

and shook it out. He sensed she judged him poorly and his temper flared again. "Gladly, I'll gladly offer my advice on all this. Let's pretend I am just any man, a man you've decided might be worthy of you."

"Please, no."

"Come, come, you have more courage than that. Let me see. *Does he accept and love my family?* That's a good question from a faithful daughter and I'm sure I should love your family—I would certainly respect them. Then we have, *Does his family respect mine and accept me?* Another man just might answer differently, although I doubt it. Where I'm concerned the answer is obviously, yes, and I like cats and dogs and I've never been accused of being a prig, although I try to be an honest man and I'm sure I've had my moments."

Fleur wouldn't look at him but she smiled a little and said, "I think we can all be a bit priggish sometimes. You don't have to go on. I can see how silly I was to write all those things down."

"You are only silly if you don't stand by decisions you considered as carefully as you did these. There are ways in which I think men are superior to women and there are matters no man should attempt because they can only be dealt with by a woman."

She raised her face. "What kinds of things? Looking after babies and taking jam to sick people?"

"Among a great many more, yes," he told her. *She didn't give up.*

"I am good with numbers," she said. "I kept my father's books for him and made sure what we had was enough…."

"You don't surprise me," he said, studying the questions again. "*Does he love and like me more than anyone else?* Whoever he is, he had better because that's what you deserve.

And your opinions, hmm, I do believe I could give them a great deal of weight."

She hid her hands in the folds of her skirts. When she looked at him, just as quickly, she looked away and pain shone in her eyes.

"As for walking in the rain with you, I believe I should like that." He would. He visualized her skirts trailing through wet grass and her damp face turned up to his, laughing and chattering. He doubted he'd find many words to say himself. "And lying on the grass to feel the rain on our skin? You'll just have to invite me one day, then we'll both find out.

"I think children are the greatest gift that comes to a marriage. Children are an extension of their parents' love for one another and they are the continuation of hope."

"Please," she said, holding up her hands. "You have shown me how a man should be able to answer—thoughtfully and as honestly as he can. Forgive me for my forwardness."

"There's nothing to forgive. I would be very gentle if I taught you to love and I should most certainly insist upon sharing your bed. When I drink, it isn't usually to excess and I'm not fond of raucous company, although I won't lie and say I've never indulged in wild times."

Fleur inclined her head. "You will be quite the catch for a lucky lady, Dominic. And I hope she does ask some of my questions just so she can have the pleasure of hearing you answer them."

His heart contracted. "I could convince you I don't have a mistress," he said offering his hands and enfolding hers when she reached for him. He drew her nearer. "I'd be a liar if I said there haven't been women in my life, or that I haven't lived fully in every way."

Perhaps she was a priest in disguise. Just being with her gave him an urge to confess.

"A man in love couldn't ask for more in a wife than her love of him in return," he said, consulting the list again. "And I do believe he would count his blessings daily and nightly if this woman was also deeply sexual."

She tried to retreat but he wouldn't let her.

"Will he join me in learning exotic ways of lovemaking?"

"It sounds so silly," she murmured.

"It sounds wonderful," Dominic told her. "I am a confused man, Fleur. I never expected a woman like you to simply appear, now, when such a thing has been the last thing on my mind." Listen to his drivel! He had all but told her he wanted her.

"I am a burden." She raised his hands and ran her thumbs over the smooth tracing of dark hair on the back of each one. "You knew I would be but you were too kind to refuse your help."

Dominic turned her hands and bent over them. With great care, but knowing he trod on the most dangerous ground of all, he settled his lips on the knuckles of her right hand. Her other hand he took to his heart and held it there.

The sudden pressure of her cheek on his hair destroyed him. What did he have to offer her but money? She needed so much more. She needed everything, and he was a man with distractions he couldn't promise would allow him time to be a good husband to her.

With a mad rush of heat through his veins, he looked up and took her by the shoulders. "To be the one to teach you everything you want to learn about being a passionate woman with a passionate man would be a dream. I will see to it that the man who marries you is up to the task."

Her smile gentled the tension in the room. "Thank you," she said.

"And now I must go." He took his watch from his waistcoat pocket and realized he should not have stayed so long.

The door flew open and banged against the wall.

There stood Nathan, his eyes aflame, his neckcloth askew, his hair wild.

Fortunately, although he still faced her, Dominic had dropped his hands from Fleur's shoulders.

"You *bounder*," Nathan said through his teeth. "You despoiler of innocents. I should have known better than leave this house when I knew you would return and could well decide to come to this girl."

Fleur giggled.

"What have you done to her?" Nathan demanded. "Speak up. She's hysterical."

Fleur laughed louder and the corners of Dominic's mouth twitched.

"I'm going to thrash you," Nathan said, advancing. "We'll see how funny you find that you little snot—"

"Nose," Dominic finished for him

Her silk gown rustling, Fleur hurried to stand before Nathan, held his arm and struggled for breath. "You see," she managed at last. "Dominic came marching in here just as you did. And he was looking for you because he thought you had taken advantage of me."

"Me?" Nathan said, scowling.

"You weren't in your rooms," Dominic said, feeling ridiculous.

"And when I came back, you weren't in yours," Nathan said.

Fleur stood between them and said, "And if a man isn't in his rooms it always means he's ravishing a lady?"

17

Fleur continued to chuckle. The look on Lord Nathan's face had been priceless when he was told that Dominic had come to her room because he thought Lord Nathan might have gone there for nefarious reasons.

They really were fascinating men—honest, too, and willing to laugh at themselves. They'd laughed a good deal before they left.

Then Dominic said, *"Lock the door after us, Don't open it for anyone but a member of the family or a servant if you recognize the voice."*

That one was also overbearing.

Fleur frowned and pulled her eyebrows closer and closer together. She had become really good at scowling…when she remembered. "Ouch!" A hairpin had come loose and pricked her nose when it fell.

She was accustomed to dealing with her own toilette, but at home that didn't mean unwinding her hair from what felt like a porcupine 'do or struggling out of impossibly restrictive clothing. Snowdrop would happily have stayed to help her get ready for bed but Fleur didn't want to keep her up late and away from her husband.

"Fuss, fuss. Hover, hover. What is the matter with me?"

She gave the same squeak she'd given since childhood when indecision frustrated her.

Dominic, he was her trouble—all of it. He could be infuriating. He said things guaranteed to belittle her. He let her know she would never be someone he'd consider as a wife—even though she had never suggested she wanted him.

"I do want you. You've made me want you." Control, she must control herself. If Rosemary and Letitia could hear her talking to herself, they'd know just how agitated she was.

Wonderful, she was in love with a man she couldn't have, and he might even be perfect for her. When he'd gone through The List, some of his answers brought tears to her eyes. Her eyes were filled with tears now. And he thought any potential suitor she might have should make his own list, did he? How enlightening it would be to know what questions Dominic might ask of a woman he hoped to marry.

Fleur took measured steps around the room, nodding her head slowly as she went. "And you said you would be very gentle if you taught me to love." She clenched her hands together over her stomach. He had sounded almost as if he wished he could be that man. What a confusion.

Dominic had been torn while he was with her. He had wanted to stay, she'd felt that, but he had pressing business elsewhere. She stood still and thought about what he'd said and the way he'd looked at his watch, and how she'd mentioned Olivia Prentergast and Dominic had said he would find out if there was a problem there other than illness. What if he'd decided to go after the answers now rather than wait for the morning?

She chewed a fingernail and a whole strip peeled off. Oh, dear, now it would look terrible and she'd been doing well overcoming her old habit.

The thought of Dominic going out to search in the dead of night, alone, frightened Fleur. She wished she could see him, see that he was safe, touch him and feel his solid, warm body.

He was special to her and she doubted she could change her feelings even if she wanted to.

Chloe's experience had angered and unnerved him—as it had Fleur. There had been a mention of Vauxhall Gardens. She knew where they were because Hattie had asked Albert to drive them past. In the daytime little seemed unusual but, according to Hattie, at night the gardens were wild and could be very dangerous. Dominic could plan to go there.

She had to find out if he'd left the house. It wouldn't change a thing but at least she'd know if she had to stay up and find a place to watch for his return.

Fleur unlocked her door and closed it quietly behind her. She dared not take a candle and had to find her way with no more help than the puny candle sconces spaced widely on the walls—except for places where there weren't even those.

She made rapid progress to the center of the house and the staircase leading to the third floor. Only when she reached the top and slid into the circular corridor did she stop to wonder what on earth she'd say if she encountered Dominic face-to-face. *I'm looking for a handkerchief I think I dropped up here.* Oh, just thinking of the way he'd look at her then made her skin crawl. *I thought I'd check the water in the bowl of greenery in that chest.* Mortifying.

The chest. If she could make it that far she would hide inside the double doors. She already knew there was nothing inside because she'd peeked—wicked, curious girl that she was.

If she was meant to be caught, she would be and she would tell him exactly why she'd come. Tripping along rapidly, holding up the front of her skirts and wishing they didn't swish so, she passed Dominic's suite and raced on to the cupboard. At once she opened both doors and climbed inside, with some difficulty since the space was quite small.

Once she had the cabinet closed again, she rested on her side with her knees clamped to her chest. She prayed the heavy odor of camphor would not make her sneeze.

Silence closed in around her. Other than an occasional creak or crack, or the rattle of a window, nothing suggested there could be another human anywhere nearby.

Her shoulder ached and she pushed it forward so she lay more on her back but with her legs in the same position as before.

She recalled how frightened she'd been when Dominic pulled her from behind the draperies over that window seat. Her heart had stopped, she was sure of it.

What made her so certain he had not left directly from her room? He would have needed a cloak and for that he would have returned to his rooms.

But he could have managed such a small task very quickly.

He'd gone to meet a lady. Of course he had. "Widgeon," she whispered and immediately pressed her lips together. A man like Dominic undoubtedly had a beautiful female he kept somewhere to fulfil his needs. Fleur felt hot all over. It was her own fault because if she hadn't spent so much time delving into matters she had no business knowing about, she wouldn't think of such things as Dominic's dalliances.

He had said he could convince her he didn't have a mistress.

Good heavens, he might well be in love.

Perhaps some terrible impediment stood between him and marriage to the lady. Tears prickled at her eyes. How sad if that were true. On the other hand, it could be that eventually they would give up trying to be together and look elsewhere for affection. They could both end up completely happy, more happy than they would have been together.

Oh, her hip felt as if it rested on a pointed rock. Fleur wriggled.

"Will you please hurry yourself?" *Lord Nathan.* She would know his voice anywhere. He and Dominic were together and she felt weak with relief.

Dominic didn't answer Lord Nathan but she heard them walking, walking toward her cupboard rather than the stairs. She held absolutely still and, when she sensed they were immediately beside her, stopped breathing.

The footsteps passed on and she dared to open one of the cupboard doors a fraction.

Fleur almost exclaimed.

Not more than a few yards from her, at another window seat, Lord Nathan waited with a candle in one hand. In front of him, Brother Juste had already lifted the seat and leaned it against the window. Lord Nathan held his candle higher to better light a space beneath the lid and the monk put first one, then the other foot inside. "Make sure you're right behind me," he said, sinking lower, walking down steps. "Close the lid as quickly as you can."

"You can be damnably irritating," Lord Nathan said, shocking Fleur since she wouldn't have expected him to speak to a monk in such a way. "Do you think I'm less concerned about Olivia than you are?"

Brother Juste paused. His shoulders were level with the opening into the seat. "I think you still care for her in your own way. She would take you back in an instant."

Lord Nathan shook his head. He stared straight ahead at

the darkness outside. "It would not have been a happy match. My fault, not hers. I wasn't ready. Anyway, now she has her officer."

"When she forgets herself, she still looks at you with warmth." Brother Juste raised his head to look at Lord Nathan. "Enough of this. We haven't time to bicker. I must get to the Prentergasts'. And remember our understanding. As far as our routine is concerned, this is no different than any other part of the investigation. You wait with the carriage and keep out of sight. Don't come near the house."

Fleur held a hand tightly over her mouth. That was Dominic. There was no Brother Juste, only Dominic wearing a monk's habit and calling himself Brother Juste. And he had involved himself deeply in The Silken Cat intrigue. Lord Nathan went with him but only to provide transportation. If Dominic continued his reckless behavior, he could face terrible danger. He already did. She must find a way to help him.

18

"Aren't you going to ask where I got this rattletrap?" Nathan said.

"Since you're going to tell me anyway, I might as well. Where did you get the thing?"

Nathan pulled the collar of his greatcoat high around his neck and sunk his chin into it. Then he gave his hat a firm tug on either side and all but rammed it over his ears. "I saw it in a farmer's field, all rusted and with a wheel missing. Bought it from him. He threw in a wheel—"

"A different size wheel." Dominic interrupted.

"He threw in a wheel—which I put on myself—and he was still chuckling about cabbage-brains when I put my horse between the shafts and drove away."

Each time they hit a rut the cart tipped from three big wheels to Nathan's bargain smaller one. Dominic planted his hands on the rotted plank seat and used his locked arms in an attempt to save his bruised derriere from further collisions. "Well, we're anonymous, all right." He grunted. "Which is a good thing. But you might have said you got an old vegetable cart that stinks of manure rather than the carriage you led me to expect."

"Didn't," Nathan said, apparently content to bump up and

down throughout the not inconsiderable trek to Mayfair. "You assumed and I couldn't bring myself to disappoint you."

"Olivia Prentergast may not know it, but she's lucky that thing you once had for her fizzled." The last thwack on the seat all but stole Dominic's breath. "You aren't normal. You're never happier than when you're making someone else suffer."

"Look, if you don't like what I manage to scrounge up, you take over the job of making sure our modes of transportation change constantly. We agreed that in case someone catches sight of us coming or going, it's important to have nondescript vehicles."

"Ouch! You've outdone yourself this time. Look, when we get to Grosvenor Street, don't actually turn in. Wait on Charles Street and I'll go the rest of the way on foot—if I can still walk."

"Thank you for telling me what I intended to do anyway," Nathan said. He looked over his shoulder. "It's quiet tonight. There are usually parties going late but things look buttoned up."

"Maybe gossip about our Silken Cat has gone farther, faster than we expected. It's bound to create a certain panic." Lights showed in the windows of some great houses but no revelers paraded past on the inside of those windows or swarmed at the front doors. And there was no coach activity.

"The fires are all stoked, though," Nathan remarked, angling his head toward spirals of inky smoke snaking out of chimneys into the purple night sky. "Dominic, five minutes and we're there. I know that house well. I'd feel better if I was closer to you than Charles Street—"

"No. It wouldn't be safe."

"It's not safe for you, dammit! I'll be a shadow you don't even see but at least I'll be close enough if something goes wrong."

Dominic put a hand on his brother's arm. "Thank you," he said. "I think a great deal of you, but you already know that. If I thought it wise I'd accept your offer, but I don't. We'll stay bound to what we decided when you first asked to join me—at least for now."

"Whoa." Nathan pulled up the horse. "I accept what you say but this worries me. Attempting to gain entrance to a private house at this time of night? You could be shot as an intruder."

Dominic jumped gracefully from the cart and went rapidly to Nathan's side. "Since I can't go to the front door and gain entrance as myself, I don't have a choice. It would be wrong to know as much as I do—inadequate though it is—yet do nothing to help Olivia. Wish me well."

He hurried away, around the corner from Charles Street to Grosvenor Street, staying close to walls and railings in front of the handsome houses there. He already knew how he would investigate the Prentergast establishment.

The house rose four stories from the street and a gate in shiny black railings opened onto stairs that led down to the entryway outside the kitchens.

At the gate he pulled farther into the shadows and studied the whole house. There had been no party here tonight yet light blazed at most windows. He saw Sir Malcolm Prentergast at one window with his hands behind his back, staring out but repeatedly turning back to talk to someone.

His instincts had been right, Dominic thought. There was trouble here.

The gate opened smoothly. Not people to scrimp on oil for hinges, the Prentergasts. He descended to the flagstones quickly and stood with his back to the building. A sideways look into the below stairs showed utter confusion. Servants ran in to stand by a handsomely appointed home steward who pored over a diagram spread on a big table. The steward issued orders and servants, mostly flunkies in green livery, left to be replaced by others. The cook and her minions scurried and paced, their faces drawn.

The front door opened and Dominic bent low into a black corner. At the same time carriages arrived, three of them, one after the other. Human shapes slipped silently down to the flagway and left in those coaches.

Dominic gave a single tap on the tradesmen's door and a man opened it, a flustered underbutler by the look of him. "What is it?" he said, ready to slam the door.

"Have you some scraps for the Brown Monastery?" he said, keeping his voice soft. "The brothers are having a difficult time of it and my Abbot suggested the people at this house might help."

"Oh, what is it?" The woman he'd decided was the cook pushed the man aside and said, "What d'you want, then?" to Dominic.

"I'm sorry to have intruded," he said, "but the brothers are desperate for food, and—"

She looked at him more closely and said, "Come in right now, Brother, and sit yourself down." She closed the door behind him. "Just here out of the way. I'll get you some things. And while you wait would you please pray for the safe return of our Miss Olivia what's been stolen away by some ruffian."

"Oh, my dear lady. Of course I will."

He bowed his head and put his hands together in his lap.

"She'll not have expected to get caught sneaking off like that," one maid said to another.

"Caught?"

"Don't be daft. She's sneaked off with that handsome officer of hers. Spending the night together, they are. I'd bet my life on it. I don't know what all this talk about kidnapping is but I don't believe a word of it."

The other girl spoke up. "We've been told not to say a word about any of it outside this house. We'd best be careful or we'll lose our places."

The question was, Dominic thought, had Sir Malcolm taken the probable ransom demand seriously? The man was known to be hardheaded and a fighter.

Dominic considered leaving the kitchens, shedding the habit and entering by the front door after all. He could rush in and say he'd heard a rumor Olivia was missing, then say how dangerous it would be to withhold a ransom.

And run the risk of being identified all over London as someone who knew more about The Silken Cat's antics than he should.

He saw the cook approaching, her arms filled with food. A kind soul. He knew exactly where it would be most appreciated.

"She's here! She's back!" A footboy tumbled from upstairs with a big grin on his ruddy face. "Just. She's coming up the front steps. She just—"

Dominic didn't wait. He accepted the food from the cook then slid out of the house and up the entryway steps. A lone figure separated from deep shadows across the way and dashed toward the only vehicle Dominic saw on Grosvenor Street. This carriage stood near a row of trees at the side of the road a good distance from the Prentergast home. Catching up the skirts of the habit, he regretfully dropped the food and ran, too. If he was heard, so be it. This could be their quarry.

The figure jumped onto the box beside the coachman. The small carriage immediately sped away and turned left on Charles Street just before Dominic arrived at the corner. Yelling at Nathan and gesturing, he urged him to get the horse moving then jumped up beside his brother when he drew level.

"You'll kill yourself, blast you," Nathan shouted.

"Never mind that. Follow the carriage ahead. I don't see how they'll fail to see us but we've got to try to find out where they're going. Olivia's all right but I think The Cat had her. And I think he just watched her go into the house. He's the one who ran to that carriage."

Nathan let out an oath and urged the horse on, keeping the cart close to the curb. "We could be on his blind side here," he said.

"If we can't find this fancy house of his, we'll never stop him," Dominic said. "That's where we have to trap him." Minutes passed before he said, "I'm damned, I guessed right. Or I think I did. Remember I told you about the smell of chocolate? Well, he's heading for St. James and if St. James Street is his destination we know what to expect there."

Nathan nodded. "We should," he said. "White's, Lock's the hatters, J. Lobb the bootmakers and Wirgman's the goldsmiths." He leaned far forward on the seat, intent on encouraging the horse to greater effort. "Any others?"

"*Chocolate houses,* you looby. And chocolate shops. And the *smell* of chocolate everywhere."

"That, too," Nathan said. "I think they're heading for St. James Street."

A blast of hope exhilarated Dominic. "Please don't let us lose him now."

"You can't confront the fellow, y'know."

Dominic thought about that. "You're right. But I can come back and surprise him soon enough. For… Look, Nathan, someone fell off the box."

"Or was thrown off. If we stop, we'll lose the carriage."

"We have to stop. He's not moving. And now the carriage is turning onto St. James Street. At least our search is narrowed. Stop."

The cart still moved when Dominic leaped to the street and ran to fall on his knees by a sniffling, groaning creature inside a bundle of rags. "It's all right," Dominic said, not at all sure anything was all right. "We'll help you."

"Get away!" A thin lad materialized with bony fists swinging. "Don't yer touch me or I'll beat yer t'death. On yer way."

Dominic grasped the boy's shoulders firmly and waited until he stopped for breath. "We saw you fall off the coach," he said. "Where do you hurt?"

"Lemme go. You'll be gettin' me into trouble, you will."

"You have nothing to fear. I shall not tell anyone we met."

Nathan arrived and stood over them. "How badly is he hurt?"

"I don't know about his body, but his mouth is in perfect condition. Can you stand, Harry?"

"I expect so." With Dominic's help he scrambled to his feet. Taller than expected, and perhaps thirteen or so, he saw Dominic's habit and said, "A bloomin' monk. Thank yer for yer trouble. I'm all right now."

Dominic looked at Nathan and raised his eyebrows. So this was the lad Jane Weller had spoken of. "We'll walk with you till you get home, just to be sure you haven't injured yourself badly."

The boy shrugged free and limped away without a word. Dominic and Nathan caught up and walked one on either side of him.

Harry led them past high class shops frequented by the distinguished, coffee shops and those chocolate shops with their sweet aroma, and the occasional alley beside a great house.

"Hey," he said suddenly, turning to Dominic. "Why did yer call me 'arry?"

Dominic had known doing so was risky. "Because I thought I heard someone in the carriage call your name."

The boy narrowed his eyes. Bruises marred his face and old blood crusted one nostril. "Well, yer wrong. And I'm not tellin' yer me name because it's none of yer business. Get off, both of yer." He speeded up, shuffling as fast as he could with a limp. When he looked back, Dominic saw awful fright on the boy's face.

"Let him think he's lost us," Dominic said, falling back. When they could, he and Nathan pulled into a shop entrance where they could still watch Harry through a window, at least for a little while.

"His name is Harry," Nathan said. "Poor little ruffian's terrified."

"He is, but he'll lead us where we need to go. Come on or we'll lose him."

They slipped onto the flagway again, just in time to see Harry duck into an alley. By the time Dominic skidded to a halt and peered down the narrow gap between two buildings, there was nobody to be seen. He signaled for Nathan to stay back and ran, crouched over, the length of the buildings.

Something creaked open. A mews ran parallel behind the buildings and Dominic turned in the direction of the sound he'd heard—just in time to see a gate slam shut in a wooden fence.

A tap on his shoulder all but stopped his heart. He swung around with his fists raised—and Nathan took several steps backward. "It's just me," he said and pointed to the gate. "He went in there."

Dominic didn't trust himself to say anything so he peered through the fence slats. There was nothing to see except the back of some sort of warehouse.

"Do you want to follow him in?" Nathan asked, without enthusiasm. "He's obviously leading us on a merry chase but if we catch him we can try to get his trust so he'll talk to us. He's frightened. Why wouldn't he want some protection?"

"There's no point in following him. He'll cut back and forth until he reaches the creature's house. He's well away by now and he knows every inch of this place. We don't."

"So we give up?"

"We never give up," Dominic said. "We need clues and the only ones who may have them are the women who don't want to be identified. Jane may have more to say, something she's forgotten. And perhaps Gussy. But we need the others and we don't even know who some of them are, or how many of them there are." He pushed back his hood. "Hell, there may not be anyone else for all we know."

They walked back to the cart and Dominic half expected to find that the horse had been stolen.

"Someone's made off with our cart," Nathan said. "The bounder. I hope all the wheels fall off for him."

"Bless him, is all I can say," Dominic said. "Although taking that rusted trap must mean the fellow should be in an asylum."

The horse, his bare back gleaming, stood by a hedge chomping his way through the privet. Dominic walked directly to him, caught the trailing reins and with his habit pulled up around his waist leaped astride the animal. Nathan followed suit and they began the long ride to Heatherly.

"All we have to do is be persistent," Nathan said. He held on to Dominic.

"Exactly. Persistence in all things, say I. Now, since this is a journey that has to be taken slowly, we might as well pass the time dealing with a pressing issue."

"I thought we were."

"Another issue. I saw your outrage when you thought I had forced myself on Fleur."

Nathan took his time before saying, "I may not be the one Mother asked to help launch the girl, but I feel some responsibility for her."

"You like her?"

"Very much," Nathan said. "Don't you?"

"She's passable."

Nathan chuckled. "I suppose it's all in the eye of the beholder. She's obviously a handful, an independent miss with a lot of spirit, but she's a lot more than passable. Every eye was on her at the Herberts'. She's a looker with a brain, my boy, and a prize to be sure. Hattie called her an *originale* and so she is. But she's also an incomparable. A diamond of the first water."

Dominic listened to Nathan extolling Fleur's person and asked himself what he really wanted. Was he sure he wasn't cut out to be a husband—not now and perhaps never?

"You're quiet," Nathan said.

Dominic breathed deeply and looked up at the stars. "Don't explode until you've thought about it, but I think Fleur Toogood would make you a perfect wife."

19

A week had passed since Fleur saw Dominic and Nathan climb inside the window seat and disappear. Their invitation to go with them to their mother's today had surprised and pleased her.

Who could help feeling happy in the Dowager's brilliant sitting room early on a sunny afternoon, Fleur wondered. Then she looked at the Elliot brothers and had her answer.

"Would you two mind settling somewhere?" the Dowager said. "What *is* the matter with you?"

Dominic and Nathan sat on a pillow-strewn divan—as far from one another as possible.

"You look well, Fleur," the Dowager said. She reminded Fleur of an exotic butterfly, a blue-and-green butterfly all flowing and glimmering. And her turban showed off her fine features. "The air and all the walking you do must agree with you." Lady Granville spoke to Fleur but cast repeated, irritated glances at her remote-faced sons.

"Walking is my favorite thing," Fleur told her. "And look at this day. This room was made for sun through its windows."

The Dowager smiled her pleasure. "It really is too bad that so many parties have been canceled this past week. But you did go to the Crewe-Burnses' do, and what I understand was an intimate little gathering at Franklin Best's. Then the Butterworths' rout. They're one of the few families I know of who serve excellent refreshments at such affairs."

"The place wasn't even crowded," Nathan said. "Wretched. Only a handful of interesting women there. And no cards."

"Fleur was there," Dominic said, popping to his feet again. "She's interesting."

He confounded her with his abrupt compliments, particularly since they invariably sounded grudging.

Nathan showed more of his teeth than usual. "Of course Fleur is interesting. Was she supposed to entertain a houseful of men?"

"Oh," Fleur said, anxious about the direction of the conversation. "I found the evening really pleasant. Such a lot of nice people."

"You mean you enjoyed having crowds of eligible males vie for your attention, and more than a few who weren't eligible?" Dominic didn't even look at her when he spoke.

"No—"

"That was despicable, Dominic," Nathan said. "Fleur has been to only a handful of parties and she's coped very well. Just how many men does she have to meet to find the one meant for her—if there is one?"

"What do you mean?" Dominic said. "*If* there is one? Of course there's one meant for her, but we both know that, don't we? I think Fleur's quite taken with Best. It's obvious that a last-minute gathering like that, sumptuously done as it was, had to be because he asked his parents to do it—and his only motive was to have Fleur there."

"*You* were the one who introduced Franklin to Fleur," Nathan said.

Dominic ignored him. "You will have noticed Noel wasn't invited."

"He wasn't there. That doesn't mean he wasn't—"

"Yes, it does. He wasn't invited," Dominic said. "Nor any man she may have spoken more than a word or two with. I'd stake my life on it."

"Mr. Best's parents thought it would be wonderful to have a small gathering to help fill in the gaps left by the canceled events," Fleur said. She also got up, planted her feet a few inches apart and swayed. Dominic had made her furious. He was mean. "They spoke with me at length and they are charming people. And it *was* a lovely party. The music swept me away—Hattie, too." Hattie had insisted Fleur use her given name.

"And from what I could see, young Best also swept you away," Dominic said. "I never heard so many waltzes played—one after the other. Or, as far as I can remember, seen the same unattached man and woman dance together so often. I thought I had warned you about men who seek to take advantage by any means they can."

"He didn't," Fleur protested.

"No, he didn't," Nathan said. "Seems to me some soul-searching might be in order for you, dear brother. You think you can hide the truth about your motives—"

"Enough of your damnable bibble-babble," Dominic snapped. "Why did you want to see us, Mother?"

"I declare it's hard to remember with the two of you being so unpleasant," the Dowager said. "No, really, I think I must stop this entirely. You should be ashamed of yourselves, behaving so in front of Fleur. She cannot be accustomed to such nastiness. Nathan, I wish to talk with you alone. Dominic, you look pale. Kindly take Fleur for a walk—perhaps in Green

Park. Relax. It will do you good. Also, I know Hattie would appreciate your help in dealing with this wretched redesign of the grounds. I understand the tenants are complaining because the landscapers are dropping mountains of debris around their cottages."

"Then I must tend to that at once," Dominic said. "I'll take Lawrence with me since he collects the rents and he knows everyone by name. Nathan, take care of Fleur, please."

"The tenant issue can wait," the Dowager said sharply. "Lawrence has already reassured them that their problem will be taken care of. You can speak with them later. I asked you to walk with Fleur since I need to speak to Nathan."

Fleur retied the strings on her bonnet—tighter—and picked up her reticule. "I don't need anyone to take care of me," she said, making sure she didn't sound miffed. "I have a great deal to do this afternoon so I must start out now. I should say, I'd like to start out now," she amended, dropping a curtsey to Lady Granville.

She hardly took a step or two when Snowdrop came in with Chloe, who held her yellow-eyed black cat in her arms and seemed in immensely good spirits. She took Raven and nestled among some pillows.

Fleur positioned herself so that only Snowdrop could see her face. Then she mouthed, "Well?"

"Fleur," Snowdrop said, "I saw a color as I came in and I think it would look wonderful on you. Excuse us a moment, please." She led the way into the hall, then popped her head back into the sitting room and said. "My lady, I was just sent to let you know your sisters are expected from Bath tomorrow."

Absolute silence followed but Fleur was too busy rushing behind the staircase with Snowdrop to care.

"That green," Snowdrop said, pointing to the silk wall hangings. "In case they ask you. We've been lucky. Lord Dominic doesn't seem to have taken off in the night all this week."

"He's going to," Fleur said. "I overheard him saying to Lord Nathan that it's time to get Olivia Prentergast alone—and that he intends to return to St. James Street and search for 'the place.'"

"When?" Snowdrop leaned close and her dark eyes filled with anxiety.

"After the ball here on Saturday evening. Did you come up with an idea for me to be anonymous in the street?"

"Yes. I'm afraid for my health if any member of the family finds out, but as long as we're careful we shouldn't be discovered."

"You are not going," Fleur said. "No, don't argue with me. Just tell me what you think I should do."

"Pretend you're a nobody, and drunk, and practicing the oldest trade in the world."

Fleur stared at her. A noisy barrage of conversation had broken out in the sitting room. "What is that trade, exactly?"

Snowdrop rolled her eyes. "They've even got 'em in the Bible so you must have read about 'em. An article, a baggage, a bit o' calico. A lady of easy virtues."

"A prostitute," Fleur whispered and sucked in a breath.

"Exactly. I've gathered some cast off maids' uniforms—scullery maids—and dolled 'em up a bit. Strings around the necks of the bodices—real loose—and gathered the skirts up in the front—leaving a petticoat, of course. I even got some of them beauty marks and there's caps with lots of ribbons. *And* a Chinese box of color to paint up our faces. Juicy red mouths we'll 'ave to 'ave."

"But, Snowdrop, we're likely to get approached by men. Dressed like that we'll be more obvious than if we went as we are."

"You know we can't go as we are. And you're wrong. We'll melt into the background."

"You're not coming," Fleur said and frowned.

Snowdrop gave her an innocent look. "Then I'll just have to make sure you know how to behave, won't I? I used to know one, y'know and I saw her about often enough."

The last thing Fleur could imagine was posing as a prostitute. But she supposed Snowdrop was right when she said such people were part of the London night scene.

"That is if you don't want to dress as a boy like I suggested first."

"Absolutely not. That's silly."

"I agree," Snowdrop said.

"Very well. This afternoon I have another fitting with Mrs. Neville, then we can get together in my room and see what you intend. After the ball on Saturday evening, I shall be quickly in place to follow Dominic. I may be able to do nothing to help, but there's a chance I can be invaluable. Did you get it?"

Snowdrop looked more miserable than Fleur recalled seeing her. She looked at the marble floor and crossed her arms.

"Snowdrop?"

"Oh, dear."

"You do have it?" Fleur pressed Snowdrop.

"If the Marchioness finds out, she'll never forgive me."

Fleur chose her words carefully. "Hattie doesn't give me the impression she's a stranger to worldly matters."

"She isn't. Oh, no, she's known an 'ard life. She almost died an 'orrible death but the Marquis and Lord Nathan and Lord Dominic helped her get away, not that she wasn't fighting for herself."

"So."

"Oh, all right, then. Yes, but it's a bit bigger than I'd like, and heavier. I'll have to take you somewhere private and show you how to fire it."

"I've fired a pistol before," Fleur informed her. "My papa is a man of peace but he believes his girls should be able to defend themselves in any dire situation. He taught me just in case he was ever away and someone tried to get into the rectory."

Snowdrop's surprise almost made Fleur laugh. "Bring it with you to my room."

"The last thing we need," Dominic said loudly from the sitting room, "is the aunts mixing everything and everyone up. Sorry, Mother, I know they're your sisters, but you've managed without them quite well for a long time so I don't know why you feel it's such a good idea to have them here now—when we're already stretched so far beyond comfort."

He meant by her presence, Fleur thought.

"Good old Aunt Enid and Aunt Prunella will liven the lot of us up," Nathan said.

"Well said," his mother agreed. "And I don't think I have to ask your permission to invite my sisters here, Dominic."

"Auntie Enid and Auntie Prunella," Chloe squeaked, apparently thrilled that these latest relatives were coming. "It will be just like home. They make me laugh and I make them laugh. Most agreeable."

"Fleur, where are you?" Dominic strode into the hall. "There you are. Let's go now, please. Snowdrop, keep an eye on your charge. Don't let her out of your sight, mind."

"Yes, my lord." Snowdrop curtseyed and managed to give Fleur a sly wink.

Once they were outside—and alone—Fleur said, "I only intend to walk right here in the immediate grounds. There is no need for you to accompany me."

"You are not to walk alone. My mother has assured me there is always a servant close enough to assist you when you are out on the estate."

"Yes," she said, her mind tumbling to find a way out of having this unpleasant person accompany her anywhere. He walked beside her like some great, furious animal, perhaps a big cat (she smiled at the thought) like a black panther.

"You meant what you said when you declined going to Green Park?"

"I certainly did. My afternoon is far too busy for such a long excursion."

"Good. Lead on then, and I'll stay with you."

How charming. How exhilarating. She did hope she would be a match for his sparkling conversation.

She set off for the open spaces, the fields where no animals grazed and no crops were sowed. Tender grass grew there where the land lay fallow until next year. In each field a track, she assumed used by the tenants, cut through from gate to gate.

"Where are you going?" Dominic asked when they left the formal gardens and the stands of trees behind and set off to the left and an empty field. "You said you didn't want to leave the immediate grounds."

"It's easier to stretch one's legs when there are no obstacles," she said. "So I use the beaten paths through the fields. The grass smells sweet and one gets a little more sun than is strictly approved of. I love it. I've even been known to make a daisy chain or two." She smiled, more to herself than at him.

At the gate he took her hand and helped her climb over. "You do enjoy forbidden fruit, don't you, Fleur?"

"Because I make daisy chains?" She thought of the biblical connotation of forbidden fruit and smothered a grin. "Forgive me for being flippant. I supposed I'm opposed to rules, if that's what you mean."

The field sloped upward. They crossed to the other side, climbed the gate and walked through oak trees to another field. Fleur marched on, over stiles and through narrow trails in knee-high grass. She heard her skirts swish behind her.

"A mountaineer, are you?" Dominic called out. "Well, I think you're almost at the summit."

"I am," she told him. "It's beautiful up there. Have you ever seen it?"

He laughed. "I grew up here. I could probably name the rocks on the ground. Of course I've been to the top. Not recently, that's all."

Fleur reached his "summit" and leaned on a stone wall built to keep livestock from wandering.

"I'm glad you like it up here," Dominic said, standing beside her with his elbow almost touching hers. "Appreciation of something like this view shows you have a heart and an imagination."

Until now he doubted that? "How odd it must be to look around and know that all you see is yours."

"It isn't," he said. "It belongs to John, to the Marquis. But it has always been my home."

He was a straightforward man.

"Nathan and I each have property but it's worked just as it has always been worked—without a master in residence."

"I see."

The wind blew hard up here and ballooned in Fleur's skirts. She noted how Dominic's long, black hair whipped beneath the ribbon tied at his nape.

"If you want to go back," she said. "I shall be perfectly safe finding my own way down."

"That is a guess, Fleur, because you don't know you're right. Anyway, I'm perfectly happy where I am, thank you."

"Do you keep your hair back when you sleep?" she asked, and wondered why her tongue was so reckless.

"No." Muscles in his jaw tightened but he didn't look at her.

Fleur pushed her bonnet off and let it trail from her neck by its strings. She turned her face to the wind and closed her eyes. When she opened them again, she found Dominic watching her. "Do you understand how complicated life can be?" he said. "How we can't always have what we might like because we have duties we must not neglect?"

"I'm not sure." She turned sideways and leaned on the fence again. Watching the wind have its way with him excited her. "I believe we must balance our lives. If, for example, we don't allow ourselves any pleasure, our hearts will eventually break."

"Piffle." He drew his lips back from his teeth.

"You're entitled to your opinion." But his protestation made her sad. He feared admitting to human needs.

"Do you wear a nightcap to bed?" he said.

She grinned at him. "No. I hate them. I do like to pull the covers over my head, though."

He raised his chin and looked down at her, his gaze speculative.

Fleur wondered what he was thinking.

She changed the subject. "I don't think it will be long before The Cat starts giving away the identities of his victims. He'll spread them throughout the beau monde just to enjoy the embarrassment and gossip he causes."

Dominic tipped his head to one side. "Yes," he said. "Just what I've been expecting. But you surprise me. It would seem you can think more like a man than a woman."

"Because I don't always look for a pretty picture so that my sensibilities need not be troubled? You don't have any idea how I think."

"Perhaps not, or perhaps I do. Tell me this. If the Cat releases the names of the women he kidnaps, why will families continue to pay ransoms?"

"To keep their daughters alive."

Dominic looked sideways at her. "Quite. Are you a heartless woman?"

"Because I don't simper or avoid the truth?" she said. "Or swoon at the mention of unpleasant things?"

"I interest you because you find me challenging, but you don't like me." He faced her and his eyes turned a burning blue in the sunshine.

She hadn't seen the statement coming.

"You don't have to like me, Fleur. You do have to listen when I say things in your best interest."

"Why do you provoke me?" she asked. "Is that part of what I must do, too? Listen to you when you're mean?"

"I'm not—"

"You are, my lord. You make no attempt to cover your moods or to wait until you are alone to deal with them. I am powerless here. Do you think yourself brave to pick on a powerless person? I know you're trying to please your mother by watching over me but you *hate* it and it is you who don't like me. And I don't think I can continue this charade, not for anyone's sake."

His fingers, settling gently on her lips, shocked Fleur.

"Can you do it for me?" he asked softly.

Fleur didn't try to answer but her eyes filled with tears and she was *so* angry at her weakness.

"I can't make you believe me, but I want you to be happy and I want to know you're cared for." His hand went from her mouth to the side of her face. He smoothed her wildly blowing hair. "I wish I were free to do whatever I want to do."

Her legs turned shaky. "You are free."

"Not completely." His thumb brushed over her cheek. "I entrap myself. I wonder if you could ever understand that. My commitment to the duties that fall to me, and certain other responsibilities, mean that choosing to do what I want—for myself—would be selfish. And it could be dangerous, not for me but for another."

Fleur inclined her head a little and pressed her lips into his palm. She squeezed her eyes shut and felt his other hand settle on her neck. He must think she wouldn't guess that he was giving reasons for not allowing himself to love her.

Her heart set up a desperate pounding. She could not bring herself to look at him. She said, "I do like you," but stopped herself from saying more. The less she said, the less there would be to regret.

"I'm a man who is accustomed to spending time alone.

Lots of it. I would never ignore someone I cared for out of malice, but I might forget to be attentive."

Dominic slid a hand around her neck and exerted enough pressure to tip her against him. She didn't resist. Neither did she attempt to hold him.

"Remember how I said I believed any man who thought to marry you should have his own list? Questions to ask you in response to the ones you intend for him?"

"Yes. It was a good idea. I still think so."

He raised her chin and waited until she looked at him. "Should I give you some of the questions I think a man might ask? Just as practice?"

"Yes." Fleur let out a shaky breath. "Yes, please."

"Would you marry a man who didn't always show his love for you?"

Surely there shouldn't be so many ways for love to hurt. "No, I wouldn't."

"Would you know your place and not question your husband's decisions?"

"No."

"Would you be happy to raise children with little interest from your husband?"

"No."

"Would you love, honor and obey your husband?"

"Love and honor, always," she said. "Obey, rarely."

"Would you share your bed with a man who sometimes ignored you?"

This was Dominic's way of crushing any affection she held for him. "No."

He pushed his fingers into her hair and looked straight into her eyes. "If you knew a man loved you but he couldn't share all of himself with you, would you marry him?"

"You torture me," she whispered.

"Do I? Tell me to stop touching you, then."

Fleur shook her head.

"Then I won't stop." He loosened her pelisse, undid the buttons that closed the front of her dress, and slipped his hands over her breasts. He held them, inciting her nipples with the very tips of his thumbnails, while he teased her lips apart with his tongue, then kissed her deeply and drew greedily on her lips.

Fleur held him then. She clutched him and hung on for fear she would fall if she didn't. Her breasts felt hot and swollen and his thumbs made her burn deep inside. With each flick across her nipples, she strained to get closer to him, and he drew on her mouth as if to take her inside him. The sounds she heard could not come from her. Dominic groaned. He groaned and buried his face in her breasts. She did cry out. Soft, broken moans. And she looked down at his dark hair blowing across her white skin.

Dominic made circles on her aching flesh, smaller and smaller circles and when she thought she would die with wanting something for which she knew no name, he suckled a breast, nibbled at its tip until she called out his name again and again. He moved to the other breast and Fleur's knees dipped. With her hands beneath his jacket, she clawed at his sides. Without warning, he jutted his hips against her and through the fine stuff of her dress she felt the hardness of him, the possessive pulsing. She had never seen a man's private parts, other than on statuary or in paintings but Fleur knew what was happening.

Straightening, he embraced her, held her so tightly she could hardly breathe. "I want you," he said. "I want you for myself." He pulled up her skirts and slipped his hands over her bottom, driving her ever more tightly against him.

But he had posed his questions and she had answered. What she felt was love and lust. What he felt was lust and he'd already let her know how empty a life with him would be.

"Please stop," Fleur said. They were the most difficult words she had ever spoken.

He closed his teeth on the side of her neck and she felt him struggle to collect himself. She didn't move except to take her hands away. Dominic let her go and stood back. He leaned forward to help straighten her skirts, and went to button her bodice again but she pushed him away.

"Forgive me," he said, breathing hard. "That wasn't fair."

"There's nothing to forgive." If only her voice held conviction. Trembling and weak, she fumbled with buttons, pulled on her bonnet and tucked up stray locks. "I…I am sad. Perhaps my heart is broken at this moment. But you can't change who you are and I shall recover." No, she wouldn't. Not ever.

"I was carried away," he told her. "You're a very desirable woman."

She struggled against tears.

"You answered the questions I asked with honesty," Dominic said. "You are prepared to give all of yourself to a man you love and you ask the same in return. That is fair."

20

"Where is Fleur?" Dominic demanded.

Hattie and his mother sat in Fleur's two blue chairs. They looked startled when they saw him in the open doorway.

"She's not here," the Dowager said. "Her fitting is over but we're too comfortable to move."

After delivering Fleur home he had retraced their steps through the fields. He'd stood again where he'd been with her at the top of the hill. Surely he had not stayed there so long that the fitting could be over.

"Is there something wrong?" Hattie asked him quietly.

A maid slipped past him to deliver a tray of tea things. She set the tray on the table between the ladies and quickly retreated.

"There's nothing wrong." Dominic took a step into the room and looked around. "Where is she?"

"Riding," his mother said.

"She can't ride."

Hattie got up but remained by the chair. She cast disturbed glances at Dominic.

The Dowager said, "Did you ask if she can ride?"

"No."

"Well, she can. And I gave my permission for her to go riding in Hyde Park."

"Hattie, will you explain this to me?" he asked.

"Mr. Mergatroyd called," Hattie said. "Fleur agreed to receive him, and he was given permission to take her riding. Neville had already made her two habits."

"Mergatroyd?"

"Mr. Mergatroyd," Hattie agreed.

"The fellow with the laugh?"

His mother waved Hattie back into the chair. "That would be the one," she said. "And very polite he is, too."

Dominic crossed his arms. He had to do something with them. "He sweats."

"Most people do," Hattie murmured.

He stared at her. *"Profusely."*

"You introduced Mr. Mergatroyd to Fleur at the Herberts', or so I understood," his mother said.

"No, he didn't," Hattie said at once. "He asked me if he could dance with her and I agreed."

"Blast." Dominic threw his head back and spread his arms. "Forgive me, ladies. But surely if Fleur meets a variety of men she should learn which ones to avoid. Don't you think that a lame example or two might help her pick out the real, er, gem?"

"Only you would think of a thing like that, my son."

"Mergatroyd is no gem," Dominic said.

"Neither is he a monster," Hattie told him.

"What if he's The Cat?" He met Hattie's eyes and she frowned. He had never mentioned the name to his mother before but he noted she showed no surprise at hearing his name now. So be it. There was no reason for her to tie the gossip to Jane Weller and that would be the only reason to keep the story from the Dowager.

"Calm yourself," she said, making him even more inflamed. "You aren't thinking. If Mr. Mergatroyd made off with Fleur then demanded a ransom, we should all know the identity of this Cat person, shouldn't we?"

"Which horse did she take?"

"The gentleman brought one for her just in case she could accompany him."

"I can't believe it." He absolutely could not. "You let her go with a strange man and his strange horse? At the very least you should have insisted she use a horse from our own stables, a horse we know. And an escort should have been sent."

"Albert Parker is keeping them in sight. And you, Dominic, sound…well, you don't sound yourself," Hattie said.

"You mean he sounds insane," the Dowager added.

The dapple-gray mare had difficulty keeping up with Mr. Mergatroyd's considerably larger horse. "Good girl," Fleur said and stroked Lolly's neck. "Could you try to go a little faster?" She hadn't the heart to press the animal too hard when she was doing her best.

This was Fleur's first time on Rotten Row although she had heard a great deal about it. People dressed in the height of fashion rode and drove all around her. She would rather sit on the grass and watch the scene than deal with an unresponsive animal and feel like a spectacle. Her escort's horse pranced ahead and Fleur might have well been alone.

Mr. Mergatroyd laughed, and Lolly stopped altogether. She tossed her head and whinnied. Fleur could scarcely stop herself from laughing. Evidently the mare thought Mr. Mergatroyd intended to communicate with her.

He had realized his companion had fallen behind and wheeled around. His wave reminded her of a flagpole against a clear blue sky. The man was pleasant enough but had almost nothing interesting to say and he was even taller than she remembered from the Herberts'. All arms, legs and neck. Even his face seemed unreasonably long, not that she was in the habit of holding a person's appearance against him. It was the laugh and the way he ignored her as they rode that irritated her.

"Miss Toogood? What can be holding you back?" he called, trotting toward her.

At least he was talking. Fleur caught up with him. "I'm afraid dear Lolly is no match for your Thoroughbred."

"Park hack," Mr. Mergatroyd said. "The finest in Town."

"He is very fine indeed." She had only agreed to come because she wanted to please the Dowager—and show Dominic how quickly she could recover from their shattering encounter.

"You haven't ridden a great deal, Miss Toogood," Mr. Mergatroyd said, pulling on his mount's reins.

No, Fleur thought, she would never recover from realizing she'd met the man of her dreams but that he could never be hers.

"Miss Toogood?"

Ooh, this man was a boor. "I have ridden a great deal, just not sidesaddle very often."

"*Not* sidesaddle? Well, after all, you're a country gel. And a beautiful country gel." He looked down at her from his considerable vantage point and laughed while he assessed her body. Mrs. Neville fitted every garment perfectly, but too tightly for Fleur's taste.

Mergatroyd snorted and actually winked at her. "Come on then, Miss Toogood. You look well enough on the mare but I must teach you to be competent. And, for reasons I'm sure you understand, it's time for you to forget about riding other than sidesaddle."

The effort hurt but she smiled at him and said nothing.

He flipped Lolly with his crop—hard.

"No!" Fleur hitched her leg more firmly between the pommels. "She is doing her best."

Mergatroyd used his crop again and this time the mare whinnied and tossed her head. And she took off with an uneven gait.

Fleur gripped the upper pommel tightly with both hands. For all the world it felt as if Lolly intended to throw her!

"Hold on, Miss Toogood," Mergatroyd said loudly. "Show her who is in charge."

The saddle slipped. Only the slightest bit but it did slip. Fleur scarcely dared to breathe. She carefully took her hands from the pommel and put more pressure on the reigns.

"That's the way, Miss Toogood. Spot on."

What a wretched man.

Fleur heard chuckles from passing riders, and giggles. A yellow phaeton went by in a blur.

She slid another tiny distance closer to the mare's side. "Lolly," she said in as soothing a voice as she could manage. "Whoa. *Whoa.*" The horse bucked, threw herself around and took off in the opposite direction. Fleur's veiled hat toppled backward.

"You have spirit, Miss Toogood," Mr. Mergatroyd declared as she passed him. "I like that. Yes, indeed, I like that."

Fear sickened Fleur. "Help," she managed to cry. "Oh!" The saddle jolted even lower. If she continued as she was she might actually slide beneath the beast's belly, but if she jumped there was a good chance of being trampled by another horse or run over by a carriage—or both.

Pounding hoofs came to her through the horror. Why didn't anyone come to her aid? "Mr. Mergatroyd," she shouted.

"Please, help me." She abandoned the reins and clung to Lolly's mane. Slammed against the saddle and the horse, Fleur opened her mouth to scream but another thump winded her.

Someone shouted, "Hold on, Fleur. It's all right. We'll get you."

She heard the voice, knew what it's owner meant but couldn't see. Pain drew a haze of moisture over her eyes.

"Got you! Let yourself go limp."

A strong arm snaked around her, plucked her from the horse, and she landed in front of Dominic who held her tight but glared ahead with fury in his eyes.

"Got the mare, Parker?" he yelled.

"Yes, m'lord. Er, m'lord, the lady's safe now."

Dominic glanced at her but his features didn't soften. "Stay with me," he called to Albert Parker. "I have business to attend to. I shall need your assistance with Fleur and the horses."

"Thank you," Fleur managed to say. "Could we go back to Heatherly now?"

Dominic's back remained stiff. He didn't answer her. "Mergatroyd," he cried. "Hold up." He sounded calm but deeply, immovably angry.

The man reluctantly pulled up his mount and Dominic stopped beside him. "Get down, man," he said. "Now."

"I say." Mergatroyd gave one of his braying laughs and Fleur could see perspiration running down his face. "You sound threatening, Lord Dominic."

"Get down," Dominic told him, his voice filled with menace. "Parker, hold my horse and see to it that Fleur isn't disturbed further."

Parker dismounted. He held his own reins and the mare's while he reached up to take Fleur from Dominic and set her down beside him. "You'll be safe, miss. Just stand close to me, please."

Dominic jumped off his horse and Albert Parker made sure it didn't bolt.

"Albert, I think there could be a fight," Fleur said.

"I know, miss. Best start saying your prayers—for Mr. Mergatroyd."

Before Fleur's horrified eyes, Mr. Mergatroyd attempted to ride on, only to be pulled to the ground in a sprawling heap by Dominic who stood over him, shining black boots braced apart.

"I say," Mergatroyd said, scrambling to his feet. "Steady on, old man. Looks bad, y'know."

"I do know," Dominic said in low, smooth tones. "How dare you bring my charge riding and put her on an unsuitable horse? And what the blazes are you thinking of to allow Miss Toogood to suffer mortal danger and public humiliation while you did nothing to help her."

"She was quite all right. I was on my way to make sure of it when you rode up making enough fuss to completely unnerve the mare."

"Parker," Dominic snapped out, "can you check the mare's girth and the backstrap on the saddle?"

Immediately Albert said, "The backstrap's come loose. If it had been properly fastened, the saddle wouldn't have slipped."

"I should thrash you," Dominic ground out through his teeth, standing toe-to-toe with his adversary. "Did you intend to *rescue* Fleur to ensure she'd think of you as her hero and throw herself into your arms?"

The traffic slowed, and some stopped to allow onlookers a good view of the spectacle.

"Can't we do anything to stop this?" Fleur whispered to Albert.

"No, miss. I've never seen his lordship so angry."

Mergatroyd made the mistake of breaking into one of his huge laughs and punctuating the racket with snorts. Fleur wanted to close her eyes but couldn't bring herself to look away from Dominic.

"You call her Fleur and she's been heard to call you Dominic," Mergatroyd managed to get out. "Do you know you're being talked about, Elliot? You squire *Fleur* around and introduce her to eligible men, but you behave like her overprotective father—or lover."

Fleur gasped.

"That tears it," Albert muttered.

"You, sir, are a cad." Dominic threw a dark gray glove to the ground. "Name your second."

Mergatroyd stared at the glove. He shook visibly. "The deuce, you say," he murmured unsteadily.

"I think I should enjoy beating you to death," Dominic said. "The choice of weapons is, of course, yours."

"I've got a weak heart," Mergatroyd stuttered. "I'm a sick man." And with that his eyelids fluttered and he collapsed.

A great collective gasp hissed from the onlookers. Several men crowded around while Dominic went to a knee and felt Mergatroyd's neck. "Just a swoon," he announced. "Someone get him home."

Fleur broke away from Albert and scurried around the circle until she saw Dominic's glove, which she snatched up and bore away, but not before meeting Dominic's steely gaze.

"You shouldn't have done that, miss," Albert said when she rejoined him. "It's not the thing to interfere in such matters."

"This male posturing nonsense must be stopped by whatever means necessary. Foolish creatures."

Several men bore Mr. Mergatroyd away to a carriage and tied his horse behind. "You did the right thing, Elliot," someone in the crowd said while another applauded and told him, "Well done. The man should know better than to tangle with you and insult your lady friend."

"Oh, no," Fleur moaned. She turned to Albert and rested her brow on his chest. "Has another fight begun? I just know Dominic didn't like that comment."

Albert patted her back but held his tongue.

"Tie the mare beside the hack," Dominic said from behind her. "I'll get Fleur home. Make your own way as quickly as you can."

Albert nodded and went about his business.

Dominic's hands closed on Fleur's waist and he lifted her to his saddle before mounting behind her. He clacked at his horse and they rode on at a faster clip than was comfortable for Fleur's frayed nerves.

The wretched tears sprang along her eyelids again. They stung and she blinked. And the devil take it, she was angry. Who decided that men would rule the world when they were clearly such a silly, arrogant, territorial bunch?

"So," Dominic said at last. "The *ton* gossips about us."

"They have nothing to gossip about," she told him. "It's just that they become hungry for a some new *on dit* and things are a little quiet about The Cat right now. I'm beginning to think he's grown bored and stopped altogether. I expect he's collected a great deal of money."

"He will surface again. And when he does he will be more dangerous. You told me you think so, too. I will know he has stopped when we capture him."

"It's too dangerous and I want you to stay away from any-thing to do with him." She knew her mistake at once.

Dominic raised one brow. He slowed and walked his horse to the side of the road. "Listen to me and listen well. My pri-vate affairs are none of your business. Don't interfere. And I think I should correct a comment you just made. Society has tied our names together. I don't know why or how."

And she would not tell him that cutting in on other men at dances and hovering over her as he did was bound to make people wonder at their relationship.

"I see you think a great deal more than you say but that's your decision."

"It is my decision," Fleur told him. "You make me angry. Such arrogance. Such sauce."

"*Sauce?*" His sarcastic little grin incensed Fleur. "I don't think I've ever been told that before, miss. You'd best be quiet and remember your place."

"Behind you? Of course, and preferably telling you how important you are, how wonderful you are, how fortunate I am that you allow me to grovel in the shadow you throw. Ooh!"

"You," Dominic said, "have no sense of danger. Any other woman would fear my response now."

"I'm not afraid of you or anyone else." There, now he knew. Well, perhaps she was a teeny bit afraid of him—but not very much at all. Pompous, that's what he was.

He smiled and narrowed his eyes to glittering blue slits. "Is that so? We-ell I shall have to decide how to change your mind about that." His knuckle beneath her chin, forcing her to look straight back at him, didn't cool her down at all. He sighed. "However, we both know that there is definitely some-thing to gossip about—about us."

She swallowed and held her head high.

"Your hair is the color of fire," he said and looked pleased with himself for it.

"Thank you. Unless you have blabbed about us we are the only ones who know… We're the only ones who know we have been more familiar than we should have been."

"Is that true?" He inclined his head. "Yes, I suppose it is. But I must say you are fearless in your attack on me."

"Please take me back to Heatherly." To Heatherly where she could shut herself away with her desperation. "I lied. I am not fearless. I am overwhelmed and more than a little sore. It's time for me to assess my position and decide what to do next."

"Yes, of course." He returned the horse to the road and they traveled in silence.

Once Dominic asked if she was asleep and she glanced at him before staring ahead at something only she could see: her return home to the dashed hopes of her family.

"My mother and Hattie should have known better than to allow that man to take you anywhere. He could not possibly be the man for you."

They reached the estate and started up the long driveway in the shadow of oak trees. "And who," Fleur said, "do you think might be the man for me?"

"You should not have picked up my glove as you did."

"Who do you think is the man for me?"

"I don't know, dammit!"

"No, I suppose not." No matter how much he wounded her, she wouldn't turn back from her determination to try to save him from his own bravado. Snowdrop would be waiting in her room by now and she should have brought everything Fleur might need when she followed Dominic on Saturday.

"I returned to the top of the hill, Fleur," he said. "Just to stand where we stood."

She couldn't breathe. A pulse at her temple hurt.

"I needed to think. What happened…it was wonderful, but it wasn't enough and it wasn't right. I took advantage of your innocence. I'm the man who is supposed to be safeguarding that innocence."

"I must safeguard myself," she said, feeling broken. "And I regret nothing of what passed between us."

"You are a passionate creature and I excited you in the ways I know so well to excite a woman."

When they drew closer to the house, a groom ran from the direction of the stables and waited for them to arrive.

"Fleur," Dominic said. "I didn't expect your fitting to be over so I came to see you. My mother and Hattie were there."

"They are so kind to me."

"Who wouldn't want to be kind to you?" He smiled at her and her own lips parted with the sensation that his mouth had touched hers. "Your ball is less than two days away. It will be our opportunity to show you off as you should be shown. And I shall be on my best behavior. Fleur, how much do you like Nathan?"

There was that question again. "Very well indeed. Your mother and father produced unforgettable sons." She blushed. "Nathan is admirable yet he doesn't take himself too seriously. And I'm sure the Marquis is also a man to be reckoned with."

The groom met them in front of the steps.

"Yes," Dominic said, lifting her down. "I am sorry to have made your time here harder. Please forgive me."

Was that the way of all men, to dally, even if only a little, with a woman and then apologize with the expectation that she would accept that apology and feel nothing for what he had aroused in her?

"I forgive you," she said.

"Fleur." His tone became urgent. "Don't do that. Don't tell me something so important in a way that suggests you will never forgive me. I am truly sorry."

"Perhaps if you weren't quite so sorry, I should not feel empty and bereft."

She left him and ran up the front steps. Inside the house, she didn't stop until she reached her room and all but threw herself inside.

Snowdrop, her eyes wide, rushed to her and held her hands. "What has happened to you? There's tears on that lovely habit. And dirt! Oh, Fleur, did you take a terrible tumble?"

"Oh, yes," Fleur told her calmly. "A terrible tumble, but I shall recover quite quickly. Where did this come from?" She picked up a daisy chain from the foot of her bed.

"I thought you must have made it."

"There wasn't time," she said and turned away to hide her blush. Dominic said he'd returned to the top of the hill, then come here looking for her.

He had made the chain and brought it to her. She held the fragile thing in her hands, closed her eyes to experience its soft weightlessness.

Snowdrop held up a rough cream dress with garish red and yellow ribbons threaded at the neckline and at the base of the laced bodice. A heap of frightful clothing rested on one of the chairs. "I added all the ribbons and lace," Snowdrop said, although the worry didn't leave her eyes. "We have everything we'll need. If you still intend to go."

"I shall go," Fleur told her. "He doesn't want me, but I am a strong-willed woman and I have appointed myself his guardian angel. I'll try some of these things on and be ready for a quick change on Saturday."

Snowdrop, her hair hanging loose almost to the backs of her knees, shook her head. "Oh, Miss Fleur," she said. "You 'ave fallen in love with him. Hattie and me were afraid you 'ad."

Fleur walked to the top of the bed and pulled back the coverlet. She kissed the daisy chain and arranged it on her pillow.

21

The newspapers arrived early. Fleur had discovered that McGee would not allow any servant but himself to bear them to the breakfast room table. That, she had been told, happened around dawn.

Wearing one of the wretched, beribboned nightcaps she hated—with most of her disheveled hair stuffed inside—and a chintz morning dress from home, Fleur had left her room in the near darkness. The object was to gain possession of the *London Ladies' Voice* before it could fall into other hands.

"Mornin', miss," a sleepy-eyed tweeny said when Fleur reached the hall.

"Good morning," Fleur said as the girl scurried by with a broom in one hand. Two more maids headed in the opposite direction. Of course the house was alive with servants. How else would they get their cleaning done but before the family got up?

Fleur passed the salon and walked hurriedly toward the breakfast room. She had never eaten there because Snowdrop always brought her a tray.

"Miss Toogood." McGee caught up with her. "Er, may I help you?" His expression didn't change but she had no doubt the entire below stairs would know she had been seen about in a nightcap. Was it her fault if she'd been unable to find a morning cap when she had no idea if she even had any?

She smiled and bore her head high. "I'm on my way to the breakfast room, McGee." After all, they had one servant at the rectory in Sodbury Martyr and she certainly did not bring breakfast to anyone's room. They all ate together downstairs.

"Yes," McGee said. "I see. I expect we couldn't sleep. But you'll remember that Lord Dominic doesn't want you abroad at such hours, and on your own."

"Well—"

"Allow me to send you some warm milk with honey. I'll have someone go with you and make sure you're comfortable."

"Well—"

"Whiskey. If I might make so bold, a little whiskey in hot milk is famous for its sleep-inducing qualities."

"Thank you, McGee." He didn't want her downstairs, that much was obvious. "But I'll carry on to the breakfast room."

"That's not... I mean, of course that's a perfectly splendid idea, miss. Was there something special you'd care for?"

Just the London Ladies' Voice *and a speedy retreat before someone really does arrive for breakfast.* "I'll have some coffee, please," she said. "But there's no hurry. I'll read the paper." Brilliant, now he'd know who took the thing before it could be picked up by Hattie's maid.

So be it. Borrowing a paper was hardly a sin. And it had been Hattie herself who mentioned that the episode on Rotten Row might be reported. Fleur sped the last few steps and rushed into the ebony-paneled room with its massive Jacobean sideboard, heavy table and chairs and windows where the green tapestry draperies were still closed.

The heavy fragrance of fresh coffee filled the room, and Dominic sat at the table behind a copy of the *Times*.

"What are you doing here?" Her voice came out as a squeak.

Dominic looked at her over the top of his paper. For the first time she saw him without a black ribbon tying his hair at the nape. He wore shirtsleeves, a buff-colored waistcoat—and no neckcloth. Fleur tried not to stare but he took her breath away.

"What are *you* doing here, Fleur? You breakfast in your room like all the ladies." Her appearance got amazed scrutiny. "It is barely after five in the morning. Why are you up at all and wandering around in the corridors on your own?"

Fleur looked about, searching for the *Voice.* Silver coffee service stood on the sideboard, together with several covered chafing dishes. Yes, she also smelled food and hunger gnawed at her.

"Fleur! You aren't yourself. Must have been all the excitement yesterday. Come, I'll take you back to your room. Go back to bed and I'll have something sent up to you—some chocolate and perhaps toast? Chocolate has great restorative properties."

"So you've told me before. I feel perfectly well enough to be up, thank you." Not true because she had a few nasty bruises and a sore behind her knee where the pommel on Lolly's saddle had dug into the flesh. "I often get up this early at home." *Now that was a whopper!*

Dominic shook his paper, fiercely, Fleur thought, and returned to reading.

Well, now this was a pickle.

"You'd be better without the cap," Dominic said from behind his paper screen. "Take it off and let your hair do whatever it does at times like this."

She stood as tall as possible, poked more locks of hair beneath the cap, and went to the sideboard. "I like the way you look this morning, Dominic. Quite—swashbuckling. Yes, I shall think of it as your pirate look."

"You, Fleur Toogood," he said, "say the first thing that comes into your head. Pirate, hmm?"

"I'm impetuous, that's what you mean. My father always says so." With two hands she lifted the heavy coffeepot and carried it carefully to the table.

A hand shot out, Dominic's, to take the pot from her and pour from it. "Why not ask rather than struggle with something you can't manage?"

"I was managing it," she protested. "I'm no weakling."

"Hmm."

An awful, terrible thought struck her. "You aren't going out to duel with Mr. Mergatroyd, are you? Please say you aren't." If he were, it would explain his early arrival for breakfast. "Seriously, Dominic. Duels and all that old-fashioned nonsense make men look foolish. All posturing and puffed—a bit like male pigeons mating. And duels are against the law."

"Thank you for your opinion. I'm impressed you know the mating habits of the pigeon. That's what I get for defending your honor."

"Poppycock. You were having a wonderful time marching about, throwing down the silly glove and glaring while people looked on. You loved having the women simper over your daring masculinity."

"Sit down, drink your coffee and watch your tongue," he said. "The coffee may unscramble your brain. Mergatroyd did not accept my challenge, the coward."

"On the other hand," Fleur said, "I am grateful to you for such a wonderful rescue. If I hadn't been frightened I should have found it thrilling. It had a sort of mythic, larger-than-life quality about it. You should have worn a golden breastplate and helmet—and some of those little puffed trouser things with long hose. Parti-colored, I should think."

"I'm not aware that men ever fought in body armor and parti-colored hose, Fleur. Bit of a mishmash, wouldn't you think?"

What has happened to the Voice?

"Have you considered," she said, "that The Cat may be at the ball tomorrow evening?"

He looked at her again. "You make my head spin. We go from men in long hose to your ball and The Cat. You must make allowances for my much slower mental abilities."

"Sorry. I'll try to speak more slowly in future." She sat down and poured cream into her coffee. She would have to brazen this out now. "Mmm. Breakfast smells good," she said. "Do you suppose there's enough for me to eat here?"

"I doubt if your little pickings will be noticed," he said. "This is what the men eat for breakfast."

"Really? Let's hope there's something other than bones to sharpen the teeth on and lumps of raw and bloody meat to chew."

He laughed. "Ah, Fleur, what should we do without you here? It used to be so dull." Dominic's lips remained turned up but his eyes grew somber while he looked at her. He made it all but impossible to look away.

Should she mention she'd found the daisy chain? Instinctively she knew the man who had picked flowers yesterday had hidden himself safely away again and wouldn't appreciate any reminders from her.

He did play such games with her. Fleur popped up, took a plate and returned to the board. "Kidneys! I love them. And kippers. Oh, yum." She filled her plate until the food showed signs of falling off the sides and returned to her place. Dominic had made sure he poured coffee into a cup on the opposite side of the table and two chairs to the left of his.

The kidneys were delicious. She spread butter on several pieces of toast from the rack and placed scrambled eggs on top of one. Mama would scold if she was here, but she wasn't. And Dominic wouldn't notice. She crunched her teeth into the toast and barely caught a lump of egg before it would have slopped to the plate. This she poked back on the toast and popped into her mouth.

"Congratulations," Dominic said. "You have a quick hand with a falling egg."

She inclined her head at the same angle as his and smiled. "Thank you. Um, I hate to bother you when you're so busy, but have you seen the other paper?"

"The *Post* is here." He pointed to the chair beside him and began to pull out the paper.

"No. Actually I wanted to look at the *London Ladies' Voice.* I know it's a silly gossip rag but I only look at the advertisements."

"Good morning, Fleur." Nathan strolled in, also minus a jacket or neckcloth. "I say, what brings you here at such an hour?"

"What brings her here at all?" Dominic added without looking at his brother. "Or you, come to that? I looked forward to a quiet breakfast alone."

"Charming," Nathan said. "Such a gracious welcome." He got a plate of pheasant with eggs and ham.

Finally he took a good look at Fleur and smiled broadly. "I don't know why you're up early, either, but I'm so glad you are," he said quietly and sat down beside her. "You look splendid. Warm and soft and just out of bed. And dare I say it—

cuddly." He gave her the most disarming smile and poured himself some coffee.

"What a nice thing to say," she told him. He was such a nice man who always knew how to make her feel comfortable.

An icy stillness caused her to look in Dominic's direction. He frowned at Nathan until the two of them stared across the table at each other. Nathan shrugged but Dominic's expression didn't soften. He pointed a long, threatening forefinger but said nothing.

"Good gracious," Fleur said, shaken by Dominic's hostility. "What's that about? All that glaring and not saying anything? How unpleasant."

"You," Dominic said, "are naive and this oaf takes advantage of the fact."

"He has never taken advantage of me," Fleur said heatedly. "Nathan does his best to make me feel at home."

"I expect he does. Could you make time for me later, Nathan?"

Nathan rolled his eyes. "Again?" He took a piece of pheasant on his fork and held it before Fleur's face until she opened her mouth and took the meat off with her teeth. "Good, hmm?" he asked.

"Ooh, wonderful."

Another cool sensation reached her from Dominic's direction. His nostrils flared, his knuckles turned white, and for all the world Fleur expected him to produce another glove from somewhere.

"I was hoping to have a little time with the papers myself," Nathan said.

Dominic tossed the *Post* across the table.

Nathan unfolded it but Fleur noted how he glanced around

the room, even turned sharply to check the sideboard. Surely *he* couldn't be looking for the *Voice*. She pressed her lips together rather than giggle at the thought.

The soft swish of Hattie's skirts preceded her. She came into the room looking at envelopes in her hands but stopped the instant she discovered she wasn't alone there. Her hair had been brushed and coiled in a simple chignon at the back of her head and she looked as beautiful as ever.

"I came for my paper," she said, her gray eyes round. "Why are you all eating breakfast at such an hour?"

"Don't ask," Fleur said. "It's so boring to hear the stories all over again. Each of us came looking for a paper to read. Except Dominic who came for breakfast, too. Enough breakfast for a dozen or so, actually." She would never, ever again give in to her impulsive urges and venture forth like this.

"In other words," Hattie said, "we all want to see if the fiasco in Hyde Park got into the paper."

"Not at all," Dominic said at once.

"I should say not," Nathan added. "It's the shipping news I want."

"Where's the *Voice?*" Hattie asked. "We'll soon see."

"That's what I came for really," Fleur said in a burst of honesty. "I do hope there isn't anything. It'll be so embarrassing if there is."

"Why?" Dominic asked. "Because I stopped you from being killed on Rotten Row?"

Hattie sighed. "I'll ring for McGee. He'll know where the paper is."

"I saw it when I came in," Dominic said—hastily, Fleur thought. "It's got to be here somewhere. Check around, Nathan."

"I have." Nathan took hold of Dominic's copy of the *Times*

from the top and pulled it away. With it came an open copy of the *London Ladies' Voice* which, being a smaller publication, slipped and fell onto the table.

"Dominic," the rest of them cried.

He swiveled sideways in his chair and crossed his legs. "I was merely trying to save the rest of you from becoming overwrought."

"Liar," Nathan muttered.

Hattie plucked up the *Voice* and carried it with her to the sideboard.

Nathan sprang from his seat at once and said, "Do sit down, Hattie. I'll pour you some coffee. What would you like to eat?"

"Nothing," she said promptly. "Just the coffee." She sat down once more, closed the paper and clutched her throat. "On the front page," she said, her voice fading.

"What does it say?" Fleur asked. "Is it so terrible?"

"Let me read it for everyone," Dominic said, reaching. "No need to bother with the details. I'll just hit the high points."

Hattie whipped the newspaper out of his reach. "The *low* points, you mean," she said. "This particular headline reads ARE THEY STILL VIRGINS?"

"Gad," Nathan exclaimed, setting down Hattie's coffee. "Someone's leaked it."

"We don't need to go into this now," Dominic insisted.

"But we do," Hattie told her brother-in-law, never taking her eyes from the page. "It's essential that anyone in potential danger be informed of all this. Young girls aren't safe."

"Perhaps The Cat's victims really aren't virgins anymore," Nathan said. "After all, a man will be a man, and—"

"Shut up," Dominic said. "Use your head, man."

Hattie ignored them and continued: *"'A communication was secretly delivered to your humble correspondent and after much deliberation I feel it my duty to share the contents with my faithful readers. Since the missive was placed on my desk in my absence, I have no idea who penned this information or if it is reliable. I shall leave you to make up your own minds.'"*

Dominic clasped his hands behind his neck. "In other words, Amanda Mercury is happy to have everyone in London believe the young ladies in question have been violated." He glanced at his brother and they exchanged nods. Fleur thought they looked quite pleased with themselves but couldn't imagine why.

"This is the letter she talks about," Hattie said and read on: *"'It is time to give credit to those whose families have generously contributed to my favorite cause. Me. By their generous donations, these families have shown the esteem in which they hold their daughters' virginity. This is an example of devotion we would all do well to emulate and I will continue to make sure that many of those who are eligible will have an opportunity to do so.'"*

"Good grief," Nathan said.

Dominic's comment was "Slimy barbarian."

"This is dreadful," Hattie said. "Monstrous. Mercury goes on, supposedly still quoting from the secret missive. *"'Lady Sylvia Smythe, Miss Augusta Arbuthnot, Miss Constance Fitzgerald, Miss Olivia Prentergast and Lady Wilhelmina Soams have all been returned home safely and in perfect order. Bravo, ladies. I did encounter one family who doubted my seriousness and came close to receiving damaged goods on their doorstep. This tried my patience. In future, if my sincerity is questioned, no goods at all shall be returned.'"*

Fleur said, "I'm so sorry the names have been printed. He means he will murder anyone for whom he doesn't get money, you know."

Hattie kept her eyes lowered but she sensed that her two brothers-in-law were already scheming. No great feat on her part since she knew they were. If only John were here to help with this disaster, and also to make sure his brothers didn't put themselves too deeply in danger.

She glanced at Fleur and found her watching Dominic. A fine conundrum they were all in. Fleur besotted with Dominic. And possibly Dominic besotted with Fleur, only he wasn't ready for marriage and the girl needed a husband now. Then there was Nathan. Who knew exactly what he thought of Fleur? He certainly paid her enough attention and Hattie knew the Dowager worried that her sons would become enemies over one woman.

She remembered the letters she'd found in the hall. "Three of these are for you, Fleur. Snowdrop tells me your family write a good many letters. How nice."

"Thank you," Fleur said, taking them almost greedily. "Sodbury Martyr. From Letitia, Rosemary and from my mother. I do love to hear from them."

So why, Hattie wondered, did Fleur frown over the envelopes and swallow frequently?

"LORD DOMINIC ELLIOT IN ROTTEN ROW ALTER-CATION," Nathan read, having deftly removed the paper from in front of Hattie.

"I haven't finished with that," she told him. "I'll take it upstairs now but you may have it later."

"Please, Hattie," Fleur begged. "May I just read that article before you take it?"

"You?" Dominic said, actually grinning. "I thought the headline contained my name." Like most males, the rattle enjoyed the idea of getting his name in the papers for some supposedly daring act.

Hattie couldn't bring herself to leave Fleur overwrought from wondering if she had been mentioned in the most read ladies' paper in London. "Very well." Hattie sighed and opened the paper again. "There is a subheading. *FRIGHTFUL FUROR IN HYDE PARK—WHAT MIGHT LOVE HAVE TO DO WITH IT?*"

Dominic smacked his cup into its saucer and said, "Good God!"

"He is good," Hattie said. "And I doubt He's much interested in your petty squabbles."

Laughter erupted from Nathan who had the sense to slide his chair far enough back to take him out of Dominic's easy reach.

"'Late yesterday afternoon, on Rotten Row, eyewitnesses were shocked to see the usually remote Lord Dominic Elliot in a war of words with Mr. Fritz Mergatroyd. Although many insist that Lord Dominic called Mr. Mergatroyd out, the latter was unable to retrieve the glove due to a fainting spell and the said glove could not be found following the disturbance.'"

"Did you call him out, Dominic?" Hattie asked. "Very foolish thing to do if you did."

"The coward only pretended to pass out," Dominic said but Hattie noted a rare flash of pink over his cheekbones.

"Dominic rescued me," Fleur said and her face turned red, probably from rushing to Dominic's defense. "If he had not come along—and if Albert Parker hadn't been there to help out—I should undoubtedly be dead."

"You *might* be dead," Nathan said, his tone smug. "I wonder what happened to the glove."

"I couldn't leave it there, could I?" Fleur said, breathing heavily. "Dominic might have got into trouble for it."

Hattie saw Dominic draw in a sharp breath and make a fist on his thigh. She read on: "'One Miss Fleur Toogood is in London for the Season as the guest of the Dowager Marchioness of Granville. Yesterday's contretemps happened while Miss Toogood was out riding with Mr. Mergatroyd. Her horse bolted and a nasty mishap seemed inevitable until Lord Dominic swept the young lady into his arms and placed her before him on his horse.'"

"How romantic," Nathan murmured.

Dominic started to rise but Hattie caught his eye and he subsided.

She thought the story romantic, too, but Nathan made the comment to bait his brother.

With her elbows on the table, Fleur hid her face in her open hands.

"Let's get this over with," Hattie said. "'Lord Dominic has assumed the duty of squiring Miss Toogood around London during the Season. She is already a sparkling success and has suitors vying for her attention (one gentleman's parents even threw a party for the purpose of helping their son court the young lady?) and all under the watchful eye of Lord Dominic and his sister-in-law, the current Marchioness of Granville.

"'From reports of Lord Dominic's remarks at Hyde Park, may we take it that defending Miss Toogood's honor until she meets the man she will love and marry is of the utmost importance to him? Or could there be something quite different on Lord Dominic's mind?'"

After a short silence Nathan said, "They're suggesting you want her for yourself, y'know."

Dominic got up and headed for the door, but he stopped and turned back to Nathan. "We have work to do. If you're not otherwise engaged, I'll find you after I finish going over things with Lawrence."

Hattie could hardly wait to be alone with Fleur and to comfort her.

"See here," Dominic said. He shocked Hattie by sliding into a chair beside Fleur and resting a hand on her shoulder. "This town thrives on the latest bit of gossip, but only until the next piece of scandal broth comes along."

"You're kind," Fleur said without lifting her face. "But I am a nuisance here. It will be best for me to leave as soon as a coach can take me."

Dominic guided Fleur's head against his chest and patted her back. He smiled at Hattie but ignored Nathan. "No such thing, Fleur Toogood. Whether you know it or not, you've arrived. Your name will be on every Society tongue in London. Nathan and I shall be turning away the hopefuls in droves, am I right, brother?"

Nathan crossed his arms and gave Dominic a speculative stare. "Almost always," he said.

22

Since the arrival of their first letter, Fleur's family tried to make sure she received one each day. Back in her room, bundled in her bed with a candle burning brightly on the table beside her, she opened all three envelopes and compared the dates.

The same.

There could not be a disaster or Papa would have written.

Fleur slapped a hand over her heart; unless there was something wrong with Papa. Letitia was the most direct, she would read her letter first.

Dearest Fleur:

I promised myself I would not trouble you with my problems. How can I keep that promise when you have always known my very heart and I, yours?

Something dreadful has occurred and I am frightened.

First, how are you, dear sister? I know you did not want to make this trip to London for the Season but my greatest wish is that by now you have started to have some fun. Keep your mind and heart open and a gentleman who is exactly right for you will come along. I'm just sure you are a huge success.

"Come on, come on," Fleur murmured. It was Letitia's way to start out by writing what was really on her mind, only to interrupt herself with enquiries about the health of others before returning to her topic.

Fleur, sometimes I find myself wishing you were here, but there is nothing you could do. This is for Christopher and me to deal with. Or rather, according to him, entirely Christopher's concern.

Papa is angry. And this alone feels so unusual I am beside myself, but I must remember that he loves Mama a great deal and I think he cannot bear to have her slighted—especially when she turned her back on her own fine family to be with him.

"She would do it again," Fleur said while tears overflowed down her cheeks. She'd been right earlier when she had said she should return home. They needed her there.

This is how it is. As you know, Squire Pool has high aspirations in life. To be fair, Mrs. Pool is an unaffected lady who has always been most kind to me. In fact, she has treated me like a daughter and said she looks forward to my becoming a member of the family.

The lump in Fleur's throat grew huge. Apparently Letitia and Christopher had pledged to each other and were engaged, but she could see where this story was going. Squire Pool, a big, florid and overly hearty man, made her nervous. But if he hurt her sister, he would learn the kind of spirit wrapped inside "that opinionated little one with the garish hair," as he had called her on more than one occasion.

I waited to tell you this—even though I've known it. Perhaps that was wrong but I didn't want to spoil your fairy-tale journey and I hoped the storm would pass. Apparently the marriage of his only son to the daughter of an impoverished vicar is not what the Squire has in mind and he is doing everything in his power to break off Christopher's engagement to me.

Fleur, Christopher is making plans for us to go away, perhaps to India, where he would offer his services as a cartographer to our military people there. But then, he also talks about South America.

I cannot speak of this to anyone but you. The Squire doesn't know of Christopher's enquiries. To be honest, I don't want to go to those faraway places but if that's what I must do to be with my beloved, then I shall go.

The Squire says I'm not good enough for Christopher and that he should marry a lady. That gentleman has gone so far as to hold "evenings" at the manor and invite whatever important people he can find. I, of course, am not invited. Each time Christopher has refused to be at the manor at all. Instead he sleeps in our barn all night and if Papa finds out, and discovers that I know about it, he will be furious.

Dearest Fleur, please send what advice you can.

Your loving sister,
Letitia

India? South America? Letitia's fair skin and delicate constitution would not fare well in such places. Fleur remained calm and thought hard. Christopher's skills as a cartographer were well thought of. She understood his wanting to escape his father, but if he secured a good job elsewhere in England, Squire Pool wouldn't find it easy to interfere with that. He could, however, make the lives of a young married couple miserable by cutting Christopher off from any support.

The squire wanted his son to marry into an influential family. Fleur screwed up her eyes and bared her teeth in a mock growl. Squire Pool should kiss the ground at the thought of Christopher marrying someone so wonderful as Letitia, and at the chance to count their father and mother as relations.

Rosemary's letter should come next and Mama's last. Rosemary made Fleur laugh with her girlish talk of meeting the man of her dreams and how she could scarcely wait. Mama, the Toogood voice of reason, was likely to help Fleur feel more calm.

After tapping the door Snowdrop came in, a surprising vision in a peach-colored wrapper edged with yards of expensive lace and with her black hair gleaming and hanging loose to her knees.

"Good morning, miss," she said softly. "Lord Dominic told me you have had a disturbed night and asked me to bring you some—"

"Hot chocolate for its restorative powers."

Snowdrop giggled and Fleur couldn't hold back from giggling with her.

"That's exactly what he said," Snowdrop said. She raised her chin. "I've seen the *London Ladies' Voice* and the mention of my Albert. He and Lord Dominic must have cut ever such dashing figures."

"They did," Fleur conceded, anxious to resume reading her letters from home.

"Let me plump up your pillows," Snowdrop said. She placed the tray she carried beside the bed and straightened Fleur's covers. Then she made a face and whipped off the nightcap. She took a comb from the dressing table, scrambled to kneel on the bed and smoothed out Fleur's hair as best she could. "There," she said, winding some locks around her fingers, and leaving shining red ringlets behind.

"Thank you," Fleur said.

"Now, the chocolate with the restorative properties. And toast with honey on it. You are to be coddled today. Lord Dominic's words, not mine."

If she were to marry a man with an impeccable pedigree—like Dominic—no doubt Squire Pool would change his mind about Letitia. Fleur rubbed her forehead hard. Like Dominic or another of the gentlemen who had shown interest. She thought of her list and trembled. What other man would answer the questions as Dominic had, even if he didn't intend to represent his own feelings?

"Fleur," Snowdrop whispered, standing close beside her, "I'll help you in any way I can. Hattie said you are going to need our support."

"Why did she say that?" Fleur asked, more sharply than she'd intended.

Snowdrop turned pink. "I'm sure I don't know, but I know she senses things other people don't even notice, and we are here and we will not let any harm or heartbreak come to you."

Fleur sipped the chocolate and it did make her feel a little better.

"You should try to get some more sleep, but later in the morning I'll return to help you dress. Today you must look especially pretty."

Fleur replaced the chocolate cup in its saucer and set it on the tray beside the bed. "Why?"

"Of course, you always look pretty, but this will be one of those trying days, I'm afraid."

As if it wasn't already trying. As if they weren't *all* trying. "You'll have to explain. I don't have any idea at all what you mean."

Snowdrop cleared her throat. She smoothed the skirts on the gorgeous wrapper and said, "My Albert bought me this. The Marquis is most generous and I'm afraid Albert is too fond of turning me out like a lady."

"You are a lady," Fleur said. "And Albert's proud of you. He likes to make you happy."

"Oh, yes, miss. Just like I think Lord Dominic and Lord Nathan like to see you happy." She closed her mouth and stood like a statue.

Fleur avoided Snowdrop's comments. "Why must I dress more carefully today?"

"Well—oh, dear. You've forgotten, I suppose, what with you having so much on your mind. But the aunts arrive today. The Misses Worth, Miss Enid and Miss Prunella. They are kind and caring but…critical. You mustn't mind anything they say that might seem hurtful. They don't mean a thing by it."

"I see." When she had set out for London she'd had little idea how many obstacles she might confront. "But they won't arrive for some hours."

"No. Would you like me to go now, miss? So you can get your sleep."

"If you wouldn't mind." And so that she could finish reading her letters.

She had to get out of bed because Snowdrop wouldn't

leave until she heard Fleur locking the door behind her. Such silliness. The Cat, if he suddenly decided to snatch women from their bedrooms, would hardly take Fleur when she was penniless.

Back in bed and chewing on a delicious piece of honey toast, Fleur read Rosemary's letter.

Dearest Fleur:

I might as well be completely honest. I am green with envy that you're whirling around London, from ball to musicale, from route to assembly, wearing fabulous dresses and being courted by literally dozens of handsome and titled men.

All I ask is that you save one or two for me—although I suppose I only need one, but should like to have a choice!

The image of her sister, two years younger than herself, giggling as she wrote, amused Fleur. Of all of them, Rosemary was the most carefree and perhaps the biggest romantic.

I do have a real request to make of you, Fleur, and I beg you not to repeat it to Mama or Papa who would be furious with me. Do you think I might be allowed to travel to London to attend just one of the parties? It would have to be one given at Heatherly, of course, but I promise I would return home immediately afterward. I am so curious and I get so excited just thinking about it. I have made over my daffodil yellow and it won't embarrass you. I could sleep in your room and stay out of the way and just watch at the party. Dear Fleur, I would be no trouble at all.

The letter went on and on in the same vein, leaving Fleur quite exhausted, and torn. On the one hand there was nothing she would enjoy more than having her younger sister with her for a day or so. On the other hand, the idea of making such a request of her hosts made her feel quite sick.

By day's end she would decide what to do and write her replies.

Mama's letter was so brief it left Fleur with more unanswered questions than if her mother had not written at all.

Fleur dear:
I have little doubt that Letitia will write to you about this wretched turn of affairs with the Pools. Your father is beside himself that anyone should call the worthiness of one of his beloved daughters into question. For my part, yet again the shallowness of human beings disappoints me.

I am not destroyed by all this because I believe that if love is strong enough it finds a way. In fact, I have proof that it does.

Mama referred without subtlety to the love she and Papa shared.

I wonder how determined young Christopher is. Family pressure has broken apart many a supposedly passionate love. He looks at her as if there is no other in the world, and she at him. But will he break with his father to be with Letitia, and if he does, how will he care for a wife and then children? This talk of faraway places frightens me. She has never been strong.

There are too many questions and I have no answers. And you, my pet, remember your standards and do not settle for less than a love match. The fortunes of this family do not rest on your shoulders.

Your loving Mama

Fleur pushed down inside the bed and pulled the covers over her head. Yes, the fortunes of her family absolutely did rest on her shoulders and all her fine rules might have to be tossed to the wind. Please, let her be able to marry a man she could love and who would love her, and be kind to her family.

This time the knock on her door sounded insistent.

Why, oh, why had she allowed Snowdrop to make her lock the thing? Fleur slid to the steps and the floor and went groggily to the door. "Yes?" she said.

"This is Dominic. Can you open the door?"

With a heart and stomach that executed impossible tricks, she let him in and stood back. "I'm very tired," she told him. "I was about to go back to sleep."

The only light in the room was from the candle beside her bed. Snowdrop had not opened the drapes. Dominic planted his hands on his hips and stood sideways to her as if preserving her modesty.

The fraud. Her demure nightrail covered her from neck to toe and even if he could pretend there had never been any intimacy between them, she would never forget.

"Is there some new development?" she asked.

"I was unable to find Snowdrop. Hattie thinks she's with Albert."

"Quite possibly." Did he think she didn't know he had chosen to come himself this time rather than send a maid?

"She left me a few minutes ago. Would you like me to go and look for her?"

"You're not here to search out servants," he snapped, glancing, then staring at her. "That hair is amazing. Promise me you'll never hide it in a nightcap again."

"You're here for a purpose," she said. She could not and should not promise him anything. "I know your aunts will be coming today."

"Ridiculous," he said. "As if we don't have enough to contend with already. Wait till you meet them. A hundred years old apiece if they're a day. Demanding. Opinionated. And the only possible reason they can have left Bath for London is because they can't stand not knowing what's going on here now that Hattie has joined us."

Fleur looked up at him. "Not quite a hundred, surely?"

His tense features softened a little. "Not quite. But close. And you'll have your work cut out for you. They pride themselves on championing the underdog, but not until they've given it a few swift kicks."

"Oh, dear." Fleur frowned. "Everything is becoming so complicated."

"And it will become more so. Can you dress yourself? Or should I ask for another maid? Or I could always stand outside the door and you could let me know when to come in and fasten things."

"I can dress myself," she told him promptly. "But I thought the aunts weren't coming for hours."

"They aren't." He sniffed and looked at his watch. "Franklin Best has called. He wanted to take you for lunch in Town but I told him you haven't time. He's keen on you, Fleur. I've given my permission for him to eat with you here. McGee has spoken to cook and Mrs. Skinner says she'll put on a nice luncheon in one of the garden rooms. On the other hand, I can always send him away if you don't want to see him."

"He is a nice man and I'll be glad to see him." Fleur swallowed. "He's waiting for me now?"

"Yes." Dominic bowed his head to look at her more closely. "Remember what I told you once. The lady always keeps the gentleman guessing—and waiting. Or I think I said something like that. Take your time and come down when you're ready."

"Very well." He was close and she smelled the clean scent of soap and his well-tended linen.

She doubted she would ever know what made her do it, but she stood on her toes and tweaked the ribbon undone at his nape.

He made a grab for it but she put it behind her back. "I told you I like to see you the way you were this morning. Don't ask me why. Yes, grin at me. You look irresistible and evil all at the same time."

Dominic laughed, showing his strong white teeth and driving dimples into his cheeks. And before she could prepare, he caught her by the shoulders and brought his face very close to hers. "You play with fire, Fleur. I truly believe you are a spontaneous spirit with no sense of danger, but danger exists."

She pressed her lips together and looked up at him through her lashes.

"Absolutely no sense of danger. You seem to know so much yet you know so little about the nature of men. Kiss me."

Fleur's eyes opened wide. She tried but failed to think of a witty retort, anything witty that would lessen the tension and get her out of this new pickle.

Still holding her shoulders, he pulled her closer and whispered, "Just a little kiss to help me through a difficult day?"

What could she do but scream or grant him what sounded like a simple request? She parted her lips a little and lifted her face closer to his. Dominic slowly lowered his head, his black hair falling forward to touch her skin and make it tingle.

"Kiss me," he said again, his voice low and gravelly.

Fleur stood on tiptoe until their lips met and it was the last moment in which the initiative was hers.

Dominic opened her mouth wide and plunged his tongue inside. He explored every inch of the smooth inner skin, her teeth, her lips, and he breathed so heavily, Fleur's heart pounded. The pressure of his mouth on hers forced her head from side to side and she pushed her hands into his hair, and kissed him back with all the strength she had.

Dominic swung her against a wall and framed her face with his hands, traced her cheekbones with his thumbs. He weakened her, yet he also sent a rush of strength and urgency through her.

At last he stood back, his hands still holding her shoulders to the wall, and he panted. Fleur fought to catch her own breath and stared into his eyes. They stared at one another as if each of them was afraid to look away.

"Fleur," he said, "you are the biggest problem ever to enter my life."

At least she'd made an impression on him.

"I have no idea what will come of these strange urges you bring out in me," he said.

"You seem to enjoy them," she told him. "I enjoy them myself."

He slapped the heel of a hand against his brow. "Get dressed. I'll wait outside to escort you downstairs. But, Fleur," he slid a hand around her neck and rested his mouth on her brow. "Remember this. Better to settle for nothing at all than to settle for second best. Think of the kiss we just shared when you're with Franklin Best."

"Stop it." Fleur slipped between Dominic and the door. "You laugh at my unworldliness and my rashness, but you don't question yourself. Since you are so sophisticated, why do you encourage these encounters?"

He took a step backward.

"Men like you are…are…"

"Are what?"

"You don't care what you do to a woman," Fleur told him. "I am nothing to you but a thing to be toyed with when you're bored. You think my life is not as important as yours."

She opened the door and averted her gaze from him.

"We'll continue this discussion at another time," Dominic said. "Franklin Best is waiting for you."

"I'm going home. I must. My family needs me."

"Your family needs you here and you will not let them down."

23

Another pickle.

Mr. Best seemed quite comfortable having lunch with Fleur while Hattie sat at a distance, almost obscured by a lush potted shrub, working over her embroidery.

Fleur felt ridiculous.

"The Marchioness is fortunate in her cook," Mr. Best said, cutting a bread-and-butter point with his knife and fork, adding a piece of ham, a slice of cucumber, and eating as if he and Fleur were alone.

He raised his light brown eyes to hers and smiled. Then he made a comical face and after she remembered that he sat with his back to Hattie, she giggled. She pressed her lips together, trying to remain ladylike, but Mr. Best rolled his eyes, first in one direction, then the other and she burst into chuckles.

Mr. Best laughed with her and leaned across the table. "You are a charmer, Miss Toogood, and I agree with you that ritual can become painful."

"I didn't say that," Fleur whispered.

Mr. Best whispered back, "You didn't have to. All I have to do is watch your face. You must never play cards, Miss Toogood—at least not for money. Your opponents would all know whether you had a bad or a good hand."

"My face is a problem," she said, liking him more and more. "It does whatever it wants to do. You should have seen how long I worked to perfect a frown."

He grinned. His blond hair fell over his forehead and there was no question but that he was a good-looking man with a devil-may-care manner.

"Frown for me," he said.

"I can't." She dared a glance at Hattie who didn't look up from her embroidery.

"So you didn't perfect a frown after all?" Mr. Best said. "I am disappointed."

Fleur cut her caraway cake with her fork and ate a piece. Mrs. Skinner and the rest of the servants below stairs were indeed wonderful. She set down her fork, pushed her head far forward and scowled at Mr. Best. She scowled so ferociously that her eyelids itched.

"Gad, you're incredible," Mr. Best said explosively. He laughed and choked on a piece of his food.

"Drink something," Fleur hissed, pushing a glass of wine toward him.

He drained the glass and wiped tears from the corners of his eyes.

A servant slid quietly forward to pour more wine.

Fleur lifted her teacup and felt another presence. She turned around in time to see Dominic enter the glassed-in garden room and begin a ponderous walk of its length. He passed the table without so much as a glance, although he did nod at Hattie before departing through a door to the room where the Dowager's shell collection was kept.

"How is the caraway cake?" Mr. Best asked. The humor in his eyes didn't match his straight-faced expression.

"Very good," Fleur said.

Carrying her black cat, Chloe ran from behind Fleur, and Snowdrop followed the girl. They rushed to Hattie and Chloe said loudly, "We are to replace you, Hattie. Snowdrop will pretend to do the embroidery now."

"Don't laugh," Fleur said under her breath. "Poor Hattie and Snowdrop. Chloe is awfully blunt."

"Honest, you mean," Mr. Best said. "I'm grateful Lord Dominic agreed to my seeing you. There are things I must say to you."

Hattie walked toward them, smiling wryly at Fleur. "Enjoy yourselves," she said and carried on to the hall.

Like the sensible woman she was, Snowdrop ignored the embroidery in favor of playing cat's cradle with Chloe. Raven batted a ball of yarn across the carpet, unraveling it as she went.

"Isn't this an interesting room?" Fleur asked, nervous about what Mr. Best might want to tell her. "There's a matching one on the other side of the hall but the family doesn't seem to use that. They often come in here."

"A very interesting room," Mr. Best said.

"My home in Sodbury Martyr is quite simple. The rectory, of course. It's an old house and the windows aren't well proportioned. They're so small that in winter the cost of candles becomes prohibitive."

"Miss Toogood?"

"I should love to have a room filled with plants and trees like this one," she said hurriedly. "It's very soothing."

"I find *you* soothing, Miss Toogood," Mr. Best said. "And I wish I could calm you and help you to understand that you couldn't be more important and worthwhile than you are— even if you were the wealthiest woman in the land."

He silenced her. She couldn't think of a response.

"My main reason for seeking you out today—other than a desire to see you again—was to apologize. The purpose of the party my parents held was too obvious. My fault, not theirs. I asked them to do it because I wanted you there and they agreed as they always would if they thought they could make me happy."

"I like your parents." Impulsively, Fleur put a hand on top of his on the table. "They remind me of my own. Generous and kind. You are not to apologize when I had such a good time at your home."

Mr. Best smiled. "I should be honored to visit your family one day."

"They would love to have you. Mama is an excellent hostess and Papa has a greedy appetite for good company and good minds. My sisters would probably wear you out with questions."

"If your sisters are anything like you I'll wear out graciously."

"My goodness," Fleur said, staring at him. "I've just had an idea, an absolutely wonderful idea. It's also disgraceful for me even to suggest such a thing."

"I insist that you ask me at once."

Good heavens, he would be so easy to fall in love with—for any girl but me.

"Forget I even mentioned it," she told him and her face throbbed with heat. "Please, just forget it. I do live up to my reputation for saying whatever comes into my head. Have some fruit, Mr. Best."

"Oh, no. No, no, no, you shall not get away with that. If you don't ask your question you will cast me down. I may never recover."

Fleur tapped the back of his hand. "Listen to you pile on

the guilt. You could give lessons in guilt making. All right, but I'm telling you my silly idea, nothing more. I shall go down in your estimation even more but I ask you to remember that I tried to withdraw this. My younger sister Rosemary, who is eighteen and as interested in everything as I am, wrote to ask if she could possibly come to London to attend a party. Just one was what she asked for. There, you see what an outrageous subject I had in mind."

"No, I don't." A bunch of grapes caught his attention and he put it on his plate. "You haven't told me your question."

She closed her eyes and groaned. "All right. If I can arrange for Rosemary to come here for a party, would you ask her to dance? It would have to be a party where there is dancing for that's what she likes the very best. But she gets shy in company and does not show herself well. She wants to go so badly but she will likely wish she hadn't if she does."

"Yes. I'll ask her to dance as many times as you want me to. In fact, I shall keep watch and whenever I see she is not taken, I shall see to it that she is."

"I've withdrawn the question, though, Mr. Best. It would be entirely unfair to you."

"If Rosemary comes, it will be my pleasure to pay her some attention."

Unbidden, a little truth came to Fleur. Mr. Best was too nice for her. He would be the kind of husband who got his pleasure from seeing his wife's pleasure, and never say a harsh word to her. They would never marry, but if they did, she would become bored.

How horrid she was. "Thank you for being so kind. I doubt it will happen, but if Rosemary does come I shall alert you. But you don't have to do more than dance with her once. Or perhaps twice."

He grinned and bit off a grape.

With the clearing of his throat, Dominic let them know he had arrived near the table again. He didn't pause but looked meaningfully at Fleur's hand where it rested on Mr. Best's. Once more Dominic proceeded through the long, narrow room with measured steps. He did stop to pick up Chloe and let her kiss him soundly. He kissed her back and whispered in her ear until she giggled. Then he put her down and continued on to the shell collection room.

"One wonders what Lord Dominic fears," Mr. Best said. "We are chaperoned. There are servants about."

"He takes his responsibilities seriously," Fleur said, chagrined by Dominic's behavior. "Oh, my goodness. You read the *Voice* today, you must have. That's why you thought you should apologize."

"My mother read the piece in the *Voice* to me," Mr. Best said. "First of all, I am grateful you were not badly hurt. I'm sure it was a frightening experience and Mergatroyd should be pilloried. Secondly, I want you to know that rather than detract from you, that silly Mercury woman's article will help make you even more of a success than you already are, so don't be upset by it."

"You are the nicest of men," Fleur told him and meant every word.

"And you are a delight. With luck we may become friends. But I did hope to have a chance to point something out to you, and my visit here makes me more determined to do so regardless. Of course you may choose to ignore me but I think you would do well to consider this question. Does Lord Dominic want you to find a husband? And if not, why not?"

24

"You should have asked my permission first."

"I beg your pardon?" He should have known it was a mistake to allow a woman to think of herself as his partner. "I have no reason to ask your permission to do anything, Mouse."

Without taking her eyes from him, she undid her bonnet and threw it aside, then removed her pelisse. "You seem to forget that this was my idea in the first place. You are becoming a rich man and you have me to thank for it. And don't call me Mouse. I told you that for our purposes my name is Owl."

"Cat and Mouse. Much more appropriate."

She let out an agitated sigh. "What you have done will have everyone in London watching for you. Let me remind you that we are becoming a power to be dealt with and you will need me more than you ever have. Do not make the mistake of acting without me again."

"My Mouse shows her little teeth," he said. He would have the upper hand here, always. He sat while she stood beside him, her head held high. "What I chose to reveal to the papers was part of the plan," he told her. "As long as there was any doubt about my intentions—or even the fact that I exist—they could pretend they were safe."

"Fie," she said. "Who could doubt your existence? Some say the women you took were probably making up stories to cover some indiscretion. Those people are like animals who close their eyes and assume they are invisible. I don't see how threats in the newspaper will convince anyone of anything."

He spread his arms along the back of the couch, deliberately making sure his Chinese silk robe gaped open. This woman posed as a lady but, as he already knew, her sexual enthusiasm was rivaled by few. He looked forward to an exhilarating game of cat and mouse. He laughed at his own little joke. First he would establish his superiority and her weakness, then he would toy with her.

"My plan," he told her, "is to carry out a mission in the near future and to take it to its ultimate conclusion."

"Your plan? We make these decisions together. The moment I arrived I told you that we must make sure our threats are taken seriously."

So she had, but that was beside the point. "I had already made up my mind how to proceed."

He had her attention and she was angry—just the way he liked her best. She wasn't fast enough to move out of reach when he gripped the back of her skirts and began to lift them slowly.

"Stop it! Stop it now."

"The Cat does as he pleases," he told her, gathering the material and raising it to the level of her waist. "And, as we've agreed, we have a great deal to discuss, so why not make the best of the time we have together? I can do more than one thing at a time and I'm sure you can, too"

She batted at him, wriggled, pulled. He enjoyed it when she tried to fight him off. It gave him a deep thrill, even if her ill-hidden smile belied her outrage.

With a single yank he landed her facedown across his knees and tore her silk drawers apart while she shrieked at him.

He slapped her white bottom, leaving red marks, and his Mouse reared up, her face red and eyes bright, oblivious to the way her large breasts billowed against his thighs and all but fell from her bodice.

"Hit me again and I'll—"

He slapped her several times. "And you'll love it?" Smoothing his hand between her legs and finding just the right spot to make her spread her legs wider apart excited him. "We must take our time preparing for our next adventure because it may be our last."

"Yes," she panted, reaching back to hold his hand more tightly against her while she jerked her hips. "Hurry up. Do it."

"I was talking about our next adventure to punish the ton."

"I know what you were talking about," she said. "You never said why you are angry with the ton," she said.

"And neither did you," he pointed out. "You are quick to remind me that it was your idea in the first place. What made you so angry with them?"

Evidently tired of his measured pace, his Mouse swung herself to straddle one of his thighs. "History doesn't matter. Only the future." She rubbed herself against his leg. "I want you to get rid of that boy."

Her mind couldn't stay with any subject but her own pleasure. "That won't happen," he told her.

"He creeps about and just looking at him makes me sick. All those scabs. For all you know he carries diseases."

"Harry doesn't carry any diseases." Taking her bodice and camisole in both hands, he tore them in two all the way to her belly. Now he was the one who must concentrate. "Don't mention the boy again."

"*Well, I don't like—*"

"*You have nothing to do with him. How do you feel about riding?*"

"*Don't change the subject.*" She managed to fill her eyes with tears. "*Look what you've done to my dress. How do you suppose I'll explain this?*"

"*I have faith in your ability to lie your way out of anything, my dear.*" He bounced her on his naked thigh. His sash had worked loose and the robe hung from his shoulders.

Her face turned pale and she closed her eyes, let her head hang back. "*Yes, yes,*" she murmured.

"*No, no.*" He laughed. "*I am not in a hurry today and I intend to take my time.*" He pulled the sash free, looped it around her breasts, and raised them until her puckered nipples pointed up. "*Look at that, Mouse. How many women could I do this to? Firm white mounds with cherries begging for attention.*"

She leaped away from him, inflamed him with her teasing smile and the way she touched herself. "*If you really want me you'll have to prove it.*" Her voice slid higher. "*Prove it, Mr. Cat. Make me stroke you. But first we have to concentrate on our plans.*"

He rose from the couch and advanced on her. "*I'm not sure I want to make plans first. Perhaps I want more of this instead.*" He closed his large hands over her breasts, held them like pieces of fruit and ignored her shrieks and the ineffectual flapping of her hands. She waved her hands but allowed him to squeeze her flesh, to nip and suck it, and didn't try to get away.

Her fingers took possession of him. "*The masthead is eager today,*" she told him. "*And it's still the most impressive in the land.*"

"*So you have seen every contender in the land? Congrat-*"

ulations." Breath hissed in through his teeth. She pushed him between her thighs in a parody of sex.

"Give me the sash," he told her, stopping himself from letting go and taking her, but with difficulty. "I'm going to show you something in a little while. First I have to get it ready. We can talk at the same time."

"Mmm." She pretended to consider without ceasing the rhythmic squeezing of his rod between her rounded thighs. "Well, I suppose I'll give it to you, as long as we can get our business done. I want it settled."

When she dangled the sash in the air, he took it from her, slid the coarse Chinese silk through her fingers. And while she continued to slap herself against him, he tied the first knot, then another and another.

"What are you doing with it?" she asked, and looked him in the eye. "Oh, I think I know. You are so naughty, but I may enjoy what you have in mind."

Some of it, he thought.

"I have chosen our next victim," she told him and chuckled when he removed himself from the grip of her thighs. "This time everything will be different. We will leave all the beautiful people breathless, terrified—afraid for every woman of marriageable age."

"You have decided?" he said, continuing to make knots in the long sash. "Feel that." He held out the sash and she touched one of the sharp, pointy knots he had made.

Her frown pleased him.

"This woman presents us with a rare opportunity," she said. "She is unlike all the others, and what happens to her will be unlike anything that has happened to the others."

It was her fault he couldn't wait until the discussion was finished. "Take off the rest of your clothes."

She started to wrap them around her but he spun her around and yanked the clothing away. Holding her elbows to her sides, he sank to a knee and bit her derriere.

"First we talk," she said, squirming to get away.

In response he tipped her to her back on the floor, pinned her shoulders with his calves and pushed inside her mouth. "You know what to do. No, just suck, I'll do the rest." He moved in and out and put his hands behind him to pinch her nipples. She drew up her knees and rocked them from side to side.

"Stop," he ordered, panting, on the brink. But he had always been in perfect control and he gave nothing he didn't want to give. "Come. There is so much more."

He pulled her to her feet and walked her rapidly backward. At each step she stumbled and held his arms tighter. Now he felt her fear and he grew so hard, so tight, he dragged in his gut to distract from the pain. To his delicious spiral staircase he took her and there he lay her back against the treads.

"You're hurting me," she whined. "This isn't fun anymore."

"It will be," he told her and pushed the first knot inside her, then the next.

"I don't like this."

"Who is it you really seek to punish? Not the woman, surely." Another knot entered her.

"I want to punish them both." She hitched her heels beneath her and pushed higher up the stairs, attempting to get away from him.

"Are you cold?" he asked.

"Yes. Very cold. I need to get warm or I shall take a chill and be of no use to you."

"We can't have that." Rising over her, he allowed the robe

to cover them both. "Like a desert tent," he said, grinning. "And I am some warrior who has born you away to help me with my fantasies."

"You are ill."

"And you aren't?" He positioned another knot at the entrance to her vagina and pushed it home with his rigid cock.

She screamed, but she wrapped her arms around his neck and opened her mouth to receive his tongue.

A man's job was to oblige a woman in such situations.

Slowly they ascended the stairs and slowly, thrusting harder each time, he buried the sash inside her.

Pushing up on one arm, he gathered her up and half dragged, half carried her the rest of the way. She gasped. Her head lolled back. He feasted his eyes on her ripe body and felt some slight regret that within days or weeks that body would be lifeless, but it had to be. As long as she lived she would be a threat to him.

At the top of the stairs he considered setting all of his music boxes to tinkling but decided he couldn't spare the time. Instead he pressed this woman without scruples backward over a leather chair, the chair where he sometimes came to listen to his inhuman musical chorus. He bent her so far that her hair brushed the seat.

"I can't breathe" she panted.

With the weight of her breasts lying as it did, he had no doubt breathing could be a feat. But breathe she would.

Again he penetrated her, sending the sash, wet and stiff with the essence of her sex, and of his, scraping high into her darkest places.

He hadn't expected her to turn mad on him. Slapping his face, pulling his hair, his ears, she set out to get him off her. And he only slammed into her more ferociously than he ever had with any woman.

"Calm yourself," he told her grimly. "Relax and enjoy. If you don't panic, what you're feeling can take you to paradise."

He felt the instant when her orgasm began and moved faster. "Come to me. Let me lift you. Put your legs around me and use all those lovely, strong muscles of yours."

"Yes," she all but whispered, but she did as he asked and soon, as he bucked her up and down and their cries mingled, his climax let go, flooded into her, and not a second passed before she joined him, bouncing up and down like a deranged mare mounted by a stallion.

She grew still. Cold air slid around them. Reaching his fingers inside her, he removed the sash, knot by knot, while she moaned at each fresh assault on injuries to her most tender skin.

Now he would tell her how things would be. She lay on the carpet and he covered her with his robe. "There will be three more victims. Then I shall stop."

"One more victim," she said. "This time I will help directly."

Keeping quiet stoked seething anger in him, but he clamped his teeth together.

"This one will prove to all London that we have always meant what we threatened."

We? There was no we. He could kill her now and she would never be found.

"The girl is Fleur Toogood. And I can't think of a better time than at the ball they will hold for her at Heatherly tomorrow."

"Too soon," he told her immediately.

"Tomorrow!"

This one could already be a liability, this vengeful woman who had shown no interest in the money they had received in ransoms. "You must count on the Elliots to pay her ransom. I didn't think her family had money."

"The ransom request will not go to the Elliots. We will send it to her family, just as we've done with the others."

"But if they have no money, they'll go directly to the Dowager or Lord Dominic."

She curled up on her side and rested her face on her hands. "The note will be explicit. If the ransom is not paid within twelve hours—"

"She will lose her virginity," he interrupted. "To me."

"If that's what you want." Mouse sounded huffy. "But this must happen tomorrow. I cannot wait any longer."

"It will happen when everything is carefully prepared," he told her. "If that can be tomorrow, all well and good. If not, then soon."

"Tomorrow, I say."

"That decision is mine."

She breathed hard. "The ransom note will not be received in time for the Toogoods to plead for financial help."

"Meaning?"

"They don't live in London. I have managed to get their address. By the time they get the note, it will all be over."

He expanded his chest silently. "The Granvilles will pay up."

"The instructions will not be sent to the Granvilles. They will start a search for her, of course, but they will have no notion where to look—any more than the rest have."

He shrugged. "If that's what will make you happy. You wound me. I had thought you wanted to keep me all to yourself."

"If you rape her, it is for your own satisfaction. What will

be in the letter that arrives too late and too far away, is that within twelve hours, Fleur Toogood will die. Only the twelve hours will already have passed."

25

They arrived at the top of a hill and Lawrence, standing in his stirrups, pointed ahead to what looked like a black scar in the shape of a crescent flanking the tenant cottages. "I thought you'd want to see, m'lord," he said to Dominic. "Noel De-Beaufort tells me his men have to have a temporary open space to collect soil and rocks. And he reckons that's the best spot because it doesn't interfere with livestock or crops."

Dominic had seen what he needed to see. He leaned forward and crossed his arms on his horse's neck. "It's also closer to the grounds than any other place he could choose. Helps keep his labor costs down, although I doubt we shall see the benefit of that. Regardless, these people look to us to protect their interests."

"Aye," Lawrence said. Usually his lean face showed little emotion but today Dominic could see his steward's anger. Lawrence's thick hair had turned gray at an early age and, together with his bright blue eyes, gave him a commanding presence. Dominic had seen any number of ladies look at the man with longing but Lawrence seemed wedded to his responsibilities.

"I'll deal with DeBeaufort," Dominic said. "You can tell the tenants the rubble will be moved in short order."

"It's right where the children like to play," Lawrence said. "And it's blocking light from the vegetable patches."

Dominic nodded and checked the time. "I have an appointment with Nathan now and I want to talk to Noel before the afternoon's over. And my aunts are coming."

Lawrence grinned at that.

"I see their reputation precedes them. They have not chosen a good time to pay us a visit."

"Seems to me some distraction might be just what's needed here at the moment," Lawrence said.

Dominic studied him with interest. "I suppose there's a lot of chatter about the goings-on at the house, the evident dissension?"

"Not a lot. You've a faithful staff and the people in those cottages feel safe because they're on Elliot lands. A testimony to the way you treat them, my lord."

Dominic shrugged. He believed he did what any fortunate, well-born man should do: treat all men as equals while recognizing there were often massive differences in their lots.

"Yes," Lawrence said. Sometimes the steward seemed much older than Dominic when, in fact, they were the same age. He cleared his throat and looked in Dominic's direction while avoiding meeting his eyes.

Another thorny issue was about to rear its head. Dominic could feel the tension and expected something even more worrisome to be announced. "Something is on your mind. Let's have it, man. You know you can speak your mind to me."

"Aye, I've always been able to do so but we may be about to enter a delicate phase between us."

"Wonderful," Dominic said. "Just what we need, more conflict when we have real evil abroad."

"The Cat?" Lawrence said at once. "Whatever happens, we

must stand together to overcome and capture that one and we have no time to waste."

This was the first inkling Dominic had come upon that Lawrence was at all concerned by the damnable Cat. "You're right and I'm open to any suggestions you may have."

"I'm working on the problem and hoping my enquiries will help."

"Good. Well, I'm delighted. I thought you intended to add something more to the difficulties we're already aware of. Thank you. If it becomes necessary, I'll ask for your help."

"Yes," Lawrence said. "There is another point. Jane Weller, who is so well cared for at the Dowager's house. From what she tells me, you have never met her but I assure you she is a delight. And she is both brave and sensible."

Dominic took time to organize his thoughts. He quickly overcame a notion to seek out his mother and demand to know if she was aware of Jane's acquaintance with Lawrence. But the fact remained that Jane's presence, for her own good, was supposed to be completely secret except for the knowledge of immediate family members and Lymer.

"I am aware of Jane Weller's presence in my mother's household. Before you say what's on your mind about the girl, will you reveal who it was who told you her whereabouts?"

Lawrence looked heavenward. "I wasn't told by anyone who wanted to do Jane ill and I have made sure my informant understands the details must not be mentioned again."

"And you trust… Did my mother tell you?"

"No. Little Miss Chloe did. Apparently she and Jane have become friends during the visits Chloe pays to the Dowager."

Dominic ran his hands through his hair, pushing the blowing locks away from his face. "Very well. I understand that, but what I don't understand is why Chloe felt she should talk to you about it."

Color stained Lawrence's cheeks. "Sometimes Chloe comes with me when I make my rounds. The Marchioness approves of this. One day I was at the Dower House because her ladyship wanted to discuss the condition of some windows. While I waited for her, Jane walked in—and ran out. Chloe was with me and told me about Jane."

For Dominic a battle raged between knowing and absolutely trusting Lawrence, and his own need to keep control of the situation. "You saw Jane once and now you are overwhelmed by her virtues. I don't understand. What can you really know about her under the circumstances?"

"Later the Dowager sent for me again and asked me to occasionally get Jane out for air and a break from the monotony of spending such a long time hidden in dark places with only Mrs. Lymer and occasionally the Dowager or Chloe for company. Lady Granville told me Jane had been recommended to her by a monk."

"She did, did she? I understood she needed a refuge, somewhere safe where she would not be found by certain people. But my mother completely disregarded danger and sent Jane around the countryside."

"Jane," Lawrence said, "is a reader and has a good basic knowledge of mathematics. To allow her mind to go to waste is a damn shame. I did not take her around the countryside. First I made sure she spent some time in the open air right here on the estate, then I took her to my sitting room where we talked about the things that interest her—and me. The Dowager allowed such an unconventional arrangement because she threatened me with the most terrible reprisals if I betrayed her trust." He grinned and Dominic laughed out loud.

"So," Lawrence said, "I would like to request permission to court her."

"Sounds to me as if you already are."

Lawrence sat straighter. "I assure you I have not pressed my advantage with Jane, not that she would be impressed if I had."

Dominic thought about all this. "I am not Miss Weller's father or even a relative, but I am taking responsibility for her since she is alone in London and under my mother's roof. If you think she is the woman for you, I wish you luck. But be careful. When she is with you, her life is in your hands."

"Just as Miss Toogood's life is in yours," Lawrence murmured. "But neither of us will make costly mistakes."

"No," Dominic said. "We can't."

Lawrence smiled and looked younger to Dominic than he ever had before. "I know all about Jane's abduction. And I have seen the new scar where that devil cut her. Tomorrow evening at the ball for Miss Toogood, I suggest you allow Jane to be in evidence as one of the servants, and—"

"No. What are you thinking of?" Dominic asked him. "It would put her at risk and that I will not do."

"The danger involved sickens me but Jane cannot hide forever. Until The Cat is caught he will be a threat to her. She wants to do this for herself and for others."

Dominic shook his head. "What you say is right, of course. Jane will not be free while he remains at large. But we cannot jeopardize her life."

"Do you deny that The Cat is proving clever at disguising himself?" Lawrence asked. "Not one of the women he grabbed knows what he really looks like, and we need ways to draw him out of the shadows. If Jane is recognized tomorrow as she most certainly will be, by Victoria Crewe-Burns if by no other, the word will sweep the ball. We would have to watch more closely than we have ever watched but I would be surprised if no move were made to make sure Jane is removed and silenced."

"And if a ghastly error is made and Jane really is captured again?"

"You will be watching, and Lord Nathan. I believe I can get away with being dressed as a footman since your peers do not look beyond uniforms."

Dominic knew the comment was not intended as a criticism and did not take it as one.

"There are not enough of us to make sure she doesn't slip from our sight for even an instant. Unless..." This cowardly endeavor had fostered suspicions among friends. "There are other men who would gladly help us—men whom I trust implicitly."

"For one, you could enlist McGee," Lawrence said, "And Butters. They are both men of honor who respect this family as much as they do their own."

"I hadn't thought of that, but you're right. And Albert and Snowdrop Parker, and the Marchioness. Not a careless or fearful soul among them."

"Franklin Best is beyond reproach, isn't he, m'lord?

Dominic winced but said, "Yes, of course he is. And Noel DeBeaufort is a man of honor who will not turn his back on a call for help. And Olivia Prentergast's Captain Sommerfield. I hear he is incensed by the terrible ordeal his fiancée endured and anxious to bring down The Cat."

"How about Bertie Crewe-Burns?"

"I am not sure he is ever sober enough to be serious about anything," Dominic said. "I'll ask Nathan his opinion. But you're right, we can make sure there are plenty of people keeping an eye on Jane. We shall have a great deal to do between now and tomorrow evening."

"It will be worth the effort," Lawrence said, looking across the valley again.

"Look," Dominic said. "I'll go down to see the tenants personally tomorrow. You can tell them that."

"You'll please them," Lawrence said. "They all like to see you, especially the children—and the ladies."

"Off with you," Dominic said, chuckling. He wheeled his horse around and started back down the incline they had climbed.

A curtain of gray hid the sun and a blustery wind blew.

Damn Noel for his cheek. His art must go before the comfort of others. Even the clients' wishes were to take second place to the man's decisions.

"Speak of the devil," he said under his breath. Riding at him from the direction of the rock gardens which had become twice as large as Dominic had expected, Noel DeBeaufort waved an arm. The wind tossed his curly hair and by the time he reached him, Dominic saw the healthy ruddiness whipped into the man's tanned face.

Noel's horse danced, as undisciplined as his master. "I know where you've come from," Noel said. "The Marquis instructed me to get the job done as soon as possible so I chose the only reasonable space to use during construction. It won't take so very long, then the area will be cleared again."

"When the grass is all dead and the children are left with mud to play in?"

"Well." Noel seemed to encourage his mount's high spirits. "At least they'll have the spot back. New grass will grow eventually."

Dominic grew angry. "Eventually? When will that be—

when there are no children to trample the area, and drive their overworked mothers mad with extra dirt and laundry?"

Noel quieted his animal and sat back in the saddle. He spread his hands on very solid thighs. "You're an odd one sometimes, Dominic. The land is yours to do with as you like. Why do you concern yourself with what your tenants think?"

"You're right. The land does belong to us and we decide what will be done here. As my brother's advocate, I choose to respect those who make their living here. Have your men move the mound to a fallow field."

"But—"

"Have them start today. They should do nothing more in the grounds until they have cleared the debris from any area close to our tenants' homes."

Noel stared at him, his dark brown eyes speculative rather than annoyed. Finally he smiled and said, "I'll get them right on it."

"Are you planning to attend our ball tomorrow evening?" Dominic asked.

Noel's smile became a grin. "You think I might miss a ball at Heatherly, particularly a ball in honor of the delectable Miss Toogood?"

"How could I have been so foolish," Dominic responded lightly, although he detested Noel's interest in Fleur. But then he didn't truly like any man's interest in her. "Good—do you think I could enlist your help with a matter of some delicacy?"

Noel was aware of The Cat, and of the recent threatening material printed in the paper. He didn't know anything of Jane Weller but did agree, instantly, to join the small army of watchers at the ball. "There must be an understanding about how we proceed if something does happen," he said.

"Go directly toward Jane," Dominic said. "Don't let anyone get in your way and don't take your eyes off her. I will inform the others. Whatever happens she must not be removed from the ballroom."

"Very well," Noel said. "We shall prevail." And he rode off.

This had already been a long, tense day. Dominic turned his horse and went in the direction of the stables. Next came an appointment with Nathan. Then he must find a way to convince Fleur that his close watch over her was appropriate given the uncertain times.

He heard the pound of more hoofs and Nathan met him by the trees that separated the ornamental gardens from the rest of the property.

"Thought I'd better come catch up with you or there'll be no time to talk before the aunts get here," Nathan said. "They'll be determined to arrive before sunset and that means within a couple of hours."

Dominic nodded. His brother was right.

"They aren't so bad," Nathan said. "I like to see them with Mother. She behaves like the senior sister rather than being younger by so many years."

"At any other time I'd be delighted to have them," Dominic told him. He gave Nathan a rapid sketch of the conversations he'd had with both Lawrence and Noel."

"Old Lawrence in love, hmm?" Nathan said. "The only time I saw the girl was when you had me rush her away from the house. You made a wretched fool out of me. But—" he held up a hand to stop Dominic from breaking in "—she is a most wholesome young woman. Perhaps a little too serious but pleasant and with intelligent eyes. Actually, she's quite attractive."

Dominic didn't have time to discuss Jane Weller's finer points. "I'm glad you approve of Lawrence's taste. And you understand what we will all expect of one another tomorrow?"

"I understand. I also question the wisdom of putting one young woman in danger, but I will do my part—you can rely on me."

"I know," Dominic said and slapped his brother's back. "Now to the other."

"How foolish of me to hope you'd forgotten."

Dominic riffled the short, coarse hair on his horse's neck. "Fleur respects and admires you," he said.

"I always knew she was a woman with impeccable taste."

His brother's flippancy irritated Dominic. He looked away.

"Sorry," Nathan said. "But if you don't understand my undisciplined tongue by now, you never will. I hold Fleur in high regard."

"Do you?" Dominic looked at Nathan sharply. He almost felt ill. "I have seen how she defers to you and laughs with you—and how she never says an ill word about you. I also know about the flowers you took to her room after the three of us had exchanged words."

Nathan turned the full force of his narrowed green eyes on him. "Who told you about those?"

"I wasn't told. I saw them—that night you came storming into Fleur's room ready to accuse me of ravishing her."

"Ah," Nathan said, "that night. The one when you went storming to Fleur's room to accuse *me* of ravishing her."

"Don't try to distract me. You gave her flowers. I don't recall another recent occasion on which you did such a thing for a woman, or any other occasion, come to that. Can you blame me for making assumptions?"

"No."

Dominic waited, but Nathan didn't add more.

"She's really lovely," Dominic said. "Inside and out. Her father has seen to it that she is educated and she is self-possessed enough to be quite at ease in any company. She admires you and you admire her. She needs a husband and although you don't seem to think so, you need a wife. Let me promote a match between you."

Nathan looked at him direct. "The job Mother gave you is arduous. You want it over with. If I courted and married Fleur it would answer your prayers."

What would Nathan ever know about his prayers?

"Dominic, I think you care for Fleur yourself. Your behavior when any other man attempts to show her attention is almost an embarrassment to the rest of us."

"No such thing." Dominic scowled at him. "You are making excuses for yourself to take as long a time as possible to do what you know you want to do."

"Why not court her yourself?" Nathan said. "You're right when you say she's lovely, but I could not be equal to her needs."

"Aha." Dominic pointed at him. "She has shown you her list, hasn't she? That means she is serious about you."

"List? Fleur has shown me no list. Why should she?"

Dominic let the air out of his lungs where he realized he'd been holding it. "Forget I mentioned it. Ask Fleur about her list and I'm sure she'll be glad to share it with you."

"I admit to being enamored of Fleur, but I also know that you are in love with her. There, I shall not beat about the bush again. You love her and I don't know why you don't pursue her. Why, Dominic, tell me?"

The light grew noticeably more dim and the air cooler. Dominic didn't want to speak of his feelings to anyone, not even Nathan, but he supposed he owed him some measure of the truth. "Brother Juste spoke with Jane earlier in the week—in the chapel once more. And this time I knew more so that I could ask better questions and receive more useful answers. I have also spent time on and around St. James Street. My concern has been that the boy, Harry, might have told his vicious friend about a monk who came to the lad's aid. I deliberately revealed myself to see if I encountered trouble. I didn't, which makes me believe Harry didn't mention the two men who came to his aid."

"You haven't said a word about this," Nathan said. "How do you think that makes me feel?"

"If I had told you, you would have insisted on coming and that could have made my job more difficult."

"Really?" Nathan said, in his most sarcastic tones. "That's all very interesting. We were talking about you and Fleur."

"Not only do I intend to continue my investigative work, but I have spoken with Brother Cadwin who arranged for me to visit the Abbot at the Brown Monastery. I am considering entering the order."

Nathan caught Dominic's arm. "Bloody coward," he shouted. "Now I have all the proof I need that you love Fleur as you could never love another. And your feelings for her frighten you. You, a passionate man who has loved and lost before. Oh, not a woman you had declared for, but at least one you intended to make your wife eventually. So now you try to close your heart away inside a brown habit. Very well, try, but I shall dedicate myself to tripping you at every turn."

The words, the ferocious onslaught from his brother, shook Dominic. "You're wrong about being in love before. If you mean my affection for Lady Vivian Simpson, well, that was something between people who were young and immature. I have never pined for her."

"Regardless," Nathan said. "I shall not accept this vocation nonsense. Not from you, not ever."

Dominic couldn't continue the argument. He no longer knew his own mind and the feeling was unfamiliar.

"Is that our mother?" Nathan said, moving his head to look through the trees. "Yes, it is. Running this way and that and, if I were a betting man, I'd say she's looking for us."

Dominic scrubbed at his face. "Why do you think she may be looking for us?"

"The *aunts*," they said together.

26

The Dowager Marchioness elbowed Dominic from one side, and Hattie poked him from the other.

"Rearrange that dreadful face," the Dowager said before checking Nathan's expression. "And you, my boy, can do better than that. Remember how excited Chloe is to have my sisters here. And Hattie has looked forward to seeing them, as have I."

Fleur, caught up in the middle of the family and their remarks, leaned to see Hattie's face and couldn't have said that she looked particularly ecstatic.

Catching Fleur's eye, Hattie said, "As you saw when they arrived, they're amazing ladies. Audacious, and they say whatever they please. The only reason I'm apprehensive today is because there is good reason to be anxious, afraid even—which will pass, of course," she finished hurriedly.

They had met the two ancient sisters, Miss Enid and Miss Prunella Worth, when they arrived with their ladies' maid, Mrs. Gimblet, and now the family waited in the salon to be summoned for an audience in the ladies' boudoir.

McGee presented himself and Mrs. Skinner put in an all but unprecedented appearance.

"I hope you will forgive this intrusion," McGee said. "Mrs.

Chambers suggested we make sure you approve of what Mrs. Skinner is preparing for the Misses Worth and that there is nothing you would care to add."

"Mrs. Gimblet did pass a bag to me on 'er way in," Mrs. Skinner said. "A bag of roots."

Hattie chuckled but controlled herself quickly. "For root tea. The aunts' gentlemen friends swear by it and believe that both the aunts and themselves owe their extraordinary vigor to the brew."

Mrs. Skinner hmphed and said, "It's being prepared as ordered. I might mention that from the quantity of roots, the ladies aren't planning to go 'ome soon."

Fleur observed the way the Dowager refused to make eye contact with any other family member, while they made a variety of faces at each other. In her experience, very old ladies didn't usually have gentlemen friends with whom they shared "brews" to increase their vigor.

"A large variety of cakes will be taken up when the ladies are ready," Mrs. Skinner said, holding her ample figure very upright. "They said they wanted *only* cakes since they don't want to spoil their dinners."

"I thought they would want to stay in their rooms and rest this evening," Hattie said, and looked pained. "After we spend a little time with them, of course. But we'll be eating anyway and I'm sure they'll enliven the meal."

"I'm sure they will," Nathan said, giving his sister-in-law a smile Fleur was certain he intended to be reassuring. The result was a lopsided effort that quickly melted away.

"Miss Prunella Worth wishes me to tell you that the audience in their rooms will be limited to fifteen minutes, although Miss Chloe and Raven may stay as long as they like." McGee delivered the instruction in agonized tones, probably because he felt embarrassed to be caught in the middle of such a pickle, Fleur thought. "I'm sure you know Miss Chloe and her cat are already with the ladies," he said.

"Yes," Hattie said, rather stiffly.

"Miss Prunella is also pleased with most of the dinner menu," Mrs. Skinner said. "Particularly with the lamb cutlets which she 'opes will be tender. The green goose delights Miss Enid who said the food at Worth 'ouse in Bath depends on the humor of the cook—a Mrs. Whipple, I believe—and that she 'opes the same is not the case 'ere."

"Oh, dear," the Dowager said.

McGee said, "We have everything in hand, milady. The turbot required by Miss Enid and the lobster Miss Prunella must have will be served. Also the plover eggs in aspic. Fortunately we were able to obtain what we need quite quickly. Do you have any further instructions, Lady Granville?"

"Mrs. Skinner, is there time for you to make a treacle pudding? The Marquis's aunts are particularly fond of that."

Mrs. Skinner bobbed. "Yes, milady."

"And—" Hattie considered before saying "—strawberry syllabub always goes down well."

"Yes, milady." Skinner actually smiled. "We make sure we always have some of those now."

"And some cheese-and-egg pies. Not a soul in the land makes those the way you do."

"Of course, milady." Mrs. Skinner's even broader smile transformed her. When she and McGee finally left the salon her cap flapped up and down on her graying hair, so enthusiastic was her walk.

"*Well,*" the Dowager said the instant the doors had closed. "Such demands and rudeness toward their hosts. You have been with my sisters most recently, Hattie. Are they much changed?"

"They are exactly the same as when I first met them."

Nathan said, "In *all* ways, d'you think, Hattie?" and reclined on one of the couches.

Hattie ignored him. "I wonder how long it will be before they send for us."

"Pah." The Dowager, renowned for her gentle nature, her easy charm, scowled as Fleur had never seen her scowl. "I shall give them a few more minutes then send McGee to say we'll see them at dinner. Such nonsense. Age is no excuse."

She wore her favorite tangerine color today and looked lovely, although her manner suggested she might leave for the Dower House at any moment. "I was an afterthought to my parents, you know. Your father, boys, considered himself a great wit when he called me an accident. A shock might have been closer. There are twenty-five years between Enid and Prunella—and me. Naturally enough my sisters have thought of me more as their child than their sibling. It's time to teach them the order of things."

"Bravo, Mother," Nathan said.

"What's the matter with you, Fleur?" Dominic asked. Dressed for riding, his tall boots shining, he shifted to the edge of his seat and rested his forearms on his thighs. "Speak up, now. What's happened? Are you ill?"

Mesmerized by all the unexpected attention, Fleur took a moment to remember herself. "Oh!" She lifted her brows and blinked several times, then she rubbed the space between her eyebrows. "The Dowager Marchioness had such a magnificent frown. I suppose I must have been trying to copy it."

All the strain in the room evaporated and they laughed together. Fleur noted that Nathan laughed the loudest while Dominic looked at her as if he thought her amazing in the best possible way. He confused her.

"You, Miss Toogood," the Dowager said, "are spontaneous in the most charming manner. Unaffected. A prize. How blessed will be the man who becomes your husband."

Fleur could only lower her eyes and blush but she heard both men say, "Here, here." Now her discombobulation was complete.

"It's bound to be a little while before we're called," Hattie said. "After all, the *large quantity of cakes* must be carried from the kitchens all the way to the aunts' rooms." She turned to Fleur. "Their rooms are close to yours. Just two doors down on the opposite side of the corridor."

"Lucky Fleur," Dominic said. He appeared to be counting and recounting the pieces of furniture in the salon.

The sound of many feet on stone tiles came from the hall. By the time what must be the entourage of cake bearers started up the stairs, the noise resembled muted thunder.

"All that for two women," Nathan remarked. "Two really old women."

Fleur had been quite taken with the imperious ladies, one tall and one short and both with eyes that missed nothing. "The old hold a treasure in memories," she said, looking at Nathan but quite happy with the notion that the entire gathering could hear. "They are our link to history and if cakes are what it takes to keep them alive and sharp, then give them all the cakes they want, say…I. That is…there are cultures that revere…their…old, because…"

"A young philosopher," Dominic said, but when she looked at him, resigned to her own brilliant cheeks, he showed no amusement. With his eyes narrowed and turned black by the shadow of his thick lashes, he ran the tip of his tongue along the edges of his upper teeth. He regarded her like a large animal eyeing a potentially filling meal and she shivered.

"My son, the cynic," the Dowager said quietly, as if she'd been deciding whether or not to comment. "You would do well to study Fleur's generous spirit and see if you can't find something similar in yourself. Or—" she framed her mouth with her forefingers "—could it be that you know you have a great gentleness within you and it makes you feel vulnerable?"

Dominic seemed about to protest his mother's assessment but he stopped and his expression grew distant. "I don't think *gentle* is the word I'd use. But I respect Fleur and her regard for all people. She is not like any other female of her age I have met. How fortunate we are that you have such good taste, Mother, and that you showed your own generosity in bringing her here. We are all blessed to know her and take part in launching her."

Fleur felt her blood drain to her feet. Such a speech from Dominic overwhelmed her and she couldn't look at him.

"I heartily agree," Nathan said.

"Wait till John learns that his brothers have developed such good taste," Hattie added and she, too, didn't smile.

Fleur gathered her wits and said, "Other than my own, you are the most special family I have ever met. However, do not take me for a fool to be fobbed off with pretty words and fine speeches, Dominic—and Nathan. You are rogues, or I am much mistaken."

The Dowager smiled delightedly.

"I feel peaceful," Hattie said suddenly. "I'm grateful. I need to relax now."

Fleur looked at her sharply and so did the Dowager. Then they looked at each other and a possibility dawned. Hattie existed almost entirely on strawberry syllabub these days, and the egg-and-cheese pie she had complimented Mrs. Skinner on. And now she admitted she needed to relax. The Dowager's eyes filled will tears and she quickly looked away. Fleur felt an extraordinary welling of happiness and anticipation.

"I'm going to see the aunts, and to dinner, dressed exactly as I am," Dominic said.

Dominic looked too handsome and powerful to be allowed in public at all, or so Fleur decided.

She realized his announcement had been for his mother's ears. He was testing her.

The Dowager got up and shocked them all by going to pour herself a sherry. She turned and said, "Hattie, Fleur?" With the decanter still raised. Fleur felt daring and said, "Yes, please." Hattie declined.

This time the Dowager sat beside Fleur and they both sipped their drinks. Warmth flooded Fleur's veins and she felt quite deliciously giddy.

The Dowager arranged her flowing yards of silk in graceful folds and said, "I believe I shall spend the rest of the evening as I am, too. You, Fleur, look marvelous, as does Hattie. We would be well dressed wherever we went."

"That's a relief," Nathan said.

"I don't recall mentioning you," the Dowager said, then smiled. "You never appear less than devastatingly handsome, you wicked boy. Now, what on earth is keeping Prunella and Enid?"

As if she had rung a bell, there came the rapid return of footsteps, accompanied by chitter-chatter loud enough, Fleur thought, to be heard throughout a goodly portion of the house. "Not above stairs," McGee's voice rose clearly over the din. "Return to the kitchens in a quick and orderly fashion. I will be down to speak to you shortly."

It took some minutes for the footsteps to fade away. At that point there was another tap on the salon doors and McGee slipped quietly inside. His brows rose like question marks and his mustache turned severely down. Every bone in his face was white from the rigid way he held his features.

"What is it, man?" Dominic asked.

McGee put his hands behind his back and bowed. Fleur saw him trying to soften his expression. "There's nothing to be concerned about. There's been a small change in plans, is all. The Misses Worth have decided to take their tea and cakes alone—with Miss Chloe of course. And the cat. They want me to tell you that they will arrive for dinner in approximately an hour and a half and that they hope you will all be ready to answer the considerable number of questions they have for you."

"Gawd," Nathan said. "The bloody Inquisition."

"Language!" Dominic said sharply and Nathan mumbled an apology. "They just don't change, not really. Very well, an hour and a half. We will be there to eat our dinner and if they aren't prompt they'll be left eating theirs alone."

"Dominic!" Fleur said recklessly. "They are your elders."

"And you are my younger. Watch your tongue."

She started to get up but the Dowager eased her down again. "Calm down. All of you. I shall take some time for reflection right here. The rest of you, why not go to your rooms for some peace and meditation—and prayer that we will manage to navigate this dinner with the minimum of unpleasantness."

McGee shifted from foot to foot.

The Dowager looked at him. "McGee, is there more?"

"I think I should speak to Lord Nathan and Lord Dominic alone," he said, casting beseeching looks at the brothers.

"Is this about my sisters?" the Dowager asked. "If so, it is to me that you should speak."

"Right here?" McGee asked.

"Just so. We are a family here." She glanced at Fleur. "You, too."

"Very well. Miss Prunella Worth requested a conversation with me in private, to ask me a favor. Miss Enid was also present." He flipped the tails of his coat. "You're sure you want to discuss this now?"

"Absolutely," said the Dowager.

"I expect the gentlemen will be the only ones who understand what I'm going to say anyway."

Fleur caught Hattie's smirk and felt she might pop with curiosity.

"Oh, you don't think…" Nathan pulled himself to his feet and went to whisper with Dominic. The pair of them slapped shoulders and laughed.

"McGee," the Dowager said, casting disgusted glances at her two younger sons, "please proceed. Too much is being made of this, whatever is it."

"The ladies are enquiring about gaining entrance to Gentleman Jackson's Rooms." McGee spoke in a clear, determined voice. "Apparently they have a great interest in pugilism, pugilism and placing bets on the same. I should like your direction in this matter."

The Dowager's eyes grew wide and she said, "You must be mistaken."

"Not so, Mother," Dominic said, and Fleur was pleased he had the sense to put on a serious face. "But I consider this interest harmless and try to remember that we stay young by having hobbies."

"Hobbies?" the Dowager said weakly. "Gambling on men fighting each other?"

"At least they don't invite the victors to their rooms like—"

Nathan was drowned out by the rest and Dominic pretended to take him by the throat and shake him.

"Shame on you, Nathan," Hattie said, the corners of her mouth twitching.

"Ahem," McGee said. "Could you please advise me? And I should mention that the ladies are hoping to view a private match. Arranged so they may watch alone."

"They were wrong to burden you," Dominic said. "Forget their request, please. If they should mention these things again, come to me direct."

McGee regarded his employers with apprehension and hurried toward the door. He was about to allow the doors to swing shut when he said, "Please don't let them know I mentioned what they said." He stepped into the hall only to return.

"I forgot. Dinner is in the scarlet dining room. The ladies requested that I tell you to dress accordingly."

27

Dominic kept his voice down. "I should like you to come with me tonight. We should have plenty of time to examine the area around St. James Street again." He had pulled Nathan into the orangeries and to a spot near the north doors where they had a good view of the entire area—or would have if it hadn't been full of shadows. At least anyone approaching them would be revealed.

"I'll be ready," Nathan said. "If we leave immediately after dinner, I'll take a hack and wait in Roman Lane. No, we can go together. You won't need a disguise this evening?"

"Both of us need it tonight. Brother Cadwin brought a habit for you so I have no need to go after any of the ones I have hidden about. If you and I go as we are, we could well be picked out no matter how late we may be on St. James Street or how in their cups most of the people abroad are."

Nathan's "Um-hm" didn't sound enthusiastic.

"Regardless of my experience when I went alone, Harry may have mentioned us to The Cat, Nathan. The boy doesn't know who we are but if he sees you with a monk again, rather than just two monks hurrying on their way, he could make our lives more difficult."

Nathan caught him by the arm. "Look at me," he demanded. "I fully understand your point about this evening. Whatever you want me to do—within reason—I will do. But you do not have my support in this ridiculous talk about entering the monastery. Escaping to the monastery would be closer to the truth and that is the wrong reason to go."

"Thank you for your opinion," Dominic said. "Now is a good time to speak of tomorrow when the stakes will be very high. I hope there will be no necessity to rush away from the ball. There should not be if everyone does as they've promised to do. But in truth, I expect to go after the man and to catch him."

"I am concerned for Jane Weller's safety," Nathan said.

"You think I'm not? This malignant coward of a man has done more than enough damage. I will keep Jane safe, but I shall be watching to see if there's an attempt to get her away by a particular door, and act accordingly."

"Then I'll have horses waiting," Nathan said.

"I believe I know where The Cat lives and does his deeds."

"What?" Nathan stood in front of Dominic, looked him in the face. "Why didn't you tell me? How do you know this?"

"I was lucky. I saw Harry again and went after him. Tonight I'll show you the route he took. You'll be surprised. Now, let's separate and get a few quiet minutes before dinner."

"Dinner," Nathan said through his teeth. "How many more irritations can be tossed our way when we have no time for them?"

Dominic waited for Nathan to leave the orangeries and sat on a stone bench beneath the spreading limbs of a tree with night-scented blossoms.

The abbot had expressed some of the same reservations as Nathan. A deeply spiritual man, the monk had asked Dominic to think and to pray before he made a final decision. The man had said that since Dominic's cases were taken on to relieve hardship and to protect the innocent, he could continue with his investigative work from the monastery. There would be tasks to perform while he was there but once they were finished each day he would be free to come and go as he pleased.

But was it what he wanted?

Rapid, light footsteps, the scuff of slippers, alerted him to someone's approach and he sat quite still with his face down and his arms crossed so his hands were beneath his arms. He should not be seen unless the newcomer held a candle aloft.

No candlelight revealed him, but the swish of skirts and soft sound of slippers came straight in his direction. Resigned, he looked up in time to see Fleur arrive. She sat beside him. He felt her tremble and she slipped her hands around his upper arm. She leaned close to his side.

"It's all right," he said. "Just dark, that's all. Why didn't you bring a candle?"

"For the same reason as you. I was here when you and Nathan arrived, sitting on the other side of the rock river. I wasn't at all afraid until I heard the two of you."

Damn it. He stared ahead into the gathering darkness. "Didn't your parents tell you it's wrong to eavesdrop?" Even as he chastised her, he rubbed her cold fingers. "If you don't listen to other people's conversation, you don't hear things you're not supposed to hear, things that may frighten you."

She clung to him tighter. "Please don't go out there tonight, Dominic. Don't go after that Cat person. He has declared that he intends to kill people and I don't suppose he'd mind if one of them was a man. Please."

This was what scared him, this dependence when he didn't know if he was capable of being what a woman needed—outside the bedroom. "Don't concern yourself with me, please. Attend to your own affairs." Her pleading, her obvious concern for him, did other things to him. He felt violently protective of her and touched that she cared about him.

"You have become my affair."

Surely she knew how reckless she was. "Promise you won't repeat a word of what you heard here," he said. "You would do no good and you might cause a great deal of harm."

"I would never do something to harm you. And no matter how harshly you speak to me, you cannot make me stop caring about you," Fleur said.

"Be cautious," he told her, and his heart beat too fast. "Such declarations of affection can leave you feeling foolish and vulnerable. I don't wish that on you, not until you find the man you want to spend your life with."

Fleur didn't answer.

"I want you to look forward to your ball. It will be beautiful. Wait until you see all the preparations. They'll start early in the morning."

"Who is Jane Weller? I know a little about her but not the whole truth."

"She is someone you have no need to know. It would be dangerous for you to as much as mention her. Dangerous for her and for you. Do you understand?" Best not to tell Fleur she knew almost as much about Jane as he did.

She didn't speak, but she turned on the bench and took his face in both of her hands. In the gloom he could still see the radiance of her eyes. She got up and bent over to place a light kiss on his brow, then kissed his cheekbone, his jaw, the corner of his mouth and, finally, his neck. Fleur slid her hands over his shoulders and held her face in the crook of his neck.

"Fleur—"

"No. Don't say anything. Thank you for all you've done for me. I'd better go now."

Fleur entered the hall and Hattie pulled her aside. "We have to be strong for the men," she said. "Mother may have a few acid words for her sisters about their earlier behavior, but if the ladies become difficult, the men will only contain themselves for so long before we get some total disaster."

Fleur blinked several times, fast. "Disaster? What kind of disaster?" Her stomach felt jumpy. Surely Dominic and Nathan wouldn't resort to some sort of violence. "Might they, well…throw something?"

"No." Hattie shook her head and frowned. "But they could do something intended to be funny and to divert attention from whatever annoyance the aunts may cause."

"How can we help?" Fleur said. "I don't know what to expect."

Hattie patted Fleur's hand. "I have been through what Nathan called 'the Inquisition.' I will do my best to lead you, and to head off the aunts' questions about you. But I need you to help me deal with Dominic and Nathan who—if they remain true to their history—are likely to make this dinner a misery."

Fleur had long ago decided that people like the Granvilles led very complicated lives. "I will do my best."

Hattie pressed her hands to her bosom. "They have been known to burst into song. Rude song."

Fleur drew in a sharp breath. "Whatever should we do about that? Anything I can think of would only add to the confusion."

"Pretending to faint might help." Hattie bit her bottom lip and Fleur had a suspicion the Marchioness was containing laughter rather than tears.

She could play along with the game, although she would have preferred a serious plan just in case they needed one.

"I mean it," Hattie said, bringing her mouth close to Fleur's ear. "And it will have to be you who swoons. I would happily do it but there are reasons I shouldn't—not until after John gets home, anyway. I promise I'll explain later."

"Mmm." Fleur felt like smiling now. Hattie must definitely be increasing but she thought her secret was still safe and wanted her husband to be the first to know. Or something like that.

"I don't know how Nathan does with a swoon," Hattie said. "I know Dominic is splendid, very gallant and caring. I'm sure he'll forget all about singing in his rush to rescue you."

"Mmm." She wished she need not think about Dominic and she certainly didn't want to look at him across a dinner table. And as for having him pick her up in his arms and…carry her… "I do believe I could manage to swoon if I had to."

"That's the spirit," Hattie whispered and patted her back strongly. "We'll manage."

At that precise moment, the gentleman in question appeared. Fleur decided he had remained in the orangeries until the last possible moment.

"Hello, Hattie," he said and met Fleur's eyes. "Fleur."

He would enter a monastery. Because he was moved by religious fervor? Or because he wanted to escape the expectations his family and the world placed upon him? Did Lord Dominic Granville fear the responsibility of a wife and children of his own so much that he would withdraw completely?

"Look at all this," he said. "Enough servants scurrying around to throw a party for all London."

"This is a big event for the aunts," Hattie said. "I can't remember the last time they went out—that I was aware of."

Dominic snorted. "It is all the times you aren't aware of that should concern us. Mother is spoiling them—and catering to their whims. Old bats."

"Dominic," Hattie cried but her grin ruined the shocked tone of voice.

Fleur stepped out of the way to allow a string of maids to pass, their starched aprons crackling, and she felt Dominic watching her.

Footmen wearing light-blue-and-silver livery stepped out smartly. Buckles shone on their shoes.

"Where is Mother?" Dominic sounded furious. "And Nathan. Hell and damnation—I beg your pardon—why is it that we are here and Nathan is not?"

"I'll ask him when he arrives," Hattie said, all innocence. "I thought your mother was in the salon but she isn't."

"Hell and—yes, well, I suppose we can't expect those we trust most to back us up at such times. Is your family close-knit, Fleur? Do they rally round in times of trouble?"

"They do," she told him promptly. "But dinner with some relatives wouldn't be considered a time of trouble at the rectory."

"We'd best change the subject," Hattie said quickly.

Dominic took out his watch and held it in a palm. "It is ten minutes past time. In we go—after all, someone must be first."

"You mean you want to go directly to the dining room?" Hattie asked. "Surely we should wait in the salon and behave as if nothing's amiss. For the sake of peace?"

"I'm going into dinner," Dominic said. "You may come with me or continue to hover somewhere."

Fleur looked at Hattie, who said, "Let's not hover."

The scarlet dining room was reached through the salon. Dominic offered each lady an arm and strode toward closed doors where flunkies stood at attention. Dominic turned his head to look down at Fleur and the unreadable, unblinking quality of his stare excited her—and sent shivers down her back.

The flunkies saw Dominic with his two companions scurrying—unceremoniously—to keep up, and threw open the doors.

A lustrously shining table stretched before them. Flowers in highly polished silver bowls and tiered dishes of sugared fruit were bright splashes of color and silverware shone by the light of a hundred candles in the crystal chandelier.

Seated between the Misses Worth, Nathan got up at once. Fleur had never cared for smirks, but Nathan smirked then turned up one corner of his mouth. "Better late than never," he said cheerfully. "Aunt Prunella and Aunt Enid couldn't wait any longer for their dinner."

"And neither could I," the Dowager said, but her eyes smiled. She sat opposite Miss Enid.

"Nor I," Nathan said rapidly.

"Traitor," Dominic murmured, for Fleur and Hattie's ears only. "He's enjoying this. But he won't for long."

"Let it go," Hattie whispered and took a seat beside her mother-in-law and opposite Nathan. "Take the head of the table, please, Dominic, and, Fleur, you sit next to me."

Which meant Dominic was to Fleur's left and she felt completely out of place.

"Good evening, Aunts," Dominic said. "I trust you're both somewhat rested now."

Miss Prunella Worth, a tall, ample lady with white hair and

whiter skin, bent close to her soup plate and said, "Do you see anything in it, Enid?" A puff of bright pink rouge decorated each cheek and lights bounced from the lenses of her pince-nez.

"I'm not sure," Miss Enid said, patting the soup with the back of her spoon.

Her voice reminded Fleur of someone doing a duck imitation. Small and very brown, Miss Enid's bright eyes looked out from a web of wrinkles. No rouge there. She looked at Dominic and said, "You are very late for dinner, young man."

"What's that?" Miss Prunella's spoon landed in her plate with splat, sending thick little waves across the surface of her soup. "Got it!" A quick swipe of her napkin over the spoon and she continued eating.

They aren't well. How can the family get cross with two old ladies who aren't quite themselves anymore? Fleur's soup was served, and Dominic's and Hattie's. And still the old ladies kept their faces bowed.

"You must be very tired from your long journey," Fleur said. "I know my grandmother tires very easily now."

"Your *grandmother?*" Miss Prunella raised her face to give Fleur the blinding impact of the pince-nez lenses. "No doubt she does, poor thing. She must be quite ancient and, of course, she's had *children.*"

Dominic leaned in Fleur's direction and whispered. "Good going. Now you've done it."

He got a prompt smack to the back of the hand from Miss Prunella. "Don't whisper in company. Henrietta, you poor dear, that husband of yours had no right to die so young and leave you to bring up these brutish sons."

"Brutish?" Nathan said. "*Brutish,* Auntie Pru? And I thought you doted on us."

"That is the first and the last time you will be disrespectful to my sister," Miss Enid said. "Henrietta, I assure you we had no idea how rebellious the boys had become. In Bath they behave quite well."

"How has the weather been in Bath?" the Dowager asked, all serene oblivion. And, Fleur thought, very clever to turn the conversation in a new direction.

"It's probably the fine weather that settles the boys down there," Miss Enid honked, not to be diverted. "And I'm sure the sulphur from the baths gets into the air and has some sort of calming quality."

"The baths and the bloody water are foul," Nathan said. "But I do think that since they're so convenient to Worth House, you two should take advantage of them. I'm sure you could get Mrs. Gimblet and Boggs to wheel you down there."

A dreadful silence followed until Miss Prunella said, "Do you think we don't know when we're being goaded, Nathan? We have no need to be *wheeled* anywhere. You know perfectly well how we detest even the thought of those filthy baths. Henrietta, can't you—"

"Yes, I know," the Dowager said. "I've always felt exactly the same about the baths. Nathan, dear, eat your soup or it will be cold."

"It's already cold," Nathan told his mother.

"Henrietta!" Miss Enid's voice silenced everyone. "Before I forget, how is your painting progressing?"

The Dowager didn't look happy. "Well, thank you."

"Prunella and I are looking forward to seeing your little efforts. What is it you paint?"

"I don't talk about it," the Dowager said, her face stony.

"Come on, Mother," Nathan said, apparently oblivious to

the danger he invited. "We know all about the fruit and vegetables that come fresh to the Dower House each day. And the flowers. I'm sure you paint very pretty pictures and I agree with the aunts, it's time you shared them with us."

"Is it?" the Dowager said. "Is there nothing you prefer to keep to yourself, Nathan? I am not a woman who cares to make a spectacle."

Nathan cleared his throat and looked at his empty plate, which was quickly removed and replaced with a tiny dish of water ice to clear his palate.

"Miss Toogood," Miss Prunella said, "who are your people?"

"Blast," Dominic muttered. "Here we go."

Fleur supposed this must be how the Inquisition began. "My parents are Reverend and Mrs. Toogood of Sodbury Martyr in the Cotswold Hills. I have four sisters. Letitia is older than I, Rosemary, Zinnia and Sophie are younger. We do not have a great deal of extended family although the grandmother I mentioned, my papa's mother, has played a significant part in our lives and we love her very much."

"A country parson's daughter," Miss Enid said. "On the hunt for a fine catch to ease the family fortunes, no doubt."

Fleur looked at the lady until she met her eyes, then said, "That does seem to be the primary reason for all this partying and rushing around, and pretending you like people you consider feckless, and spending time with people who are self-centered and rude. The Dowager Marchioness and my mother are old friends and the Dowager—with great generosity—offered to give me a season. My family could never afford such a thing."

A slow smile pleated Miss Enid's thin brown skin. "A girl who can speak up for herself. The first point goes to you."

Fleur's stomach sank. The questions were to continue.

"Come now, Enid," the Dowager said. "I didn't invite you here to embarrass this sweet girl who will make some man the best of wives."

"You didn't invite us here at all," Prunella said, raising her thin beak of a nose. "We decided there is too much afoot in this family and we should be with all of you before some dreadful disaster comes along."

"And what would that be?" Nathan asked. His thunderous expression only deepened Fleur's unrest. "What possible disaster could be about to occur?"

Don't sing. Please don't sing. Fleur pressed her palms against her skirts.

"That's why we're here, isn't it?" Prunella said. "To find out the nature of the impending disaster and decide how best to deal with it. We have decided something is afoot, something you're all keeping from us. Well, be secretive but we shall uncover the mystery."

Servants came forward to remove plates. Thick cutlets of venison were served and for a few moments the succulent meat took precedence over conversation.

Fleur longed to escape. She tried to keep her attention on her food but the force of Dominic's attention made it impossible. From time to time she glanced up, and every time he was studying her with an unfathomable gaze. She tried a little smile, but his eyes only darkened even more.

"Tomorrow there is to be a ball here. Am I correct?" Miss Enid asked.

"You know you are," the Dowager said, mildly enough. "I told you as much as soon as you arrived. Of course you will be in attendance. I think you may enjoy all the fuss and the splendid decorations. The food, also, will be outstanding since Hattie and I do not believe in these pathetically sparse efforts put on by so many who know better."

"I shall wear my rich hyacinth," Prunella said at once. "It is a masterpiece. And Enid plans on her new fading sunset. I've always liked her in yellow."

"Not fading sunset, sister dear. Not *fading* anything. I shall be in colonial mustard."

Fleur visualized a mustard gown with Miss Enid's nut brown skin and all but shuddered.

"Good," Hattie said. "That sounds lovely and we shall have a marvelous time. You'll get to see all of Fleur's suitors. She is the toast of London, you know."

Both aunts set down their knives and forks and considered Fleur until her cheeks throbbed. At last Miss Prunella said, "She is a beauty. Fortunately she doesn't have the freckles one expects with such red hair and pale skin. No, I'm not surprised the men are sniffing around her as if she were a dog in heat."

"Aunt Prunella." Dominic whipped his head around. "Miss Toogood is young and such comments as the one you just made are distasteful—and they're upsetting to her."

"And you care a great deal about Miss Toogood's feelings?" Miss Enid said. "I rather thought so. Did you know that Miss Toogood's mother is from a good family who disowned her for marrying Reverend Toogood?"

"And the family is as poor as church mice," Miss Prunella added.

Rather than feeling abashed, Fleur's temper rose.

"We have done our homework and discovered a good deal," Miss Enid said. "The older daughter is about to be passed over by the son of the local squire because the father wants better for his son than a penniless nothing."

"Letitia would be a wonderful catch for any man," Fleur said, explosively. "And the squire's son in question knows as much. If that mean man doesn't realize the wrong he's doing, he'll lose his son altogether. I can't imagine how you know such personal things about me."

She snapped her mouth shut, annoyed with herself for the outburst. The only way Miss Worth could know about Letitia was from the contents of the letter still on Fleur's writing table.

"Family loyalty is always admirable," Miss Enid said with no sign of being at all ruffled. "As far as how I know what I know? A word dropped here, a letter left there. Houses with large staffs have no secrets. What sort of dowry could you bring to a marriage, Miss Toogood?"

Hattie made a strangled noise.

"Nothing," Fleur said, more disappointed than angry about the invasion of her privacy, "Not a single bean or family heirloom. If I should ever marry—which is doubtful—it will be to a man who wants me only for myself and my strength of character, the fact that I will be tireless in my love and loyalty, and an unshakable friend."

Not even the sound of silver on china followed.

Fleur looked around at sympathetic faces, all but Dominic's which showed something entirely different and overwhelming. He stared as if he might see into her mind. A sniff caught her attention and she was amazed to see tears coursing down the aunts' faces.

Miss Prunella turned to her sister and said, "Wasn't that beautiful, Enid? And I believe her. We must do all we can to help make sure she marries the perfect man for her."

Miss Enid's muffled sob caught at the back of her nose and she sneezed. "We shall not rest until that is accomplished.

Henrietta, dear sister, you are a woman of uncommon insight. A husband for Fleur Toogood. That is our mission." They shook hands.

28

If she couldn't get where she needed to go quickly, she would be too late. She had pleaded a headache and left dinner before the rest. Changing her clothes and getting to the chest outside Dominic's rooms had been easy. The rest of her mission seemed overwhelming.

Even more cramped than before, pillowed in the billowing mass of cheap and gaudy petticoats she wore beneath a modified scullery maid's dress, with a thin cloak over the top, Fleur kept still inside the nasty chest. Dominic and Nathan had come upstairs and gone into Dominic's rooms.

Fortunately Fleur had told Snowdrop she wouldn't need her this evening. She had no intention of involving the young woman in her own reckless plans but convincing Snowdrop she couldn't go would have slowed Fleur down.

Also, it seemed possible that Snowdrop had been the one to spread personal details from letters Fleur received. Who else could have done it? The idea sickened Fleur and made her feel even more alone.

The real hurry would come when she had given Dominic and Nathan a head start into the tunnel beneath the window seat. She knew just the horse she would take from the stables to go after them. The pistol was hidden in her clothes and she wouldn't hesitate to use it in the defense of Dominic—and Nathan, of course.

The men would be slower in the hack but she'd still be at a great disadvantage. Fortunately she had a fine sense of direction and already knew the road to the center of London. She had even located St. James on a map in the library.

There they were. She heard Dominic's door open and the low hum of men's voices. They moved quickly, too. She watched them through the crack between the chest doors. Not knowing how difficult it would be to follow them down through whatever lay beneath the window seat didn't help.

She couldn't do it.

Apprehension gripped her stomach and squeezed. She dared not take a candle because they would see it. This meant she must set off after them while there was hope that their candles would give a faint illumination for her.

How heavy would the window seat be?

The instant she saw it moved into place over their heads, Fleur tumbled from the chest and ran to the seat. She put an ear to the wood and listened. From underneath came faint scraping sounds.

She swallowed and swallowed, but still felt sick.

Now it was time to go. When she tried to raise the solid wooden seat her arms shook, yet she could not let it drop. Slowly Fleur opened it a few inches then managed to crouch and push her shoulder into the gap. She hissed at the pain but kept on lifting and, in the end, sat on the edge of the frame with her feet dangling inside and leaned forward until the seat rested against the window.

Below she saw several steps of a downward flight and without giving herself time to think, jumped to the top step. She looked up but knew there was no way she could close the seat after her.

Reaching out to touch rough-hewn walls, Fleur took the

stairs as fast as she dared. At first the light from above helped, but all too soon it faded. She moved by feel, sliding one foot after the other across a step until her toes found the edge. The way was narrow and she could keep contact with the walls on either side of her.

She went almost straight down to a tiny landing and made a sharp right turn along a tunnel to another downward flight. Fleur carried on, her heart thundering, her palms and back sweating. It would all be for nothing, she was sure, unless she could follow at enough distance not to be heard, but not at such a distance that she lost them.

The faintest of wavery candlelight stroked stone walls. The men weren't so far ahead and she must proceed with great care. If they were speaking their voices should rise to her, but she heard not a sound.

Fleur decided that this passageway must have been made when Heatherly was built. Simple in design, it followed the outside wall, paralleling a floor then sinking by means of two rough flights of steps to the next level. At any moment she would reach ground level.

The hint of light snuffed out and Fleur stood in darkness so thick it seemed to touch her skin and she shivered. Scraping echoed back to her. It didn't sound like a door being opened but more like a stone moving.

Cautiously, she moved on—and realized she was below the ground.

Stone clinked and clunked and slid into place. She heard it thump.

Dominic and Nathan were already outside and she remained cocooned in nothingness that had its own sound, like hoards of gnat-size crickets. It pressed in to paralyze her.

A stone tomb. She could die here and possibly never be found.

And she was a maudlin fool. Edging forward, she scraped her forearm and breathed hard. She bent over her arm and hit her brow on a point of rock—and she cried out before she could stop herself. Warm blood trickled down her face.

The only choice was to carry on, and quickly if she was to do any good at all.

The tunnel ended and there was, indeed, no door. Feeling overhead, fresh dirt fell through her fingers. Painstakingly she outlined a slab of stone and soon felt a metal ring set into its center. Fleur grasped the ring with both hands and pushed with all her might. The stone didn't move.

Abandoning the ring, she concentrated on one side of the stone trapdoor, pushing, pushing, straining until it shifted the smallest amount. It tilted and rested on a lip, and Fleur saw a tiny sliver of pewter sky. The little rush of cool, fresh air invigorated her.

But getting out there would take so long and that assumed she would be able to pull herself out by her arms.

Already she was too late to follow them and be the lookout they would never know they'd had—unless something went wrong.

Crying would show defeat or she'd cry right now. And, fiddlededee, she was not a person who gave up.

Fleur toiled. The blood from her forehead dried on her face but sweat took its place.

She *would* get out—at least she'd accomplish that much.

Standing on tiptoe, with both arms braced, she counted to three and gave a mighty shove. The stone actually swung around and one end dropped into the hole.

Fleur threw herself back against the unyielding wall, covered her head and screamed. The slab of rock slowly overbalanced and began to fall down into the tunnel.

What happened next went so fast she lost her bearings completely. The slab stopped falling and, instead, disappeared outside the hole. Two hands and arms reached into the tunnel and she was plucked into the open air. One large hand clamped over her mouth while her captor lifted and ran with her away from the house.

Fleur kicked. She squirmed and flailed, but he held her fast and he didn't speak. Curls of fog drifted through the oppressive blackness and all Fleur heard was the rasping of her own breath.

The Cat had her.

He could well have been loitering and looking around, getting ready for whatever Dominic thought would happen at the ball tomorrow night. She had surprised him.

Perhaps he'd seen Dominic and Nathan leave and planned to enter the house by the tunnel. Or perhaps he hadn't seen them, but he'd been looking for a secret entrance for tomorrow evening and, thanks to her, he'd found one!

She made as much noise as possible with her throat. Pathetic sounds she scarcely heard over the roaring in her ears. Fleur bit his hand. She managed to get a small piece of a finger between her teeth before she closed them and locked her jaw.

The great, grappling man roared with pain. Fleur would have sneered at him but that might loosen her grip on the piece of skin.

He wrenched his hand away and she shouted at once, "I'm worth nothing, you *bad* man. My family has no money so they can't pay you for me. You might as well let me go. I'm absolutely *no one,* do you hear me?" She took a deep breath to scream only to have his hand cover her mouth again.

But she had the pistol. She wrapped her right arm over her middle and drove the business end of the weapon into the man's chest. At the same time she bit him again, and again he whipped his hand away.

"That's a pistol in your scurvy ribs, my man, and I know how to use it. My papa taught me. My finger's on the trigger and if you're to have any chance at all you'll put me down carefully and back away. I may still shoot you, but I may let you go. That's a fifty per cent chance of staying alive. Worth the wager, don't you think?"

"Fleur!" The instant he spoke her name she fell limp. Slowly he lowered her until her feet met the ground. And the lout began to laugh. "Scurvy ribs," he said, his chest heaving. "*Scurvy* ribs?"

Dominic's voice changed everything. Instantly she smelled his familiar clean scent. "Don't you laugh at me," she said, hoping she sounded threatening. Terror had made him unrecognizable to her.

"When someone captures you and you think he may intend to do you harm, you don't start long conversations with him," Dominic said, placing a finger and thumb on her gun-toting wrist and moving her aim toward the ground.

"You're a monster," she told him.

"Am I?" He turned her to face him and she looked up at him in the dark. "Villains don't care who taught you to use a pistol. They can easily overpower you and take it away. You had been attacked already and you should have got off a shot at once while you had the benefit of surprise on your side."

Fleur tutted. "Why didn't I think of that? You would probably be dead by now and ever so much less trouble to me." Whatever he said, she had managed to stop him from courting danger, at least for tonight.

"The biting was excellent," he said. "You should always try to hurt an assailant and get away. But a lot of talk is just not on."

"You're doing a fair amount of jabbering yourself," she said. "Why did you come back?"

"I never left. Nathan and I heard someone following and from the feminine sounds and your history, and the fact that you eavesdropped earlier, I assumed it was you. Poking your nose in where it doesn't belong as usual."

"It does belong. Someone has to look after you."

His fingers tightened on her shoulders. "You don't know your place, Fleur, and I fear you would never learn."

You would never learn. "I learn quickly," she told him, with a nasty sinking feeling inside. He had given thought to having her in his life. "All I wanted to do was back you up. You know, like in some of the stories. The daring seeker of justice goes forth after the villain but he has someone in the shadows to back him up—just in case."

"You couldn't do that, Fleur. You heard Nathan and me talking. We decided to leave by hack. What did you intend to do—run along behind?"

"No! And I'm not a fool. What I tried to do was with the best of intentions, but I had already decided—before you scared me half to death—that there was no way for me to follow you. I had given up, much as it pained me and all I wanted was to escape from that hole and get inside the house again. Why didn't you say who you were at once, instead of terrifying me."

"Because I wanted to terrify you," he said and she could make out his angry features.

"Why? What have I ever done to you?"

He chuckled, then laughed louder, and he folded her tightly

into his arms. "Why? To make sure you never do anything so foolish again. You have ruined this night's efforts for me. Nathan has gone ahead with Albert. I hope they'll get at least part of what needs to be done out of the way. Lives could depend on this."

She looked straight ahead at his chest. "You didn't have to stay behind."

"Yes, I did. I could not risk you injuring yourself in that tunnel. You might have managed to creep back the way you came but without light anything could have happened to you."

"And you were concerned for me," she said softly.

"I am a gentleman."

"Of course, and you would have done it for any foolish female."

"You thought I was The Cat. Very flattering, I must say. Please don't ever let me hear you say you are no one and you aren't worth anything again. You infuriate me. Your worth is incalculable and I assure you that if you were to fall into that man's hands there would be no difficulty fulfilling ransom demands."

Now she got a lump in her throat

"Give me the pistol," he said.

Fleur handed it over and said, "I had to try to be there." It sounded so pathetic. "Somehow I thought I might take a horse from the stables and still manage to get within following distance of you. No, I didn't think that—I hoped, that's all. Now I've made a mess of things."

"Yes, you have. I think it would be best if we went back through the tunnel. I'll light a candle."

"Why can't we just use a door? Where is your habit?"

"Albert is wearing my habit," he said, in an even enough voice although she felt something icy behind his politeness.

"How do you think it would look if we were seen entering the house together at such an hour?"

Unfortunately I doubt if anyone would think a thing about it.

He lit a candle in a holder, turned toward Fleur and paused only an instant before half dragging her back to the walls of the house. He held the candle aloft and peered at her. "You…" He looked closely at her forehead. "What have you done to your face?"

"Cut myself on the wall down there," she said very quietly. "Anyone could have done the same thing."

"Anyone who was hurrying and didn't know the twists and turns, and who had *no light.* Well, it doesn't look too bad but the rest of our ladies won't be pleased when your ball is tomorrow evening."

"I'm sorry." What else could she say?

"You've got a beauty mark on your face!" He was astounded, no doubt about that. "A black heart. And…paint. Thick paint. Frightful. You need nothing of the kind—not ever."

To her amazement, he produced a large handkerchief and wiped at her face. So shocked was she, that she hardly winced when the pressure pulled at her injured forehead.

"Lick it," he commanded, stuffing the cloth against her mouth. She did as she was told. "You look like a person from a circus," he said, concentrating until her skin stung. "Much better," he concluded at last.

"I'm glad you're pleased."

He took in the rest of her. Leaned closer and lifted away one side of her cloak. " Why are you dressed like that? Gad, you absolutely must not be seen until you've changed."

"It's my disguise," she said darkly. "Who are you to be horrified by a disguise, *Brother Juste?*"

"You intended to go to St. James dressed as a…well…"

"A lady of the night," she said promptly. "You could have said it without hurting my feelings."

He choked, but collected himself quickly enough. "Yes, exactly what you said. What were you thinking of?"

There was no point in telling him the idea had not been hers. "I would have blended in very nicely. Don't tell me there aren't plenty of other such women there. Oh, I know another name for them. *Strumpets.* My mama got quite cross with a lady who said a maid at the manor was no better than she ought to be, and a strumpet."

"I can tell you're well versed in these matters," Dominic said. "When I get you inside we shall continue this conversation. We can't be here like this."

More was the pity.

He led her back to the opening in the ground, gave her the candle and jumped down first. "Now give that to me," he said and took the candle from her. He set it aside and held up his arms. "Sit on the edge."

Fleur shuddered. "You go that way. I'll go to the front door and say I've been to a party."

His face gave away nothing of what he might be thinking. "Sit on the edge," he repeated, his deep voice sinking even deeper. "Not another word of argument out of you."

She did as she was told.

Dominic said, "Lean forward until I can take you by the waist," and snatched her the moment she did so. "Sit there." He plunked her, none too gently, on a ledge beside him while he dragged the slab back into place.

They would climb back up to the inside of the house and he would rush her off to her room with orders about how she should behave and what she should or should not do. And he would withdraw even further from her.

And it was *stupid* because she was convinced he felt something more than duty toward her. He was making her so… Oh, what an awful pickle.

"There," he said, not looking at her this time. "Go ahead of me but go slowly."

"I don't want to go." Her own words surprised her.

"Don't be foolish. It's cold and it's late and you should be in your bed. Also, that cut needs to be cleaned up and tended to so it isn't too noticeable tomorrow."

"I don't care if it is."

Dominic took her by the elbow, hauled her to her feet and set her firmly in front of him. "Off you go."

The instant he released her, Fleur ducked under his arm and sat on the ledge again.

"This is outrageous," he said. "If you want to be sure I'm angry—I'm angry. Now stop this."

There might never be another opportunity to be completely alone with him. He was too busy pretending he wanted to be a monk and trying to put distance between them.

"Fleur, are you listening to me? If I carry you it will be over my shoulder. The way is too narrow for anything else. And it's also low, so the trip may be painful."

"Put a hand on me and you'll wish you hadn't," she said.

"Good grief." Head and shoulders bent over, he paced in the cramped space, glancing at her frequently. Then he sat on his haunches and put the candle down beside him.

"I want you to give me some assurances," she said.

Dominic frowned.

"Tell me you will do your best to think of me as a friend—always."

"You didn't need to ask that," he told her.

"Thank you. You are the best man I've ever met. Hard-headed, but dear and—"

"Please don't go on with this, Fleur."

"And I shall pray for you and for your safety. Please look after yourself. You think you can solve all the bad things in the world, but if you get seriously hurt—or killed—you will solve nothing."

He stood again, his head bowed beneath the low rock ceiling. "Enough. You have no need to worry about me. I know how to look after myself and those who need my help. I don't need your lectures."

His words stung. "You think affection between a man and a woman is some sort of weakness." She got to her feet and stood close to him. "What you don't know is that giving love is a risk. Accepting love is a bigger risk and only the brave can do it well."

"*Damn it.* You don't understand, you little fool."

"Not fool—*champion.* I want to be your champion, the one who will always put you first. And that's what I am whether you want it or not."

"I don't," he snapped. "Now move."

She slapped his face, hard, and without thinking. Never before had she struck another person like that.

Dominic caught her by the wrist and put her hand at her side. He took her by the shoulders and shook her till she cried out, "Dominic, I didn't mean—"

He kissed her with bruising force, swallowed her words, sent his tongue deep into her mouth. And he held her head still with his fingers driven painfully into her hair.

Anger and fear drove Fleur. And a wildness while she fought to hold her own with him.

She tasted the salt of her blood on her lips—or was the blood his? Kissing him back, meeting his tongue, nipping at the skin inside his mouth, she clung to him or she would have fallen to the rocky ground.

He ripped off her cloak, let it fall and tossed his own on top. Their rasping breaths mingled and his groans joined the sounds she made and had never heard before.

The cheap dress tore in his hands, ripped apart with her chemise until she felt cold air cross her breasts. The urgency turned to frenzy. Dominic shredded her clothes until she stood naked, but she had done her own damage and his shirt hung from his wrists. She fought with his trousers until he helped her, stripping himself, and all the while staring at her with dark fire in his eyes.

Holding her away he said, "Do you know what's going to happen?"

Fleur could scarcely draw in a breath. "Yes," she said, and lied. His body shone in the flickering light. His hair, loose of the tail, swung forward to drive deep shadows into his face, beneath the sharp bones, and to shade the contours of his sensual mouth and arched brows.

He kissed her again, deeply, and stood back a little once more, looking at her, studying every part of her.

His shoulders were wide and muscular. Soft dark hair spread across his chest and grew narrow over his belly. His legs, braced apart, looked as if no force could move them, and she could not imagine any force which might lessen the solid thrust of his manly part.

She raised her eyes to find him watching her, watching him. A slight smile lifted the corners of his mouth and he took one of her breasts in each large hand.

The moment before his face was hidden from her, and he sucked a nipple into his mouth, she'd seen a kind of madness in his eyes. It shook her, but with aching anticipation.

He moved his hands to her bottom and parted the cheeks. He moaned and lifted her, snaking his fingers forward, into the hair between her legs, and over slick flesh that leaped and burned at his touch.

"I can't wait." Dominic, his face stark, stared into her eyes. He guided her legs around his waist. "Cross your ankles. Please don't let me go." And in a spear of fiery, stretching pain he forced himself up and into her.

Fleur grabbed handfuls of Dominic's hair. She gritted her teeth and fought back tears. It hurt so, but it pleased her so. Holding her hips he began to move her up and down on his rod. She stared at his face but saw no recognition there. He was not lost to her, but lost in her and she wanted to keep him forever. She didn't care what the future held. There need only be this.

Faster, he moved and his feverish lips pressed, nipped, sucked each inch of skin they found. Their bodies slipped together until, with a great heave, Dominic cried out and jerked. He rested his face in her neck and the great panting went on and on.

Fleur plucked at him. Sensations swelled in her until she couldn't keep still. "Dominic," she keened, and at last he looked at her with clear eyes.

"Yes," he said, a statement not a question, and he lowered her to the heap made by their tangled clothing. He remained inside her. "Poor, sweet, beautiful creature," he murmured, his voice broken.

He put a hand between their bodies, went unerringly to the place where they joined and slid fingers inside her. Once again their rhythm began while he found a spot with his hand and caressed it harder and faster. A shard, a knife, a sweet, sharp weapon struck a divine wound. Helpless, Fleur's limbs fell from Dominic. She strained against him while searing eddies rushed into her, through her, over her.

"Don't stop," she cried to him. "Dominic!"

The sensation broke into waves that left her shaking and weak, but still pulsing. Dominic slumped on top of her, a crushing weight but one she wanted to bear.

Perhaps for only minutes, they drowsed. Fleur felt heavy and sore, but satisfied. Dominic was a large man and her body had stretched to accommodate him.

She drifted, warmed by his skin and flesh on hers.

Darkness made her open her eyes and turn her head.

"Stay still," Dominic whispered. "I'll light another candle."

Light flickered to life again and he sat beside her on their destroyed clothing. With one knee raised and the other leg beneath him, he studied her, stroked her gently, bent to place a light kiss on her lips.

"I failed," he said quietly. "I'm sorry."

"Failed?"

"To be gentle when I introduced you to love."

She didn't know what to think or feel. "That was on my list," she told him. "I don't think it applied to you."

"Yes, it did. I told you that if I were the man in your life, I would be gentle. Regardless, I should have stood by my word and not hurt you. And I did hurt you, didn't I?"

Lying didn't help anything in the end. "Yes, but I liked the way it felt. And I played as much a part in what happened as you did."

"You are young, inexperienced, curious and wild. You're wonderful. But I know better and I should have controlled myself. Fleur, when did you last bleed?"

Her hands flew to her scalding face and she closed her eyes.

Dominic pulled her to sit up and rested her face against his chest. "These are practical things. But it doesn't matter. I know what must be done. The wedding will be arranged at once."

Her head ached suddenly and so severely she pressed at her temples.

"You're overwhelmed. Of course you are. This is all too much for you to deal with at once. I shall travel to see your father and ask for your hand on Sunday, the day after your ball. You have nothing to worry about. We shall manage well enough."

If she weren't so tired and achy Fleur would be angry. She would be furious. She would think up terrible, hurtful things to say to him. But she was all of those things.

Pulling away from him, she searched out wrecked pieces of her clothing from among his and started covering herself as best she could.

Dominic watched her in silence and she felt embarrassed.

At last she swung the cloak around her, grateful for its cover.

"I know how you feel," Dominic said. He had pulled on his trousers, given up on the shirt but put on his coat and cloak. "You're overwhelmed. But you will become accustomed to the idea and then you will settle down and be happy."

"Stop it." She turned on him. "I'll be happy because, out of duty, you would marry me? Out of duty you would change the plans you've made for your life? And you would never resent what I had caused you to give up, would you? No, you would never feel I had somehow trapped you."

"No, Fleur, I wouldn't."

"You are a gallant man." She turned from him and started along the passage. "What happened was a mistake, but I shall remember it with awe and I shall not regret what we did."

"It was just a beginning." He walked behind her holding the candle aloft.

"It was also the end," she told him. "Thank you for your kind offer, but I cannot accept it."

29

"Sounds as if every cart and carriage in London—and every horse—is making a visit to Heatherly this morning," Lawrence said. He slid another document in front of Dominic for signature.

Dominic signed and said, "That will go on all day." He glanced up at Lawrence. "You're all set for this evening? And the others?"

"Yes, milord." He removed the document again but let it dangle from his fingers while he stared into the distance. "Would it be better not to hold the ball?"

"I've thought of little else but that question for days," Dominic said. "The Dowager points out that there are a number of events this evening and they will all go on as planned. The *ton* appears to have grown quickly complacent about The Cat."

"Could it be that his activities add to the general excitement?" Lawrence asked.

"Yes. You were always a man who understood the workings of certain minds. I think there are some who even look forward to more bad news."

Nathan walked in and an extra dose of ill humor came with him. He flipped back the tails of his coat, slumped into a chair and stared at nothing in particular.

Dominic raised his brows to Lawrence who responded with the faintest of smiles before gathering papers and leaving the room.

"How long did you think you could avoid me?" Nathan said.

"I haven't been avoiding you." That was a lie.

"Where were you last night? Whose bed were you in—you were never in your own?"

Neither was I where I wanted to be. He put his elbows on the desk and laced his fingers together. "How did it go for you and Albert?"

"I bloody well asked you some questions first," Nathan said, his mouth tight, a muscle jerking in his cheek.

Wonderful. Nathan filled with righteousness and criticism. Just what Dominic needed after he'd managed to wreck one life and turn his own into a hell. "It was Fleur who came after us last night," he said. "When you see her you'll note the wound on her forehead. She followed us without a light of her own."

Nathan's expression changed to one of speculation. "Was she trying to kill herself?"

"Don't be flippant!" Damn. A man would have to be a rattle not to hear defensiveness in Dominic's voice. Defensiveness of Fleur.

"You don't think a person could fall and break her neck in the passages?" Nathan rested his head back against his chair. "If she didn't have a candle with her, that is? Or even if she did, but she took a wrong step?"

"Of course." Best be careful what he said until the other, what had happened with Fleur, was taken care of. "She overheard us discussing our mission at St. James and decided we needed her to stand guard. In case we got into trouble we couldn't handle."

Nathan blinked rapidly and said, "Now who's being flippant?"

Dominic opened the second drawer down on the right side of his desk and took out Fleur's pistol. He held it up for Nathan to see. "Our country parson's daughter has courage and ingenuity," he said, replacing the weapon. "And she is too fearless."

"I would have said reckless," Nathan said, but he smiled. "I'll lay odds you didn't get angry with her. How could you?"

"She was dressed like a whore with a pound of paint on her face and a heart-shaped beauty mark."

That stole Nathan's words. He gawked.

"When I got angry with her—you'd lose your wager on that—she insisted she knew there were plenty of whores around St. James and her plan had been to blend in."

"I'll be damned." Nathan gave a low whistle. "Who would have expected her to have the word in her vocabulary."

Dominic threw up his hands. "She *didn't—doesn't*. It took her a while to come up with *lady of the night* and, eventually, *strumpet*. She is such an innocent, it's painful." He caught his breath and looked away from Nathan. Fleur wasn't an innocent anymore. The passion, the instinctive sensuality had always been there, but he should not have awakened it and must blame his own weakness for their lovemaking.

She had said she wouldn't have him. At first, after he'd seen her to her room, he'd felt a kind of relief. After all, what were the chances that she'd be with child after one encounter? Then, when he couldn't face his own bed or even his rooms and he'd wandered the house for an hour, he found he also couldn't face the thought of having Fleur gone from his life.

He glanced at Nathan and found his brother looking straight back. "What's on your mind?" Nathan asked. "Something is troubling you."

Dominic only missed a beat before he said, "It's The Cat, and this ball we shouldn't be holding. If you must know, I hardly slept at all last night, I was so worried. I walked the house. Finally got an hour or two on a couch in John's old room."

For longer than Dominic thought necessary, Nathan watched him with half-closed eyes. "Last night was a success," he said abruptly. "It would have been better if you had been with me, but you'll be pleased. I understand John's attachment to Albert Parker—the man is solid and, I believe, capable of anything."

"Tell me," Dominic said. He got up and went to lean against the front of his desk.

"We went to the gate behind St. James Street—the one where I met you the night you followed Harry. Then we went inside and stayed close to the walls until we reached the building. You were right, it's a sort of warehouse. Huge."

Dominic gripped the desk with both hands. "Did he come or go? The Cat?"

"No. And we waited almost three hours. But the boy did."

"Harry? You're sure?"

"I'm sure. Straight to a door he went, and inside, but not before he lit his candle. He looked better, but his clothes didn't. Anyway, in he went and closed the door behind him, only there's a window in the door. Dominic, it's the strangest thing you ever saw, like a miniature house built inside another building. At least that's what it looks like. Fancy front door, columns. Only two floors."

"Did you follow the boy?"

"No. I decided—"

"Good." Dominic cut him off. "We think alike. No point in getting into something unless we're sure we can catch the man red-handed."

"As you say," Nathan said. "Let's hope we can resolve something this evening. Tomorrow I intend to go to Sodbury Martyr. I have business there."

Dominic turned cold.

"Hattie ascertained that a maid, who has been working for her while Snowdrop looks after Fleur, read letters sent by Fleur's family. The maid's name is Blanche and Hattie says the girl confessed to sharing the contents with the aunts after they arrived. They asked what she knew, of course. Since she told the truth the girl's to be given another chance."

"I've been too preoccupied." Dominic shook his head. "I heard what the aunts said about Fleur's family and I should have done something about it."

"Mmm." Nathan's bald stare wasn't intended to reassure. "Fleur will have to be told the truth."

"I'll be glad to do that," Dominic said.

Nathan stood and gave one of his secretive smiles. "I'm sure you will. My mission will be to make sure Squire Pool decides Letitia Toogood will make his son, Christopher, an excellent wife. You can tell Fleur that, too. Now I must see how the preparations for the ball are progressing and try to keep the ladies and the staff calm."

"Thank you."

"It's part of my job, remember? When I return from the Cotswolds it will be time to take care of another matter. I cannot see a girl like Fleur return to that village unmarried after the Season, and I'm afraid it could happen because she shows no particular interest in any of the men who call. She likes Franklin Best but not enough to marry him. It seems the rest don't make much impression at all."

Dominic knew he must not reveal his feelings but desperation gnawed at him. "What exactly do you intend to do about Fleur?"

"I'm not ready to discuss it yet," Nathan said. "We'll talk within a few days. I shall be expecting to hear your plans for the monastery once our current unpleasantness is solved."

Dominic knew when he was being baited. He seethed, and only minutes after Nathan left, Dominic strode from his study—and all but collided with Fleur. She turned about as if confused, and showed signs of rushing away.

"Good morning, Fleur," he said, and she stopped. "I think we have a fine day for our ball preparations. I expect you've heard all the activity going on."

"Good morning." She faced him and her pallor concerned him. The wound on her forehead had bruised but it wouldn't detract from her appearance that evening. Not that he cared what anyone else thought of her.

He found his voice again. "It has been discovered that someone read your letters from home." Dominic explained exactly what had happened and a flush rose in her cheeks. "Please don't be embarrassed. Nathan is going to see the squire mentioned. He will make sure Letitia and Christopher have nothing more to worry about there."

"How?" She looked hopeful and fearful at the same time. "I cannot allow anyone to make my parents feel indebted."

Nathan was right to see something very special in this girl. "That won't happen. Nathan knows how to be subtle. I assure you his visit will never be mentioned by the squire or anyone else."

Her eyes shone through a sheen of tears. "Thank you then. I shall also thank Nathan when he returns."

He lowered his voice. "Have you thought about what I said last night?"

"Constantly. But I know what's right and what's wrong and

I also know that sometimes, what we want the most can make us eternally unhappy."

"Not this time," he told her urgently.

"Let it go. It will be for the best."

He saw that she would leave him there, and that her mind was made up. With great care, convinced she would push him away, Dominic rested his fingertips on the soft, white side of her neck. Fleur bowed her head a little and stood still.

He turned his fingers and brushed lightly with the backs of them, then left them there, unmoving, a curl at her nape caught between finger and thumb.

A moment more and she sped away.

Another movement caught his eye. Just barely, he saw Nathan move quickly across the end of the corridor.

So his brother was his rival. Fate had an evil sense of humor but now Dominic must play his own game. He strode into the hall—in time to see Nathan bend over Fleur and place her hand beneath his elbow.

"McGee," Dominic roared, producing the butler almost instantly. "Kindly tell the Marchioness and the Dowager that I have business in Town. I shall return in plenty of time for this extravaganza."

30

Dominic cleared his throat and made sure his expression was bland. If he appeared smug then later, when an unexpected lady guest arrived, some member of his family would make connections he didn't want made.

The hour grew late but the ball at Heatherly was the event of the evening, perhaps of the Season, and most guests would arrive late after making rapid rounds of other parties. They would save the best for last and stay a long time.

He suffered another inspection by Merryfield who picked more invisible specks from his master's black coat.

"May I go now?" Dominic asked, but he smiled at his man.

"I should think so, milord," Merryfield said and opened the door. "The timing should be perfect."

Dominic nodded and left his rooms. He went directly to Fleur's door and knocked, knowing full well that every female member of the family would be gathered there.

His mother opened the door and frowned at him.

"I wouldn't be doing my duty if I didn't reassure my charge on such a night," he said, and congratulated himself on his smoothness. The Dowager inclined her head and opened the door wider.

He walked in, saw Fleur before a full-length mirror and stiffened his suddenly weak knees. Fleur looked back at him in the mirror and caught her bottom lip between her teeth. She busied herself twitching the skirts of her flame-red chiffon gown.

Both of the blue chairs in the room had been turned for the aunts to sit in and have an unimpeded view of Fleur. Each of them repeatedly dabbed at their eyes with lace handkerchiefs.

"Mrs. Neville told us the red was your idea," Hattie said, gorgeous herself in dark green satin flounced and beaded at the hem.

Dominic didn't find it easy to speak but he said, "I believe I did mention it."

Leaning on the arm of Aunt Enid's chair, Chloe propped her chin and wriggled back and forth. She looked at Fleur with admiration. "I'm to go to the ball, Uncle Dominic," she said. "Snowdrop will look after me."

"But not for long," Hattie said, wagging a finger. "Just long enough to see all the ladies and gentlemen."

Chloe gave Dominic a twinkly smile he couldn't resist. "I've always liked you in navy blue, Chloe," he said. "It suits your coloring."

The child dimpled.

The Dowager looked at Fleur from all angles. "There's no adornment on the gown," the Dowager said. "So plain and so clever. I am not sure about this." She lifted a diamond collar from its box.

"What about this instead?" Dominic said, and produced a blue velvet box. "I had decided tonight was an appropriate time to give Fleur a gift to celebrate her Season and, in honesty, I did know a little about the dress."

If only Fleur didn't appear to be steadily losing her composure. He removed a necklace from the box, approached her and lifted it over her head. When it settled in a V to match her neckline he fastened the chain of perfect diamonds so that a single, large, teardrop-shaped gem rested perfectly in the shadow of her decolletage.

Every woman in the room sighed—except Fleur. Fleur met his eyes and he waited for her to tell him she couldn't accept the necklace. Instead she said, "Thank you, you're much too kind to me," and his heart stopped beating in that instant.

The aunts twittered about what a thoughtful "boy" he could be when he tried. Hattie and his mother watched his face, and Fleur's, and he was sure they saw too much.

"Very well," he said lightly. "I shall go down to help Nathan be a perfect host. Don't be too long. We shall need your company."

He hadn't fooled one of them with his excuse for the gift but Dominic found he didn't care what anyone thought. Tonight he felt pleased with himself, apprehensive, threatened, but pleased. He also felt as if every nerve and sinew in his body sprang as he moved. This could be the night when they caught The Cat, but the burden of protecting Jane Weller weighed heavily on him.

Slipping around a group of loud gentlemen, he entered the ballroom. As he'd assumed, the *Beau Monde* arrived in droves, chattering and exclaiming as they climbed the flower-draped staircase to join the other guests. From their jolly countenances he decided he had been right in thinking they would have made the rounds of a number of parties before arriving at Heatherly.

Nathan spied him and made a "help me" face, but before Dominic could reach his brother, Lady Barbara Jacoby and her mother accosted him. Groaning wouldn't be the thing. Raven-haired Barbara could hold her own in any group of lovely girls but he wished she would find another man to lavish with her longing.

"Everything is quite beautiful," Barbara told him. "You said you've never seen such buffet tables at any function, didn't you, Mama?"

"The Dowager has always put on the perfect do," the woman said. A waltz began and she fell silent, giving Dominic a meaningful look.

Barbara lowered her big, brown eyes and he saw her tremble. Damn it all. "I don't suppose you're free for this dance?" he asked, and with that he went unwillingly to the dance floor.

With the aunts, Hattie and the Dowager surrounding her, and Chloe holding Snowdrop's hand, Fleur suffered through the master of ceremonies' loud announcements of their names.

The dance floor lay below a gallery where blue-and-silver chairs surrounded tables with bowls of roses at their centers. Flunkies circulated, some wafting fragrant-smelling potpourri burners, others removing empty glasses and plates. More tables and chairs circled the dance floor on its own level.

"Where should we sit?" the Dowager asked.

"Down there," the Misses Worth said at once. "We like to be in the middle of *everything*," Miss Prunella added.

"On any other occasion, that would be in the middle of nothing at all," Miss Enid commented. "Since we never go anywhere."

Miss Prunella ignored her and they made their way slowly down wide steps and to a table in the second row from the dancing. Immediately gentlemen emerged to help the ladies get seated. Fleur couldn't help smiling at Franklin Best who was the first to reach her, but her smile disappeared at the sound of a braying laugh. She couldn't believe Mr. Mergatroyd had come at all but there he was, trailing a handkerchief from an upraised hand.

A Mr. Stanton, whom Fleur remembered from several events, bowed over her and asked to see her dance card. Dutifully she put it on the table but the gentleman seemed slow to remember that it was not Dominic's diamond he'd asked to see.

"I see young Dominic is already cutting quite the figure," Miss Enid said in her unforgettable, squeezed tones. "Pretty enough girl he's dancing with. Who is she?"

"Lady Barbara Jacoby," Hattie said. "I think she has a serious case on him."

Fleur saw Dominic, a striking figure in black and the only man likely to tie his hair back to keep it from his shoulders. And the girl was more than pretty enough. Lady Barbara looked even more beautiful than when Fleur had last seen her dancing with Dominic. "I might be bold enough to say she's in love with him," Fleur said, hurting too much to curb her rash tongue. How could she presume, even for a moment, to think she'd make him a suitable wife?

"Pish posh," Hattie said. "Every woman in the room is in love with him—and with Nathan, from what I can see."

"I'd be in love with both of them if I wasn't taken," Snowdrop announced, swaying the skirts of the lovely mint-green dress "her Albert" had bought for her. She caught the amused looks of Hattie and the other ladies and said, "There I go again, forgetting my place." Her naughty smile made them all chuckle.

The chatter continued and Fleur was almost grateful when Franklin gleefully told her the next dance was his and flourished her card in front of her nose. With her hand decorously placed on the back of his wrist, he led her through the marvelous brilliance of the ladies' dresses, and past perfectly dressed men, many in dashing uniform.

He faced her, put one hand at her waist, and whirled her into the waltz. "It seems everyone only wants to waltz these days," he said.

"Yes."

"I agree with them." Franklin's expression was gentle and engrossed in Fleur. "Why would a man want to trot all over the floor trying not to fall over his feet or miss a step when he can whirl a girl around like this?"

"You are so agreeable," she told him. "I love the waltz. It's gay and makes the best of all the swirling dresses. I'll tell you a secret, though. I never waltzed before I came to London and I'm sure my parents would disapprove."

Franklin twirled her with even more vigor. "You must have been born an expert at the waltz," he said.

When she had seen the ballroom for the first time, after she'd arrived at Heatherly and Dominic showed her around, she hadn't gone down to the level of the dance floor and didn't realize how deeply it stretched beneath the gallery. There were open doors around the sides. "I hadn't noticed the doors until now," she said to Franklin.

He glanced about. "Yes, they open onto balconies."

"Yes," she said, "of course. I've seen the balconies from outside, but I didn't realize they were outside the ballroom. I expect you can walk down to the grounds from there. How lovely."

"It is," he said and she thought he seemed sad now. "Do

you know anything further about when your sister may visit? I shall keep my word and make sure she gets enough attention."

"I've written back but it's too soon to hear from her again," Fleur said. She saw Dominic and Lady Barbara dancing for the second time in a row. "I doubt if Rosemary will be able to join me while I'm here but thank you, Mr. Best."

"Do you think you might call me Franklin?"

"Franklin, and I'm Fleur."

"I know. Thank you. The name is perfect for you."

No matter how Fleur tried to stop herself, she searched for Dominic at every turn, and found him easily enough. He laughed with his pretty partner and she looked at him with open admiration.

Franklin swung Fleur around again and there he was, Dominic, not feet from her and looking straight at Fleur over Lady Barbara's head. He raised his chin and stared. Fleur stumbled over Franklin's feet but kept her eyes on Dominic's. His intense, silent communication undid her. She wished she didn't regret being with him the previous night, and in ways she didn't. But she detested that the most memorable night of her life must be ruined by the conventions of Society— even as she knew she had been wrong not to stop the love-making.

The only graceful way to cope was to finish the Season, keeping her distance from Dominic, thank the wonderful family for their kindness and go home. Once she was out of sight she would soon be out of mind. He would get over the guilt.

"Franklin, may I sit down, please?"

"Of course." Immediately he ushered her from the floor and found another chair for the table, which had become crowded. "Sit there. Would you like some lemonade? Have you eaten? You don't look too robust, Fleur." He glanced at the bruise and cut on her forehead but didn't mention it.

"Lemonade, please," she said, realizing how thirsty she was. She had not missed the vigilance of the men Dominic and Nathan had chosen to be on watch this evening. Franklin frequently swept his attention across the room, as did Nathan, and Noel DeBeaufort, who stood behind Hattie.

Gussy Arbuthnot and Victoria Crewe-Burns were already at the table. Nathan didn't do a good job of pretending he didn't see the way Gussy looked at him. Olivia Prentergast and her officer stood nearby. Fleur had heard that they were to set a date for their marriage.

"Are you happy?" Hattie whispered, close to Fleur's ear. "I mean entertained, anyway. I think there is something else on your mind and I wish you would confide in me."

"I am very happy," Fleur said although Hattie was one of the last people she wanted to lie to. "I will never be able to thank you and your family enough for all you have done for me."

"Oh, I think you will," the Dowager said, making Fleur jump and look over her shoulder to where the lady sat close behind her. "Difficult decisions must be made but made they shall be. Trust us, Fleur, and trust your family. Whatever happens will be for the best."

Fleur frowned at Hattie who wouldn't look at her. They were hatching plots and that made Fleur nervous.

"Oh, my," the Dowager said, keeping her voice low. "Nathan." She looked up at him until he bent over her. "Do you see who is here? An invitation was sent, an invitation is always sent, but she never accepts."

Nathan sank to his haunches beside his mother and looked gingerly over his shoulder.

"Not there," the Dowager said. "Just arriving."

The rapid drain of color from Nathan's face intrigued Fleur a great deal. She ought to chastise herself for her curiosity but Society was so interesting. She looked to the top of the gallery stairs where a very slender woman stood, holding the bannisters. She wore black and all Fleur could make out from here was blond hair and a graceful carriage.

"Lady Mary Eaton," Hattie said. "I'm glad she's here. It's wrong that she decided to shut herself away for good after Charles Bennet was killed."

Nathan didn't say a word. He continued to stare at Lady Mary.

The Dowager leaned forward until her mouth was beside Fleur's ear. "Mary Eaton was seriously injured three years ago when the phaeton her fiancé was driving turned over. Charles was a lovely man but he was driving too fast around Marble Arch. He died at once. Mary almost lost the use of her legs but we understand she can walk now—with difficulty. She retreated from the world after the accident."

"How horribly sad," Fleur murmured. "Isn't it nice she's here this evening?"

"It's strange," Hattie said. "I know the invitation went out but I also know it was declined. So why did she change her mind—and without letting us know?"

"She's here," the Dowager said. "That's all that matters."

"You're whispering because you want to exclude us," Miss Prunella said loudly. "Really, Henrietta, you are not making us feel at all welcome."

"You are welcome," the Dowager said shortly. "I love you both very much. Now use your heads and stop behaving the way you think old people should behave. You're too intelligent for that."

Miss Enid and Miss Prunella smiled a little and managed to look entirely too wicked. But they subsided and emptied two glasses of champagne apiece, rapidly.

"Excuse me," Nathan said, too loudly and too anxiously. "I must greet an old friend."

As he walked away, his big shoulders swinging as he threaded his way through the crowd, the Dowager said, "He loved Mary deeply. Her engagement to Charles Bennet was a terrible blow. Sometimes I think Nathan still loves her."

"She's a cripple," Aunt Enid said.

Chloe, who had been keeping quiet to make sure she stayed as long as possible, popped up and said with her pretty French accent, "It is not kind to speak so of a lady with a hardship. So her legs do not work as she would wish. The rest of her is beautiful and there is such sweetness in her face. I expect that is because she has suffered so much."

"The mouths of babes," Hattie said, gathering Chloe to her side. "You're quite right, of course and now we should speak of other things."

"Well, I don't see why Nathan thinks he must rush off to Lady Mary," Gussy said. "Do you, Vicky? He certainly couldn't love her now, if he ever did."

Vicky had the grace to appear awkward. "I'm sure he's just paying his respects."

Both women stared slavishly at Nathan whenever they saw him.

"Let's go and see who we can find," Gussy said. "Everyone is too busy gossiping, Vicky. They'll never notice if we pop off for a bit."

"I shall notice," the Dowager said, but she waved them away and said, "Go. But not for long and remember—decorum."

Fleur searched the faces of the servants, trying to decide which one must be Jane Weller. The maids wore black dresses, white aprons and starched caps and they all looked the same.

Nathan and Lady Mary distracted Fleur. He had greeted the woman at the top of the stairs and she continued to look up into his face while he talked. Sometimes he bent over her to speak into her ear. He held her by the elbow and she rested a hand on his arm.

He looked to the lower floor but Lady Mary shook her head and Fleur guessed she was saying she didn't want to go down the stairs.

What happened next caught the attention of a good many people in the room. Nathan picked up Lady Mary and carried her effortlessly down to the lower level of the ballroom. Fleur heard ladies sigh all around her and heard her own indrawn breath, too, and felt her throat tighten.

The two made a breathtaking couple.

"Mmm," the Dowager said in a low voice behind Fleur. "What do you think, Hattie?"

"I see the fine hand of another in this," Hattie responded. "We'll discuss it later."

Rather than bring Lady Mary to join the rest of his party, Nathan set her down beside a small table for two and settled her there. He pulled up his own chair and sat, never taking his eyes from his companion's face.

"Oh, dear," the Dowager said. "Let's pray his heart isn't broken again."

Gussy and Vicky rushed back to the table and Vicky said, "You'll never believe it but one of our old servants is over there. Jane Weller. She used to be my maid and made up all sorts of stories. She had a young man and stayed out all night with him. Oh, Lady Granville, I'm sure she gave you a false name to get employment but she really shouldn't be here."

"Where is she?" Hattie asked, exchanging a glance with her mother-in-law.

"Over there," Vicky said. "She has a tray of champagne glasses in her hands."

Fleur looked at once and saw the young woman they meant. In the chapel she'd been able to make out very little and all she saw now was a pleasant-looking girl with light brown hair pulled back.

"I employed Jane," the Dowager said and she was no longer smiling. "I suggest the two of you forget she's here."

Looking at each other, Gussy and Vicky went slowly from the table and walked toward one of three alcoves where refreshments were arrayed.

Dominic threaded his way from the dance floor, constantly stopped by men and women who wanted to talk. He bowed politely, said a few words and moved on—until he saw his brother and Lady Mary. At once he went to them and kissed the lady's hand. He beamed at her and she at him. Nathan said something and they all laughed. Dominic spread his arms, bowed and left them, but he glanced back in time for Lady Mary to cast him a meaningful look and give a slight nod.

"Aha," Hattie whispered.

The Dowager said, "Indeed."

Fleur almost informed them that even she wondered if Dominic has somehow persuaded the lady to attend this evening—for Nathan's sake. Dominic had the kind of gentle, caring heart that would forever steal her breath, and her soul. Her eyes filled with tears just thinking about his selfless efforts.

Before he reached them, Dominic turned away again, briefly, no doubt checking Jane Weller's whereabouts. Fleur tried to pick out Lawrence but failed. The livery and wigs were equalizers—apart from varying height, all the men who wore them looked the same.

Dominic arrived and bowed all around. "I am the luckiest of men," he said. "I have the most beautiful women in the room all to myself. What's the matter with the men here? Why aren't you all dancing?"

Aunt Enid whacked him with her fan and both Worth sisters tittered.

"Would you care to dance, Hattie?" Dominic said, offering her his hand.

Hattie blew him a kiss and said, "I'm saving my dancing for John."

"Mother?"

"I'm saving my feet," the Dowager said. "Ask Fleur."

Her heart speeded up. "I believe I'm promised to Mr. Stanton for this one," she said.

Dominic picked up her card, checked it and said, "No. You have no excuse not to dance with me."

Fleur could think of many reasons why she shouldn't dance with him. She couldn't say any of them aloud and neither could she make a scene by refusing to dance. "Thank you," she said and accompanied him toward the floor.

Her short train twisted. She twitched it straight—and saw knowing looks passing between the Dowager and Hattie. Even the aunts appeared fatuous.

31

Bless Mary Eaton. Dominic faced Fleur and drew her lightly into his arms. Unless Mary realized too soon that he had fabricated—just a little—in telling her he worried deeply about his brother's state of mind, she was the perfect diversion. Let Nathan struggle with his feelings for her, and let him try to melt her heart again. The reentry into his life of his old love would keep his mind off Fleur, at least while Dominic's drama with her played out.

The girl Dominic danced with scarcely seemed to touch the floor. And her features were as remote as a marble sculpture. He turned his head to make sure he could locate Jane Weller. She stood at one side of the entrance to one of the alcoves where food was served. Lawrence stood on the other. All was well and Dominic didn't know if he felt relieved.

"I have been foolish," Fleur said, startling him.

He enjoyed dancing with her, enjoyed the envious looks from other men. "Why do you say that?"

"From when I was a little girl I've been strong. Strong-minded I suppose you'd say."

"I won't argue with that," he said and smiled. A wasted effort.

"You wouldn't have made love to me if I'd told you not to."

He glanced about. "Have a care."

"Yes," she said and at least a little color came into her cheeks. "Please remember that I caused us—"

"No, you didn't," he said rapidly. "And this isn't a good time and place to discuss such matters."

"I most certainly did. Why can't you accept that you aren't less of a man because you were seduced by a woman?"

He moved her across the floor so fast she was too breathless to speak. "Now," he said when they were finally in a less populated area of the floor, "listen to me. You cannot do what you don't know how to do. But the question of who did what is immaterial. At least to me. It happened."

Mr. Mergatroyd danced close with Victoria Crewe-Burns. "Lovely evenin', Elliot," he said. "Top-notch. Absolutely top-notch."

Dominic gritted his teeth and nodded, and turned Fleur until they were too far away for conversation with Mergatroyd.

"Why did you go to great lengths to get Lady Mary here?" Fleur asked.

Damn the girl for her cheek—and wits. "One day I'll tell you all about Nathan and Mary. Not tonight."

"Is that Lawrence on the other side of the alcove from Jane?" Fleur asked.

"Yes," he said shortly. Why try to pretend nothing was going on?

"There's plenty of time for an attempt to be made on her— or someone else."

"You know too much," Dominic said.

"True," Fleur said. "But I am curious about everything and I seem to fall onto information. I don't plan to eavesdrop, as you call it."

Dominic sighed. "Would you ever be able to stay out of someone else's business?"

"Not if I cared about the person. Or I thought a wrong might be committed."

"Gad, you're impossible."

She tilted her head and looked at him. "Will you enter a monastery or is that what you threaten whenever you're afraid a woman is getting too serious about you?"

"Dammit, miss! You are enough to drive a man to a monastery."

She smirked. "I don't think they'll have you."

"I beg your pardon?"

"I don't think they'll have you. You're too wicked. You'd keep falling asleep in prayers or something awful. And you are a very sexual man."

He checked behind him. "Those are not things a young lady says to a gentleman."

"Even if they're true?"

"*Especially* if they're true."

They stared at one another and he fought not to laugh. Fleur's smile helped him. Sadness lay in her eyes.

"I love you, Dominic," she said.

He stopped dancing and swallowed. His skin felt icy and tight. And at the same time his heart began to bump faster. "Then why not—"

"I don't expect anything from you. The memories you've given me won't be enough, but I'll learn to live with them. I don't belong in your world."

He hardly reacted to a thump in the middle of his back. "Yes, you do."

"Come on," Nathan said in a startlingly agitated voice. "It's happening."

Dominic raised his chin to see over the crowd and saw Albert Parker, wigless now, running toward one of the doors to the balcony.

"Go back to the other women," he told Fleur. "Quickly. Try to behave as normally as you can or we'll have panic. Go!"

Fleur struggled through the crowd toward Hattie and the rest of the family. It was too late to stop the panic Dominic had mentioned—already people surged across the big room talking loudly, appearing shocked, clutching at one another. They went in the direction in which Dominic and Nathan had gone.

For a brief moment she saw Franklin Best. He dodged those in his way and made speedy progress.

By the time she rejoined the others Snowdrop had already left with Chloe and Hattie was on her feet with an aunt on each arm.

"What's happened?" the Dowager asked Fleur. "Did you see anything?"

"Yes. Dominic says we're to stay calm."

Hattie pressed her lips together and narrowed her eyes to peer across the press of people. "You know all about it, don't you?" she said.

"I think so," Fleur told her. "This is too much for Miss Prunella and Miss Enid."

"It's too much for all of us," the Dowager said. "We must leave it to the men. They know what they're doing. We can't persuade our guests to be calm, but we will pray everyone is safe."

The side of the ballroom where they stood was all but empty. The Dowager led the way to the stairs and the others followed.

All but Fleur.

She was grateful they failed to notice she wasn't with them. She couldn't leave as long as she didn't know if The Cat had been caught and Jane was safe.

She noticed that Lady Mary Eaton continued to sit quietly at her table. A few servants hung back. Above her, faces ringed the gallery and the din from anxious conversation rose and fell. She thought the music had stopped.

A maid moved between tables with a tray, carefully removing plates and glasses. Fleur noticed the woman never looked in the direction of the crowd at the other side of the room.

"Fleur?"

She turned around to see Gussy Arbuthnot with her hands pressed to her cheeks. "Oh, Gussy, this is frightening."

"Do you think it's The Cat? You know he got me, don't you? You probably read it in the newspaper."

"Yes, and I'm so sorry you had such a scare."

Gussy came and put an arm through one of Fleur's. "My family blamed me for it. Can you imagine? They still think it was somehow my fault and my father is furious that I cost him so much money."

"Poor, poor Gussy." Fleur took the other girl in her arms and hugged her. "I'm sure he'll get over it and see how much more you're worth than the silly money."

"He never will," Gussy said. "He hates me. I want to get out of here."

"We will." There seemed little point in continuing to wait there.

So many people had started to crowd down the stairs that leaving that way would be difficult, even dangerous.

"We can get down from the balcony outside," Gussy said. "Then we'll go in by the front door and find somewhere to wait quietly."

Lawrence held Jane Weller tightly. He buried her face in the pale blue coat of his livery and glared at the guests milling around them. "M'lord," he cried when he saw Dominic. "Can you make them get back?"

Nathan went to work at once, urging people back inside the ballroom. Franklin Best worked the groups as did McGee and a band of male servants. Gradually the balcony cleared.

"Thank God you're safe," Dominic said to Jane, patting her back awkwardly. "Did you see him?"

Jane raised her face and began to cry. "I'm so sorry," she said. "It wasn't anything. Not really. Just a nasty joke."

Dominic waited while Lawrence murmured consoling words to Jane.

"I shouldn't have stepped outside but I forgot for a minute. I heard someone crying, see, so I looked."

"And?" Dominic said.

"He pulled me. The boy did, the one from the night The Cat got me. I'm sure it was him. He pulled me across the balcony with me screaming all the way. I thought that man would get me again. But then the boy let go and ran away. He ran down to the grounds and I didn't see which way he went."

Dominic and Lawrence frowned at each other. "A diversion?" Dominic said. He spun around and ran into the ballroom. The music played again and guests returned to their tables. The dance floor began to fill up.

When he reached the place where he expected to find his

family, they had left. Nathan arrived and said, "The chaos must have been too much for the aunts."

Dominic felt uneasy. "I suppose it must." He expected to see Fleur emerge from somewhere.

"Nathan! Dominic!"

"Mary," Nathan said. "I forgot she was there alone."

On her feet again, Lady Mary walked awkwardly toward them, steadying herself on the backs of chairs and swinging her feet forward. "Is everything all right?" she asked.

Nathan met her and stood as if ready to catch her if she fell. "We think so," he said.

"Dominic. That lovely girl you were dancing with left through that door onto the balcony. I am most concerned. Another young woman was with her but your young lady tried to change her mind and come back."

"You mean, Fleur? She wore red."

"That's the one. I'm almost certain she was forced to leave."

Dominic started to move. "By whom?"

"Someone outside. I saw a hand shoot out, then she was gone—and the other girl."

32

Wicked people wanted to see fear in the eyes of their victims, to hear them beg for mercy.

Fleur didn't know why she sat, tied hand and foot, in a carriage that rumbled through London's meanest streets, or why Gussy Arbuthnot perched on the seat opposite, her face filled with hatred. Whatever the reason, Fleur would remain quiet and composed for as long as she could. If it was to be her lot that suffering lay ahead, she prayed she could give her kidnappers as little satisfaction as possible.

If only it was as easy to quiet her heart as to control her face. She hid her steady trembling by holding her body rigid. The palms of her bound hands were moist with sweat.

The carriage lights outside cast ghostly shadows over the shabby interior, over Gussy's pinched features. Her eyes glowed with an inhuman fervor.

Along one street, through a small square, an alley where the conveyance barely fit, and another street and another.

"Don't you want to know where you are?" Gussy asked at last. "And where you're going?"

"If you'd like to tell me," Fleur said. "I'm sure you have a plan."

"You're so reasonable. So sweet and submissive."

Fleur wondered how Gussy could have formed such a wrong impression of her. "I expect I seem so," she said. One thing she would not deliberately do was to bait Gussy. "When you grow up in a small place and you're one of the minister's daughters, you learn to be seen and not heard." She shrugged and looked from the window. Rain had begun to fall hard.

"You won't be so sweet after tonight," Gussy said. "Not that it will matter."

"I see."

"No, you don't. You can't imagine that there are people who would hurt you because you're such a sap and such a nuisance. And because you're in the way. Guess what will happen in the end?"

Fleur made an amazed face. "I don't know."

"I will take your place with the Elliots—the place that should have been mine in the beginning—and would have been if you hadn't come to London. This was my year. Everything was arranged."

Fleur shook her head. Gussy's presence, the way she poured out facts she should want to keep secret, convinced Fleur that she was never slated to return from tonight's horror.

"One of them would have asked for my hand two years ago, or last year, if I'd been more mature and more cunning. This year I set everything in motion to be sure they would concentrate on me. But the country mouse came to Town and stole all the attention. I was to be the brave one, the one who put aside her own fears to help save others. No matter, the plan will still work and I shall be the heroine in the end, taken into the arms of the family for good. Do you know why?" Gussy grinned.

"No," Fleur said. Her ankles alone, where the rope dug into her skin, were enough to make her want to cry.

"Because I will be the one who tried to save you." She laughed until she choked. "When they find us, I'll be holding you and sobbing over you."

"Why?" Fleur asked quietly.

"You know why." Gussy gave her a sly, sideways glance. "Because you'll be dead."

All of this because Gussy meant to marry Dominic or Nathan? Fleur couldn't imagine what part the girl had played in The Cat's escapades, other than to capitalize on her own abduction by currying sympathy. Yet now she traveled with the man and a boy dressed in rags—and she went willingly. Gussy had helped hold Fleur while the man wearing a shiny black mask had tied her up. How could she not believe they intended to kill her?

"It's Nathan I want," Gussy continued. "I have always wanted him. But he pined for Lady Mary Eaton. Now she has reappeared but he won't take a cripple as his wife. Olivia Prentergast tried to capture Nathan's attention and I'll never forgive her for it. She knew how I felt. She moved on to her officer, but only because Nathan didn't know she was alive. Still I made sure she suffered. Her father almost refused to pay for her return."

Fleur tried to close out Gussy's voice.

"Vicky Crewe-Burns escaped her punishment because she got frightened she'd be caught leaving the house. She set her cap for Nathan, too, and I made sure she thought it could be he who waited for her in the park, but she has no courage. She sent the maid instead. Jane Weller was a nuisance who should not have been set free, but she proved most useful this evening."

The carriage ground to a halt.

Gussy knelt on her seat and called through the trap to the driver, "Why are we stopping? I haven't finished."

"Indeed, I think you have," came the cultured reply. "Step out of the carriage. You can wait up here with Harry."

Gussy gave a shriek of fury. She flounced around on the seat again and lunged forward, her teeth bared, to slap Fleur's face. She pinched her cheeks and pulled her nose, took her by the neck and shook her. "We're driving around to make sure we aren't followed," she cried. "You'll never be rescued."

Fleur tried to put her bound hands between them but Gussy bit the fingers.

Do not cry out, do not beg, do not say anything at all.

Gussy punched Fleur in the stomach and pain caught under her ribs. She couldn't breathe. Gussy punched her in the same place and Fleur doubled over.

She heard a coach door open and slam back. "Enough. I told you not to touch her," the same male voice as before said harshly, and Fleur looked up. A man in a black leather, full-face mask leaned into the carriage and lifted Gussy. Promptly Fleur suffered a flurry of painful kicks to her shins before Gussy, her arms and legs still flailing, disappeared outside.

For a moment she was left alone and she wasted no time wrenching open the other door with her bound hands and throwing herself from the coach. The fall to the ground shook every bone. Expecting someone to grab her at any moment, she rolled and kept on rolling away over muddy ground, with rain beating down on her. The soaked chiffon gown wound around her. There was nothing to see but falling rain and a leaden sky that felt inches from her body. The coach had stopped in an open space but Fleur couldn't guess where she might be.

Yells came from the direction of the coach and Fleur imagined the struggle going on between The Cat and Gussy. Gussy, the friend who had said she would take Fleur under her wing.

Would they ask the Elliots for ransom money, even if they had already killed her? Of course they would.

If only she could see Dominic just once more. She closed her eyes and her heart ached. He was there, in her mind, his dark hair blowing in the wind, his eyes so very blue. And he held a hand out, his white sleeve billowing from his arm. He offered her his hand, asked her to hold it and let him take her away.

She would hold him in her heart and in her head and fight as hard as she could. Fleur gave herself another shove, and barely held back a scream. She hurtled downward, slipping and sliding, catching on roots and revolving until she landed, facedown, in a gully filled with rocks where a trickle of water ran.

She felt the sting of many cuts and bruises, her head hurt and her eyes ached, but her mind didn't waver. Wearily, she rested the side of her face on the rocks and kept still.

Dominic read two o'clock in the morning on his fob watch. He pounded the back of the chair where he hid. He longed to act, to find the madman who had Fleur and crush him.

The Cat, and he was sure it was he who took Fleur and Gussy, had done the unexpected and stayed away from the cavernous warehouse with its lavishly decorated but flimsy little house built inside.

Convinced the man would eventually bring her there, Dominic remained inside the hidden St. James Street house. Franklin Best concealed himself on the gallery with the bizarre collection of music boxes, ready to back up Dominic who sat on his haunches behind a large easy chair facing the door, waiting to attack. The front door was the only way in or out of the building within a building. Not even the windows opened.

The place had no available water and, apart from liquor and chocolates, no sign of anything to eat or drink. The scent of chocolate Jane Weller had mentioned hung in the air from the chocolate houses on St. James Street. He would find a way to reward Jane for her bravery.

"This is unbearable, this waiting," Dominic said, loud enough for Franklin to hear. They knew the sound of the creaky warehouse door opening would alert them to anyone arriving.

"Too much time is passing," Franklin said. "But perhaps they have found her elsewhere."

Dominic bounced to his feet and bent over, loosening the muscles in his legs. "If they had, someone would have come directly here to tell us."

After they'd found The Cat's house empty, Nathan left to organize a search. The effort seemed hopeless, but they had to try. At Heatherly, Hattie and the Dowager kept a lookout for any sign of Fleur's return.

"I can stay here and watch for them if you want to join Nathan," Franklin said.

"You don't think they're coming back, do you?" Dominic said bitterly, voicing the notion he didn't want to believe. "You think she's already dead."

"Don't say that."

Of course, Franklin was very taken with Fleur himself. "I don't want to say it or think it," Dominic muttered. "But if there had been a demand for ransom, I would have been informed at once. I can only think the worst."

"Do you want to go?"

"It's the waiting and doing nothing that destroys me, but I'm sure he will bring her here—in time." He closed his eyes against thoughts of what the man might be doing to her now—

or already have done to her. Lady Mary had insisted that Gussy pushed Fleur outside. Dominic didn't know what to think about that.

"Why have you introduced Fleur to other men?"

Dominic raised his face toward the balcony. "I beg your pardon?"

"You heard me. You have introduced Fleur to other men yet you don't want anyone else to have her."

"That's—" Why tell another lie? "You're right. I want her for myself."

When Fleur opened her eyes, the earliest gray light turned a dribble of water to quicksilver beneath her head. She shook from the cold and couldn't feel her hands and feet.

Click-clicking sounded. She raised her head, turned her stiff neck with difficulty, and saw a hedgehog cross the rocks with several almost grown young in its wake.

Before she had slept, if that's what it had been that stole her consciousness, she had listened to curses and yells from those who had brought her here. Twice they had come quite close and she waited to be found, but they'd missed the gully in the darkness and at last they gave up searching.

No human sounds reached her now. She dared to hope they had left in the night.

Fleur raised her hands, inch by inch, until she could look at them. Her hands had swollen and turned blue. She moved the white tips of her fingers, almost crying from the pain, but she must try to get free.

"Are you alive?" a voice whispered.

She jumped so badly she thought she would be sick.

Someone poked her gently. "You're alive. Best stay quiet."

"Who are you?" Fleur asked.

"That don't matter. Keep still and I'll untie your hands. I can't do no more for you. It'll be up to you then, and if I'm asked, I never saw you."

A pair of battered shoes came into view and their owner crouched near Fleur's head. The hem of a torn and filthy coat settled among the wet rocks. It was the boy who traveled with The Cat—and Gussy. Harry. His hands looked as cold as hers and his dirty fingernails moved slowly when he worked with the rope that bound her wrists together.

"Thank you," Fleur whispered. She wanted to ask why he was doing this but dared not risk that he would change his mind.

Slowly the bonds loosened until, eventually, she could start to rub her hands together. Slowly, blood started to return and the pain made her gasp.

"I got to put it back on," the boy said after a short while.

Stricken, she shook her head and looked into his face.

The lad who stared back had intelligent hazel eyes and long, curly hair that might be blond if it were washed. He put a finger to his lips and listened. Then he bent closer. "I got to. I'll put the rope on so you can get out of it again yourself, but I don't know what he'd do to me if he ever found out I let you go."

So it was useless. Barring some miracle, she would remain a captive—until they were ready to do whatever they planned for her. Fleur tried not to think of death.

Lashed together once more, even if more loosely, her wrists burned where the rope sank into punished flesh. The fire and ice in her hands was unspeakable. She looked at the boy and said, "Thank you." She was grateful for the risk he had taken for her.

"Harry? Harry, where are you?" The man shouted and he wasn't far away.

"That's me," the boy whispered. "Gawd. He'll kill me for

sure if he finds out what I did. You close your eyes now—I'm going to call back to him. Over here! This way!" He scrambled up and waved his arms. "I've found her."

Fleur closed her eyes and felt her hot tears. She blinked, squeezed her eyes shut tight trying to dry the evidence.

The heavy thud of feet on muddy ground vibrated in Fleur's ear. He was coming for her again, The Cat, and this time he would be angry because she had foiled him, at least for a few hours.

"Get back to the carriage, Harry. If the Arbuthnot woman tries to get your sympathy—don't speak to her."

Fleur heard Harry scramble away.

Fingers settled on her neck. "You're alive. Little fool to try to escape in such circumstances." A heavy, warm blanket—or, more likely, his cloak—covered her. When he lifted her, Fleur hung heavy and limp. She scarcely believed her good fortune when he put her over his shoulder rather than carrying her in his arms. At least her face would be hidden and they wouldn't see if her eyes moved.

The creature had broad, strong shoulders and he carried her from the gully as if she weighed nothing.

Suddenly he bellowed, "Harry! Get that woman out of the carriage."

Gussy's furious shouts didn't make sense to Fleur.

"On the box," the man shouted back. "You'll ride with me. We've got very little time. We lost anyone who tried to follow, but I must reach our destination before there are too many people about."

With a pistol in his hand, Dominic examined the warehouse—and found nothing, not even leftover materials from the work that had been carried out there.

Four o'clock had brought first hint of light and he'd been unable to remain in the make-believe house a moment longer.

"Dominic?" Franklin joined him. "If we go out there, at least we can do something, we can search and keep on searching until she is found."

"Dead or alive," Dominic said tonelessly.

Franklin rubbed his eyes. "Yes."

"I shouldn't have left her behind when the commotion started last night." If only he'd held her hand and kept her with him.

"Of course you should," Franklin said. "Any man would have done the same thing when he thought he was going into danger."

"I assumed The Cat always came back here." Dominic looked through a grime-filmed window onto the large patch of ground behind the warehouse, where grass and weeds grew to the height of a man's waist.

"Could he have changed his mind because he found out Jane Weller was there?" Franklin said. "He may have thought she'd told you about this place."

Dominic watched a spider outside the window. It vibrated at the center of its dewdrop web. "I wondered the same thing, but he would expect Jane to keep quiet about what happened to her, not talk about it when she was trying to get a place after being let go from another household. The Crewe-Burnses told lies about the girl, remember, and Gussy knew it."

"Mary must have been mistaken about Gussy—"

"They're coming," Dominic said, casting about. "Get back inside the house quickly. There's no cover in the warehouse."

"We can jump him here," Franklin said.

"Move," Dominic replied and ran with a hand on Franklin's shoulder. "Go back where you were. We'll only get one chance and he'll likely be armed. I think he's carrying Fleur. Gussy's there, and that boy."

They were barely in their places when The Cat and his entourage entered the warehouse.

Dominic had extinguished the only candle he'd lit.

Footsteps sounded on the front steps and the door opened. Dominic saw The Cat go to a table in the center of the room and bend to put a spark to several candles there.

"Over there, Gussy," he said. "Sit on the floor. Harry, tie her up till I've got what I want from her."

"Don't you put a finger on me," Gussy told Harry. Her voice got higher. "I warn you, if he comes near me I'll scratch his eyes out."

"I doubt it, although you're good at scratching, aren't you? I told you not to touch Fleur but you did it anyway. Sit still and keep quiet. Harry will tie you up. I can't keep my eyes on you all the time. I've got things to do."

Dominic wanted to rush the man. He wanted this over now, but he wanted Fleur away from The Cat first. He was bound to put her down while he did whatever he'd come to do and Dominic would take advantage of the opportunity.

"Let me help you." Gussy whined and hit out at the boy when he approached her with lengths of twine. "It'll be quicker. Then all you have to do is drop me in the woods near Heatherly, with her, so I can wait for them to find me."

"And welcome you into the bosom of the family, and be forever grateful that you tried to save Fleur."

Dominic looked at the bundle The Cat held over his shoulder. It was Fleur all right. Her red hair hung loose from inside a heavy cape that swathed her.

Tried to save Fleur. Was she already dead?

The Cat lowered her from his shoulder and set her on the

floor. Dominic's heart pounded. The man set Fleur down much more carefully than he would a dead woman.

Dominic raised his pistol, then lowered it again. Rather than move away, The Cat went to help Harry tie Gussy up.

Dominic needed a clear shot. And he wanted to wound the man, not kill him. There were questions to be asked.

The man tore the leather hood from his head and Dominic sucked in a breath. He pulled farther back behind the chair. Noel DeBeaufort, his blond curls flattened to his head, returned to tying up Gussy.

"The money's all here, isn't it?" Gussy said. "That's what you've come for. Take your pistol and kill Fleur now. Get it over with. Then take the money, leave me as we planned and you're away. Untie me. I don't know why you've tied me up, anyway."

"Get something to gag her with," Noel said. "I hate the sound of her voice." He sank to his haunches, took Gussy by the shoulders and shook her till she cried out. "You're the one who dies. Right here. Who knows how long it'll be before your body's found. I've changed my mind about everything. Fleur goes with me. We'll get away by sea and eventually she'll come to love me. We'll be rich and she'll have everything she wants."

"The letter has gone to her family," Gussy said, her voice shaky. "We worked everything out. They will find out too late to do anything, too late to reach the Elliots and ask for help. It will all be perfect."

Dominic positioned himself to see Noel as clearly as possible. Fleur was in the clear, but if he fired now, the chances were high that he'd hit Gussy or Harry. Loathsome creature that she was, he had no desire to kill Gussy and the lad deserved a chance.

He saw the slightest movement and stared at Fleur. He could see her face and her eyes were closed, but beneath the cloak something shifted. *Don't move. Don't try to do anything, my darling.*

No sooner had the thought gripped him when she rolled toward Noel where he crouched beside Gussy. Dominic realized Fleur's ankles were tied but she lunged at Noel's back and hung on to him, hit him with hands that moved in slow motion. Noel stood up with her clinging to him.

"Kill her," Gussy cried. "Kill her now. I told you she was trouble. Take me with you instead—you know how good we are together."

Dominic had no choice but to reveal himself. He slithered from his hiding point and threw himself at Noel and Fleur. Noel swung around in time to see Dominic. The man reached back to grab a handful of Fleur's hair with one hand while he raised a pistol and stuck it into her neck with the other.

Harry yelled, "No, don't hurt her."

Noel looked at Dominic's pistol and said, "One inch closer and you know what I'll do."

"You can't get away," Dominic told him. "Put Fleur down and we'll talk."

Noel's face twisted. "The likes of you don't want to talk to the likes of me. You tolerate me because of my family but you know I've been cast out. I wanted to show them how well I could succeed. I still will in my own way, only this time I'll make sure they aren't welcome in any polite company afterward—in Town or elsewhere."

A shot rang out.

Dominic turned his head in time to see Franklin fling himself to the gallery floor.

Noel swung Fleur around him and held her like a shield while he lined up his pistol, aiming straight for Franklin.

In the second left to him, Dominic leaped on top of both Fleur and Noel, knowing how he would hurt her but wanting only to save her life, and Franklin's.

Noel's shot went wild. He snapped his fingers at Harry and said, "My other pistol," in a panicked voice, but Dominic thrust Fleur aside and pinned both of Noel's arms to the floor and sat astride the man's hips.

Franklin slithered and slipped down the curving steps and Dominic saw a bloodstain spreading on his right shoulder. He had been hit after all.

"Stay where you are, man," Dominic told him. "Put your left fist into the wound and press to help stop the bleeding."

Franklin sat on a stair and did as he was told.

"Dominic," Fleur said and he gave her his full attention, hating to see how she had been hurt by these people. "The boy tried to help me. Be kind to him." She sounded weak.

Dominic stared into DeBeaufort's frightened eyes and considered beating him to a bloody pulp. He restrained himself, brought the butt of his pistol down on Noel's nose and took pleasure in hearing the man's cry, and watching blood spurt.

"Sir?" Harry stood in front of Dominic, "It's all over now, isn't it?"

Dominic nodded, although he wished he had one more able-bodied man to help him get Noel DeBeaufort into the hands of the law, sorry as those hands were.

"Sir," Harry said. "I'd be obliged if you wouldn't kill my father. My mother died when I was a babe, but she would want me to ask you to spare him."

Noel's son. Who would have thought such a thing?

"He's not mine," Noel said. "His mother was a maid. I did her a favor by taking him in."

The likeness between the man and boy was unmistakable but Dominic didn't say anything. "Harry, would you undo Fleur's ankles?"

"Don't you dare, you snot," Gussy snapped, then she met Dominic's eyes. "It's not the way it looks. He made me help him."

The sound of the warehouse door opening came to Dominic again. He held his breath and prayed to see friend not foe.

With both hands Franklin trained his pistol on the door and Dominic did the same.

Nathan was the first to appear, his green eyes narrowed to furious slits. To Dominic's amazement, behind him came their brother John, Marquis of Granville. His handsome face bore deep, weary lines and he'd obviously been traveling, but he surveyed the scene rapidly.

"I'll tell you the whole story later," Dominic said.

"Nathan already did." John went immediately to haul De-Beaufort to his feet, spin him around and pull his arms up behind his back. "Take care of your lady." John was accustomed to giving orders and having them obeyed.

Dominic was too exhausted to argue.

Nathan untied Gussy's ankles and pulled her to her feet.

"She's his partner," Dominic said, indicating Noel. "She must be punished. The boy is Noel's son. He's suffered enough. He'll come back to Heatherly with us for now."

He lifted up Fleur and went to Franklin. "Put your good arm around my shoulders and let's get out of here."

"Take Franklin first," Fleur said in a hoarse voice.

"I'll take you both," Dominic said, and there, in front of all assembled, he said, "I love you, Fleur. Will you be my wife?"

John showed signs of laughing and Dominic shot him a look promising punishment if he did. John straightened his face. "She's a very brave girl," he said. "Nathan told me about her."

"I'm sure Nathan told you about everything," Dominic said. What had possessed him to ask for Fleur's hand here?

"You need time to think," she said through swollen lips. "Your emotions can't be trusted at such a time."

Dominic's temper began to simmer. "I asked if you would be my wife and I've never been more sure of my emotions in my life. Answer me properly or I'll leave you here."

John, Nathan and Franklin sputtered and Fleur bowed her head, to hide a smile, Dominic suspected.

"Fleur?"

"Well," she said in a small voice. "I certainly don't want to be left here."

33

"You are sure Fleur meant to accept you?" John Elliot Marquis of Granville asked. One corner of his mouth jerked down and ruined the serious effect.

Slumped deeply in one of the study chairs at Heatherly, Dominic waited for news from the sawbones who had been called in to attend both Fleur and Franklin. Franklin, who was determined his wound would not be serious, had asked to be patched up before returning to his parents' home.

"John asked you something, old man," Nathan said. "You seem to think Fleur accepted your pathetic proposal. Wouldn't be at all sure if I were you."

Dominic studied first one, then the other and gave a self-satisfied grin. "I might have expected jealousy from you, Nathan. But you're a married man, John."

"Miss Toogood is a lovely girl," John said. His black, curly hair showed signs of the rough night he'd had. "However, as you've noted, I'm a married man and in case you've forgotten, my wife is Hattie. I assure you I shall never have need to look elsewhere."

The Dowager came into the study. She paused a few moments to examine her brood and her pleasure radiated. "John," she said, holding out her arms. "I didn't have time to greet you properly when you arrived. Welcome home. How was Vienna?"

"Productive," John said with his customary brevity on the subject of the diplomatic work he did for the Crown. "We are seeing the world change before our eyes."

John hugged his mother and Dominic felt that his life was complete for the first time in weeks. Almost complete.

"Hattie had just gone up to take a rest before you arrived," the Dowager said to John, taking the chair Nathan held for her. "I'm told she fell asleep and I decided not to awaken her. You'll be able to surprise her all on your own." Her eyes twinkled.

John breathed in slowly through his nose, giving Dominic the feeling his brother was more than ready to "surprise" his wife. "And Chloe?" John asked.

"She entertains us all and she's in the best of health," the Dowager said. "We dote on her." She turned to Dominic. "I am so grateful you found Fleur in time. What a terrible experience, for her and for you. She tells me you are to be married."

Dominic took a moment to collect himself. "She did?" He grinned. "And she's quite right, too."

"You haven't spoken with her father yet," Nathan said, but he slapped Dominic on the back and said, "Bravo. Congratulations."

"She's giving the doctor a terrible time," the Dowager said. "Insists there's nothing wrong with her but a few bruises. She admits to painful wrists and ankles. But she told him that since she has no broken bones she need not be in bed. Snowdrop is all but sitting on her to make her stay there."

"That's Fleur," Dominic said.

"She is exhausted, though," the Dowager said. "You'll have to insist she take life easy for a bit. At least until the wedding—which I understand will be soon."

"Me?" Dominic looked around. "You want me to insist Fleur does something?"

Nathan started passing drinks. When he gave one to Dominic he said, "You're going to marry her. You'd better find a way to control her—at least some of the time."

Dominic frowned. He did not intend to lose sleep over Fleur's high spirits—and he already had an idea for making sure they understood one another's needs well. "How is Franklin?" he asked his mother.

"Asleep," she said. "More from shock than the wound, I think, although he lost some blood. The doctor says it's a *lucky* wound, whatever that means."

"Did Nathan tell you the aunts are here?" Dominic asked John. "And they haven't changed, unfortunately."

"He mentioned something about it. I've told you that all you have to do with them is be patronizing. They love it."

Everyone laughed.

"They may accomplish something we've all wanted," Nathan said. "If they get their way we'll see Mama's paintings."

"Really?" John said. "I don't know why you're so humble, Mother. It's about time you shared your work with us."

"So that you can laugh at me?" the Dowager said. "Most unlikely."

"You are too shy, Mother," Nathan said. "You always have been."

"Perhaps," the Dowager said, sobering. "McGee is finding Harry a place to sleep. He'll have a bath and get some new clothes. But we shall have to decide what is to become of him. I wonder if he'd enjoy a place in the country."

Dominic spread his fingertips on top of his desk. "It won't be an easy task, but I think we should inform the DeBeauforts. They may choose to ignore the boy, but there's no doubt he's their grandson. Just look at him."

The Dowager said, "A little sherry, please, Nathan." She sighed hugely. "Things will go badly for Noel."

"Yes," Dominic put down his own glass. "And for Gussy. But all that will be up to the law."

"There will be plenty of people to bring charges," Nathan said.

They didn't meet one another's eyes.

John left the salon and barely stopped himself from running to the wing beyond the orangeries, up two long flights of stairs, and storming the extensive suite of rooms he and Hattie shared when they were at Heatherly.

Instead, when he got to the suite he let himself quietly into the anteroom, walked through the sitting room and Hattie's softly lit boudoir, and lightly pushed on the door to the bedchamber. A wedge of yellow light slowly widened into the room and he saw the big, red lacquer chinoiserie bed his wife prized. As usual, Hattie slept in a ball with the covers pulled over her head.

Deep warmth, edged with arousal, came as a familiar—and urgent—friend. John no longer tried to soften his footsteps, rather he walked purposefully, knowing his habit of scuffing his heels would wake up Hattie and she would smile and reach for him.

He got all the way to the side of the bed before the bump under the covers moved. A hand appeared, and another, and two softly rounded white arms stretched.

"Mmm," came from a muffled place before Hattie caught

the sheet between a finger and thumb on each hand and edged it down until her gold hair, then her sleepy gray eyes came into view.

"John?" she said, squinting. Then, "John, oh, John," and she scrambled out to throw herself at him.

He laughed and took a steadying step backward. "I hope that's not, "Oh, No, John, No, John, No-o, John, Nooo!" He sang the line from a raucous old ditty he and his brothers had been known to use when they wanted to be annoying.

Hattie giggled, at least, he thought she did. Kissing every inch of him that she could reach made other activities all but impossible.

"Allow me to carry you with me while I lock the doors, madam. We need privacy so that we can discuss important matters."

"Hah. John Elliot, you are a buffoon. But you'd better lock the doors anyway since we don't want to be caught doing nothing but…well…" She buried her face in his neck and clung to him while he secured the suite.

"Now," he said, returning to the bedroom and managing to remove at least his neckcloth at the same time. "Stand there and prepare to be adored." He stood her on the bed and took hold of the hem of her nightrail.

In a moment it came off over her head and she plopped to sit down—and covered her breasts with her folded arms.

John didn't allow himself to frown but it wasn't like Hattie to be bashful at moments like this. He stripped quickly, dropping his clothes and kicking aside his boots.

"John," Hattie whispered. "Just to see your face is to want you. To see you naked is a raging need in me."

Beside her on the bed, he took her in his arms and stroked her hair. "You know I'm a man who relishes the work he does, and the travel. But I can hardly bear to be away from you."

Hattie placed both hands on his chest and pushed him back, but only a little. "I've changed," she said and her blush was like fire. "Surely you can see?"

He could feel the tightening in his throat and the fear that crept around his heart. "What do you mean?"

She touched his lips and smiled. "Look at me, all of me."

"With pleasure." What he saw was the same woman he saw in his dreams when they were apart. Perhaps she was even more beautiful. He smoothed her breasts with the pads of his fingers and leaned to kiss her deeply. "I love you," he murmured.

"Look, John," she said, and her lower lip trembled.

Puzzled, he did as she asked and concentrated. He glanced from her breasts to her belly and back again, and traced the blue veins on one breast. He weighed it, then spread his hand over her faintly but definitely swelling belly.

"A baby?" he said, barely able to find a breath.

Hattie spread herself on her back and pulled his face to her tummy. "A baby," she told him.

The household slept, apart from the servants and the Dowager Marchioness of Granville. The hour was noon and she had been busy since nine. She could not have tried to sleep longer when there was so much to do and it could be done much more quickly without help from her family.

Already a rider was well on his way to Sodbury Martyr to see Reverend and Mrs. Toogood. Another had been dispatched to Squire Pool at the manor house in the same village. Both riders would deliver detailed letters of explanation, quite different in content, and the Toogoods would be urged to travel to London as soon as possible. The Dowager had little doubt that the letter she had written to the squire would turn the manor house upside down in no time.

But now she awaited visitors and already she heard the wheels of a carriage crunching over the gravel driveway she could see from the garden room.

McGee had waited with her throughout her vigil, as had Mrs. Lymer.

"I think that will be your visitors, milady," McGee said. "Will you receive them in the salon?"

"Here will do," she said. "This is a beautiful room. Very welcoming. You know what to do, Lymer."

McGee went quickly into the hall and opened the front door, while Lymer left the garden room by going through the shell room.

The carriage that rolled sedately up the drive spoke of wealth and good taste. Black, impeccable, and the horses perfectly matched. The coachman also wore black but with a crimson cape over the shoulders of his greatcoat.

McGee ran down the steps and waited until the coachman ushered his master and mistress to the ground. The gentleman spoke briefly to McGee while his wife looked up at Heatherly with her arms tightly crossed.

The DeBeauforts had arrived from Buckingham Street to see the boy they'd been told was their grandson.

The Dowager stood in readiness to greet her guests and she wouldn't have admitted it to a soul, but her stomach rolled dreadfully.

"Mr. and Mrs. Werther DeBeaufort," McGee announced, standing back to let the couple enter the garden room.

Bowing, DeBeaufort led his wife forward and said, "We're grateful you sent for us, my lady."

His wife's eyes were red from crying and her pale skin

blotched, but Mrs. DeBeaufort had the same naturally curly blond hair as her son—and her grandson—and despite the damage done by tears she was an elegant-looking woman.

"I'm sorry," the Dowager said. "There's nothing more I can say to help with what you're going through."

"Noel has always been difficult," Mr. DeBeaufort said. "We never considered he might be a criminal. But that's not why we're here."

"Where is the boy?" his wife asked.

The Dowager detested the pain these people must suffer. Perhaps in time she could help them, but a great deal must be resolved first.

"Will you see Harry now, my lady?" Lymer asked, approaching from the shell room with her hands on the lad's shoulders.

"Come along, Harry," the Dowager said. She could not imagine the boy's or the DeBeauforts' feelings.

Harry had certainly been washed. His hair, still long, curled to his shoulders and shone the color of bleached corn. As handsome as his father—and the likeness was striking—he needed to eat a good many nourishing meals to fill out his lanky body. He wore good clothes well but the mutinous expression on his face was still that of the unhappy boy who had arrived early in the morning.

Mrs. DeBeaufort burst into tears.

"Good Lord," her husband said, staring at Harry. "How old are you, boy?"

Harry looked about as if he might dash away, but turned back to the couple and said, "I think I'm twelve, but I could be thirteen."

"Werther!" Mrs. DeBeaufort swayed as if she would faint. "He's ours. Just look at him."

"Yes," her husband said, putting an arm around her. "Very well. Nothing to worry about, Harry. You'll call us Grandmother and Grandfather. Now we must get on. Where are your things?"

Harry turned red and shook his head. "There's nothing."

"I see," his grandfather said. "No matter."

"He'll have everything he needs, won't he, Werther?" Mrs. DeBeaufort said. "I know you must be frightened, Harry, but you're going to have a good home."

"My father did his best," Harry said. "Things made him unhappy."

The DeBeauforts looked at each other. "They always did," Mr. DeBeaufort said. "Thank Lady Granville for her kindness. We'll take you home now."

34

Four weeks later

"How much longer must we stay?" Dominic whispered in Fleur's ear.

Fleur said quietly, "I don't know about these things. I've never had a wedding or a wedding breakfast before." She did know that although she dared to hope, she must not be too sure the dream of today could be more than that, a dream. Once he was faced with the reality of doing his duty by her, he might regret his chivalry.

She had heard all about what happened with these Society marriages forged for expediency rather than love. Theirs was a different kind of expediency. She would bring no advantageous family liaison, no rich dowry. The truth, or at least part of it, was that Dominic felt responsibly for having made love to a virginal woman under his mother's protection. But in the weeks since the nightmare in St. James he had treated her with deference and shown her so many small and not so small kindnesses.

And he was happy now. Even through the tedious wedding preparations he'd remained in high spirits.

Fleur clung to every promising sign.

A silver-and-blue-clad flunky slid quietly beside them to place a tiered silver dish arranged with chocolate-dipped strawberries and crystalized apricots.

Dominic waited for the man to withdraw before he said, "You've been to weddings. Women know about these things."

"Village weddings, Dominic. They last all day and into the night. The bride and groom dance the night away."

He groaned. "This bride and groom won't."

"You must have been to lots of weddings like this one," Fleur told him. "You decide what we should do."

His attention became fixed on her face. "I have to get you away from here."

"Why?" She wasn't in a hurry to leave. "Everyone is having a wonderful time because they're here celebrating with us. Wouldn't leaving them so soon be thoughtless? The preparations took such effort and so many people to complete. It's all beautiful, too, and meant to be appreciated."

Dominic leaned away a fraction. "All I want to appreciate is you, and I do," he said. "I also have to make up to you for a broken promise."

"Have you drunk too much?" she asked, and used one of her perfected frowns.

"Not yet," he told her archly.

"What promise have you broken? I don't think I like the sound of that at all."

"I'll explain later," Dominic said, "and I promise you won't mind."

Fleur kissed him quickly but not so quickly that no guests noticed. Applause rippled from flower- and food-laden tables in the orangeries.

"Now look what I've done," Fleur said. "I've made a cake of myself."

He returned her kiss, but for such a long time that laughter and the clink of silver on crystal rose to a roar.

When Dominic pulled back, Fleur buried her face against his chest and he held her. This time a distinct sigh gusted across the air.

"We should say our goodbyes," Dominic murmured. "Your mother is enjoying every moment of watching us but I'm not sure your father approves."

"Oh, dear." Fleur sat up at once and smiled at her parents who were seated on the opposite side of the wedding party's table.

Papa was slower than Mama to return the smile, it was true, but she could tell he was happy. He had performed the marriage in the estate chapel with many of the guests standing along the walls or even spilling outside into the sunshine.

To Papa's right sat John with Hattie at his side. Talking to them would be pointless since they were wrapped in their own world. Even the aunts had commented on the couple's preoccupation since John's return from Vienna. The news that Hattie was increasing brought the Dowager and Fleur great satisfaction over their intuition.

Fleur turned to look through doors that stood open onto a terrace. Aunt Prunella and Aunt Enid had excused themselves to go outside and "get some air." They had been gone a long time.

Nathan sat at Fleur's left. He caught her eye and wrinkled his nose. "Probably can't stand it that they're not getting all the attention," he said, reading her thoughts.

"Perhaps," Fleur said, aware of the empty chair beside him. She knew he still hoped Lady Mary Eaton might arrive but felt certain she wouldn't come now that the ceremony was long over.

"I heard Jane Weller's to be a permanent member of the staff here," Franklin Best said. Fleur had insisted that he be included in the wedding party. "And there's talk that she may soon take up another position as well."

Nathan snorted. "All this romantic nonsense must be in the air."

"Jane is a lovely girl," the Dowager said. She raised a glass of red wine to her lips and took a long swallow. "Good for the blood, this," she remarked. "Jane will remain at the Dower House until she marries Mr. Lawrence. An appropriate match, I believe."

Dominic drummed his fingers on the table—close to Fleur's hand. "I don't think we shall leave today, after all," he said. "It's getting too late and Fleur is still recovering her health." He raised a finger to catch McGee's attention.

"My health is perfect," Fleur muttered.

"Kindly tell Snowdrop to have my wife's things moved to my suite," Dominic told McGee a moment later. "She should be ready to attend her there. And make the necessary arrangements to defer our departure until tomorrow…tomorrow afternoon, that is."

Every man at the table cleared his throat. Fleur couldn't imagine why but she did feel embarrassed at the idea of spending her wedding night under this roof—with the family, hers and Dominic's.

"I couldn't *believe* we had to wait two weeks to come here," Fleur's sister, Rosemary, said brightly. "Of course, it was all very exciting—especially for Letitia and Christopher—but they were busy gazing at each other and getting ready for their wedding journey so I wanted to get *on* because I knew you would need me, Fleur dear." While she spoke to Fleur, she faced Franklin.

"I'm sure Mr. Best doesn't want to hear about all our little happenings," Mama said with a speculative gleam in her eyes when she looked at Franklin, who leaned back in his chair looking pale and like a handsome soldier returned from a war.

Franklin came through as Fleur had known he would. "I am honored to be included at this table," he said. "And to meet Fleur's family. She does little else but talk about you so, of course, I couldn't wait."

"Wounds are ever so dashing, you know," Rosemary said, eyeing the way Franklin wore his coat loose over his injured shoulder to accommodate a sling. "Does it hurt very much?"

"Well." Franklin caught Fleur's eye and she saw a devilish glint. "It does rather but it's certainly much better than it was."

Rosemary's dark hair and eyes gave her a dramatic air and she knew what colors suited her best. She'd chosen to wear pale green for the wedding and once Chloe saw the material and the fashion plate, she'd begged for a dress, "just like that one," too.

"I'm so sorry you've been hurt," Rosemary told Franklin. "We believe fresh air and a relaxing atmosphere are good for convalescents. If you like, I'll gladly read to you in the gardens later."

"I should like that very much, Miss Toogood," Franklin said and Fleur noted he gave Rosemary quite the assessing stare.

"Zinnia and Sophie are such babies," Rosemary said of her younger sisters. "Quite embarrassing, really, running all over the place exclaiming. Now they're in the grounds with Chloe. I suppose she's showing them all sorts of things."

"Would you like to join them?" Fleur asked.

Rosemary bit the chocolate-covered end off a strawberry, chewed and swallowed. She looked at Franklin and said, "Oh, no. My older sister eloped, Mr. Best. That's Letitia, but I already told you that. She and her fiancé eloped and there was such a fuss."

"Rosemary," Mama said grimly.

Rosemary continued as if she hadn't heard her mother. "My father followed them with Christopher's father but they were too late to stop the marriage." She hunched her shoulders. "Isn't it romantic? But then they asked them to return to Sodbury Martyr where my father could marry them properly—and they agreed. Letitia and Christopher are much too nice. I should have floated off on a mist of mystery and the power of love and nothing would have made me go home."

"Rosemary!"

This time Papa addressed Rosemary who gave him a sweet smile.

"Now they're off on their wedding journey and they're going *everywhere*. The squire insisted." She grew quiet and looked at her hands. Tears sprang into her eyes. "I'm so glad for Letitia and Christopher. They really are the loveliest couple and they've had difficulties. But now those are over." She sniffed, blinked, and smiled once more.

"You talk too much," Fleur said. "But you're a love with a soft heart."

"Bosh," Rosemary said. "I'm a harridan. Ask anyone."

"Don't ask me," Franklin said. "Not if that's the answer you want."

Dominic really did need to get away from these well-meaning people and be alone with his wife. There didn't appear to be a way to do that quietly so he supposed he'd just have to cause an uproar by carrying Fleur off. The fleeting shadows that crossed her face didn't comfort him. The sooner he found out what those were about, the better.

He started to move his chair only to be stopped by the return of his aunts, who were both flushed and twittery.

"Sit down at once," the Dowager ordered. "You don't seem at all yourselves."

Hattie roused herself and said, "What is it, darlings? Have you had a fright?"

John and Dominic rose to hold the ladies' chairs.

"Of course not," Aunt Enid said, shocking her companions by lowering her voice. "A surprise, that's all." She and her sister sat down.

"Yes," Prunella said. "And we did something we probably shouldn't have done so we've decided to confess. With the reverend here that seems appropriate."

Seated again, Dominic rested an elbow on the table and ran his hand over his face.

"I don't usually hear confessions," Reverend Toogood said. "Certainly not in—"

"But you can," Aunt Prunella said testily. "Henrietta, dear sister, we have wronged you." She looked back at the reverend. "We've wronged our sister by using our nephew's wedding breakfast as a diversion while we got into her studio to look at her paintings when she didn't want anyone to do that." She caught her breath and pressed her hands together.

Mother actually slid down in her chair, crossed her arms and wouldn't look at anyone. She said, "I expected this to happen while you were here. You are so predictable. Thank you for apologizing. I don't want to talk about it ever again."

The more they drank and ate, the louder the other guests became and Dominic gave thanks for that. Nathan leaned forward to send him a questioning glance and they both turned toward John who looked at the ceiling and shook his head.

"They're really good, you know," Aunt Enid said. "The paintings. Warriors on horseback. Muscular men—like pugilists. And they're *huge*. I think Henrietta should have one of those exhibitions. You could have it here, John. In the long room. There are quite enough paintings for that."

"If that's what Mother wants, that's what she shall have," John said promptly. "I want more champagne."

More champagne was poured at once, all around the table.

"There's something we don't understand about your paintings, Henrietta," Prunella said. "The boots."

Fleur slid her hand into Dominic's and squeezed. "I don't think I can eat or drink another thing," she said. They had sat through nine courses and the dishes continued to come.

"The boots," the Dowager said darkly, "are necessary since the fields and hillsides are often muddy and there are rocks. If it were necessary to dismount, one would need boots."

"Well," Aunt Enid said, "I should think riding bare-bottom—"

"And bare everything else." Aunt Prunella interrupted her sister. "Not that we didn't find that most interesting and well done. I'm sure painting from life must be difficult—particularly with the horses. Do you send the grooms away and paint in the stables?"

Aunt Enid continued, "As I was saying, I should think riding bare-bottom would be more dangerous than standing barefoot in the mud."

This was absolutely not the time or place to laugh.

"The boots are representational," the Dowager said. "They denote masculine power and the allotted—if ridiculously so—superiority of the male sex."

Aunt Prunella appeared cross. "But you just said the mud—"

"I was trying to give you a simple explanation that would keep you quiet."

"Henrietta," Enid whispered, "where did you find that perfectly marvelous young man? You've painted him so many times."

"They are not all paintings of the same man," the Dowager said and Dominic almost groaned with relief at the humor in her eyes.

Reverend Toogood didn't quite hide his smile before he said, "I've got one question, then I think we should pack you off, Dominic."

Dominic could have kissed the man for changing the subject, particularly to the subject of leaving. "Yes, sir?"

"Do you understand your wife?"

Dominic blinked a few times. He doubted that was a standard question for a man to ask of his new son-in-law. "I think so," he said. "But I'd be a fool to say I don't expect to be surprised by discovering more unusual things about her."

"Will they bother you?"

"Absolutely not. If I'd wanted a boring wife, I'd have found one."

Reverend Toogood gave a satisfied nod. "Then you've both chosen well."

Arguing was pointless. Dominic insisted on carrying Fleur all the way to his rooms where Snowdrop sat quietly waiting in the sitting room, supposedly reading a book.

"Snowdrop will help you change," he told Fleur quietly when he set her down in the largest bedroom she had ever seen.

Despite the early hour, the draperies had been closed and candles lighted.

An excited, panicky, fluttering sensation attacked her stomach and her limbs didn't seem too sturdy.

Her trunks stood with the ones that must belong to Dominic and Fleur said, "It's not really too late to start our journey today."

"We've already started our journey," he said. "Don't you like our first stop?" He indicated the room.

"It's very nice," she said, feeling inadequate.

"Will you be happy living here at Heatherly?" he asked.

Fleur hadn't thought about where they would live. "I love Heatherly."

"You did say you didn't approve of separate beds for a husband and wife. If you've changed your mind I can have one put in the dressing room for myself. There is no second bedroom in this suite."

"I haven't changed my mind," she said in a small voice.

"Good. I'll call Snowdrop and you can change here. I'll use the dressing room."

"Change?" She glanced down at her lace gown. "Oh, you mean I should put on an ordinary dress, of course."

"That's not what I mean," he said. "It's time to prepare yourself for bed. Snowdrop—"

"No!" she said. "No, thank you." But she pressed a fist into her stomach and couldn't take her eyes from his face.

"What is it?" He sounded patient enough.

"It's still afternoon. Why would I get ready for bed?"

Something close to frustration darkened his eyes. "Why do you think, Fleur? We are man and wife and I want you in my bed. The time of day or night is immaterial."

She set her feet apart, put her hands on her hips and stared boldly into his eyes. "I do believe you're cross with me."

"I'm not cross with you." His voice got louder. "I could never be cross with you."

She put a finger to her lips and whispered. "Then why are you shouting at me?"

Before he could answer her, Fleur opened the bedroom door and went to Snowdrop. "You don't need to stay, thank you," she told her and the other girl bumped a chair in her hurry to leave. But she paused to kiss Fleur's cheek and say, "It's ever so romantic."

Dominic waited exactly where she'd left him. "Fleur?" He took a step closer. "I'm not shouting. But your voice is shaking. I can't bear for you to be frightened of me."

Fleur turned her back to him and said, "I can't undo all the buttons myself. Hurry up, please."

With her feet close together, her nightrail smoothed down and tidy all the way to her ankles and her arms at her sides, Fleur lay still beneath the sheet.

She started to jiggle, but deliberately made her muscles relax.

Dominic shouldn't take so long. His clothes were much easier to remove than hers. And he didn't have to take at least a hundred pins out of his hair.

She rose to her elbows and peered toward his dressing room.

Dominic gave up trying to wait. He wanted to be with her and the sooner he was, the sooner she would relax and stop being nervous. He shook his head and opened the door.

He was coming. Fleur heard him open the door and dropped to her back again and pulled the sheet to her chin. She closed her eyes.

"Fleur?" he said gently. "My love?" He stood beside the

bed and looked down at her. Her hair rested across the pillow in a thick, loose braid and her eyes were closed. He touched her cheek lightly and shook his head again. As long as he lived, he would never understand women.

His wife of a few hours had fallen asleep before her husband could join her in bed.

Fleur opened her eyes the tiniest bit and tried to see him through her lashes. Not easy—except that she could tell he was naked. He had answered that question honestly, no nightshirts for Lord Dominic.

Her breathing grew shallow and rapid. The sheet was too heavy for her tingling nipples. No, not too heavy, the weight made the sensation more exquisite. Oh, my, she felt moisture flow in heavy, throbbing places.

The minx wasn't sleeping.

Not unless she slept with her eyes partly open. Dominic saw the hint of a glitter where her eyelids didn't quite meet and crossed his arms. His arousal made itself known and he braced his feet apart. Let her peek at him and think she did so in secret.

He could look at her for a very long time. Her face, her shape beneath the covers, filled him up with a warmth so possessive his throat tightened. So this was what it felt like to love. This was the beginning—and he did feel they were just starting their life together—and this incredible woman would be in his bed every night.

Dominic sat on the mattress beside her. "Fleur, I know you're awake."

Her eyes opened wide. "Of course I am. Who could sleep at such a moment? I was just resting my eyes."

She put a hand on the side of his face and stroked him. With fingers that shook despite her brave words, she pushed into his hair.

No more waiting.

He surprised her. Thrilled her. One moment he sat beside her, quietly watching and waiting. The next he vaulted over her and slid beneath the covers. "This is the best moment of my life," he said. "I have been afraid of what it would mean to commit to one woman. Now I know why. I hadn't met you yet."

Dominic lay on his side and Fleur turned to face him. She slipped an arm beneath his and wriggled until she pressed close.

"I love you," he said, squeezing her against him. "I love you, love you. Why didn't you make me admit it before? I've been wasting time."

"I knew it, I think. That was almost enough." But it hadn't been. Nothing could feel as finished, as complete as this moment. Tears welled and she didn't stop them.

She pushed her face against his neck and whispered, "I don't want my nightgown, either."

"Whatever you don't want, wife, you won't have."

The nightrail all but disappeared. Unbuttoned and whisked over her head, it landed somewhere on the floor and she put herself back where she'd been, her skin to his, her heart beating with his, her body crying out to be joined with his.

Somehow she'd managed to get both arms around him. And she hooked a leg over his hip. "You're driving me wild," he told her. "How do you know to do that?"

Fleur didn't know what he meant. "I only want to be so close to you we feel like one person."

His manhood rested on her thigh, positioned where he felt the mad-making texture of hair and the slickness of her moisture mixed with his. He trembled from holding himself back. How easy it would be to slip inside her.

Fleur gasped. Dominic used his hands deftly, carefully, but he used them to draw her ever closer. His fingertips caressing her face, her neck, her shoulders, driving her mad when he didn't touch her breasts but traced her ribs, lightly touched her belly, pulled her close and held her bottom, stroked it and the backs of her thighs.

He could touch her forever—as long as he didn't have to wait forever to touch her in that dark, drugging place where he would find release.

Dominic pushed her to her back. He looked down at her, his face stark and possessive. Slowly, he bowed his head and licked circles around her breasts, each circle a little smaller, but never quite small enough to let him reach her nipples.

He raised his face enough to look up at her, and he smiled, a smile of pure, wicked delight. Extending his tongue, knowing she watched him, he delicately flipped the very tip of each nipple and he did so again and again until she held his head to her and strained upward against his mouth.

His. His wife. His lover. His friend.

Kissed, he kissed her thoroughly, stealing her breath, panting with his ardor, and then he lifted his head, squeezed his eyes shut and she saw a mix of ecstasy and sweet pain cross his features. She had taken him in her hand and guided him where he should be.

Fleur couldn't close her eyes. She must watch emotion and sensation have their way with him.

He could not have stopped the drive of his hips, the burying of his rod deep inside her. Their pace speeded and he braced his weight on his arms, a hand either side of her head. They looked into each other's eyes, their teeth gritted, the power of their joining rippling through their flesh.

She called out his name. He heard it as an echo in a dream,

and fell on her, gathered her up and rolled to his back, nestling her on top of him.

Her hair had escaped the braid and spread over him, over his neck and shoulders. Her breasts rested soft and full on his chest and their legs tangled together.

"Dominic?" Her voice was muffled. "What promise didn't you keep?"

He frowned then recalled what he'd said at the wedding breakfast. "I promised I'd be gentle if I taught you to love."

"Oh."

"Mmm, well, it gives me something to strive for. I'll just have to practice until I get it right."

"That sounds like a good idea," she said.

"Sleep, love," he murmured.

"I am."

"But not for too long."

"Ten minutes, perhaps five. One?"

They slept much longer and when Dominic opened his eyes the candles had burned out and the room was dark. He settled a hand on Fleur's shoulder.

"Are you awake now?" she asked.

"Mmm."

"Do you hear the rain?"

"Mmm."

She kissed his chin and wriggled her hips the slightest bit. "Would you like to go for a walk with me? We could lie on the grass and feel the rain on our faces."

He held her tight and said, "I'd really like to do that—some other night when it rains."

MILLS & BOON®
Live the emotion

SUPER
Historical
romance

Look out for next month's
Super Historical Romance

THE NINEFOLD KEY
by Rebecca Brandewyne

A Dream… Ariana Lévesque has been haunted for years
by a recurring dream about a handsome young man and a
dark, forbidding castle. But when her nightmare begins to
come true, Ariana is caught up in a dangerous intrigue that
began over two hundred years before she was born.

A Quest… Malcolm Blackfriars barely escaped with his
life after his father was murdered and his home burned
to the ground. He must discover what lies behind these
devastating events – even if it places his own
life in jeopardy!

A Ninefold Key Ariana and Malcolm are fated to meet
and to fall passionately in love. But will their search for the
ninefold key unlock the deadly secrets of their past – or
utterly destroy them both?

*"…a lush novel brimming with rich historical details and
written in the grand tradition of the Victorian gothic"*
—Romantic Times

On sale 3rd February 2006

*Available at WHSmith, Tesco, ASDA, Borders, Eason,
Sainsbury's and most bookshops*
www.millsandboon.co.uk

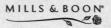

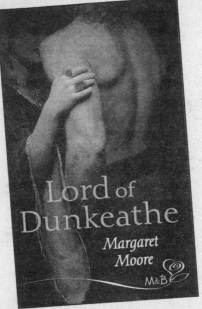